– Liverpool –
MMXXIV

dead ink

First published in Great Britain in 2024 by Dead Ink,
an imprint of Cinder House Publishing Limited.

Print ISBN 9781915368515
eBook ISBN 9781915368522

Cover design by Emma Ewbank / emmaewbank.com
Typeset by Steve J Shaw / white-space.uk
Editing by Jack Thompson
Copy edit by Dan Coxon

Printed and bound in Great Britain by Bell and Bain Ltd, Glasgow

www.deadinkbooks.com

Supported using public funding by
**ARTS COUNCIL
ENGLAND**

Funded by
UK Government

MIX
Paper | Supporting
responsible forestry
FSC® C007785

ABOVE US THE SEA

ANIA CARD

dead ink

For Tomasz & Ralphy

I

It's my picture right before I got old

1

Eight months before
December 2013

I first met Gav three years ago, on the dance floor of Pulse, Cardiff's loudest gay bar. Gav's face flickered in the whooping disco lights and his body whirred in a dance to the sounds of Divine, a lithe body wrapped tight in a velvet red turtleneck and black leather trousers, unrestricted in a spectrum of motion drawing men around him close. I admired the freedom in his movement, free from all of us dancing, free from our eyes on him, his face drowned in sound, eyes closed, lips mouthing the words with a smile as if he had never danced before and the dance was the answer, it was all there was.

I took a sip of my beer, dizzy with my new freedom clanging in my head clumsy and heavy, so loud despite the music punching the air with beats, despite the eyes of women on me, despite the invitations, despite the scents of new territories palpable at the tip of my tongue, the particles of heat between bodies, it was all there was, freedom of everything finishing all at once.

I glanced at a woman looking at me, afraid to make a move, to make a decision, struck by my stillness, keeping the future at bay, batting it away with another beer I took outside into the wet and mild Welsh winter.

I looked at the swarms of men and women outside, groups guaranteeing safety. I moved to the edge of the beer garden, flanked by two circles of gossip and drama running with passion and detail funnelling through my brain with images of people and places I didn't know. I took out the last cigarette I had haggled off a man on my way in and placed it between my lips, its taste always reliable.

There he was again, and to my surprise he was walking straight towards me with a confident stride, heeled leather boots clopping against the cobblestones.

'You look lost,' said Gav, a warm Welsh voice reverberating around me. There was something in the way he was looking at me, as if he needed to rescue something that night and here I was, everything he'd been waiting for. He had the kind, affectionate eyes of a rescuer, a frown of attention above them lining his high forehead beneath short blond spikes gelled upwards.

'Is it that obvious?' I smiled and asked for a lighter.

'Come here,' he said, bringing his face close to mine and cupping my cigarette with the palm of one hand, cool December air pushed in between my face and his neck, the flickering lights behind him highlighting the angles of his face, bony and pointed, blue eyes sunk deep in the cheekbones, eyelids covered in golden glitter, eyeliner climbing high above each eye.

'There you go.' The flame struck. I inhaled and blew the smoke away from his face.

'You're a beautiful dancer,' I said.

'Oh, thank you, pet.' Thin lips spilled into a wide grin. 'My god, I've missed it,' he said and frowned in my direction. 'Having a look around tonight?'

I smiled. Was I having a look? I had never dared to look.

'Maybe,' I said, acting coy when everything in my body screamed in fear.

'I'm Gav,' he said, holding the cigarette by his face, head tilted to the side.

'I'm Toni.'

'Are you a student here?' he asked, grabbing my hand and walking us away from the cackling voices, snaking into the quieter corner with a cha cha step. 'That's better, now.'

'I was,' I said, my voice louder, the statement definitive, pushing me forward. 'I quit today.'

Gav's eyes widened at the revelation.

'What are you going to do now?'

'I don't know,' I said, forcing a smile, hoping smoke concealed fear. I looked around, stamping the cigarette to the floor. 'I hated every minute of my degree. I had to break free. You know?'

Gav's face flashed with something else, eyes narrowed, inspecting me closely, in recognition, something in his face longing.

'What is it like to be free, then?' he asked.

I looked down, teetering on my feet.

'Right now,' I said, 'it's mostly scary.'

Gav squeezed my hand and looked away, smoke dispersing into the starry night, his grip strong, wiry hand enveloping mine.

'Let's dance, darling,' he said, pulling me gently towards the music. 'Let's dance.'

We quenched our hunger with greasy burgers, alcohol dulling the edges of his face, tired now in the brash light of Burger King, skin glistening under its assaulting brightness, my head still dancing next to him, relieved of the future, grounded in the burnt meat and sweetness of the bun.

'Where are you from?' he asked, my accent always making an introduction.

'Poland,' I said. 'Are you now going to tell me how good my English is?' Good, adequate immigrant.

Gav laughed and slurped on his monstrous cup of Pepsi filled up with ice, rattling like dice in a casino.

'I know better than that now, pet,' he said, a mischievous flicker in his eyes. 'My boyfriend is Polish.'

'You have a type,' I said and sent him howling, the rattle of the ice falling into the cracks in his laughter.

'I certainly can't resist those cat eyes,' Gav purred, which made me laugh in return.

'I'll take it as a compliment.'

'You should,' he said.

'You said you'd missed it,' I said, starting on my cardboard box of fries, dunking them one by one into a pot of watered-down ketchup.

'What?'

'You said you'd missed it, dancing? What happened?'

Gav pouted away from me and returned with a smile.

'Oh, life, darling,' he said, a tinge of fleeting sadness in his voice, and I wanted to know more about this life forbidding dance, but he was quicker. 'Sorry to have interrupted your conquest tonight.'

'I am not coming home empty handed.' I winked at him and our drunk tired bodies curled in laughter again. I thought about the room in my halls, everyone still away for Christmas.

'How long have you served?' he asked, hand landing in my box of chips. 'I'm having some, come here.'

I nudged the box forward, closer to him.

'Three long months,' I smiled.

'Where's home for you in Cardiff?' he asked, a handful of fries landing in his mouth all at once.

'Senghennydd Hall,' I said and paused, confronted with the impending conclusion being said out loud, 'for another two weeks.'

'How come?' Gav slurped on the plastic straw.

'I'm not a student anymore, so they're kicking me out.'

'You're having a bit of a moment, aren't you?' Gav laughed and I couldn't help but join him despite the fear nestling in the crooks of my joints, in every delayed decision, a hesitation, every drunk night, creeping into tonight.

'You could definitely say that.'

We took a beat above our plastic table of carnage, tired eyes meeting in defeat of the night in the incoming notes of dawn, peering through even here, into the den of the sleepless and the drunk.

'I have some lager back at mine if you want to come over?' he asked, eyelids lowered halfway, clinging on to the energy of the night.

I didn't want to say goodbye and I didn't want to go back to my room in the deserted halls, empty of students having somewhere loving and more comfortable to be.

I looked at Gav, his hand already squeezing mine, and in that moment I hoped it took only one hand to guarantee safety. Safe and drunk and half asleep I followed him into the hailed cab.

Gav's hand squeezed mine harder when we came closer to the blue door. Number 8. I struggled to keep my eyes open. My phone was dead and I had no idea what time it was. Gav patted the pockets of his leather trousers in search of his keys, and just when he found them the door flung open revealing a tall man in a white T-shirt and black boxer shorts, his dark hair combed back neatly. He looked like a ghost, pale with baggy eyes, horror slashed across his face in lack of sleep and worry and anger that spat out when he said:

'Where have you been? I've been calling all over for you.'

It was an exasperated sigh, hands resigned to the sides of a body that looked like a threat under a tone in muscles weaving themselves in knots and threads, tense now. Gav swayed on his feet, not letting go of my hand. 'Who is she?'

Gav smiled and pushed the eyelids open to glance at me with a wide grin.

'She's another Pole I've found,' he said and looked up at his boyfriend. 'Now I've got two.' My cacophonic drunk laughter was quickly stamped out by the boyfriend's icy stare.

'I told you not to drink, Gav.' The sentence befell us like an order. 'What the fuck are you thinking?'

'Can a girl never have a dance?' Gav's head fell to his right shoulder, the body swaying from side to side and with it mine, its little puppet. 'Can I step into my own house now, my lord?'

I glimpsed the boyfriend throw his face in his hands and move away from the doorframe which we stepped through, hands still linked, my body following Gav's.

'Thank you, sir,' boomed Gav, leading me into the bright hallway, dappled in the fresh light of the morning.

'Fuck you, Gav,' came the reply. 'Can I have a word with you?'

'Can I show her to her room first?'

I exchanged glances with the boyfriend, foreigner to foreigner, Pole to Pole, the ground tested, shaking underneath our feet. He hung his head first and disappeared behind a door at the end of the hallway.

'Fucking hell,' I whispered in Gav's direction.

'Don't pay him any attention,' said Gav, leading me forward and up the narrow, carpeted staircase. 'He's not usually like this.'

'What's his name?' I asked, huffing behind him, ready to lie down right there on the small landing and stay there, quietly and comfortably with no future and nowhere to be.

'Karol,' said Gav and his face brightened with a smile.

2

The room I woke up in was completely white, afternoon sun beaming through an enormous window, adding to the sense of unreal. The sheets were white too, soft and clean, fresh laundry scent permeating the air. Unable to resist their comfort, I buried myself under them to breathe nothing else of the world for a while. I could've stayed drowning in them, looping in and out of consciousness forever if it hadn't been for the fact that I was ravenous and nauseous and eventually, remembering where I was and how I ended up here, in the room with ironed sheets tucked around my body, in the bed with none of the breadcrumbs or bits of cereal I usually nestled in for the night with. I looked around the small room, the bed and a small bedside table painted white filled the space entirely. I looked out the window onto the low-lying rows of terraced houses in this area of Cardiff I couldn't recognise.

I took a deep breath and let it out, images of last night looping through my head, beautiful, dancing Gav, music jolting through my body in pleasant pulses, making everything right, making it all make sense, my whole world contained in the disco lights, in Gav's hand not letting go of mine.

I thought about Karol, edged into the night's corners, his hardened voice and tensing muscles, anger pushing at the temples and something else, easily readable when it's knotted in your stomach—

Fear.

The door opened to white walls covered in photographs in mismatching, colourful frames, a battlefield of opposing tastes and sentiments. The stairs creaked underneath my feet as I hobbled down unsteady on my toes, teeth pressed hard against my lower lip. When I reached the bottom of the stairs, I heard their muffled voices coming from behind a half-open door behind me, tense and unintelligible sentences punctuated by long pauses.

'Hello?' I said.

'Come in, darling.' I heard Gav's voice behind the half-open door. It opened to a narrow kitchen with a small round table pushed to the side tucked underneath the windowsill.

'Hello,' I said again and stood in the doorway, hugging my breasts to my chest. Karol acknowledged me with a quick glance from across the table, the threatening body crouched over, calm and relaxed now, reading. Gav was ruling the hob in a string of precise movements, pouring, flipping and stirring. He beamed at me from the opposite corner, my first sober memory of this most beautiful human creature; bold and loud, draped in a green silk nightgown, loosely tied with a golden string, so alive in the memory of that first frame.

'Pancakes, darling?' he smiled, pointing to a table with a steaming stash and three empty plates.

I reciprocated the smile and nodded, perching on the seat opposite Karol. He was older than me. They both were. In their late twenties or thereabouts. I watched them like a little timid show dog, turning my head left to right, inspecting Karol's chiselled jawline and high cheekbones and Gav's small pointy nose, much like mine, and his narrow, long face.

Karol didn't look up from his book when Gav placed two mugs of black coffee in front of us and sat down on a stool on the side, loading pancakes on his plate with one hefty scoop. His left hand grappling a fork, a waning cigarette was burning in the other hand next to the open book. His face was grey and he looked tired in the clouded light coming through the window.

Gav turned to me with an inviting smile, energetically spreading Nutella on his pancake.

'How's the beginning of the rest of your life going?' he asked. I glimpsed Karol rolling his eyes.

'Off to a great start,' I said, taking him in, a tall wiry frame containing so much life.

'Thanks so much for this.' I waved a vague circle above my pancakes and coffee. 'It's really sweet of you.'

Gav joined in with the hand-waving, saying it was nothing at all. Karol remained motionless at the end of the table, the burning butt of his cigarette close to the finish, so close to touching the skin. He was holding the cigarette butt with a light grip, focused on the text underneath.

'All I've got in my fridge is a loaf of white bread, a can of Fosters, and a half litre of Sainsbury's Basic cider,' I said, to further emphasise my gratitude. 'This is amazing.'

'God, I miss the times when I could stomach this stuff.' Gav squirmed and nudged Karol's elbow.

Karol looked up from above the book.

'I hate cider,' he said, his voice quiet and lifeless, his face still, eyes tired and red around the edges, 'and more than anything else, I hate Fosters.'

'He's a posh Polish cunt,' said Gav, taking a sip of coffee, which made Karol smile for the first time.

'You could say that.' Karol put out the cigarette in the ashtray.

I nodded, feeling my head jerk awkwardly. Poland had always been a place I ran away from, impatient to erase it completely. I couldn't believe this encounter, pulling me away from everything I ran towards, Karol's cold dark eyes glancing at me without much expression, just a quiet inquisition. Perhaps I was an interruption in his escape, too.

'How long have you been in the UK?' I asked, the standard exchange between any foreigners. Karol didn't look remotely interested in continuing this conversation.

'Six years.' He returned to his book. I took offence at his lack of interest in my first six months.

Gav cupped my hand in his, a square black stone on a silver ring glistening on his middle finger, his nails painted deep primary blue.

'This is beautiful,' I said, and glimpsed Karol checking his watch and draining the rest of his coffee in one gulp.

'Diolch, pet,' said Gav. 'It's a Welsh slate, a birthday gift from Karol.'

Gav shifted on his stool towards Karol, who stood up, not looking at Gav, a flash of colour in his face under the display of affection.

'I thought you had today off,' said Gav, a tinge of wistfulness and surprise in his voice.

'I've got a meeting with my supervisor in an hour.' Karol picked up his plate and cup and placed them in the dishwasher. 'I'm heading to the shoot later, taking some stills for this Apollo kid at uni, one of his final year films.' Karol spoke in quiet beats, bits of information floating away from one another, filling the longing silence present in the room. 'I'll be back as soon as I can.' Gav bobbed his head in acknowledgement.

Karol disappeared upstairs and came back moments later wearing a denim trucker jacket with a rucksack thrown over his left shoulder, a tripod gripped in his hand. He placed the bag on the table between us and investigated its contents with a concentrated frown, Gav cleaning our plates in silence. Karol looked at me, eyes scrutinising my face. I cowered under his gaze.

'See you around, Toni,' he said, throwing his bag back over his shoulder. 'Call me if you need me, Gav.'

'I'll be fine, darling.' Gav's pitch rang high as the front door shut with a thud. He twirled on his feet and leapt over to the chair opposite, both hands flailing in the air, battling with remnants of smoke, dispersed all around us.

Gav would soon be painting my nails, my eyes, and my lips, as I failed to draw any colour on my body besides the occasional black line cornering my eyes. He was very good at drag make-up and would be in Pulse every Friday evening, creating local queens ahead of their weekend shows, dragging me along as his assistant.

Gav had a kind, infectious laughter. He laughed at everything and with everyone. He finished all his sentences with a quick burst of laughter, and howled long and with a full heart when something was either disarmingly hilarious or horrifically sad. He was laughing the last time I saw him, too.

It was only eight months after that first breakfast.

3

Three days later, I hadn't left Gav's side. He always found an excuse for us to do something and be somewhere and I never wanted to be anywhere else or with anyone else but him, his hand holding mine away from knowing and deciding, from acting and doing, and here I was, drifting through breakfasts and film nights, nestled on their sofa in the safety of commotion, through a shy murmuration of friends, checking in on Gav, extending their kindness to me.

'It's been good having you around, darling,' Gav said on New Year's Eve, patting my hand, our glazed eyes hooked on Jools' Annual Hootenanny. 'Good old Jools,' he laughed at the TV, mouthing the words to a cover of a song I didn't recognise, cocking his head left to right.

I smiled at him.

'It's been good to be here,' I said.

I was his uplifting end to an otherwise shit 2013. When I asked him what made it so bad, he said it was an infection he couldn't shake off for ages, messed with his nerves and all, nasty stuff. 'Anyway,' he smiled a wide smile, 'all better now.'

I looked for the traces of the disease, scanned the blond hair and pale skin for any signs, messages cleaved in the skin, but everything was right, and so were we.

'Have you thought about what you're going to do?' He turned to me.

I shook my head. I had one more week to move out of halls and start something new, somewhere new.

'You know…' Gav paused and looked down, long fingers readjusting the ring, taking it off and sliding it back on as he spoke, the slate grounded in gold, not succumbing to the angles of the light. '…I'm signed off for a few more weeks still. If you were looking for somewhere cheap, look no further.' The eyeroll gave in to a coy smile. 'I will need to talk to Karol, but…' Gav gave my hand a squeeze and his voice lowered to a murmur just as Jools Holland gathered momentum to count down the new year. 'I would love you to stay.'

'Yes,' I said, sinking in the sea blue of Gav's eyes, 'I would love to stay too.' I never understood how anyone could marry anyone in under forty-eight hours but here I was after only a few days heading towards the altar without a doubt, the future safe in no plan and no logic. The studio audience broke into cheers and fireworks pierced the sky.

'Happy new year, darling,' said Gav, a smile stretching his beautiful face and mine just as the key turned in the lock of the front door and Karol walked in, carrying bags of equipment, his face flushed. He took one look at the TV and us and let out a long gasp.

'Not fucking Jools Holland,' said Karol, wincing at the old bulky set pushed into the corner of the room. 'Happy new year.'

The morning after, Honey burst in through the kitchen door with an elongated sigh. He plummeted onto a chair in the corner of the room, splaying himself all over the table opposite me.

'You and Gav are going to be the death of me,' he said, pulling himself up by the elbows and glaring at me with the bloodshot eyes of a heavy night. I miss the way we used to make friends back then, light on the feet and deep in our hearts, stories of short lifespans recounted overnight with dramatic strokes and juicy details. Honey and I had only met the previous night when he paraded through the door with a four-pack of lager and a bottle of champagne a few minutes after midnight, imposing a New Year's party, Gav's longest and most faithful companion, Phil Jones by day, Phillippa Lusciolla by night, Honey to friends, Cardiff born and bred with a soft Welsh twang that always faded next to Gav's loud valley cackle.

I smiled and offered Honey some coffee. He gasped and nodded. I poured hot water over two heaps of instant coffee and topped it with three sugars.

'You're a darling, ta,' he said, scooping it up in his pudgy hands. I always thought of Honey as a slightly uglier brother of Gav. He was identical in the pale complexion, with a round face and cheekbones that seemed too broad for his face. Immaculately plucked eyebrows drawn in thick lines flung high above small blue eyes in a permanent state of surprise, drama etched on Honey's face and coursing through his veins, sprouting through his lips at any opportune moment.

I placed the mug in front of him and sat down on Karol's seat by the window. The minute Honey asked me if Gav was still asleep, Karol came in through the door. He looked different, his face creased with sleepiness, eyes bleary, sneaking a strike of excitement, hair rumpled into a messy quiff, white cotton shirt spilling out of black jeans.

'Don't you have a home to go to?' he asked, eyeing me up and down, a smile stretching his face in an unfamiliar way, a foreign feature on this otherwise joyless face, his eyes sparking up with something new I couldn't put my finger on. My face twitched in a nervous smile. I wondered if Gav had said anything.

'Leave her be, sweetheart!' Gav's flying pitch bawled from behind the kitchen door before he pushed it open with a swing and leapt in with a sprightly jump, green nightgown flailing behind him. 'Good morning, my debauched darlings!'

'Good morning,' I smiled from above my cup. 'You look happy.' I turned to Karol. Me and Honey exchanged quick glances and gripped our mugs, pressing them to our lips.

'I'm not. I'm late,' said Karol, eyes distracted around Gav now, voice quiet. He was shuffling around the kitchen without aim, mumbling something under his breath about having photos to develop. I watched Gav watch him; there was something different in Gav's face, too, the same half-smile Karol wore while going through cupboards before announcing: 'I have no time for coffee.' With the same shadow of a smile, he leant over to Gav and gave him a quick kiss before turning to us with a sigh as his eyes met mine.

'See you later, guys.' Before he sprinted out, Karol patted Honey on the back and winked at me as he did every morning. It was different today, too, playful and light.

'Well, well, well,' Honey clucked. 'All good in the nest again?' he asked Gav, pushing his cheek out with his tongue.

'Philippa!' Gav rolled his eyes, a joyful grin on his lips.

'You two,' said Honey and took a deep breath that he held in, looking like he wanted to say something, but, giving Gav's smile another glance, he exhaled slowly. 'I've got to go, drunkheads.' Honey stood up and stretched his arms. 'As ever, don't ruin your lives without me there to witness it.'

'Love you, darling.' Gav leant in for a kiss on the cheek.

Honey circled him and came over to me with a pout.

'Ta-ra, new best friend,' he said as we blew kisses by each other's cheeks. With a whirl and an exchange of 'Ta-ras' following him all the way to the front door, Honey was gone.

I looked at Gav's face, bits of gold glitter still glistening around his eyes.

'Oh, darling, I'm not gonna lie, I'm absolutely hanging today,' he said, squinting his eyes. 'Do you fancy watching a film or something? There's a cinema down the road.'

We agreed that the cinema was a perfect thing for a week's worth of hangover. It had the comforting balance of isolation and closeness, distraction and focus, but mostly: darkness. We fancied something light and goofy but the only thing showing in the afternoon was a film about monks in Argentina and we were both too tired to wait until six. I was far too spaced out to pay attention to anything that was being said in the film, and hardly anything was said at all. Gav's head dropped on my shoulder when the lead monk died of a heart attack. It was probably only ten minutes in, but it felt like hours. The rest of the monks' story was mostly long stretches of grief, the languid, silent grief of monks on an island waiting to be flooded and submerged by the surrounding sea. It's odd to think of this film now, its title long forgotten, images of the encroaching sea vivid and menacing, crawling at my feet, turning them red. I rested my head against Gav's as the sea filled the screen.

We yawned our way out of the end credits and strolled over to the foyer cafe.

'What did you think?' I asked, as we hobbled towards a table, each with a pint in our hand.

'It certainly was a film,' he said, lips bursting at the seams in laughter already, our hands starting to shake, stirring the beer to bubble up. We reached the table with relief, our long, dangling bodies shaking in unison.

'It certainly was a film about monks,' I said, wiping a stream of tears from under my eyes. I had never laughed like this with anyone, a cacophony of sound ignorant of anyone around us, a looping roar we kept afloat as we talked, laughter becoming a part of the language between us. 'One of them died of a heart attack,' I remembered.

'Fuck off, no way!' Gav's arms flung wide in the air, attracting passive aggressive huffs and annoyed looks from the nearby tables. 'I missed the best bit!'

'The only bit, you missed the only bit. That was all that happened.'

'Next time we should take some pills,' he said.

Next time, exactly a week later, we did. The monks floated from the screen in sparkling stardust. We got reported by a long, sullen face behind us and warned we would be banned from the cinema for life if we ever ran around the aisles pretending to be nun fairies again.

I asked Gav what area of Cardiff this was and he told me we were in Pontcanna.

'Are you from Cardiff?' I asked. Gav shook his head.

'I'm a valley boy, darling, right up from Treherbert.'

I didn't know where that was. My hometown wasn't familiar to him either and for that blissful moment we were caught nowhere.

'When do you think you'll have to get back to work?' I asked, hoping it wouldn't be soon, the two of us floating in our nowhere land of no defined future and no routine, no knowing.

'I don't know.' Gav lowered his eyes, a finger drawing circles around the rim of the pint glass. 'They don't want to take any risks.' He looked at me with a smile. 'I miss sales, though. It's fun.'

'I can't think of anything worse,' I said and he burst out laughing.

'I could talk the dead back to life, love. I'm a born salesman. I always have a good chuckle and they pay me for something that would otherwise ruin my relationship with my mostly silent boyfriend,' he said, lowering his mouth to the half-empty glass, laughter echoing in its chamber.

Talking to strangers all day long was the last thing I could ever do, but Gav didn't see it like that. He liked a story in everything and everyone and was the first person I'd met interested in mine. In the cinema's cafeteria, empty and bright, I told him everything about Toni and her first six months on earth in Cardiff, meandering through stories of drinking of the most excessive and cheapest kind, of filthy halls rooms and filthy kitchens, of the many flatmates, the names of which I have difficulty recalling at all now. When he asked me if there was an origin story, I shook my head.

Gav smiled at me, meeting my grimace.

'You're just like my Karol,' he said.

I shrugged.

'Maybe,' I cautioned, determined to keep Poland at bay.

Gav drained the end of his pint and asked if I fancied a fag. I nodded and followed him outside.

We smoked in silence underneath the cinema's short roof. The persistent drizzle soaked us through despite our shelter. People were never too bothered about shielding themselves from the rain in Wales, and neither were we under the low clouds. There was a comforting sense of companionship about the Welsh rain, it never meant any harm. It was part of the landscape, the romantic melancholy of the spirit, the communal complexion.

'Alright, pet?' Gav turned to me and put his arm around me. Together, we were two skinny giants, our lanky bodies hunched under the fall of rain, my cheek glued to his shoulder, huddling for warmth. I liked how we belonged to each other in the beads of rain dissipating in the cranky air, our eyes already bleary, heads weighed by more beer. Three pints in, I dared him to race me to the nearest pub. Gav said there was one just around the corner. The loser was buying drinks for the rest of the night. I arrogantly believed in the advantage of my youth.

When we ran out onto the street, he sprinted ahead, quickly becoming a colourful dot on the horizon that disappeared through the doors of a Wetherspoons. I had never jogged in my life and got out of breath after thirty seconds, grossly overestimating my lung capacity. Every centimetre of my body was soaked by the time I got to the pub, and every man turned to me with curiosity as I walked through the door, confronted by the stench of stale lager and sweat.

Gav stood in front of me with a big grin and a glass of clear liquid in each hand. He jerked his head to the left, pointing towards a booth at the back of the pub. The penetrative eyes of men followed me as we walked, unsteady with our drinks. I was self-conscious under their gaze, aware of my wet dress wrapped around my bum in cold discomfort.

'Is this water?' I asked when we got to the table, relieved at the thought of drinking something other than alcohol.

'Cher almighty. What do you take me for?' Gav glanced at me with dramatic shock. 'It's double gin and tonic, darling. You owe me six pounds sixty,' he said. 'Oh, and an extra pound for being really shit at running.'

I sat down and took a sip.

'I hate men staring at me,' I said, running my hand through my hair and squeezing its ends, lonely droplets trickling down my neck and onto my shoulder.

'Oh, I love it, pet,' he said and his eyes sparkled. 'Anyway, how do you know they weren't looking at me?' Gav grinned as he scanned the room, blowing kisses in the air. Most men looked away, busying themselves with the football on a gigantic screen in the opposite corner, or else buried their faces in their newspapers. Gav gave a short cackle.

'God, I love the Spoons,' he said, stretching the syllables into a beautiful Welsh song and turning back towards me with a smile. 'Thanks, love,' we clinked glasses in the air. 'Karol never comes with me.'

I asked him why.

'Told you, he's a posh Polish cunt.'

I spat in my drink, laughing.

'How come?' I asked.

'It takes one look at him. Cher knows I'm at the end of my rope sometimes.' Gav shook his head and I laughed along in companionship. 'The only cheap things he tolerates are cigarettes. In fact, the most rank, disgusting ones, he'll have them, but will only smoke them in our kitchen or outside, mind. Go figure.' Gav took a beat, glancing down at his fingers splayed on the table, and added with a sigh I didn't know where to place: 'It's funny, the things you notice after being with someone this long.'

'How did you meet?' I asked.

Gav dropped his cheek in the palm of his hand, eyes glancing up as if he was looking at his own thought bubble in a cartoon.

'He was the photographer at a mutual friend's wedding. I was...' He shook his head and laughed. '...I was chewing on this massive prawn, half that bloody thing still dangling out of my mouth, tail and all, when he rocked up in front of me with a camera and took a photo before I even understood what was happening.' Gav took a sip of his gin and tonic and straightened up on the old cushioned bench opposite me. 'Once I swallowed that bloody prawn, I told him to stop being a prick like, and do you know what he said to me?' He turned back at me, his face beaming.

I shook my head.

'He said he was no longer interested in taking anyone else's photos. All photos from the evening included me, pet. I wasn't even a close friend of the bride and groom. The bride was furious, bless her.' He laughed and added with a wistful glint in his eye, 'I asked him to move in with me that night and he did. You just know sometimes.'

'To your place in Pontcanna?' I asked, my mind swelling with images of the romantic spontaneity of the night recounted.

'No, I was still living down the bay. I bought this place last year.'

'I didn't realise,' I said.

'I've always been a pretty conventional type of a guy, you know, find my perfect man, get a mortgage, get a dog, have a baby.' Gav sighed and looked up again with a wince. 'Further down the line. Don't look it, do I?'

I disagreed, telling him he looked like anything he wanted to be.

'Oh, you sweet darling.' He tapped my hand and gave a little squeal. 'My wee life coach.' I smiled. 'Karol's bloody gorgeous though, isn't he?' Gav picked up after a short pause and squirmed in delight, closing his eyes and pressing both palms to his chest, sparkly golden nail varnish sparking up in the bright pub lights.

'I think you're much cuter,' I said and gave him a wink.

'Stop it!' Gav's voice flew high above and he waved his hand, patting the compliment away, face grinning at me. 'You're such a little flirt. You know my weakness!'

'What's your weakness?' I asked, draining the rest of my drink.

Gav leant forward, elbows pushing both empty glasses to the side, his nose touching mine.

'I already told you. I'm a real sucker for those Eastern European eyes,' he whispered and kissed my lips. 'Be careful now.' He laughed and I burst out laughing, too. Gav straightened up and clambered out of the booth. 'You got me there, pet,' he said. 'I'm getting the next round. What do you fancy?'

Rum followed whisky that followed more gin. We were out to taste the world.

Gav told me that night he couldn't think of anything worse than going down on a woman. I couldn't remember how we even got there, nor could I recall how I ended up telling him that I really wanted to go down on a woman but was generally terrified of flirting with anyone other than gay men and straight women, something he repeatedly reminded me of in the months that followed as something of an issue. We stared drunk at the game on the screen and talked about football, how we didn't get the phenomenon of it, nor the wages paid to footballers, and at one point we concluded that Karol was wrong about Fosters.

We remembered we had left our phones in the flat. Mine must've still been in a bag I had with me. I couldn't remember the last time I had it on me.

Gav said he'd put it by my bed the night before and shook his head, amused.

I thanked him and it was the first time I told him I didn't know what I'd do without him.

Someone put on 'Sweet Caroline' and the inebriated pub started breaking into shy sways of heads and the modest murmurs of men whistling along, quiet still, their jaws clenched and heads jerking left to right, out of rhythm. It took Gav to erupt to the chorus in full volume for the entire room to gain confidence and join in, pints flailing in the air. I noticed a few women, too, in their forties or fifties mostly, dyed black or bleached blonde bobs swaying along between the murmuring men.

With the end of the first chorus, Gav leapt onto the table and conducted the crowd into the second verse, hands pointing at various groups scattered across the room. It was the first time I'd heard Neil Diamond and the first time I felt really foreign, too. Gav stretched out his hand towards me.

'Come on, pet! Get up here!'

Gav's hands flung high in the air again like a little kid who had just scored a goal and was having the time of his life. I envied his ignorance of the space around him. I spent every hour of my life wondering what people thought of me, whether I was too quiet or too loud, too shy or too outgoing, too boring or too anxious, assessing with each person what it was they wanted me to be so I could become it. Gav took no interest in the world beyond himself and the person he was with. It was so easy to fall in love with him. When he was with you, you became his entire world.

Drunk enough to ignore my instincts, I grabbed his hand and stepped into my worst nightmare of standing in front of an audience, hopping onto the table behind him with a girly squeal to a loud cheer from some in our male crowd. 'Sweet' and 'Caroline' were the only two words I knew, but it seemed enough to get me through the ordeal. We took our bows and plopped down on our seats to roars of 'Yeah' and discordant whistles and claps.

'There's no party like a Welsh party, pet, remember that now,' he said, gasping and scanning the bar.

It is strange to think of this now, but I knew there and then that I would always love this man.

+

'Language just isn't natural,' I tried to explain to him two more pints of Fosters later. 'Everything I am saying is memorised, and no,' I waved my finger in front of his face, pivoting on a clenched fist, 'it's not the same process as learning your native tongue, because learning your second language is far less intuitive and is learnt in translation to the native tongue, it mirrors you, whereas your native tongue is constructed with *you*, the language is, you could say, you, you construct each other, do you get me? Nothing I'm saying right now is *me*. Do you get me? Can you get me some water?' I let out a long sicky burp.

Gav was not looking at me. He wasn't looking at anything. He was gone. It was time to go home.

I got us some water that we felt too full to drink and only took a sip of. We stumbled out into the crisp night, greeting us with a gentle graze of drizzle. Gav hung himself on my shoulder and we huddled together in silence, relieved we were able to walk at all, cautious of each step.

I imagined that we had walked for miles. I half dreamt we had walked around all of Wales, round and round on the endless whirling route, which can't have been true, but maybe it was. I wanted it to be true, I never wanted that walk to end, Gav's lips pressed against my ear, his warm breath brushing against the skin on my face.

Eventually, in the middle of Wales or the galaxy, we got to the blue door of their flat.

'Cunt, I forgot my keys,' said Gav, gasping and patting his jeans. 'Fuck.'

I offered to grab a cab back to mine. I still had the keys for three more days. We were wondering out loud what our best option was, when Karol would be back, what time it was anyway, and what day it was, too, when the door swung open in front of us, revealing a toned and muscular body in boxer shorts. We froze underneath Karol's frown and started speaking over each other, hurriedly and decidedly apologetic, making up excuses, making no sense.

'The state of you two,' said Karol under his breath, barely audible, as he retreated into the flat. We sheepishly followed. Gav fell onto all fours and started crawling towards the stairs. I wanted to follow him, but Karol stopped me, his index finger right in front of my face.

'No way, kid. You're coming with me.' He looked behind at Gav clambering the stairs. 'I'll be right back, alright? You're okay to get yourself to the bathroom?'

Gav let out a faint 'Yeah' and carried on. Karol turned to me again.

'Don't move.' Karol's finger landed in front of my face again.

He popped upstairs, skipping over Gav, and was back almost immediately wearing what he had when he left in the afternoon. He had my stuff with him.

'Alright, I'm going to drive you home.'

I followed Karol out across the street to a black Volvo. It could've been something else, I called all cars Volvos. I could never understand how anyone could be bothered to remember brands of cars. Volvo was the only thing I had room for.

'Hop in.' Karol opened the door. I climbed into a tiny space, my head touching the car's ceiling. He turned the engine on and glanced at me with one eyebrow raised, asking if I was going to be sick.

I told him I never got sick after alcohol. He decided to trust me on that.

'Now, tonight, do you remember where you live? Take your time, it's been a while.'

I let out a quiet laugh but he didn't find it funny, waiting for my joy to die along with his dead face and his dead, dead eyes.

'Senghennydd Hall,' I said reluctantly. He said he knew where that was. We drove in silence for a while.

'Gav told me you were looking for a place,' he said and switched to Polish, so out of the blue that for a second I thought I'd lost all my comprehension of English.

I nodded, my eyelids heavy, body tensing at the thought of the room I hadn't been in for over a week, nothing of value in its contents, an air of wasted time settling on scribbled notes and books.

'It would be nice for Gav to have someone around when I'm at work.' Karol sounded softer in Polish, less rigid somehow.

'Sounds like you want to get a dog.'

'You smell marginally better.'

I snorted quietly and looked at him, brown eyes glowing in the deep yellow lights of the streetlamps, long fingers wrapping the wheel.

'It doesn't look like I'm getting rid of you any time soon, you might as well pay me for the pleasure.'

I looked out the window, my face pressed against the glass, the city in motion collapsing into streaks of subdued browns.

'I might be in love with your boyfriend.'

I turned to him, his eyes on the road, corners of his mouth lifting.

'Yeah, he might be in love with you, too.'

I smiled, thudding heart falling into the foreign sounds trickling out of the speakers in soft saxophone beats woven through the thrums of guitar. I asked him what the album was.

'Have you heard of Super Furry Animals?'

'Vaguely,' I said.

'It's their Welsh language album, *Mwng*.'

I said it was beautiful. He agreed.

We parked outside the big round building of Senghennydd Hall. Karol took a beat. He cleared his throat before shifting in his seat towards me. 'Two hundred a month and the room is yours.'

I smiled and pressed my hand on the handle, Senghennydd looming warmer in its imminent departure.

'Oh, and—' Karol grabbed my arm and pulled out a pen from the front seat's pocket, scribbling his phone number on my forearm. 'Get your stuff packed and I'll come pick you up on Monday.'

I told him he liked me. He denied it. I hugged him as he was pleading with me not to touch him and I waved him goodbye as he left.

4

I was surprised to see a text from Karol. Me and Karol didn't text, not then. We bumped into each other in the kitchen after mine and Gav's heavy nights in Pulse. We shared pancakes and coffee and, in time, his packets of cigarettes. Karol never said much those bleary mornings, busy reading. He occasionally lifted his head towards me or Gav and listened to our stories of debauchery and silliness with the slight irritation of someone who made no secret of his time being wasted.

Do you want to see Sunset Rubdown tonight? read the text.

I was in Primark shopping for new cheap underwear due to not washing mine nearly often enough, and when my eyes rested on the name of the band I squealed, inviting furtive glances from the women around me.

YESSSSSSS!!!!!!!!!!!!!!!! I pressed the exclamation mark button hard as if intending to punch a hole in my phone.

Cool came the reply.

We agreed to meet at seven at Dempseys around the corner from Clwb Ifor Bach, where the gig was taking place.

+

'Thanks so, so much for thinking of me!' I said, plonking down into my seat with a rum and Coke in hand as Karol lowered himself slowly opposite me with a pint of ale. He was wearing a long black cotton T-shirt that hung loose on his frame; a padded black corduroy bomber jacket hung in his hand.

'My mate Nico couldn't make it in the end, so.' Karol took a sip, eyes grazing the windowsill by his elbow. 'You said you liked them.'

He was probably referring to the time a couple of weeks ago when I screamed in his ear as we passed the poster advertising the gig.

Tonight was the first time Gav wasn't with us. He'd left to see his family the night before in triumph. He was finally allowed to go back to work, all clear, all better now.

It felt odd, as if we were both cheating on Gav, which as I thought it made no sense at all, our bodies awkward around each other, at the sudden proximity, our glances distracted, words clinging on to Gav, Karol's Polish already breaking into English, mine still young in its migration and intact.

'Do you know when he's coming back?' I asked, already impatient, unstable on my feet without him there, all my bets placed on Gav.

'They hardly saw him last year,' Karol said, eyes giving in to an imperceptible twitch. 'His grandmother owns a pub up there, he used to go up a lot to help out.'

'Do you know them?' I asked. I thought about my mother's Christmas card, two fifty-pound notes tucked between two pages of Christmas wishes 'from Down Under', her children's names scribbled underneath hers.

'Yeah,' he said and took a sip of his lager, looking away for a moment as if in idle search of something. 'You've dyed your hair,' he said after a moment of silence.

I smiled and asked him if he liked it.

'It's intense, really red,' he said. 'But sort of okay, I guess. It makes sense.'

'Thanks,' I said, draining my drink and glancing at his pint, hardly touched.

'You look good with short hair,' he said, scanning my face, his eyes narrowed and inquisitive, brow furrowed in examination. 'You've got one of those faces you can't really forget.'

'Thanks,' I said again, thirsty for another drink. I wondered what he meant by that, if he meant my teeth, pushing into one another, each protruding abreast of the other, or my eyes, one slightly discoloured with grey and blue, thin lips, everything that pushed boys away when I still wanted them to get close, everything that clashed with all other faces and their even features, matching those on magazine covers and the soap operas we used to watch, approved by my aunt and by boys. It's not always the beautiful things you can't forget, sometimes it's the ugliness you can't erase from memory. It has the power to strike. 'Do you want another drink?' I asked.

Karol shook his head.

'No, but you go ahead.'

When I returned, he was scribbling something down in his red notebook. He said he liked to note down the bands he saw, what year, where, jot down a few lines of what they were like.

I told him that sounded like a good idea.

'Why do you never come to Pulse with us?' I asked after he pocketed the notebook and checked the time on his phone, mumbling to himself that we had half an hour until the support band he didn't want to miss.

'Oh, it's a dive. It's the worst place, like an open fire sweaty gay hell,' he said, grimacing.

This made me laugh but he didn't laugh along, his face still, as it mostly was, vague with no expression. Karol cleared his throat and looked away at the cobbled Womanby Street outside. Lanky twenty-somethings in skinny jeans and oversized wool jumpers strolled down towards Clwb, their bodies hunched in the cold, their eyes glazed with alcohol, faces contorted in laughter.

'What degree did you do that made you pack it in all together?' he asked.

'European Union Studies,' I said.

'Fair enough,' he said, his voice sombre. 'Why did you do it?' There he was, eyes attending to me and detecting.

I shrugged.

'I needed to do something,' I said, my aunt ready for me to leave, handing me a ticket as far away as they could afford. 'How about you?' I said, unprepared for his scrutiny. 'Gav said you were still at uni.'

Karol nodded.

'I'm finishing Graphic Communication, technically.' He paused and sighed. 'They've let me do my dissertation project in photography, and that's my year mostly, trying to piece together my degree exhibition in July.'

'Cool,' I said. I asked him what he was working on but he wasn't sure yet.

'I've got a few ideas,' he said and looked straight at me again with a new glint in his eye I couldn't put my finger on. There was a sense of danger about Karol I couldn't place. It lay still under the cold stare. 'We should get going.' He took a gulp of his pint and left it on the table, unfinished.

I nodded and knocked back my rum and Coke, slamming the empty glass on the table, rounded cubes of ice clinking against the bottom.

'Clwb puts on local bands every Wednesday,' he said, putting on his jacket and a small blue beanie, leaving most of his tall forehead exposed. 'If you want to come along sometime?' he asked, looking down at his phone.

I did. We went the following Wednesday, and the Wednesday after that. We went every Wednesday that year, in fact, a new red notebook replacing the old. The last band we saw together were Islet supporting Gruff Rhys, four months after Sunset Rubdown.

5

Five months before
March 2014

Karol glanced up at me from behind a book, funnelling clouds of white smoke above as I walked into the kitchen. He grunted a quiet hello and returned to what he was reading.

I asked him if he was interested in a cup of coffee. He said he'd already had three this morning.

'Gav's already gone to work,' he volunteered before I asked. I poured hot water into a heap of instant coffee, watching it dissolve in the mug with a hiss. 'Why don't you use a cafetiere?' Karol didn't look up from his book, cigarette burning between his fingers.

'I can't be bothered to wash it,' I said. I put two teaspoons of sugar in my cup and stirred slowly, eyes fixed on its creamy top. I could feel him shake his head, the judgemental vibrations in the air brushing my skin, but I didn't want to give him the satisfaction of my attention.

'I don't know how you can drink that stuff. It's like drinking powdered orange juice or eating powdered broccoli. Just drink the real stuff.'

I smiled to myself. Karol could never resist saying this, to my and Gav's amusement, as we rolled our eyes in unison over our cups of instant coffee.

ANIA CARD

'How are the workers going?' I asked, sitting on the chair opposite, glimpsing Joseph Conrad's *Victory* in his hand.

'Yeah, alright,' he said, taking a slow drag of his cigarette. It was his graduation project, exploring new landscapes of the working class through the eyes of factory workers in Wales, or so he said; the way he always explored the subject made him sound vague, but he insisted on being specific, looking at immigrants and class, an attachment of Welshness to a working-class identity. Me and Gav never fully understood. Every weekend he took to his Volvo and travelled across Wales. He developed the photographs on weeknights. Now Gav was back at work, and I was contributing my two hundred quid a month to the rent, he could quit taking photos at weddings and commit to the project.

With Gav at work, I spent the weekday mornings with Karol, making us eggs on fresh slices of bread with dollops of cottage cheese with chives we stocked up on from a Polish shop across town. When Gav wasn't around, we never had toast.

All my attempts at conversation usually ended with Karol tearing out an article in the newspaper he'd found most interesting that morning and placing it in front of me, and so we read in silence, dabbing at the eggs and sipping on coffee, smoking. If it was a book he was reading, he'd ask me where mine was and tell me to get it. Nothing and no one had done more for my reading than Karol and his insistence on a lack of morning conversation.

These mornings contrasted wildly with the weekends when Karol wasn't around, days filled with loud music and even louder guests, those who'd stayed over after a night out or those living nearby who'd pop in, mornings swelled with laughter, the air pierced with its roar.

This morning was different.

Karol put Conrad down and stood up, hands on hips, fingers nervously tapping at them. It always surprised me when he did that, his capability and propensity for random neuroses, taking me out of his flawlessly performed stillness.

'Do you want to see them?' he asked. I didn't understand. 'I could show you what I've been working on.' This came from nowhere. He had never asked me to look at anything he'd worked on before.

I chewed on the egg, flushing it down with warm milky coffee. I didn't know anything about photography and wasn't sure I had anything constructive to offer, but I nodded in a reluctant yes.

I followed him upstairs. Karol stopped on the landing that stretched between their bedroom and mine and pulled down at a narrow, rickety ladder, concealed in the ceiling. He was talking about workers and their faces, fragments scooting in and out. I thought about how little I understood of what he was saying, how his Polish came out incomprehensible under an English clenched jaw and hardcoded pursuit of abbreviation.

He looked down at me, his head floating above his bum that hovered in front of my face as I followed him up the ladder. With a lopsided smile skewing his face, he told me I wasn't listening to anything he was saying.

I said that I wasn't, but if he could move his arse out of my way, I could perhaps hear him better and see what he was referring to.

Karol swung his legs into the attic, his muscled arms straddling the entrance.

'Very impressive,' I said, clambering up the wobbly steps.

The attic was an extension of Karol: a dark room, the blinds of two windows drawn but for a sliver of light piercing through. It was neatly ordered; notebooks arranged by colour, greys, whites and blacks, and vinyl and boxes on a wooden floor that was painted grey. I turned around, spotting a long black curtain pinned to the ceiling that kept that part of the room concealed. In front of me, on large paper sheets, hung the men he was talking about. Karol pulled open the blinds and the fragile Welsh sun seeped in, shedding more context on Karol's black-and-white world which I saw in detail now, dust particles setting on records, notebook covers marked with black ink, photographs clipped to a string stretching from one corner to the next in a perfect square around me.

Karol was standing next to me, completely still but for his fingers which were rapping at his shoulders, arms crossed across his body, the air thickening between us.

I glanced at the photographs, all faces in motion, distracted, as if they were somewhere else.

Karol started telling me how they were only physically occupying the space in front of the camera, its lens unable to penetrate their *real* place, scrambling at stillness, his wiry fingers pointing at the men before us. He spoke, clearing his throat now and then, his words separated and punctuated in a mechanical melody of sorts, permeated with the hoarseness of his voice. He talked me through each photograph, giving me their names, their occupation, an anecdote from the moment of taking each photo, the story cut short by the pull of a camera trigger.

I pointed at one man in the corner. His name was Gary and he had a round, jolly face, caught in the middle of a joke.

'He was full of them,' said Karol, and paused as if struck by the ease of kindness in that face. 'The general idea was fragments, fragmented conversations, a fragment of an expression captured, stuff out of context.' Karol turned away from the photograph of Gary and looked at me; my eyes were fixed on Gary's face. 'It's, I don't know, none of them seem real,' he said and bit his lower lip, his eyes darting now from one photograph to another. 'Just like our memories, fabrications.' He tapped at his shoulders again, harder this time. 'Gary's wife cheated on him that week. He was a mess that morning. Do you think you can see that now? In his eyes? I sometimes think I can, but not always.'

Karol's voice was gathering strength and speed, becoming frantic, catching up with his eyes, blinking and shooting at different corners of my face, always investigating.

I was tired. I didn't know what to say. I looked at Gary.

'I guess?' I said.

Karol needed something from me, but I wasn't sure what he wanted me to say. Perhaps he needed an impressionable audience. That I could do.

I clapped my hands and said it was all very impressive. He was too absent to detect any irony.

'It's always only observation.' He gazed out, past the photos, head tilted, and fell silent.

There was something compelling about Karol, an authoritarian way about him, a sense of prowess, his stature as sombre as his face, tall, straight, still. In a way, in those days, he was a fantasy to me, an alien of sorts on the outskirts of my experience.

My stomach rumbled but he took no heed of it.

I asked him what was wrong with observing. He was, I said, always documenting something, after all; a generation, a place in culture and a society, a figurative place and the very physical, he was keeping a record.

Karol denied it all, said he had perhaps set out to do that, but he only made up new stories, preconceptions. He landed at the exact opposite of where he intended to be. He couldn't be further from home.

'Where is that?' I asked.

'With them,' he said and cleared his throat again.

'Why are you with Gav?' I asked, my voice stronger with this question.

The impulse of my question surprised both of us. It had bugged me from the night we met through countless dinners, breakfasts and stoned nights, that no amount of touching limbs and sneaked kisses gave an answer to, the two of them so different, so far apart.

Karol usually took a while before he answered. I always found it exhausting.

'I guess, in a way...' He paused, sticking his tongue out and pressing it down his lip, his bizarre thinking mannerism. '... in a way, Gav's them.' He pointed at the men in the photos. 'He's the closest I can get to home.'

I felt the corners of my lips lift. Gav was the closest I could get to home, too, its definition slipping further and further away from me.

'Why do you ask?' He turned to me, his voice quieter.

'You're very different,' I said.

Karol shot me an amused glance.

'You know, relationships are only fleeting and fragile spaces between the lines. No one can understand them leaning in, you have to throw yourself in for that space to appear.' Karol looked away and started pulling the blinds down.

'Did you read that somewhere?' I asked. If he was right, these were our lines, veiled in deadpan smiles.

'Yeah, one of those breakfast books,' he said, the only light in the room coming from the open floor hatch between us.

'Can we grab something to eat?' I asked. I had been ravenous all morning, but I didn't want to let him go, not when he was finally here.

Karol lowered himself down the ladder with a huff.

'I've never met anyone needing so much food,' he said, feet touching the floor on the landing.

+

Our favourite was a little sandwich shop on the corner of Llandaff Fields, a ten-minute walk up the road. It was run by Andrzej Jankowski, a moustached bear of a man in his late fifties, round in the upper body and red in the cheeks, small eyes buried under generous eyebrows. Andrzej made a point of introducing himself to every new customer and so his name rang in our ears through the many hungover mornings, his migration story booming above our heads, mostly in English, sometimes in Polish, and once or twice in broken Welsh, which had gained Andrzej a whole new following instigated by Gav.

Andrew's quickly became a popular hub for the Cardiff University LGBT+ society, as well as the community of a local Queer Book and Film Club chaired by Honey's boyfriend, Rhys. Its cosy, small corners were unassumingly furnished with repurposed wooden structures peppered through with rainbow flags. Sipping on a pint of Coke one cold March morning, Gav told me that all Mardi Gras plans had been happening here for the last three years, too.

Whenever I came to Andrew's with Karol, we were offered a freebie or a generous fifty per cent off, and it never happened when I was there with Gav or Honey. Today our coffees were on the house.

'Do you think he fancies you?' I asked Karol when he arrived with our food, neatly distributing it on the table between us. 'You're the only one that gets all the free stuff.'

Karol let out a chuckle.

'Andrzej's not gay,' he said. 'It's a Polish discount. He hasn't been back in thirty years.' He sat down and gazed past me for a while before cocking his head to the right. 'He'd make a good daddy, though.'

This had me in stitches, but Karol didn't laugh along, lips pursed, eyes giving in to a fickle glint.

'Do you know why he's never gone back?' I asked. I wondered if I ever would. I wondered if it got easier with time.

'Sometimes there is nothing left to come back to.' He took a sip of water.

'Is there anything left in Poland for you?' I asked him.

Karol had been dismantling his salad into separate pieces. He couldn't stand certain items of food touching other items of food. There was a complex system to it that I never really worked out. Any dressing or sauce was a great offence, too.

He stabbed a loose piece of lettuce and put it in his mouth.

'So, do you? Have something to go back to?'

Karol jerked his head towards his shoulder and paused, looking past me again, staring vacantly into the long stretches of city park behind me.

'My father's still in Warsaw,' he said eventually. 'Some people I used to know. Carl and Jung, my mother's cats.'

I burst out laughing and he smiled the same smile, his lips pressed tight, face fighting to remain still.

'How about you?' he asked.

I shrugged and shook my head, surprised at the discomfort of that question.

'Not really. My father left when I was young. My mother, well, she left around the same time. She married.' I sighed in clumsy attempts to rush through my childhood as fast as I could. 'She lives in Melbourne with her husband and two daughters. We're not really in touch.' I took a full bite of my falafel baguette, accidentally squirting hummus from the other end all over the table. 'My grandmother raised me. She died two years ago.' I wiped the corners of my lips with the back of my hand, looking away from his face, stricken with shock and something new, sadness perhaps, trying to escape me too, and we sat in silence for a short while, trying to run away from each other. 'My aunt took me in.'

'Jesus, Toni,' said Karol, giving the pile of hummus on the table a panicked glance, his voice turning impatient, but this time he looked back at me and stopped. 'Are you in touch with your aunt?'

'I punched a guy at her daughter's wedding. He tried to feel me up when we were dancing. He was the mayor's son, rich, they said, and worked in Norway, too.' It was strange to think of them, of that night, of the man's big leery hands clasping my hips tightly as he pulled me towards him in an invitation to a dance, fear firing at my limbs, itching to run away, numb and heavy now. 'My aunt told me not to make a big deal out of nothing. It wasn't like he raped me.' I could hear him gasp at this, but I didn't want to look at his face. I didn't want him to see that scared girl in case she came back. It wasn't that long ago, after all. 'I got drunk and made out with my cousin's best friend, a German girl, Nelle. My aunt hasn't spoken to me since. It doesn't go down well with some Catholics.' I hadn't even told Gav this; that morning I thought maybe Karol was the only one who could understand. He stopped eating and was looking at me with caution.

'No, it doesn't,' he said, his hand edging closer to mine, but before it could touch it, he withdrew it and patted his trousers in search of a cigarette packet. He put an unlit cigarette in his mouth, his other hand tapping the table. He looked at me again, took the cigarette out and said: 'My first boyfriend was— Well, they beat him up outside the car factory he was working in. I picked him up after work too often. He was unconscious for a week. Then he married our mutual friend Kasia, and I came here. They have two kids now,' he said under his breath, giving the cigarette a sniff.

I scooped some of the spilled hummus off the table with my index finger and licked it off. I heard Karol squirm, and when I looked at him he was looking past me, his gaze fixed on the window behind.

'I'm honestly surprised you're still alive with your level of hygiene,' he said, placing the palm of his hand to the side of his face to block out the view of the mess, the other hand holding the cigarette to his lips. I remembered Gav telling me that Karol was still working in a Volvo factory around the time they met. I struggled to imagine him in any form of manual labour despite the leanness and muscle that weaved through his arms and chest and made so many men and women swoon as we walked through town. There was a daintiness permeating the display, underpinning every move, the frailty of something broken.

'Can you please go wash your face?' Karol looked straight at me with hilarious seriousness.

I told him he was funny.

He told me I was stressful.

I conceded and stood up. I leant over towards him with a pout as he strained backwards, both hands pushing at my shoulders.

'Go away,' he hissed, turning his head away from my face.

I told him I loved him.

He never said it back.

6

Four months before
April 2014

In just under nine months in the UK, I hadn't ventured outside Cardiff, finding safety in its familiar bricked corners and terraced houses that stretched low alongside the quaint buzz of a handful of high streets.

My random home that came to define me, Cardiff, third and last-minute choice on the list of universities, following Edinburgh and Glasgow.

I had not known a single thing about Wales beyond Super Furry Animals. I couldn't know that the rain would soon get under my skin and spawn its roots, how quickly Cardiff would become home, and how quickly I would leave it behind, too.

How I'd never be able to come back.

When we boarded the train to the valleys, ten minutes ahead of the departure time, Gav informed me that there was no specific arrival time for the party, adding that we should get there just as everything was getting into the swing.

'We had so much time!' I said, the palm of my hand landing on my forehead, thinking about the rush out of the house and our breathless sprint to the station. 'I could've done so much with my day!' I protested. 'I could've slept!'

Gav contested that I had woken up with mushy peas on my foot and it was already early afternoon.

'Well, at least I could've done my eyeliner better.'

'Could you now?' Gav narrowed his eyes at me. He shook his head and pulled an eyeliner, a red lipstick and a half-used bottle of foundation, a slightly different shade to mine, out of a small purse he had buried in his jacket pocket. 'Come here,' he said, pulling my face gently towards his, redrawing lines on my eyelids, his breath warming my face, his touch tender and soft.

It was my first trip to the Rhondda Valley, trickling up towards the Brecon Beacons in one of the many branches of the South Welsh valleys. The voices on the train sounded different from those in the capital. They cackled in high pitches, words impossible to pin down and discern from one another. Girls my age were buttoned up in tight skinny jeans and perched on high heels, their faces tanned, their make-up heavy, reminding me of our queens in clubs. Men roared in sonorous tones, screaming over each other. Most guys had a can on the go. Some younger girls squeezed small bottles of WKD in both hands.

I asked him who was going to be there tonight.

'Who isn't going to be there, more like. Half of the bloody Rhondda.'

Gav seemed slightly on edge, inspecting my face, both palms pressed to his thighs, fingers splayed wide. I told him he looked the best I had ever seen him.

'Thanks, darling.'

'Did you say Karol will be joining us later?' I asked.

'He's got a photography seminar or something. Do this.' Gav pouted and dabbed my lips with blood-red lipstick as I followed his direction. 'Now this,' he said, pursing his lips.

'I'm starving,' I yawned, tilting my head back on the seat.

'Honey was on top form last night.' He let out a short laugh.

'Yeah, you could say that,' I said, shutting my eyes. 'I think I gave his boyfriend a piggyback down Queen Street to Burger King,' I said, looking back at Gav and his perfectly manicured hands. 'What's his name, Rhys, is it?'

Gav nodded.

'Yep,' he clucked. 'The notorious Rhys Jones, slept with half the male population of Cardiff, the other half being straight, and I'm sure even some of them didn't get away.'

'Did you?' I opened my eyes and looked at him.

'I'm saying nothing to you now.' He pursed his lips and looked out the window, his lips breaking into a coy smile in the reflection. Fragments of the night sparked up, flashes of Gav grinding away to 'Alejandro' with Honey, some girl's lips sealed to mine.

Gav was gazing out the window at a long thread of stone terraced houses, tied together in identical looking villages and towns.

'We'll get you some chips and pop in a minute now. It'll sort you right out,' he said, giving me a quick glance.

I had never seen towns like these. Unassuming and low, almost uniform, no ego shooting high in Wales, its ancient landscape, vast and proud, flashing between the rooftops in long stretches of sprawling mountains, flat and heavy.

'It's only when you're out of Cardiff that you're arriving in Wales,' he said with a wistful glint in his eye. 'I miss it sometimes like.'

'It's not that far from Cardiff,' I said. I tried to understand what he meant but I wasn't sure that I did. I wondered if migration worked at such short distances.

'Once you're out, you're out,' he said, left cheek still resting against the glass, looking out at his valleys, hands pressing down at the thighs, fingers digging into the red silk of his jumpsuit, foot tapping away in an uneven beat with the other.

'Are you alright?' I asked.

Gav smiled.

'Yeah,' he said. 'I'm good.'

The train stopped for a short while in Pontypridd.

Putting finishing touches to my lips, Gav started telling me about coal and the communities built around it, for over twenty years now left to their own devices with underfunded infrastructure and centralised retail putting local shops and producers out of business.

I was taking it all in, looking at the town on the other side of the window, a comma in the valley's story, railway tracks branching out in different directions from here, each valley telling its own tale.

I asked Gav if he spoke any Welsh. I thought I heard him say a few words in Welsh to Honey once or twice.

'I did, just to piss him off. He's a Cardiff lad, he hasn't got a clue,' he said. 'I speak it, yeah, well, I get by like.' Gav smiled at the memory and his eyes glazed over. 'Most people around here don't speak it. I went to a Welsh school so was lucky that way. It's different up north,' he said and pouted at me, asking me to draw my lips in the exact same way. 'Almost there, pet, you're looking gorgeous.'

When he finished, I asked if anyone in his family had worked in the mines. We had never spoken about his Wales before, and now I was here, I wanted to know everything.

'Good luck to those poor bastards if they tried,' he said with a loud cackle. 'Daddo was a barman. My mammo owns a pub up in Treherbert. That's where the party is.' He paused and looked at Pontypridd as the train nudged forward and rolled on the tracks with a gentle hobble. 'My mammo, she's a hell of a character, you'll meet her today. No heroes in my family, just a bunch of loons partying. Absolutely feral they all are, let me tell you that.'

I smiled. I loved the song in his voice, sharpness to the letters rolling off his tongue.

'Mammo, you mean?'

'Grandmother,' he said with a smile.

I thought about my grandmother, the only character in my family if a character is measured by resistance, a degree of danger and always fun, everything I had.

'My grandmother was quite like that, too,' I said. 'Wild in her own way, lived her life by her own rules. She laid tarot cards in the most Catholic part of the country. She married a communist, my step-grandfather. She always said she liked the way he looked like Stalin, you know, a big bushy moustache, a big kind of a guy.'

Gav's slender frame shook in laughter at every detail.

'She sounds great. What's her name?'

'Paulina,' I said. 'She died two years ago.'

'Oh, I'm sorry, pet.' Gav winced and put both hands on my thighs, leaving wet marks as he straightened up in his seat.

I shrugged and said it made it easier to leave. I could never see myself staying.

'She was the toughest woman I have ever known,' I said, the stories of the deafening bombs and German soldiers stationed in my grandmother's home whirling their way to the forefront of my mind, a terrifying technicolour film looping memories that were never mine, my voice flattened under their weight.

I looked back at him and the kindness I felt pushed the words out stronger, with feeling. 'She was my everything.' I wanted to tell him that he and Karol were that now, my unlikely family behind the blue door.

'What a beautiful legacy you are to her,' he said, the blue in his eyes glazed over, lips carved into a kind smile. 'Keep dancing to your own song, pet. I'll always be dancing next to you.'

I smiled back and let my eyes shut for a minute longer. When I woke up, there was no one else left on the train. We reached the end of the Rhondda line at Treherbert.

'It used to go all the way up to Blaenrhondda.' Gav pointed at the overgrown track disappearing into the bushes behind the station as we shuffled past it. 'But that was a long time ago now.' There was wistfulness to that collective memory, sadness coating everything that lay abandoned. Gav squeezed my hand and shot me a short smile. 'Now, let's get you some chips.'

I gasped a begging yes and wrapped my arm around his, pushing my hand into his pocket. We huddled under his big purple umbrella, the only splash of colour in the vicinity, my very first picture of the valleys washed out in the rain, its corners blurry, sentences falling into sentiments.

'Gavin Evans himself, holy shit,' the guy behind the counter said, much too loud to warrant our arrival in the fish-and-chip shop, his lips parting and eyes dilating underneath the thin metal frames of his glasses.

I thought it was a strange thing to say.

Gav gave a brittle smile. He always had his act together.

'Alright, butt,' the boy said, his thin voice ringing high. 'Haven't seen you in forever like, butt.'

'Alright, Ben.' Gav nodded at him and introduced me.

We half waved at each other. Ben seemed to straddle both bewilderment and flustered avoidance, simultaneously wanting to look at me and trying his hardest not to. I smiled and looked down at the fish on display, heavily battered and greased, all in enormous portions.

'You know what it's like, butt,' said Gav, his voice higher than usual, the song containing a cackle similar to the one I heard on the train. I had never heard Gav call anyone *butt* before, either. I was trying to work out whether it was bud or butt, like a short for buddy or not. Gav and Ben shared a chuckle.

'Give us half and half, will ya?' Gav threw a five-pound note on the counter. 'And two cans of Coke, please, butt.'

'What's bringing you home from the big city, Gavin?' asked Ben, scooping out chips from the metal grille. Did he mean Cardiff?

'Mam's sixtieth, butt. Should pop down to The Dragon after. It should be a good night.'

He said he might and thanked us.

The Dragon edged proud on the corner of Treherbert's high street, the music booming in a distant echo despite the drumming rain.

'Wendy's on top form tonight,' said Gav as we caught the first notes of what vaguely sounded like 'Bad Romance'.

'Who's Wendy?' I asked, huddling closer to him, my body curling away from the rain.

'My mammo.'

Gav swung open the door to reveal an already half-packed pub. Disco balls spangled all around the room, sparkling in several mirrors hung on walls that were otherwise decked with boxing and mining days memorabilia. An old, knackered jukebox was pushed into a corner underneath a hefty portrait of a moustached man. The aroma of rich ales hit my nostrils; different from the stench of spilled stale cider and the sugary scent of Jägerbombs that marked our regular nights out, adding to the peculiar reverence. A chunky dark carpet covered the entire floorspace, which had never ceased to baffle me, this national obsession of carpeting all possible floor spaces regardless of the purpose of the rooms they adorned.

Me and Gav only fell out once and it was over carpets.

In the corner, the tiniest woman I had seen in my life was having the time of her life, a whirlwind of her own device, swirling round and round in gleeful circles behind the decks.

'My mammo, Wendy,' said Gav, pointing at the far corner of the room.

I didn't know where to begin, gawking at this woman, the age of my late grandmother, dancing to 'Poker Face', which she had presumably put on herself.

'She loves her Gaga, Mammo does,' said Gav, clocking the shock on my face.

Everyone turned towards us as we'd come in and 'Alright, Gav' soon fired at us from all directions. Gav seemed to move his way through the crowd towards Wendy with ease and a half-smile I had never seen on him, a slight lift of the chin with each 'Alright, butt'. He'd enveloped my hand in his and his palm felt clammy. I looked up at his face, now grinning across the room.

'Gavin! Sweetheart!' A high-pitched shriek blared behind us and then a permed blonde bob appeared, followed by the body of the second-tiniest woman I had ever seen, her small figure shaking in excitement, hands outstretched and reaching for Gav.

'Happy birthday, Ma!' Gav leapt in to give her a cuddle, in which she momentarily disappeared completely but for her small, wiry face, covered in uneven pockets of strong, powdery foundation, her jade eyes popping out of bright pink eyeshadow, eyebrows drawn thin and dark. I tried to work out how the tallest man I had ever known came from that tiny woman's vagina.

One of life's wonders.

She scooped Gav's face in her supple hands as if he were a little bird, beaming at him with glee. I had never seen a mother so happy to see her baby. I let go of his hand. She looked up at me with a smile and gave Gav a conspiratorial wink.

'I knew it!' she roared in apparent victory.

'No, Ma.' Gav glanced at me, stifling a sigh. He was embarrassed and it had just clicked with me why. 'This is Toni, a friend of mine I told you about. Karol couldn't come today. He's got work.' Her face went blank as he was saying it and then quickly turned cheerful again when he stopped. Then she turned to me and opened her arms.

'Toni, how lovely to meet you, darling!'

I had to crouch down to give in to her full embrace. Her body felt even more fragile and bony when I hugged her.

'Happy birthday,' I said. 'It's a great party.'

'That's nothing yet, gorgeous!' she said, sounding exactly like Gav, their voices mellifluous and woven through with patterned threads of laughter. 'I'm Gill, by the way,' she introduced herself, grabbing my arm and pulling me towards the dancing grandma, who was now having a ball of her own to 'Alejandro'. The moment the song finished, Wendy flew off the makeshift stage right into Gav's arms like a missile, headfirst.

'Gavin! I didn't see you there, my boy. Alright?'

'Mammo, alright? Rocking Gaga today, I see,' he said. 'You've got to keep the bangers for later tonight now, don't be using them all straight away, it's bloody four o'clock!'

'I've got plenty of bangers, boy, don't you worry. Can you get me some sherry, will you, love?' She fluttered her eyelashes and gave him a peck on the cheek.

Gav nodded, grinning, eyes sparking with her every word. I stood by, my left leg encircling my right so that it enclosed it completely. I couldn't help but think of my grandmother, her strong hands kneading dough, her stare intent, her hair dark until the day she died. Wendy spoke like she moved, with the vitality of an excited twenty-year-old, loud and fast, no pausing for one second.

'Let's grab a drink!' Gav shouted in my ear, leaving it ringing.

It was me who grabbed his hand now, as I huddled next to him, doing my best to tune in to the Welsh voices around the room, which seemed so foreign in that moment, so far away from anything I knew and anything I was a part of, so far away from the safety and familiarity of Cardiff, where people were just travelling through, becoming, taking a break, looking around at options. Everyone in The Red Dragon had formed a long time ago and becoming wasn't in anyone's interest, belonging was where everyone was here, with everyone that mattered sharing the same space. I wondered what it felt like, not needing to look for home.

Gav was ordering two of the cheapest pints of cider on tap and a double sherry for Wendy.

'Alright, pet?' he asked.

'Yeah,' I said, but I wasn't looking at him. 'Everyone is lovely.'

Gav smiled, handing me the pint.

'They have their moments,' he said with a wink and asked the barman to throw in a packet of Mini Cheddars.

I felt safer with a pint in hand. Soon, I would be someone I liked again, that I'd seen a lot more lately, ever since that first night in Pulse, the world a dance, Gav casting his spell. I would be chatty and asking all the right questions, giving everyone my best reactions: Did he, really? I bet! No, don't! That's hilarious. Oh, that's funny. Now, that's interesting. Innit!

My face had been versed in doing its own fitness marathons by then, making up for my lack of expression when sober: lifting eyebrows, bulging eyes out, slapping a thigh with a hand, mouth shouting 'I knew it!' or 'That's brilliant', sticking my tongue out only slightly when listening to a funny story and bursting out laughing enough to seem likeable.

I was a fastidious student of Gav's charisma; what worked with people, what made them fall in love. Mesmerised by the snow, one freezing January night outside Pulse, half conscious but smoking vigorously, he told me he could never tell whether I was happy or sad or angry, nothing was clear until the moment of articulation. Something I had in common with Karol. Were we all like that?

My brain paused at *we*.

Gav disappeared with his pint, and in the corner of my eye I saw him sit down with a group of men at the other end of the pub. I pep-talked myself into diving back in and saying all the right things again, making all the right faces, making the language mine for a second. I landed in a corner booth of men and women, one of them Gill, who introduced the rest as a vague combination of her siblings and cousins and their spouses.

I sipped on my drink, my head turning from face to face, trying to follow the conversation as it traced the family stories. They were busy talking about all the different scars on their children's bodies and how they got them, each incident more dreadful and unfortunate than the other, children falling on barbed wires, pressing their hands on hot irons and pulling cords with boiled kettles onto themselves, names and details drowning in new sounds.

Then someone mentioned brain trauma. Someone else said:

'Poor bugger.'

Gill fell quiet for a second before someone else, blurring in front of my eyes and in memory, said:

'He was top of the tops, Gill, your boy, and tonight we raise our glasses to that!'

Glasses were flung in the air and clinked against each other.

The voices cackled and crowned around me until they froze in silence, someone turning the volume off. I excused myself to the bathroom, feeling dizzy. Were they talking about Gav? Was this why he was ill last year? He never mentioned brain trauma. I splashed my face with cold water but the girl in the mirror escaped me, her edges whizzy too, it was no longer clear who she was. I needed some fresh air.

I glimpsed a sign to a beer garden and followed it out, air warmer than I expected it to be, a light drizzle grazing my face.

The beer garden was a small, concrete square, with only two tables at the back and two benches on each side of the door. A string of bulb lights hung above, flickering faintly.

'Are you Toni?' A voice rang next to me as the door creaked open.

He came and stood over me, and I could match the voice with a body, then a face. The boy was probably my age and it made me think how unattractive youth was in men, in their plump faces, naive smiles, awkward hands and soft bodies. He was wearing a Swansea FC shirt, a pair of denim shorts and black trainers, despite the weather. Madness to anyone from Eastern Europe.

'Can I join you?' he asked.

I nodded, my mind whirring back to the barbed wires and irons, wounds inflicted, no childhood left unscathed, and Gav, glasses raised to some success he had never mentioned, the meaning of Welsh sounds drowned out by alcohol.

'Do you want some?' the boy asked, lifting a pint of lager towards me.

I grabbed it greedily and started gulping it down, not knowing what to do with this boy standing in front of me, with boys and their intentions.

'People say you're a good laugh,' he said.

'I don't know any people,' I said.

He laughed again and placed his hand on my leg.

I looked at his speckled face and short red hair, gelled up, his ugly squishy boyish cheeks, wet in the invisible Welsh rain that had never stopped falling. My face and hair were wet now, too. The rain here was inescapable, we all belonged to it. I wondered whether, if it rained hard enough, it would wash us away, starting at our edges, digging into the rounded, shapeless core.

The boy leapt in to kiss me, cold lips, breath soaked in alcohol, teeth clanging against mine, small fingers crawling up my thigh.

I didn't know how it worked. I'd only had sex once before. It was a pact, calculated and sober, two people unable to get laid helping each other out. Get it over with so that at least we didn't start university as virgins, curb the fear. It didn't work; the fear was still here despite those ten awkward minutes and it came bounding back now with the boy's hand sliding underneath my bra, aggressively and fast. I froze under his touch, the strangeness of the new discomfort creeping up my body. I wanted him to stop but I couldn't make a sound, my mind escaping to the delicate soft mouths of women in Pulse, the delicate hands wielding under their firm touch, desire dancing with fear.

The door to the beer garden opened behind me, joyful fragments of The Divine Comedy's 'National Express' pouring out before it slammed with a thud, leaving the song's hazy murmur.

'Alright, pet?' asked Gav in vague proximity I couldn't determine, my head spinning with shame I couldn't understand. I wanted to cry, and before I could make any decision about this, warm tears streamed down my face, blending in with cold drops of rain.

'Fuck off, Gavin. I'm busy here, mate.'

'That's enough now, butt. She's drunk.' Gav's voice again, closer, lowered and direct followed by lightness, the boy's weight lifted off me. I tried to stand up but my knees bolted, my legs shaking as if they'd walked miles all around Wales again, and I sat back down, closing my eyes, their voices booming around me, looping in and out.

'What's your fucking problem, batty boy? Are you her boyfriend now?'

'What did you call me, butt?'

'Batty boy, you cunt!'

It was a nasty, hateful roar that sobered me. I stood up and stepped forward. Struck by the insult. Numb in my reaction.

'Watch out, Ton!' said Gav, echoing the nasty howl.

I watched Gav fold his fist and lift his arm like he'd done it before, the precision of the angle, the hand steady and slow as it pulled away from its victim, the cheek and mouth of the boy struck with such speed and force that his head bent sideways, pulling the rest of the body with it with a deaf sputter and spangles of blood splattering across his T-shirt.

I locked eyes with Gav. He was gasping for breath, bent forward now, his hands pressed hard against his thighs, squinting at me as the rain picked up.

It wasn't long before men flooded into the beer garden and pushed themselves between me and Gav, before the boy picked himself up enough to rest on all fours, before he spat more blood and stood up, before he launched himself into Gav just like Wendy hours before, headfirst.

I could barely make out their figures, tall and strong, wrestling with each other like two grizzly bears, roaring loud. More men streamed into the garden, their heads tilted forward, hands stretched out, claws out, teeth bared. Some launched themselves at Gav, others at the boy, tugging at their shirts, ripping them open, pulling them apart.

Someone asked me if I was okay. Some woman I vaguely recognised handed me a glass of water. She poked me with it first. She pressed the iced glass against my cheek. I must've talked to her at some point tonight. I thanked her and looked back at the crowd of men, still pulling at one another, shouting.

Gav was being held back by two men, their fingers clawing into his shoulders, their faces distorted in effortful squirms as Gav growled like a fighting dog, hungry for his next bite. It shocked me, the vastness of anger shooting across his face, the same face I only ever saw laugh, pout and flirt. The paunchy bar man was dragging the boy out of the beer garden, right past me, his squishy jaw loose now, mouth foamed with blood.

'Slut.' I could just make out his words as he glanced at me. I felt sick.

Affirmations of 'Alright, Gav' ensued, and for a second it seemed as though it had been the only thing said all night. I wobbled on my legs, shifting forward towards Gav, still torn away from me by men, young and old, now patting and hugging him, his own army.

Gav's eyes darted around the beer garden with a new wild look, patting some men back, hugging others. He looked unscathed. What had just happened?

'There's only one Gavin Evans! Well done, lad!'

Similar headlines flew in from around me, filling in information for those, like me, who stood there, perplexed, looking at my goddess in a red eighties jumpsuit breaking someone's jaw in one punch.

'Gavin "Jawbreaker" Evans!' said an old man in a hoarse, gruff roar. 'That Treorchy twat's lucky to be alive!'

'He was a Welsh junior boxing champion,' someone said behind me.

I overheard a gold medal and 1999 from the opposite direction, now surrounded by people. The entire pub must've emptied out into the beer garden. Someone I vaguely recognised as Gill's sister offered me her coat.

'A pretty bad brain injury,' said the same woman behind me. 'He was hospitalised for a few weeks. Never went back, bless him. He could've been one of the greats. Not sure, darling. He's down in Cardiff now.'

I could no longer tell where the voices were coming from.

'His girlfriend's just by there. That weird looking one, with two different eyes. Foreign. Russian, I think? God knows. They all sound the same to me.'

We stayed at Wendy's that night. She had a spare room which at one point in time belonged to Gav's mother and her sisters. We could stay for breakfast and then catch a train back to Cardiff. Exhausted, I thought it was a great idea.

It was a spacious room on the first floor of a terrace on Treherbert's high street, a stone's throw away from the pub. Wendy told us that Kevin, her husband, took it as a drunken challenge once and threw a stone standing at the step of the Red Dragon. It broke the front window in the middle of the most freezing January she could remember. Gill was only a tiny baby.

'Tell you this much now, sweetheart.' She turned to me as we walked into a small beige hallway. 'Men are a bloody nuisance, this much I've learnt.' She shook her head. 'I'll leave you some pancakes in the oven tomorrow. Nos da!'

She screeched, waved at us, and disappeared upstairs before we even managed to take our shoes off.

'Bloody whirlwind,' said Gav, fighting with his right shoe, laces tied in unsolvable knots. He finally pulled it off with his other foot.

I asked him about his grandfather. He pointed upstairs, where I could make out the faint sound of snoring.

'We're upstairs, too,' he said.

The room once housed three beds with three tiny teenage girls growing up to be the tiniest women in the Rhondda Valley. It now had a double bed in one corner and a vast, chunky cream-coloured wardrobe towering over us as we undressed in silence, drunk and tired. The wallpapers and carpets were everywhere.

I had never seen Gav's body the way I saw it that night: the hard-wired body of an ex-boxer, strong, muscular, aggressive, forward, the body of steel, slender in build, the body that tricked me into being something else.

I slid into bed behind him and he asked me to *cwtch* him.

I weaved my hands around this new body, hard and strong, and kissed the back of his neck softly.

'Thank you,' I said, nuzzling into the nape of his neck, safe.

'I got you, darling,' he said, pressing my hand closer to his chest.

I asked him about boxing. About the championship. About the brain injury.

'There's not much more to it,' he said, quiet and sleepy, tucking his hands, palms touching, underneath his left cheek.

I apologised. If I hadn't let that idiot near me, none of this would've happened. I tried to remember and count the times I had to apologise to Gav and Karol in the last four months, sinking in my own old favourite, the cesspool of shame, tantamount only to moments of crinkling sin lists in my clammy eight-year-old hand before compulsory confessions.

I had fully, dramatically thrown up on the carpet in their hallway three weeks before, having not reached the toilet in a frantic hurtle upstairs.

I had made my explosive vomit stain worse in an attempt to clean it with bleach. I had never seen Karol as pale as the morning he saw it. He had a new one ordered and replaced the same day.

I had called Gav crying during their date nights, incapable of remembering which day of the week it was and not understanding the concept of a date in a relationship.

I had made Karol pick me and Gav up from various and random Wetherspoons as we were refused entry to any cab.

I had repeatedly finished all their boxes of cereal and never replaced any.

I had shrunk Karol's cashmere sweater in the wash once and never admitted to it. He had never given up the quest for a culprit.

My body was used to curling in on itself in confession, like a dog waiting for punishment.

Gav dismissed my apology the same way he always did: 'You're very dramatic, pet.' It was usually followed by the forgiveness of sins: Now go in peace. Today accompanied by: 'I'm fucking shattered.'

A whale's heart can weigh up to a hundred and eighty kilograms, the weight of a car, and it is the largest heart in the animal kingdom. Now, imagine that heart broken.

We were wrapped under a blanket made up of multicoloured squares of different sizes, Wendy's knitting triumph. Feet up on the coffee table, we were holding on to our tiny cups of tea on saucers with a chocolate biscuit on the side. Wendy got up at seven this morning. She had already had her lunch and was off to town to meet a friend. Kevin disappeared just after her, too, heading down the local if Wendy was looking for him. She never did.

'I love that about whales,' Gav said, pointing at the small screen in front with half of his bourbon crumbling in his fingers. The voice on the TV announced that the blue whale had the longest migration of all mammals.

Of all mammals. Always.

We stared at the tiny body of a whale squashed into this tiny screen making his way through the swathes of blue, pushing on, majestically, slowly and methodically, the world's largest giant, of all giants, of all gods, charging at the water so quietly, so softly, before swimming up, higher and higher to the surface; the blue pales into the pallid sky, the water erupts.

'It's amazing when they do that.' Gav crunched on the biscuit, eyes stuck to the screen. 'I could watch them forever.'

'Was your dad a boxer?' I put my cup and saucer by the flowery sofa, so old and worn our bodies had sunk into the middle of it, the coffee table too small to hold both our legs and cups.

'Plumber,' he chuckled, eyes fixed on the whales. 'He died last year. He was quite old. Wasn't your dad a sailor or something?'

I confirmed.

He squeezed my hand. A baby whale swimming close to its mother, holding tight. Their safety was not guaranteed, the narrator proclaimed as melancholic music played.

7

Three months before
May 2014

Gav had gone away for a family wedding at the beginning of the month, a tenuous maternal link, a great cousin of someone's sister, all names lost on me. It was overseas, too, Ibiza, the special place of the bride and groom, everyone staying on for a holiday afterwards.

I asked Karol if he had been invited.

He said he couldn't think of being on holiday anywhere worse, likening it to a long Pulse night out in the heat.

It was strange not having Gav around for this long. It had been almost three weeks and summer days spilled into one another, swelling under the heat, me and Karol drifting past each other in the much-too-bright morning light.

We exchanged exhausted and husky hellos before disappearing into our bedrooms until the midday sun made it impossible to sleep. It demanded action, however bleary and hazy. We converged briefly in those midday moments before going our separate ways; Karol disappeared up into the attic, I usually started my afternoon shift at Andrew's, where I'd picked up a few hours in the last month.

In an unspoken ritual, we came out onto a small concrete patio, bearing a cushion and a book each, pancakes and coffee. Then one of us would scoot out and get plates, cups and cutlery. Today it was Karol. When he came back, there was already something unusual about him. He couldn't stop talking about the book he was reading. I thanked him and slid half of the blueberry pancakes onto my plate. I wasn't awake enough to take in anything he was saying with any genuine interest or understanding, but awake enough to be suspicious of him telling me a story that breached the usual two sentence limit, the story he went into an unnecessary amount of detail about, leading me to think he was either nervous or excited, or both, neither of which he had ever been in front of me.

'Have you ever noticed you fidget your left arm?'

'What?' My head was wrapped up in the scenes of last night, replaying them out of sequence. I zoned Karol out completely. I looked at him, his black strands longer now, blowing about his face, eyes restless, darting across my body.

'You sort of do this.' Karol drew a full circle with his right shoulder. 'You do it quite a lot. I might have photos of you doing it, actually, I never asked you...' He came to a halt, reading something in my face that said I wasn't fully conscious. 'Sorry,' he rushed to add. 'What I meant to say was that I really like it about you.' He shocked and softened me with the directness of that address.

'Okay, weirdo,' I said, unsure about this turn in our midday pancakes ritual. 'You were telling me about this book.'

'You weren't listening anyway.' He poured himself another cup of coffee.

Karol had never paid me this much attention. At gigs, we enjoyed our silence. We sometimes careened safely to people we recognised at the gigs and things they had said, staying clear of each other. On the walks back home, we trod steadily on the sounds and their notes. I opened my mouth and closed it, having no defence.

'No, I wasn't, sorry,' I said, to which he picked up, unphased.

'I like the way you fidget, the way you pick your skin, all the time, so often, a lot,' he said, 'and cross your legs over each other in this bizarre and beautiful knot, the way you hold your lips tight when you pause, thinking of what to say, and the way you laugh, concealing your teeth, the way you hide... the way you hide your body, so much, all the time. You know, that's it. You – all along.' I pressed the cup to my lips but I didn't take a sip. We sat motionless for a while, fingers twitching on our thighs, as if ready to shoot.

'You notice a lot,' I said after what felt like the longest pause. 'You're the strangest person I've ever met, Karol.' I laughed at that to lighten this new tension between us. Karol remained still, scanning my face.

'You're the strangest person *I've* ever met,' he echoed, his voice belonging to him again, husky, quiet and slow.

That made me chuckle, the put-on laughter I had picked up from Gav that worked so brilliantly in the absence of words, a much-needed filler when your foreign brain goes blank and neither language volunteers to fill in the gaps.

Karol smiled, the nervous twitch stretching the angles of his face in caricature.

'Do you want to tell me something?' I cautioned.

Karol cleared his throat and looked away. He was making me nervous.

'I really want to photograph you,' he said much louder than anything else I had heard come out of his mouth.

I burst out laughing, the laughter light in my chest, dispersing thick summer air into pleasant gusts that could fill my lungs with a full breath.

'Is that it? You sounded like you were about to murder me or something. My god, Karol.' I could hear my voice rise unnaturally, high above its usual baritone.

'You know, the two are not that far apart,' he said, lifting himself up from his cushion, stretching his hand towards me.

'Precisely,' I said, grabbing it and pushing myself up, 'what you shouldn't say to anyone ever.'

The attic felt unbearable that day, swollen under the thin tin roof. I knelt in front of a neat pile of vinyl and dismantled it slowly on the floor around me, into a circle of titles, most of which I recognised or knew pretty well.

Karol was taking the working men down and forming another pile on the desk to my left, a tired and what looked like self-built structure pushed underneath the slanted roof. Its opposite slope was still concealed by the black curtain.

I asked Karol what was behind it. He was now busying himself rolling out a large white sheet of thick matt paper and pinning it onto the bare bricks behind me.

'A makeshift dark room, an amateur thing I stitched together last year,' came the answer as he lay down a similar sheet on the floor, half covering our source of air.

I turned to him and asked if he was okay with Ratatat. He asked me if I was alright to undress.

'Gladly.'

'Up to you.'

We turned to our respective corners. I lifted the lid off what looked like an old Soviet record player my grandfather had and carefully placed *Classics* on the black platter, cautiously swinging the arm across. The roaring tiger on the cover caught my eye, its fangs spread wide in warning.

'Pants, too?'

Karol gasped a quiet no, kneading at the last creases, the sheets now falling seamlessly into each other.

I opened a can of Fosters I had brought with me and watched him adjust the lamps: one tucked underneath the slant, leaning on the table, the other I was now resting against, a pleasantly cold metal pole secured by tripod legs.

He asked me to step onto the sheet and shot two streams of light at me.

'Are you okay?' he said, hanging an ironed white sheet on the thin white rail I had just spotted running along the line of the tip of the roof.

I nodded and sat down, clinging onto my warm lager with both hands, fingers rapping at the can. His figure shuffled between the lamps, partly obscured, then revealed in the blinding brightness. Karol was examining them with an attention I hadn't seen him give anything else; there was something cerebral about his touch and observation, like a priest ordaining Mass, the ritual of attending to every single detail with a reverence that was curiously performative and chillingly solemn.

Karol wasn't looking at me, his eyes darting all around me instead, following the dance of light and shadow. I thought about Gav and how he had seen me naked dozens of times, our bodies childlike and innocent in play, one of us usually ending up naked in front of the other at the end of a night out and how shy I felt now stripping in front of Karol.

I drew my knees closer to my chest and pulled my legs closer together.

'Can you pass me another beer?' I asked.

The light jittered across my body as Karol moved the lamp towards and away from himself slightly. He skidded across the room silently, picked up the can from my hand, and handed me one of the ales he kept stashed away behind the records. It was disappointingly warm.

'Thanks,' I said. 'Are you and Gav good?' I was surprised by the candour of my question.

'Why do you ask?' he said after a while, his eyes now peeled on the lenses he was holding in both hands. 'Is something wrong?'

'He's been gone three weeks and you haven't mentioned him,' I said, cautious.

'He's with his family.' Karol picked a lens and hid behind the camera he had positioned on a tripod right above me. 'He's okay though, right?' He shot me a glance.

'Yeah, why wouldn't he be?' I said. The truth was Gav hadn't been okay, and in the month before he left I had hardly seen him sober besides the weekend mornings, when he smiled his widest smiles and assuaged all worries with waves of hands.

Karol stuttered and looked up from the camera. I hugged my breasts as nonchalantly as I could.

'Right,' he said.

'Whenever he sees his family, you never go with him,' I said.

Karol grabbed the camera in both hands and pressed it close to his face, standing above me.

'And why do you think that is? You've met them,' he said, his voice hardened. 'Look at me?' The camera made a clicking sound.

I said I didn't know. It was another lie.

Karol asked me to lean back and relax, but my body straightened up in contraction and my head was dizzy. 'What's wrong?'

I didn't know.

He sat down cross-legged in front of me, camera still concealing his face.

'They've never asked about you,' I said after a while, gasping for air, my throat tightening, veins pulsing underneath my skin. 'And this is weird. It's two in the afternoon and I'm half naked in front of you.'

I felt weak, and confused, and so hot.

Karol put the camera down beside him and looked at me.

'I'm sorry,' I whispered. 'They've never asked about you,' I said, tears pushing into my eyes, thinking about the birthday parties, weddings and funerals I had been to with Gav when they talked about me as his girlfriend.

'It's okay, I know,' he said softly and looked at me, thick strands of hair falling heavy on the side of his forehead. 'I'm sorry. I don't know how to do this either. I just know what I want to get.'

My face felt sticky to touch. I was conscious of how bad I smelled but tried to convince myself that Karol smelled bad, too. He never did, though.

'We can stop now if you want to.'

I shook my head and took one more – final, I promised myself – gulp of Karol's ale.

'No, let's do this. I just—' I hesitated. 'I need you to do one thing for me, too.'

'What's that?' he asked.

'You need to hug me,' I said.

Karol flinched and clutched his camera tighter.

'Why do you think that fixes everything?'

I shrugged.

'You're spending too much time with my boyfriend,' he said, edging himself closer. 'When was the last time you showered?'

'Come on, let's do this,' I said, my voice gaining strength.

Karol heaved a sigh of resignation and clambered further forward towards me, a tamed cat prowling out into the wild, as he cautiously tangled his arms around me, pushing me a little closer to him. My chest pressed against his. His chin slid down on my shoulder, cheek brushing against my ear. He smelled of fucking soap.

'I'm glad he's got you,' he said, his voice ringing an unfamiliar sad note. 'It's good that you're here, Toni.'

'Wildcat' gave a synthesised roar from the two wooden speakers that flanked the piles of vinyl, jolting our bodies apart. We looked at each other.

'Can I take photos now?'

I smiled and nodded.

'I'm going to stand above where I was before. Look up?'

Snap. Karol was panting, tiny drops of sweat crawling down his tall forehead.

'I'll go down now, just above your face, look up at me again?'

Snap. The metallic eye of the camera gaped at me cold.

I asked him if he wanted me to do anything but he didn't reply, his figure diluted in the two blinding streams of light, blurring in the heat.

I eased into the camera's cold eye. I asked him if I could finish his ale since he wasn't drinking it, but he remained silent, his muscles tense in stillness. I caught myself thinking how strong he must've been, to hold himself so still for so long, hunched forward, knees bent. I grabbed his ale from where he was standing and took a greedy mouthful.

Snap.

Uncomfortable with his silence, I felt compelled to fill it. I started telling him about a night out we'd had last weekend.

Karol started circling around me, pulling the trigger at irregular intervals, as I recounted the night in Pulse.

'When Rhys arrived, I took him and Honey to the Student Union, they were running an all-nighter.' Quick gasps punctuated my story as I was constantly running out of breath. 'They actually let them in, they couldn't believe it. Honey said—'

'Toni,' Karol said, my name drawn with solemnity and impatience. 'Please shut up.'

My lips parted; my body stilled under the order.

Snap.

Karol lowered himself, crouching down in front of me, and carefully got down on his knees, edging forward towards my neck and shoulders.

Snap.

He pulled away again and drew closer towards my breasts and then up, the camera inches away from my chin. It was so strange feeling him this close to me, my breath lodged deep in my lungs, too heavy to rise.

'Can you turn around?' he asked. His voice didn't waiver. It came soft and steady, in a soothing monotone against the calming fuzziness of Ratatat.

Karol put the camera down, resting his arms on his lap, beads of sweat trickling down his face. His chest rose and fell slowly as he took a couple of deep breaths.

'It's fucking boiling in here,' I gasped, and continued to fan my face with my hand in silence, glancing at his figure, back shifting between the lamps and adjusting their streams.

I obliged his request, dejected, reclining into a child's pose. I hated my back, bent in scoliosis. The proof of nothing going right with my body. Karol pulled the trigger, sending an involuntary tremble across its meandering, lost vertebrates.

And again.

I closed my eyes, finally at peace, comfortable in darkness.

Snap.

'We're done.' I heard him stand up behind me.

I didn't want him to stop.

One month before
July 2014
Fragments: The Exhibition

Fragments of my body replaced the familial faces of factory workers for Karol's graduation show, his big day, one of those days that defined all further trajectories, spilled us into vast territories that seem almost grotesque with the benefit of hindsight, both of us propelled into separate fantastical worlds of our own.

Right before that happened, though, right before we got old, me and Gav arrived at Cardiff Arts Institute hand in hand in matching red playsuits we had ordered online especially for the occasion. We'd gelled our hair back and put red lipstick on, our lashes dabbed in luscious mascara, our fingers intertwined and holding tight to the other's hand as hands do in foreign spaces.

The exhibition had been garnering some heat. Karol had been invited to St Martin's and Glasgow before it even opened in Cardiff. We didn't understand the extent of the recognition, but he seemed excited; he walked quicker than usual and answered our questions immediately. He smiled more, too. We figured it must've been a big deal. We came dressed for the big deal.

It turned out I was the big deal.

My fragmented body lined four gigantic white walls of the bunker-like gallery space at the back of the cinema in

Pontcanna. The plaque by the door said it had once been a factory of sorts. Photographs were blown up into abstract shapes, blotches of greys and whites weltering through space resurfaced into lines of stretch marks and blots of scratched spot wounds, clenched fists, fingers hovering over lines, exposed and vulnerable.

The shimmering echo of what I recognised as my voice chimed in the recorded message in the background. I remembered recording it for Karol after the session in the attic, reading out loud the lines a poet friend of his had written. The accent surprised me; the dissonance of what I had always heard, belonging here, and what had always sounded foreign.

'It's not mine. *It's not mine.* It's – not – mine,' it rang. On a loop, over and over in a dizzying robotic whirr, whizzing around the thickening crowd in black T-shirts and Dr Martens, their black cotton trousers hanging just above bare ankles, faces drawn and investigating, giving in to sharp nods, purple lips sealed to plastic cups filled with wine.

'Gorgeous wine! Here you go, pet,' Gav appeared before me, squeezing a glass of 'they said it's a merlot' into my hand.

'It's like he slaughtered me and hung me up like a piece of meat, in a way. Do you think?' I asked, my head shifting from one blown-up part of my body to the next in a trance.

'He fucking did, didn't he now?' Gav knocked back his glass in one swift gulp. 'Not big on modern art stuff, not gonna lie to you. Fag?' He pulled a Rizla from the small white leather bag slung over his shoulder.

I accepted it with relief, small and alone under my exposed body, Gav holding up the other hand in front of his face, blocking the brightest piece of the exhibition: a close-up of my mouth, half open, teeth in a disarrayed assembly, not fitting in, pushing out of the limited liminal space. 'Jesus, your mouth's fucking blinding babe,' he chuckled.

'Let's get out of here,' I said and took a cigarette off him.

I T ' S N O T M I N E distorted into pixelated synth beats and followed us out of the building. We passed Karol and gave him a quick wave. He had been deep in conversation with someone looking like his older copy. The man was wearing all black and had thick-framed glasses, greying hair zhooshed into an immaculate quiff he touched occasionally with tips of his fingers, showing off a large black-stone ring. We paused for a second to take in the picture of these two pretentious clones. It was going to be Karol one day, only in his trademark Ray-Bans, his own stylised quiff and black turtleneck.

'Like an avant-garde goth Johnny Bravo,' said Gav, his voice booming into an empty wine glass, drawing attention. Karol gave a dainty wave in our direction and returned to his conversation, unphased.

Gav scooped up another glass of red from the table of unguarded free wine and we giggled our way out of the building into the July sun.

'I can't wait to see Karol in twenty years' time. He will be the hottest fifty-year-old, don't you think?' he asked as the sun struck our pale skin in spiky streaks, leaving it burning. I squinted, looking for shade. I pointed at a bench underneath a lonely oak on the opposite side of the square.

'I can't really picture him in any way,' I said, shielding my eyes with the palm of my hand.

'My gay Don Draper,' Gav bellowed, his voice filled with dreams, his gait sprightly, marching towards the bench. I thought that Karol looked nothing like Don Draper but I didn't want to take that away from him. No one should take a Don Draper away from anyone. 'I am putting out signs to be proposed to, manifesting it hard, if you know what I mean. It's going to happen.'

I put my hand around Gav's waist, dropping my head on his shoulder. His voice was cheerful and loud, thudding in my chest, *his*, through and through, like it always was, except today, in that moment, there was a tinge of sadness to his story, like there was to every vision of the future, clinging on to its fantasy when the present wasn't enough.

Gav flung his arms open and turned to me with a twirl.

'I'll say yes a thousand times and we'll have the biggest wedding bash!'

We should not have started drinking at breakfast. There was no stopping the dream I could never imagine Karol participating in.

'I will wear the most outrageous purple suit and Karol will look stunning in something black and depressing.' Gav glided through the sun-roasted square that stretched before the gallery, a concrete sun trap, his dream of the future roaring, falling into a song. 'We'll get one of those champagne fountains, a fucking free-flowing river, like, a sea of champagne!'

We reached the end of the square, edged on all sides by a string of black wooden benches facing the gallery, our bodies folding into one, as if wilted by the heat, the sun burning my head, fresh red dye pricking my skin. Gav parted his lips in childlike wonder, the fleeting faith of possibility.

'Just imagine this, darling. A sea of champagne!'

I wiped the tears off my cheek, laughing at the expanding vision of the wedding.

'Would you ever propose?' I asked.

Gav shook his head in comical seriousness.

'Oh no, darling. I can only be proposed to.' His arms jostled to the sides once again, letting an empty plastic glass bounce off the sizzling concrete. 'But enough about me.' Gav's hands now clasped mine with the speed of a mouse trap. 'You're a muse, pet! Your tits are up there! If you ask me, if that's not art, I don't know what is,' he said, the tinge of sadness gone, no trace of it when he looked at me, the lit fag stable in the corner of his mouth.

Gav watched me battle with a lighter for a while and with humoured exasperation he grabbed the lighter and the cigarette off me.

'Here,' he said, passing me his cigarette.

I said thanks and exhaled deeply, my eyes fixed on the bunker with my body on display.

'It's not even me, though, is it? It's what Karol said, it's fragments of something. I'm not sure what,' I said, smoke hitting the back of my throat hard, choking me for a moment, throat constricting in a shallow cough.

'It's, well, sort of all of it,' Gav waved at the gallery, his long slender fingers splayed, '*is* you. There's free wine inside you. It's good, too. Which reminds me.' He glanced down at the empty glass at his foot and turned sombre, a warm smile lighting his face in a new kind of joy. 'You've made it possible, darling. He's got his big opening. He's off,' Gav said and took a drag, exhaling slowly, a glimpse of longing in his eyes, fixed on the building, the liminal space of what Karol could be.

We watched the black-clad people leaving and entering the gallery.

'He's not going anywhere yet,' I said, trying to reassure him but I wasn't sure myself. Karol never felt permanent in Wales. Gav must've known that, too. 'Any of your friends coming tonight?'

He let out an amused laugh.

'No cock, no show, darling. Those tits of yours ain't gonna bring none of my boys around. It's all those,' he waved his hand in the air again, vaguely pointing at grave figures dispersing into different smoking circles before us. 'It's Karol's university art crowd. I don't really know any of them.'

I hadn't met any of them either, and it struck me that Karol had never introduced me to anyone, not even Nico the painter who was the only one occasionally surfacing in conversation.

'I know what you're thinking, pet. You've been thinking that for a long time now, but you haven't said it.' I gave a nervous laugh, averting my eyes. 'Karol told me you asked him about us.'

'I just want you to be happy, Gav,' I said.

'You're a darling.' He tapped my knee and pouted. 'He's the best there is, my Karol.' Gav pointed his cigarette at me and threw it on the ground, grinding at it with his leather boot. 'People like us, we need our anchors.' My brain paused at *us*.

It was then, between *us*, when the trajectory of the day and the future took a turn with a confident baritone, low and young, buoyant and arrogant, when the voice rang:

'Is that your back?'

I turned around and looked up at a boy, submerged in shadow, wavy strands of chestnut brown hair grazing his face in light gusts of wind, small green eyes peeking from underneath it. The boy's hand waved the exhibition leaflet in front of my face as he pushed himself between me and Gav, who had just about finished mouthing how cute this stranger was.

'You're Toni, right?' the boy asked, pivoting on the bench to face me, obstructing Gav from my view. 'I'm Apollo,' he introduced himself. I stared back at him with what I could only imagine to be a completely blank expression. The boy's teeth were the straightest I had seen, flawless in design, fitting his mouth with a terrifying ease. I didn't know how to answer those teeth, or what to say to them.

'She is Toni, alright,' said Gav, leaning forward towards me and mouthing my name as if to make sure I still remembered it before leaping upwards, his body casting a long shadow over the two of us.

'Oh, sorry man, I didn't realise.' Apollo glanced up at Gav. 'Nice to meet you.'

'Gav, nice to meet you too, stranger.' Gav gave him a wink and they shook hands. 'Wine?'

Apollo and I said yes at the exact same moment, and I was surprised at the sound of my voice ringing in sync with his, a chilling premonition of my voice submerged in his along with the rest of me, floating under Apollo's visions of the present and the future.

I looked down at the leaflet clenched in his fist, my back in a child's pose underneath the scattered

F T A M E R N S G

the letters sprawled around the page in indiscernible order. I remembered Karol going through the printed copies of the photographs spread around the lounge. I watched him shuffle between my body parts with erratic energy, the neurotic oddball, *my Karol*, so far away from Gav's anchor. *Foreign body – fragments* Karol scribbled in the corner of my back and pressed his teeth deep into the fist he was pushing into his mouth like a distracted toddler. I had never seen him more attentive and caring, cautious and focused.

Apollo inched himself closer to me, his confidence as startling as his voice that had come out of nowhere, tearing through me and Gav.

'Are you a model?' Apollo looked like the prospect excited him but it made me flinch. I concealed my discomfort under a laugh I'd learned from Gav, expansive and warm, reverberating deep inside everyone within its reach. I didn't know how to talk to straight boys. Our worlds hadn't crossed much until now, fear lodged deep between our bodies, amplified by crawling hands, the ease with which they turned into a threat.

I kept my eyes peeled at the bunker door, seeking Gav, the bright floating red blob emerging out of the concrete sheet.

'No, I don't model,' I said after a while without looking at him. The words felt heavy and awkward in the sun's gaze, foreign and strange.

'You should,' Apollo said, the tone of his voice flushed with a strike of heat in the space between us I didn't know what to do with.

Gav appeared on the horizon, a little blossom in the dystopian landscape, clasping all three glasses of white wine like chalices and gliding past the grey crowd as if he was an ancient priestess in a solemn stride on her way to the altar. He placed the glasses in front of us on the concrete slabs, shooting a conspicuous glance at me and disappearing behind Apollo again.

'Cheers,' Apollo and I said, in unison again.

'No trouble,' Gav said.

'How do you know Karol?' I asked Apollo.

'He's in my year,' he said.

'Oh, so you're a photographer, too?'

'No, a filmmaker. Karol's been taking stills on a couple of my films this year.' He smiled at me. I looked back at him this time. 'He's a bit aloof, isn't he? Lovely guy, but hard to talk to sometimes,' Apollo said. I found the boldness of that judgement intriguing.

'Why do you want to get to know him, then?' I asked.

Apollo said he was always eager to meet the mind behind the work he admired.

'And the body,' Gav threw in behind him. Apollo chuckled but held his gaze at me.

'And the body. Sometimes...' He paused, the tone faltering, his cheeks flushing along with mine. '...this time.'

I cleared my throat and said thanks, not knowing what else to say.

'The trick is to be the bait, love,' Gav edged forward, his fingers stretching out to his sequined shoes in a lengthy yawn. 'Karol's a cat, he needs to come to you first.'

Apollo turned to Gav.

'You know him well, man?'

'I'm a bit of a fangirl.' Gav now grinned at Apollo.

'That makes two of us.' Apollo leant back on the bench, gesticulating as he spoke. There was something soft about him, he felt safer than most men I knew. 'The workers were brilliant, the work that went into that, unbelievable, but I'm glad he's decided to go with... *you* for his graduation show.' Apollo locked his eyes with mine and showed his perfect teeth again, apologising as he wrote his number down on my matte paper back. He had to get back to his friends.

'I'm going to this screening next week, there'll be free wine.' Apollo held out the leaflet with his number, his lips breaking into a smile that puzzled me for a long time after, Apollo of the future having little of the bravado he showed in this very first, excellently performed, pick-up. 'If you want to come along, give me a text.'

'Sure, why not,' I said, accepting it, unfamiliar with the feeling of being asked out, unsure what to do with it, surprised at my own indifference.

'Great.' Apollo glanced at me with a different smile, freed from performance and endearing with boyish clumsiness. He clasped the edges of the bench as he lifted himself up and raised his hand at us as he said in shredded beats, 'Cool. See you then. Nice to meet you, man.'

Neither of us said anything, smiling back, the sun pushing our eyelids shut, the two of us squinting at Apollo as he sauntered away with a broken swagger, the walk of someone being watched.

'A bit like Pierce Brosnan, wasn't he?' Gav yawned, his eyes glazed, the sun making me sleepy too. 'Weird that, I've never seen anyone look like Pierce Brosnan. You ever seen *The Heist*?'

I shook my head, half listening, my eyes resting on a seagull battling a crisp packet with desperate squeals, his head all in, frantically tossing the wrapping around, unable to shake it off. At which point do we get up and help him?

'I was obsessed with that film when I was a kid. This Apollo fella, he's a younger copy of Pierce Brosnan in *The Heist*,' said Gav.

'That's very niche,' I said, and yawned too. 'He's not bad looking.' I cautioned around it as an objective truth, belonging more with Pierce Brosnan than me.

'You're going to see him?' asked Gav, pinching my hip. I tapped his hand away and laughed.

'Maybe, I don't know. Do you think I should?' I wanted Gav to tell me what to do, but he shrugged and smiled.

'You won't know until you try, so you might as well, like,' he said, pulling me closer to him and resting his head on mine now. 'Do you think he was joking with that whole Apollo thing?' he asked after a while, his eyes cracking at the edges in thin red linings, tired, so old at that moment. The seagull freed itself, triumphantly clinging onto the crisp, to our enthusiastic cheer. 'It can't be his real name. He's probably an Alan or something.'

9

On the day of
Swansea Pride 2014

Cher's 'Save Up All Your Tears' pierced the swollen air. Karol was smoking in silence, looking his usual morning miserable, some art magazine spread high and wide in defence from the conversation, a blanket of smoke lying low and still in the kitchen. Summer was at its peak, about to fall, and Cher was singing higher and higher, louder and louder, our hearts ringing in anticipation.

In the opposite end of the house, Gav was rumba dancing out onto the corridor, cha-cha-ing into the lounge and rolling out back into the kitchen in a loosely interpreted samba, lost in his dance, circling the flat with ballerina lightness defying his height, the low ceilings and narrow doors.

'Sing your heart out, Cher, darling!' Gav stormed through into the kitchen, his arms flailing in the smoke. There he was, thrusting his hips and tossing his arms in the air, up and down, always cheerleading his own dance.

'Gav.' Karol's sigh drowned in the dancing cues. I sat down opposite him, watching Gav toss the art magazine on the floor with a dramatic head tilt and sit astride his boyfriend. 'You shouldn't be drinking,' came Karol's quiet murmur behind the singing Gav. 'We shouldn't be going anywhere. Not now, anyway.'

'Oh, can I please have a day off?' Gav curved his body backwards and splayed his arms on the table towards me. 'Tell him, pet.'

'What's wrong?' I asked, stroking strands of his hair and moving the tips of my fingers in slow circles around his temples. I looked at Karol but he looked away, blowing out cigarette smoke at the window. I looked back at Gav, purring under my touch. 'Are you okay, babe?'

Gav sprung up and pirouetted himself out of the seat.

'Oh, I'm back on those dreadful antibiotics again, darling, nothing to see here.' He rolled his eyes at Karol.

'They are helping, Gav,' said Karol, his voice hardened, fingers pressing the cigarette butt into an ashtray between us.

'Yes, Daddy, they are working very *very* well.' Gav clasped his hands. 'Now! Today is the day to be super gay!' he bellowed, his lean frame now twirling back into the lounge. 'Come join me, pet!'

Karol said something that neither of us heard or cared to listen to, busy jumping up and down to 'If I Could Turn Back Time', our eyes closed, singing as loud as our voices were willing to carry us. We were halfway through the second chorus when we heard a thudding knock on the door, tapped in the rhythm of the song, announcing an arrival of colour, cheer and joy: Honey, Rhys and Owain, a real bear of a man, an old friend of Gav's from Pontypridd.

They burst through the door, small bags and rucksacks dropped at their feet. Honey, his ginger spikes mirroring Gav's carefully composed quiff, his pale skin already a victim of the morning sun, peeking from underneath white denim shorts and a bright blue net vest in burnt dots and lines, a thin golden chain wrapped around his neck. Rhys's beautiful high cheekbones stretched in a wide smile, black beady eyes sparked with mischief that could only be matched by Honey's,

Rhys's Southeast Asian genes dismissing the solar power of this rainy part of the island in glowing skin, weaving delicate threads of muscle underneath a tight black T-shirt as he flung his arms open to give me a hug.

'You look gorgeous, darling!' he said and moved past me to the kitchen, shouting multiple hellos at Karol. Owain almost filled the corridor in width and height, his big hazel eyes beaming at me, the melodious song to his voice a low bass. Everything Owain said sounded half sung, his shoulder-length hair flying about his bearded face as he spoke. I stood on my toes to wrap my arms around his neck, hairy and already drenched in sweat, his face red.

'Bloody hell, I hate summer,' he said, wiping his forehead with the palm of his hand. 'How are you doing, love? See you've got the party started.' He smiled and we turned our heads towards the squealing sounds in the kitchen. Honey and Rhys flanked Karol, their arms around his neck, ring-laden fingers tousling his hair.

'Alright, boys,' was the only thing I could make out Karol saying as he freed himself from them and stood up, his limbs jerking before he took a breath and steadied on his feet. Gav was leaning back on the counter, laughing hysterically at the scene.

That Saturday morning, we were too drunk to be subtle. All sins were yet to be committed.

'I'll get the bags in the car, Gav,' said Karol, but Gav was busy with fresh gossip from Honey.

'No, he didn't! He's such a slut,' was the only thing that reached me in the kitchen's doorway, bottles clinking on the counter, Cher booming through the flat, our lungs already contracting in the heat.

'Do you need help with the bags?' I grabbed Karol by the arm as he brushed past me.

'Sure,' he said, his mouth twitching into a half smile, his hand already reaching for his packet of cigarettes.

'You smoke too much,' I said, grabbing Rhys and Honey's bags as he bent down for Owain's big tourist rucksack.

'You drink too much,' he said, opening the door, the gushing sunshine setting the hallway alight.

'It's way too bright.' I stepped onto the concrete steps, my toes hot and sweaty in once-white second-hand Converse.

'My point exactly,' I heard him mumble, a lit cigarette pushed into the corner of his lips, shades pulling strands of his hair back, eyes squinting at me. 'You can drop them here.' He pointed to a pile of bags, switching to Polish.

We were staying in a hostel in Swansea. It was right by the sea, apparently, and Gav and Honey had stayed there the year before. I sauntered over to the car, shuddering under the morning breeze that grazed my skin. Karol pulled a motorcycle jacket out of the car and draped it over a white T-shirt. He had refused to wear any rainbow, not even a pin.

'It wouldn't kill you to show more support,' I said, taking the packet of cigarettes out of his front pockets.

'It wouldn't kill you to mind your own business sometimes,' he said, sliding the shades down on his face and handing me his cigarette. 'Here, I'll light it for you.'

I inhaled slowly and thanked him.

'I forget that you're gay sometimes.' I blew the smoke in his face with contempt that rose in my throat. I was angry with him; I thought he wanted me to be angry with him, and he wanted Gav to be angry with him too. 'It wouldn't kill *you* to have some fun with your own fucking boyfriend once in a while. Why are you even going to Pride?'

As soon as I said it, I knew I had gone too far. He dropped the cigarette and stamped on it with the heel of his black leather boot.

'You don't know half of it, Toni,' he said, his voice quieter and cold. 'Do you know why I'm going to Pride?' I shook my head, drawing my lips tighter in active resistance. Karol stepped towards me, his face inches away from mine, nostrils blowing out smoke. He raised his finger to my face and lowered it almost immediately, as if scared by the violence of the gesture, aware of his quickened pulse showing in his veins. 'I'm gay. Why are *you* going to Pride, Toni?'

I pursed my lips, feeling my hands shake. Karol averted his eyes and walked past me towards the open front door. He came back minutes later, his gait sprightly and proud, his head raised high, my backpack in his hand alongside his and Gav's. He didn't look at me when he passed me, and I looked away too. I watched him place the bags carefully alongside each other in the boot. The face that could've been sculpted, angular, its edges strong, drawn in steady lines, pale lips wide and full. A little work of art himself.

Our eyes met for a second, our faces turning towards the sounds of laughter coming from behind us, the twirling cloud of boys gliding towards the car, their faces already painted the colours of the rainbow, bodies contorted in laughter.

I can only remember that moment in slow motion; Gav, Owain, Honey and Rhys all floating down the stairs, a long yellow shawl now snaking Rhys's neck despite the heat, a rainbow cape fluttering on Owain, and a purple wide brim hat adorned with a long leopard-print-patterned feather on Gav lifted in high sail. It's an image that has replayed in my head a thousand times since, a fleeting memory that has become a whole scene, a brief pause of promise before we ceased to exist, the six of us never sharing the same space again after that moment.

'Alright, chickens?' Gav threw his arm around Karol and gave him a peck on the cheek. 'Let's save the drama for later in the evening, shall we?' He winked at me and pinched Karol, who said nothing and headed towards the driver's seat.

Honey, Rhys and Owain whirled about, throwing the rest of their things in the boot and dropping puns I couldn't understand, words often too quick to catch, disappearing into each other, broken by loud chuckles.

Karol opened the door to the car and pointed the car keys at us.

'Owain's the biggest, he's going in the front. You lot squeeze in the back and let's try not to get caught,' he said in an authoritative tone that didn't suit him.

Knots of limbs tucked in behind the seats, our bodies pressed against one another, making the already unbearable heat even worse. Gasping for breath, we rolled all the windows down, the air thinning out as the breeze came in gentle sweeps. Gav brushed the back of his hand on Karol's cheek and leapt out of his seat to whisper something in his ear as we drove out into the road.

Karol in charge of the music, we set off to the synthesised transient waves of Patrick Cowley's 'Love Come Set Me Free', a cacophony of 'But Gaga' dying out to Karol's firm head shake. He turned the volume right up and drowned out all complaints. I smiled, comforted by the sounds I enjoyed completely, the song's every note and every bridge, as Cowley looped the sounds from the limitless sky, the soothing, ethereal beat swallowing my body, floating now, empty inside, out of reach of gravity.

My leg over Gav's, his face hovered above my chest, giggling away with Honey. Rhys was busy taking selfies to my right, pouting at his phone. I fixed my gaze on the rear-view mirror, trying to catch Karol's attention, his eyes locked on the road ahead, as we started and stopped in the outcoming traffic, leaving Cardiff.

I didn't budge, staring at his still face. Karol looked directly at me. His brows furrowed.

'Okay?' I mouthed slowly, looking straight at his face in the mirror.

The corners of his mouth lifted conspicuously as his eyes met mine.

Our hostel was an old brick building on the corner of a terraced block, its floor lined with a threadbare green carpet that welcomed us into a wide hallway belonging to a bygone era, low-resolution photos of people drinking spangled on its walls, photos of pints in the air, pints on tables, shot glasses on trays and in hands, faces puffy and cheeks red, all of them sweaty, bad highlights placing them firmly in the last decade. The stench of sweat, stale beer and long dead parties hit my nostrils as we walked in, the decaying carpet crunching underneath my feet, its threads sticking to the soles of my trainers.

Before I got my bearings, still half asleep from the snooze on the way, Karol was already storming outside, shaking his head and gasping an exacerbated litany of no-ways. Gav rolled his eyes and let out a sigh, fanning his face, which was dripping with sweat, with his hat. I gave Gav a quizzical look, but he only nodded in the direction of the door, getting pulled into the drama of a room allocation at the reception.

I stepped outside in search of Karol and spotted him crouched down by the hostel's entrance, his shades back on.

'There's no way I'm sleeping there,' he said, words barely making it out through his pressed lips, his voice quiet and dejected despite the charge of complaints that started spilling out of him; something about Gav giving him his word, things smelling of piss, and other things being foul. There were more complaints, too, none of which I registered, my eyes following a tall blond boy leaving the hostel and turning a corner with a gentle swagger, his sandy waves shading half his face. The boy paused for a second, turned his face towards me and smiled. I smiled back and he walked on, looking over his shoulder at me. It felt surprisingly good to hold my gaze with him and have him look back at me.

'You're really not having a good day, are you,' I said to Karol, leaning back against the hot bricks of the hostel wall next to him. I looked out at the street, the colourful world in celebratory commotion, the hostel door opening and shutting with a bang.

Karol stood up and rested his head against the wall.

'No, I guess not,' he said.

The seafront was only a street away from us, men ambling towards it from all directions, their vests tight and netted, their pale skin burnt in the glazing sun, shorts ripping playfully above the knee, sore feet rubbing against the coarse rubber of flip flops.

I sat down, stretching my legs out.

Karol slid back down onto the pavement next to me, patting the patch of concrete beside him. He pulled a tissue out of his back pocket and dabbed at his face.

'I hate sweating,' he added under his breath, folding the tissue back into a perfect square. He held it in the tips of his fingers and eventually put it away.

I loved watching his hands, so gentle and precise, delicate but deliberate in every move as if they never knew how to move spontaneously.

'You can always take a dip in the sea,' I said.

'I—' Karol hesitated and pulled the tissue back out of his pocket, folding it in half once again. 'I hate the sea,' he squirmed. I burst out laughing, hearing my voice howl deep in my chest, tears streaming down my face. Karol's lips quivered and broke into a quiet giggle.

'You are a hysterical human being,' I said and wiped the tears from under my eyes.

A boy wearing a sailor costume appeared above us, gleaming at Karol. He must've been older than me by a year or two, but he beamed with teenage youthfulness and a lightness of being I couldn't put my finger on. He had short curly hair climbing into a ruffled quiff, its splayed tips falling to the side of his face, and enormous blue eyes accentuated by high strong cheekbones. He moved his lean body as if dancing, as if swayed by the wind, the way he leapt into the space between us and swung a can of fizzy wine to his lips. He had beautiful lips, wide and full, the colour of cherries, but it could've been the light stain of wine. He was also most definitely on something.

'Where are you guys from?' asked the boy, his voice languid and soft.

We looked at each other and replied in unison: 'Cardiff.'

'Oh,' he gasped, surprised, and laughed, his mouth half open, as he questioned our origin. He said he'd just heard us speak a language he felt instantly attracted to, he loved its harsh edges and blunt tone, the rolled r's that sounded Welsh. 'Are you guys Welsh?' he asked.

I looked at Karol staring at the boy, his lips parted too, curved into a smile, struck under the boy's spell. I had never seen him pay anyone this much attention and I wanted him to stop.

I told him we were Welsh and the boy nodded, smiling, his big Bambi eyes wide.

'We're from the Black Mountains. It's, well, it's a dialect of our village.' I scraped through my memory for the most Welsh sounding syllables I could think of. 'Llarsaw.' If anything, it sounded like a Welsh Warsaw. Karol didn't pick up on my joke, continuing to stare at the stranger unabashed. The boy said he had never heard of it, but he didn't know any Welsh, he was from Blackpool. He asked Karol if he'd seen two tigers wandering wild around the west side of the beach and he waved his long arm to our right. Once in a while, one of them gave a deafening roar and he wondered whether it was a cry or a laughter, an outrage or a plea. He couldn't place it and asked if we could help.

'I've seen one of them,' said Karol, his tone of voice unchanged, if anything softer now, carrying a melody I hadn't detected before. 'He seemed quite lonely, out of place.'

The boy's shoulders drooped and his high turned to sorrow, head nodding wistfully.

'I saw that too, his loneliness,' the sailor boy whispered and there was a surprising sadness to his voice. Then he shook his head violently, like a dog shedding water after a swim. 'I'm a sailor,' he said. 'I need to forget those tigers. I'm waiting for a whale. It's going to come, today, maybe tonight.'

'I've always wanted to see a whale,' I said, in an attempt to peel his face away from Karol's. 'My dad was a sailor.'

The boy turned around and looked me in the eye, his pupils wide and pulsating slightly, a creature in his own world, locks touching his tanned forehead.

'Did he see the tigers too?' he said and chuckled to himself so jauntily and with such disarming honesty that we joined in. 'You're the nicest people I've met all day,' he said and leant forward, cupping my face in his hands. He enveloped my lips in his, tasting of strawberries and wine. 'Take care, friends.' He peeled away from my face and turned to Karol. 'I need to be ready when the whale comes,' he said, pressing his lips into Karol's and pulling away. He clambered back to his feet and smiled at both of us. 'I'll come back and find you,' he said, his eyes glazed. We looked up at him and watched him disappear into the crowd, gone as quickly as he'd arrived.

'Maybe today isn't going to be so bad after all,' said Karol and sprung to his feet. I hadn't seen him this animated since I got him drunk in Cardiff Arts Institute, where he dismantled their Lego bridge wall. We kept finding Lego blocks in our pants all through the next morning and he could barely move for two days. It was the best money I had ever spent on sambuca.

I was about to mention his boyfriend but his boyfriend appeared in the hostel door, wiping the sweat from his face with both hands.

'All done, darlings,' he said, climbing down the small concrete steps towards us. 'Karol, I got us a separate room. I've been up there. It's as clean as you like.'

Karol said nothing, took his shades off and did what I had never seen him do. He walked over to Gav, pressed his body against his boyfriend's, pushing both of them up against the hostel wall, his lips sealed to Gav's. Karol's hands were gripping Gav's face long enough for his arms to loosen and wrap around Karol's body, pulling it tighter, Gav's hands now ruffling Karol's hair and caressing the back of his neck.

I glimpsed Honey, Rhys and Owain step out of the hostel, their eyes bulging and mouths open at the scene before us, two bodies pressed together so tight you could argue they were never apart. The three of them looked at me, their eyes becoming larger as if in question, but all I had to offer was a shrug. When Karol pulled away, he looked only at Gav, Gav's chest lifting and falling out of breath, gasping, his body still. I had never seen him speechless before.

'I'll get our bags,' said Karol and walked away towards the car, brushing past Rhys.

'Well, happy Pride, sunshines!' yelled Honey and blew a small red whistle he had strung around his neck.

Gav smiled and looked at me, out of words for a few moments longer before he asked:

'What have you said to him, pet?'

'Nothing,' I said. Maybe Karol was right. Maybe I only knew half of it.

10

The plan was to drink, quickly, out of the now-warm cans we had brought with us. I had never seen Karol drink this much or this fast, thirsty for release. Lighter on our feet and in our hearts, the world glimmering and shifting before our eyes in the sparkling summer, we were ready to march, hand in hand, mine in Gav's and Gav's in Karol's, Rhys, Honey and Owain ahead of us.

I had never marched for anything. I had escaped all Catholic processions I had been dragged along to, solemn and wallowing, and slid out of all school patriotic marches, too. I had never *believed* in anything until that Saturday, when the imposition of a different *us* that I had questioned my whole life made sense, that day *we* made sense.

Gav was leaning on Karol's shoulder, his arm wrapped around his waist, face brushing against his. I chanted along, running my thumb up and down Gav's hand, soft and hot, our steps swaying off course, breaking into a dance with the Pet Shop Boys blasting out of a speaker that had appeared behind us, turning the chants into lyrics, throats catching on the familiar loved melody, the rare sounds that united the three of us in a dance, three pairs of hands flying high in the air, steps in sync with one another.

I had never seen Karol dance before, the body I only knew as rigid and conscious was free now, intertwined with Gav's, hand grabbing mine. He twirled me around and weaved himself past me, leaving me to dance between them. Gav was jumping to the beat, his entire body consumed by the song, hands high in the air and twitching to the rhythm. Gav's hand found Karol's and they were singing out to each other now, bodies rising and falling with the same pulse, bodies that knew how to be close around each other. Gav turned to me and grabbed my hand, pulling me in with another twirl. Karol weaved his fingers in with mine and for the final notes of the song we danced to our beat, holding on to each other, bodies all around us swaying, jumping, dancing, some thrusting, the final words to 'Go West' loud and clear, bellowed at the tops of lungs, from the depths of throats, pulling at heart strings. When the speaker disappeared into the crowd ahead and the slogans returned and our steps evened, a tall dark blonde woman rocked up by my side and grabbed my hand, softly seeping her fingers through mine.

'You're gorgeous!' she shouted in my ear, letting it ring for a while.

She was beautiful, with dark chocolate eyes, hair brushing her shoulders in wavy knots, skinny jeans wrapping her long legs and Morrissey leaping out from underneath a bouquet of flowers on her chest. I lunged over to give her a kiss, alcohol surging through my body in a new bout of confidence, in all being possible, hands slipping out of Gav and Karol's knot, out of their familiar faces and amused looks. We stood embracing, letting the crowd brush past us, my head dizzy in the midday sun and drowned in what, at the time, felt like a litre of cider.

Her name was Tallulah. I hung myself on her shoulder, head hanging loose, as she shouted along in French, echoing each of the battling mantras. *Tallulah*, I kept saying to myself. It rang so beautiful.

'Toni,' I whispered in her ear, stretching my hand out in a greeting. She smiled, looked me in the eye and kissed me instead. I gripped her hand tighter. She said she wanted to have some fun. When she said that, she arched over and bit my lip, slowly, as if she was tasting it, smiling playfully. She placed her hand on my stomach, running her fingers down to my zip. I placed mine on hers with a quick peck on the lips.

'Let's have a dance.' I threw my head backwards, enacting my most camp impressions of Gav and Honey that I had studied and collected over the last few months. Everyone, absolutely everyone was dancing in the streets that Saturday, but maybe, maybe it was all in my head, because nothing was still in that moment, not least us. Tallulah sprung upwards, grabbing my hand, and for a moment we were just two girls in the playground, fun and wild, *young*.

When the sky turned red, the cider started to wear off and punters started to crawl back into pubs. I told Tallulah we needed to find my mates. Everyone seemed to be headed to the Queen's Arms that curved right across from the beach, a thirsty finish to the day-long dance.

Locating Owain wasn't hard, his trombone voice bouncing off the pub's walls in roaring laughter, brawly shoulders hovering above the crowd of half-naked men, now cheering on the drag queen doing her most faithful Cher of *Heart of Stone* era in the most touching rendition of 'Does Anybody Really Fall in Love Anymore?'

I slid through the wet bodies, air thick and puffy, breaths soaked in booze, strangers' hands grazing my waist. I dove head in, aggressively grabbing the barman's attention.

'Oi, get in a queue, pet,' yelled a familiar voice behind me, Gav's crotch pressing against my bum.

'You're here!' I spun around and threw myself on him, wrapping my legs around his waist in a knot, annoying everyone around us who had to reshuffle. Gav swayed backwards, grabbing onto me tighter.

'You're fucking mental!' he roared in my ear, steadying himself as I stumbled back on the floor, holding on to his shoulder for balance. 'So who's your girl by there?' He looked at Tallulah, who stood squeezed between two very muscly men having a very dramatic conversation right over the top of her head. She waved awkwardly across the room, gesturing that she was going to order the drinks. Gav shot her a flirtatious glance. She looked helpless queuing at the besieged bar, where only the butch, the desperate or lunatics seemed to get served. He turned to me and winked, clucking his tongue.

'Nice one, pet.'

'Where's Karol?' I asked, glimpsing Tallulah starting to push her way through with a lot of shouting in French.

'Oh, no idea darling, he'll rock up somewhere,' he said and gave a quick laugh. 'I'm sure he's alright, doesn't like crowds much, my boy. Not sober, anyway.' Gav rolled his eyes, flinging his wrists in the air, hands hanging down, a smile turning sour. 'What can a girl do!'

'What can a girl do,' I said softly and touched his beautiful face, caressing his cheek with the back of my hand. He couldn't keep a still face, eyes darting around the room.

Gav bit his lower lip and slapped both hands on hips.

'Careful, now. I only let one girl touch me like that.' He tried to lower his voice to a hoarse gruff but it broke halfway through the sentence and cracked open into a friendly pitch.

Tallulah came over with three shots of sambuca tucked between her fingers and three pints of lager locked safely in her arm.

'Very kind of you.' Gav bowed.

'No problem, friend.' Tallulah cheers-ed us in the air. '*Santé!*'

'*Lechyd da!*'

Tallulah asked what it was in Polish but my answer was drowned out under the roars of '*Lechyd da!*' sweeping through the room, shots and pints flying up in the air.

'Culprits!' bellowed the drag queen from the stage. 'You three darlings! Where are you from, gossip girls?'

'Space!' yelled Gav.

Cher tapped her long eyelashes, glancing around the room.

'I can see your Welsh cunt from up here, darling!' Gav bent over howling with laughter, splashing half his pint on me and Tallulah. 'Do you wanna sing a song with me, babe?'

Gav downed his pint and shot a thumbs-up in the air. He pressed the empty pint glass into my chest and hopped through the dancing bodies towards the stage, straight into the opening of 'If I Could Turn Back Time'.

'You're in love with him,' said Tallulah, gazing out into the crowd with an idle smile.

'What makes you say that?' I wanted to sound indifferent, but my voice came out high and broken.

'The way you look at him, like he's the most beautiful thing you've ever seen.'

I looked away, trying to locate Owain again, to anchor this moment elsewhere, the warm pint glass pressed to my lips, unable to take my eyes off Gav, now saddling the stage sideways, the drag queen pressing her sparkly red heel into his back to general cheers.

I wasn't sure how long we'd stood there. It could've been Cher's lifetime, Gav in the centre of it, all of it. Honey soon joined him on stage and started jumping up and down, Cher wrapped around Gav's waist like a festive bow, lost in manic laughter.

Tallulah clutched my hand and pointed towards the toilets. She wanted me, and in that moment it felt good to be wanted so urgently. Time stilled and I followed behind her, alcohol easing my body to submission again, obliging desires.

When her tongue touched my lower lip, fear pricked my skin. The boy in the wet Welsh valleys pushed on top of me now, his tongue riding down my neck, her hand unzipping my trousers, her teeth grazing my ear. Panic spilled into my limbs remembering girls in Pulse, their eyes hungry, hands greedy, all rushing through my head in a drunk whir as I stood frozen under Tallullah's touch, my back arched over the cold toilet seat, her hands cold and sweaty on my skin, unresponsive to her touch. Outside men were shouting along to the peak of 'Believe', Cher in charge of narrating this memory, the men behind closed doors, behind the intimacy and loneliness of the moment, Gav among them, his beautiful lips wide in the joy of fragmented lyrics.

'Are you okay?' Tallulah pulled away and stood above me, panting. 'I thought you wanted this.'

I lifted myself up, looking away from her, embarrassed, my eyes grazing the mouldy tiles papered with stickers, filthy particles crumbling on the drying glue of ripped paper reading: *FREEDOM, queerlife.co.uk, been abused? Helpline! Suicide prevention, THE ONLY LESBIAN NIGHT IN PORTHCAWL, end queer violence.* There was a drawing of an ejaculating dick, dry cum smeared all over it. My head was spinning.

'No,' I heard myself say. I didn't, no, and I didn't know why, why I felt so numb under her body, why I had the courage to punch the man with the leery hands at my cousin's wedding and why I was struck so silent under the Welsh boy and his creeping little hands, why I never felt safe and why she wasn't safe either.

'Why are you even at Pride, love?' The question rang again, urging the decision. *Dare to belong*, it said, the parting announcement, etched in my memory, as some words are, pressing, pressing so hard, over and over, their nails between my vertebrae.

11

The Sailor Boy

Distorted disco lights spangled and flashed across the room of a club I found myself in, sometime after Tallulah slammed the doors of the pub's tiny cubicle and stormed out, my throat swelling in the heat. I had no idea where the others were or how I got here. What a party, life at nineteen.

For a long time, everything around me was beaming and morphing into faces I couldn't recognise, lost in a dance and the thudding beats, forgotten Polish faces, words left behind, mouths moving in familiar syllables that no longer made sense. Body conceding control. Which bodies control which? It was too early to know at nineteen. All joined in now, to the distant lyrics I mimed to, making up Polish meaning out of unknown English words, my heart pounding, hands sweating, ears ringing, it scared me how numb my legs were, detached from the rest of me, my neck burning; now, one more time, everyone, faster—

Dance!

There came a touch, shooting through the dance, in the middle of the starred dance floor, tearing me away from dancing strangers. It was eerily tangible in the mess of sounds, abstract under a thick surge of alcohol. The touch felt sweaty and warm, it was skin that I knew, that I had learnt to recognise, lines I could always trace from memory. If I closed my eyes now I could picture that hand on mine that night, its veins bulging slightly, skin stretched across the structure of the bones, light, fluffy hair coating the wrist.

'Toni, are you okay?' Karol's words boomed loud in my head and echoed, transmuting into his familiar figure, his face sweaty, hair patted back. Something changed in his expression when he looked up at my face, something I had never seen on him: worry, the short pang of a sinking heart. 'I've been looking all over for you.' My cheek felt hot under his touch. 'What happened?'

'I don't know,' I said, trying to piece together the night ruptured by Tallulah's departure, her cold parting eyes, my shame swelling in numb fingers that had just stroked hers seconds ago. I looked away from Karol's face, glimpsing the muscles on his arms tensing.

'Let's get out of here,' his lips grazed my ear, his words leaving it ringing.

We stumbled out of a pub I didn't recognise. I had no idea how I'd got myself there. We fell into the crisp night, the wind picking up as we pushed against the human tide running in a steady current towards the clubs. Karol put his arm around me and pulled me closer, tearing through the crowd. His eyes darted across men as we passed them, his voice dropping and rising in volume, distracted.

'How did you find me?' I asked him.

'I've been asking all over for you,' he said, turning into an empty side street lined with low terraced houses, our bodies easing into an amble. It struck me and softened me, the worry and the search, the love that always nestled behind them, its safety. I wanted him to hold me in that place and I wanted to learn how to hold him too, but our bodies were too tired that night, comfortable in the practised distance. 'Then, there you were, dancing.' He paused and stilled, his eyes sparking at the memory. The night was in a disarray of broken shards of manic conversations, none aligning, the five of us spangled on its edges, dissolving in drink and pills. Karol fumbled two crumbled cigarettes out of the back pocket of his black jeans. 'Go on, have this one.' Cigarette drooping down his mouth, he leant forward to light it.

I took it out of his mouth and scooped down on the kerb. I felt sick and exhausted, a biting wind sobering me with its strikes. I needed to sleep.

'Are you okay?' I asked him.

'Yeah,' he said, lighting another cigarette and taking a slow inhale. 'Yeah,' he said again, his free hand tapping at points on his body in search of something. 'What happened?' He continued to stand next to me, looking down at me with short glances. I navigated the details of meeting Tallulah, wanting her, or maybe only wanting to want her, paralysed by her touch. Karol smoked in silence, listening.

'I'm sorry, kid,' he said eventually, sitting down next to me. 'You know,' a funnel of smoke escaped from the corner of his mouth, 'you don't have to have it figured out on anyone else's time.'

I smiled at him.

'Where's Gav?' I asked after a while.

Karol looked at me, his eyes widening at the question.

'I haven't seen him since the march, I—' He looked down at his shoes and started rubbing the tip of his black DM. 'Was he there? Was he in that pub with you?'

'Yeah, initially, not the one you found me in,' I said. I willed my memory to stitch the night into a linear timeline, but it kept breaking up into a scree of beats, words and bodies all bounding in my head.

'Right,' he said, the cigarette burning his fingers, the butt alight and sizzling between the tips giving in to a light tremble. 'Right.' He dropped the cigarette and stood up, looking out into the narrow street ahead of us. We wished we had more cigarettes, occupying our hands and mouths, now lost, longing. 'Let's get you to the hostel, kid, come on.'

I told him I'd be fine getting there by myself, but he shook his head and held out his hand towards me. I took it in mine and he lifted me up.

We strolled on in silence. Crowds had dispersed into clubs where the real fun was starting, where bodies pressed against bodies under the flickering disco balls, and where bodies straddled bodies on the threadbare leathers of corner sofas. I watched him pace beside me, hands in pockets, face pale, dark eyes tunnels into a space far away from me and far away from now.

'Are you going to be okay now?' he asked when we got to the hostel. He looked aged by our walk, the texture of the skin whiter still and dry, eyes darting from me to the building.

'Just call him,' I said and gave him a smile, but he responded with a vacant look.

'Yeah,' he said. I embraced him and he caved in this time, small and more fragile than I ever felt him. He pulled me closer and kissed my cheek and I thought, again, maybe I did only know the half of it.

'Get some sleep. I'll see you tomorrow,' he said quietly and turned towards the empty street in the direction of the clubs.

I looked at my phone.

Two texts from Honey. One from Owain. All read: *where are u?* Three missed calls from Rhys. None from Gav.

I fell into the first bunk to my left, flat on my face, blacked-out memories seeping into my dreams, the Sailor Boy sitting on the bed opposite, his face bright in the moonlight pouring in through the large window, the light parting the bunk beds on each side, his sailor stripes sopping and blurring in the rain that fell on him.

The blurred edges of his body were shaking and I knew he was excited. He couldn't wait to tell me, he said, and his voice was distant, blunted by gusts of wind I couldn't feel, he couldn't find us anywhere, me and that boy I was with. I would never believe this, but he had seen the whale! The one he was looking for!

I asked him about the tigers but he brushed it off with a shrug. They were clearly not as important. I remembered that one of them was lonely.

'No, you don't understand,' he said, shaking his head, his face fantastical, its contours washed in the rain that fell only on his body and nowhere else in the room. 'I have seen *the whale.*' He spread his arms wide to illustrate his point, water dripping down each hand. The boy was raining! I pondered this reality – how could anybody gather and contain so much water?

'The whale was enormous, beautiful, fierce, a real *force majeure,*' the boy continued to tell me. I thought that I had never heard anyone use force majeure in a sentence before. 'Have you ever learnt French?' he asked but waited no time for an answer. 'No need, English swallows and filters French like whales taking sips of plankton.' He chuckled, a drowned sound. 'I've only seen him far in the sea, he was a blob of sorts, barely perceptible but *there.* I could feel its presence.' The boy told me how he swam and swam, as fast as he could, as deep as he thought the sea must've stretched at points, but he couldn't get deep enough or far enough despite the blob still in the sea, waiting. 'There!' The Sailor Boy pointed at the moon rippling into the room in multiple uneven streams, the cosmic seed that fell into the estuary of light, now stretching to both of us, the boy's face dripping in water, wry in excitement that slid into disappointment like a missing slide, a badly cut together film. 'I had to give up, I had no strength to swim any further, any closer, but every time I went under, every time I submerged, water spilling into my lungs, I could see it there, majestic and heavy, so graceful.'

'How did you get back?' I asked, my voice coming from somewhere else in the room and echoing all around me.

The water rose up and now fell down his body in buckets, weltering down with a powerful shimmer, louder and louder. He couldn't hear me through the water falling down his face. I shouted louder.

'How did you get back?'

'*I have seen him*, do you not get it? *I have seen him*,' the boy shouted back, as if he'd just heard me and that made him whole for a while. His body stilled, eyeballs now dissolving in water, running in distorted streams. It should've been creepy, but it was only sad. He was sad. How could I tell how sad he was? Was this sadness even his? He was weeping now, his voice wallowing. 'I couldn't catch him. He was so close, but I couldn't catch him.'

I kept asking questions. Was it *him*? Was it the whale? Was he sure? How could he make it out in the darkness? Eyes fail us in darkness. Could he trust them?

I couldn't be sure if I trusted mine, but I kept squinting to piece him back into a solid human shape. It only worked for a handful of seconds, and he dissolved in the rain again, water drizzling down his cheeks. It could've been tears. I couldn't tell, I would have had to taste them. Aren't tears as salty as sea water?

He slouched now, face drooping.

I reassured him he was going to see him again, if he'd seen him once already, he would again.

'That makes no sense,' he argued.

'No, it doesn't,' I admitted. I didn't have anything better.

'I couldn't keep up, I couldn't catch the whale,' the Sailor Boy moaned, his face concealed by his hands, veiny and pale blue in the moonlight.

The boy sprang across towards me in terror, his wet hands landing on my shoulders, soaking through my skin, water cold as ice. It should've been ice, but it wasn't, it burnt getting under my skin. He started to shake me, water now spraying everywhere, dripping down my shirt, his voice scared, a wallowing cry.

'*I couldn't catch him. I tried.*'

'They couldn't,' cried Honey.

Honey? The Sailor Boy was gone as quick as he came and the room was bright, no river flooding Honey's face, now clear in front of me as I opened my eyes. Honey's face was wet, mascara dripping down both cheeks in tears. They were definitely tears.

'Toni, he's— You have to come.'

I tried to figure out where I was, who I was and where the boy was. What happened to the whale and the Sailor Boy? But time ran and it would never wait for me, seconds overlapping and overtaking each other, too few of them to make sense of Honey's face in half consciousness, of what he'd just said. Was it his wet hands on my shoulders? Why was he wet?

Honey edged himself away and stood in the middle of the room, weeping, nails clipping his hair tight, pulling at its strands. Out. He wanted them out, he was pulling so hard.

He was frightening, so much more frightening than the raining Sailor Boy; fright was all around and between us, etched in his face, stretching out mine in the unravelling sunrise.

'He's dead, Toni. He's—'

'Who?'

Anger came bounding to help, but it was too early. It needed time to process and there were not enough seconds, they existed in no order, falling like our tears, and time lacked order to create meaning, to start from the beginning, to move past the shock.

Everything died with—

'Gav's dead, Toni.'

II

The Ultimate Picture Palace presents

12

I was looking at the girl in the mirror enclosed in a heavy golden frame, her eyes, one mismatching the other, looking back at me without expression. She was wearing a short blue cotton dress, described to her as casual and elegant. She'd bought it from a small second-hand boutique on Portobello Road, where she lived now, after her boyfriend had spotted it in the window and told her he liked it. I patted my head and she copied the move, running her pale fingers through bleach-blonde hair, so light it was almost colourless. I pouted in the mirror, jade art deco tiles shimmering behind the girl, and dabbed my lips, red with lipstick, just like Gav used to do them. My eyes were painted in the same golden sparkles of Cardiff's most beautiful drag queens, a look I'd studied and perfected. I smiled and the girl smiled back, a rehearsed smile.

Her boyfriend was a nice boy close to her in age. If she was cynical, she'd describe him as handsome and rich, but I would say he was kind and quite fun, and above all else he introduced me to a new world when the old one ceased to exist. This new world spilled first into Roath in Cardiff, on the other side of town from Pontcanna and the blue door. The new world contained itself in a shared house full of boys very different from mine, boys who didn't wear make-up, boys who were into film and girls.

A week after Gav's funeral, when rain fell along with everyone's tears but mine, I texted the boy that looked like Pierce Brosnan in *The Heist* and invited him out. Tonight we were having dinner in the bizarre world of Brasserie Zedel, in Soho, London, where I was about to meet his mother, a fashion designer, Catherine de Palma. Everything about the evening was completely surreal, this new city contained in the world of fashion and film, held first in Notting Hill and now in this glamorous snapshot of 1920s extravaganza.

I curled thin blonde strands behind my ear.

The girl in the mirror winked at me and I looked away from her, now all on my own.

I climbed the spiral staircase of this underground world trapped in a Great Gatsby fantasy, and emerged facing an extraordinary room, vast in its size and busy with wealth, the ubiquitous golds and bronzes glimmering in a theatre of lights. I took one glance at a waiter who gave me a nod and I followed him through a maze of tables, laden with stacks of seafood, meats, and expensive looking alcohol, all as foreign to me as the concept of a fashion designer being someone's actual job.

I spotted Apollo in the corner of the room, his hand stretched in my direction in a heedful wave.

'Oh my god, this place.' My lips parted as I sat down next to him. The chair opposite was still empty.

'It's my mother all over,' said Apollo and rolled his eyes, his voice quiet and unassuming. 'I asked her to go low key tonight.'

This was the exact opposite of low key by anyone's standards – the colour, wealth, texture, light. Apollo and I excelled at low key, hiding from the world together. On the days we weren't working, we played PlayStation and had quick horny sex, living on pizza and Chinese food in an absolute and beautiful mess. This hadn't changed much since we moved to Apollo's place in Notting Hill two weeks ago. The house belonged to his grandmother Genevieve and was equipped with nothing beyond essentials and Genevieve's enormous, creepy four-pillared oak bed with a blue velvet canopy, a monstrum that held all our living.

I could almost feel Catherine before I could see her, gliding down the hall like an elegant dove, lines and numbers running across her face in uncanny symmetry, a museum-worthy specimen of mathematical beauty. I could picture her on a magazine cover, like the one I held in my hands in 1997, its headline proclaiming that Catherine Zeta-Jones had the most symmetrical face in the entire world, deeming her the most beautiful of all women. What a title. The most beautiful of all women.

Of all women.

In 1997.

Incredulously, this Catherine looked just like Catherine Zeta-Jones, with long dark hair and wide eyes of dark amber. She was a wonder I couldn't stop looking at, an artifice I wanted to dismantle in hope of understanding. It wasn't just the face; it was her stature too, long and ballerina straight, her neck slender and long, bust and hips the perfect proportion of a fifties housewife, embroidered black fabric veiling her voluptuous figure. She was the ultimate woman if there was ever to be one – a mother and lover to all.

'I'm sorry I'm late.' Her voice rang deep and smooth, like a voice-over actress. She had a slight accent and I wondered if she detected mine when we exchanged greetings, if she sought solace in those foreign spaces we were safe to occupy without danger of exposition. 'So happy to finally meet you, Toni,' she said, smiling, bearing a perfect set of teeth, much like Apollo's. They had the same lips, beautifully in proportion to their strong jawlines and small noses, their eyes identical.

Catherine ordered a very old champagne as soon as she sat down.

'Mum, wow, you didn't have to.' Apollo looked embarrassed, glancing at me with a half-smile.

'Nonsense,' she waved. 'I'm meeting your first proper girlfriend tonight.' My eyes widened at this. I could accuse myself of being many things, but never of being proper, to anything or anyone. 'You've moved in together.' Her fingers jutted out of her hand with alluring prowess as she counted her reasons for spending an unbelievable amount of money. 'You've come back home, you've finished another film.'

'Short film,' said Apollo.

'A film nonetheless. I haven't even had a chance to congratulate you on your graduation film. Fantastic news about Raindance,' Catherine was chirping away, love pouring through her eyes and down onto her only son with an abundance I had never seen from any mother.

'Thanks Mum,' said Apollo, smiling his usual polite smile, squeezing my thigh underneath the table. Catherine continued with the same sweeping melody.

'That poster, darling, I had it framed. It's absolutely fantastic,' said Catherine, a fork landing in a starter salad between us.

'This,' Apollo's voice rose, as if in an arm-wrestling competition, holding advantage for a couple of minutes to say, 'was Karol's idea, he's a friend of Toni's. It was one of the behind-the-scenes photos he took. It was so good it became the poster.'

This was how Karol began to inch back into my life, twelve months after I last saw him. In Apollo's words he appeared as short pangs of pain shooting at random parts of my body, which was numb and stiff most days otherwise, my brain steadily losing memories, tastes and opinions, capable only of simple commands on film sets or on the latest PlayStation game. Without interference, I had a chance of becoming a simple set of commands, too, but maybe we were always meant to be an interruption in each other's escape. 'I met Toni through Karol,' Apollo explained to his mother. 'She modelled for him.'

Catherine smiled at me.

'You have a face you can't easily forget,' she said.

'He told me that once,' I said. 'Karol.' I cleared my throat. I felt shy under her gaze, as out of place as I had ever been.

'I was a model when I met Apollo's father,' she said with a sigh, shaking her head at the passing of time. 'I could hardly speak English back then, a little fledgling from southern Spain.' She gave a short laugh.

Apollo's hand tensed on my thigh. He looked down at his vegetable pasta and dabbed at it with a fork.

'I would love to see them if you have them anywhere, Toni.' Catherine turned to me with a smile.

'I haven't got them,' I said, throat tightening again. It always did when I tried to eat. I had pills for that but I hadn't brought them with me tonight. My skin itched constantly, too, and I was nauseous nearly all the time, making my brain foggy and head heavy. It usually went away with the right pills and the right alcohol, neither within reach right now, which always made me nervous.

'I can always ask Karol for copies,' said Apollo. There hadn't been as much as a mention of Karol's name up until now, the past in the past, Cardiff in Cardiff.

'Yeah,' I said, giving up on food and reaching for one of the oldest champagnes in *The Great Gatsby*. 'He must have them somewhere.'

'Fantastic,' she said. She said 'Fantastic' a lot. 'Are you working on anything new?'

Apollo straightened up in his chair and took a sip of water before delving into what he most enjoyed talking about: film, his own or others'.

'We finished two weeks ago. It's with George, my sound guy at Ratchet Sound, now.'

'The little ginger Georgie?' Catherine chirped above her plate of chocolate fondue.

'Mum, he's like, twenty-nine.' Apollo sent her a dejected look.

'Well old,' she said.

Apollo shook his head. 'Yeah, well old.' It made her laugh and I smiled at them, keeping up with the mood of the room. 'Anyway, it might be a few months yet. We need some VFX done, too.' Apollo turned to me and placed his hand on my shoulder. 'Toni's been helping me with it. She was my first AD on the shoot.'

'Oh really? How fantastic.' Catherine's dessert spoon clinked against the glass of a small ramekin. 'Is that what you do?'

I cleared my throat and shook my head, forcing a smile.

'Not really. I quit my university degree last year,' I said, cautious of her reaction, glad when none came, 'and Apollo got me into running. So I've just been doing that since.' What I wanted to say to her was that if a job could save a person, then running saved me in a way that was all encompassing and relentless. I ran for anyone who would have me, working fourteen-, sixteen-hour days that battled my insomnia with the complete exhaustion it gave me, brain engaged with incoming tasks, one after another. They said I was good, but I was just desperate not to pause for a moment. I didn't have to eat or feel nauseous, my skin didn't itch, and my heart slowed down. When I came home, I could hear Apollo without listening to him, the ringing in my ears erasing his words, and I could have sex with him without feeling much, my body in a pleasant state of permanent tiredness, all sensations dulled.

'Is this what you want to do eventually? First ADing?' asked Catherine, drawing a map of career expansion before my eyes. There was always more in film, a bigger set and crew, a bigger budget. You never had to stop climbing. 'It's very demanding,' she said.

'I like demanding,' I said with a smile.

'I like a girl with ambition,' she smiled back, a different tinge flickering in the corners of her mouth, one of recognition. 'Us women, we need to try harder, us immigrants in this country, that's a whole different lane.'

My brain paused at *us*. I looked at the empty bottle of champagne between us and there were no further mentions of Spain or Poland. We smiled English smiles at each other before she turned to her son and changed the subject again.

'Your father's going to be back in town soon. He called me last night. He's working on a new album with Freddy, or something. I don't know, I was too busy not paying attention,' she said. Apollo's hand tensed on my thigh again.

'Cool,' he said.

'I'm sure it's all very exciting,' she said, rooting in a breadbasket and fishing out an olive breadstick she proceeded to nibble on, her lips drawn, teeth chipping away at the crust like a little bird. 'I told him about your film,' said Catherine and acknowledged a waiter to get the bill. 'Who knows, he might even turn up if there's a screening.'

'Fine,' said Apollo with a roll of his eyes. I brushed his leg with mine and he gave me a smile. 'Thanks Mum,' he said, glimpsing her settling the bill.

'No problem, darling,' she said. 'Do you want to share a cab back to Notting Hill?'

'No, that's cool,' he said. 'We're seeing some friends in Soho later.'

'Some friends' always meant his friends and I liked that. I liked being his girlfriend and nothing much else. I smiled at Catherine and told her it was really lovely to meet her.

She said it was really nice to meet me, too.

13

August 2014

The day after Pride the sun was out, glazing bodies with its midday heat, the world outside of the sea and outside of us. Swansea was back at work, Pride remembered only in yesterday's leaflets and cans that crackled underneath the feet of hurrying shoppers, crashed under the wheels of impatiently honking cars. The town stood still above the weekend's sad remnants, not a whiff of breeze, seagulls perched on the low rooftops in silent surveillance.

Honey looked at me and nudged his head forward in silence, and for a second I thought, had he not done that, we would've never moved from the steps of the police station, blocking its entrance forever so that no deaths could ever be reported and no bodies identified, no questions asked, no protocol for pain.

'Let's grab some coffee somewhere,' he said, his face unmoved as if someone had sculpted it this morning and such it would forever remain. I followed his step, eyes idly crawling shop banners, all signs strangely unintelligible, as if no words had ever been studied, none memorised, none carried any meaning. My mind wandered to everyone at the police station talking about how hot today was, and it occurred to me that yesterday must've happened, too, sweltering and still, so impenetrable it went unnoticed, and until that moment I didn't know that days carried the power to erase themselves so completely. The world was so foreign that day and so illogical in its liveliness and forwardness of direction, I feared it would swallow me whole if I even let my feet touch the road. I took a long breath and hesitated.

I looked down to double check the ground was still underneath my feet and I was surprised at just how solid the scorched concrete steps felt for a second. Honey nudged me onwards gently, conducting my reluctant legs, heavy and numb, to lift and fall in a forward motion. I couldn't remember the walk to the round metal table, white and hot to touch, and the chair beside it that Honey sat me on while he went inside to order. I couldn't orient myself in Swansea, I had no idea where we were in relation to the hostel, but I was glad we couldn't hear the sea from there. It took us a cup of coffee, black and sour, to find words again. I was zoning in and out of a conversation that followed between us, stuttered and distracted, words sputtered out falling flat on the surface, like whales out of the sea, unable to return. Our conversation sought safety, looping around coffee and the people walking past us, how interesting or dull they looked, how busy they seemed. We debated whether to get cake but neither of us could stomach anything. More things were called okay, not too bad, an interesting choice, fair enough, pretty nice, all sapped of energy to contain meaning. Then, the sentiments were repeated, more things agreed with, statements reiterated, recycled, if anything, just to make a sound in this world, to be heard, to never let the silence ring so white and never-ending as it did in the room at the police station. If we let it in, we wouldn't be able to break it again, every stretch of it more exhausting than the previous.

When it finally came, when we ran out of all things nice, alright and interesting to discuss, we knew the silence would always be there around us. There would always exist a pause, reserved for a booming melody from the very end of the Rhondda Valley.

'Where's Karol?' I heard my own voice, crackling and barely audible, as if I was learning to speak again.

'He's gone,' said Honey, his eyes screwed in focus on the bottom of the cup. 'I'm sure they must've contacted him by now, but I haven't talked to him since the march. The car's gone, too.' I looked away from the table, trying to find anyone to anchor myself in, but the street momentarily stood still, not a person in sight. I thought of Rhys and Owain, their restless bodies awake on bunk beds this morning, too exhausted to move, too shocked to make a sound in our direction as we left to identify the body. 'Let's be honest now. Karol's always been a cunt,' said Honey, leaning back in his seat, 'a hot cunt, but nevertheless.'

I looked back at him, my eyes squinting in the afternoon sun.

'I'm not even surprised,' he said, draining the dregs of his coffee. 'Who wouldn't fuck Karol?'

'What are you talking about?' I felt a lump in my throat, imagining Karol disappearing first thing in the morning.

'Did you see a sailor-looking guy last night?'

I nodded, cautious, lighting a cigarette, thinking about the boy's lips on Karol's, his wet lips on mine.

'High as a kite,' continued Honey, perked up by the sight of a second round of caffeine brought to our table. 'Wasn't making any sense, mumbling something about whales or some shit. A minute in, I was like, honey, I'm outta this conversation and good luck to you.'

I blew out the smoke and took a sip of coffee.

'Well.' Honey's eyebrows shot high above and his nostrils widened. He pressed his lips tight with a sucking sound and his fingers thumped the table. 'I saw him. Karol's mouth wrapped around that guy's dick, that weird sailor guy,' said Honey in my direction and it went through me like a bullet. 'Gav was coming right behind me when I saw Karol and stopped.'

When the question left my lips, it fell into a hoarse whisper, escaping my tight throat.

'Did Gav see them?'

Honey cocked his head to the side and looked down.

'I don't know, babe,' he said. 'I can't see how he wouldn't have.'

'Did Karol see you?' I asked. It could've been the reason why he left without us, without as much as a word or a text.

'With a mouth full of cock?' Honey's eyebrows flew even higher.

'So he doesn't know that you know.'

'He doesn't,' said Honey. He paused for a second, pouting, looking at his fingers splayed on the table. He lifted his cup with the other hand, and, holding it daintily, took a quick sip before continuing. 'When it hit me what was actually happening, I turned to Gav but he wasn't there. He was back on the dance floor.' I looked up at Honey, a single tear slowly trickling down his sunburnt cheek, voice breaking, eyes vacant, staring right ahead. 'I lost him in the crowd. I blacked out a little at that point. Next thing I remember, I was in the crowd by the beach, and then I saw him—' The story stopped there, and with it, Gav. Honey bent down in his seat, weeping, the wallows bursting out of every cell, buried deep in mine. I straightened up in my seat and placed my hand on his shoulder, rising and falling under my touch. I bit into the only bit of nail I had left to chew on.

'Let's go back, Honey,' I said and stood up, gently brushing his face. He looked up, his face wet, and gave a quiet nod. I took his hand in mine and pushed him up, leading the way this time. We wobbled out into the sun-baked street. A cobbled highway of people ran down into the sea from the peaks of shopping pleasures; Saturday Primark pop-ins, caramel-toffee-vanilla pumped buckets of iced coffees balanced on sunburnt arms, tired hands patting away children, pulling dogs and throwing orders, stop, come, come back, heads turning, let's just pop in there for a second. The waves murmured in the distance, menacing and heartless.

Up and down.

In and out.

14

One month later
October 2015

Apollo tilted his head back and groaned as I pulled my hand back.

'That was great,' he said, smiling.

'I'll be right back,' I said. 'I need to wash my hand.' I hadn't let him come inside me in fear of both pregnancy and abortion, fears, acute and compulsive, springing up in the months following Gav's death like weeds, each week presenting a new menu of dislodged discomfort trickling down my throat and sinking deep in my stomach.

He pushed himself up resting on his elbows and looked at me, his eyes narrow.

'I like you like this,' he said.

'Like what?'

'Cold,' he said. I looked at him, sunk there in his grandmother's extravaganza trip, the absurd columns of the bed twisting and weaving upwards into the canopy hanging low above our heads, as surreal and out of place as us here, two bad actors playing a couple in Notting Hill.

My body shifted across the hall and I glimpsed the girl in the mirror, her long, thin naked body framed in thick oak, her back slumped, breasts drooping, one slightly bigger than the other. I sauntered to the bathroom, its whiteness always invasive, a long bath perched on four golden legs to my right glinting in the mirror with a new compulsion. I put my head under the taps of the sink and let cold water run, its small currents filling my ears and splashing into my eyes, making them sting. I pulled my head out and shook it like a dog. The girl in the mirror smiled as her hands ran down through bleached strands to the split tips, which she squeezed into the sink.

I walked back into the room and asked Apollo if I could borrow his *Scott Pilgrim vs the World* hoodie.

'I love the way you say *hoodie*,' he said.

'How did I say it?' I asked, taking it as a yes and pulling the crumpled hoodie out of the pile on the floor by the bed. Is it an affliction, the inability to hear your own voice? Does it exist only when heard and replayed by another? How mirrored and how transformed is it in this looping exchange? He couldn't be the one to tell me.

'No, no, it's the most adorable thing. Please don't ever change that.' Apollo smiled.

There were other words. They all betrayed and pointed to something new. I just didn't know what yet. The words transcended the immigrant into foreign outlands, pronounced what they were taken for, traced literally, their identity concealed by historical layers, guarded from a deaf ear that couldn't hear its own voice.

Foot dipping in the /u/ of shoes.

Sponges sloping into operations.

World becoming worms. Unaware.

No.

Lacking a native diphthong, the melody in the rise and fall. It lacked the song.

Apollo slid off the bed, his arms stretched above him, hands curled into fists.

'Pizza?' he asked, turning towards me, his small boyish shoulders slumped like mine, pushing his bare chest inwards. It was three in the afternoon and we hadn't been awake for long, having got home from a night shoot at five in the morning. Those were my favourite days, shortened and tired, leaving little room to think and remember.

I nodded and put his boxers on.

'I'll make coffee,' I said.

'I'll have a shower,' said Apollo, brushing past me with a towel he picked up at the other end of the room. Apollo considered himself a communist and didn't believe in buying things like wardrobes or tables. This rule didn't pertain to anything film related, our second bedroom filled with what he described as a small-house-in-Cardiff's-worth of film equipment, or his parents and what he himself owned via proxy, like our film set home in Notting Hill. Film needed to rise above its commercial trade, Apollo believed; buying furniture was bourgeois, as was the cafetiere coffee I had just placed on the table we found around the corner, a tired pine construct that must have survived some very frustrated dog. I found it weirdly liberating, the possibility of dropping to your knees and biting at the legs of the table, feeling your jaw ache, teeth pressing hard, bleeding gums, single shards of wood ripped in satisfaction.

'Oh, I needed that,' he said, marching into the kitchen with a jaunty step, a laptop under his bare arm and a towel around his waist. I looked up at him from my book, lighting a long-awaited cigarette. It was the only drawback of getting up this late, sometimes I wished I could smoke in my sleep. Apollo sat down opposite me on another street find, a black leather swivel chair, weathered and loose at the seams. 'Should be about half an hour,' he said, pouring himself a cup of bourgeois coffee.

I nodded a quiet okay, blowing a ring of smoke in the air and returning to my book.

'Wait, what are you listening to?' he asked, a shadow shifting across his face, his smile faint now, fading away.

'I'm not listening to anything. It's just on,' I said, resisting silence in any way I could. When I wasn't working, I turned on interviews and news reports, spoken words pushing Gav's voice out of my head, the melody of his Welsh song singing in my ears.

I looked up at Apollo, my brows furrowed, but he turned his face towards the radio I was only allowed to buy because it was second-hand.

'...no, it's good, it's good to be back, man. I can't wait to get on with it...' I caught a hoarse male voice, blurred and fuzzy, the radio antenna jutting out of its plastic body bent and out of tune.

'This was,' picked up a voice that I had been instructed to recognise as very BBC, as Apollo pulled himself up and walked towards the kitchen counter, 'Frank Moz, everyone, back with...' Apollo twisted the knob on top, switching the channel to an analysis of bourbons and digestives, its speakers debating how they got their names.

'Twat,' Apollo said, plonking back on his seat. 'He's going to be bloody everywhere now.'

I never asked him about his rockstar father, and he never told me much about him either. There was only a name I didn't recognise. When I first told him I had never heard of Frank Moz, Apollo's eyes widened with excitement, his thin body crouched and sliding off our third-hand and possibly infested faux leather sofa.

'For real? You've never heard of him?'

I shook my head.

Apollo pushed himself up on the sofa and looked at me with a softness I'd never noticed in his face before. Back then I liked to think that it was perhaps in that moment, when I allowed him to stop being Frank Moz's son for a second, that he fell in love with me.

Today, too, I shook my head.

'Don't worry about it,' I said, steering away from fathers. When I lied and told him about my father dying of lung cancer when I was ten years old, killing Poland one family member at a time, it seemed to have the opposite effect to that intended: Apollo started to cuddle me at night. I learnt my lesson. If I wanted to keep the physical contact between us to a minimum, I should stay away from Frank Moz.

Today, too, he looked at me with the softness I was so afraid of.

'You're right,' he said, forcing a smile and taking a sip of coffee. 'It's not like we really see each other anyway.'

I smiled at him, smoke escaping the corners of my mouth.

'Anyway,' he picked up with a cheerful tone, his accent and the way he spoke, his voice quiet and friendly, belonging everywhere. I loved that about Apollo. He belonged everywhere and through him I found myself somewhere too. He came as a friend to everyone, with an amicable chuckle and ease of conversation, quiet enough not to appear put on, complementing the sharpness of his mind. He always knew what to say and how to say it. In London, I oscillated on the fringes of language, away from Wales and its familiar sounds. I was copying everything he was saying, his nods, the way he looked people in the eye when he spoke, the warmth in his voice when he asked people how they were, the way he responded, always with a smile, saying that he wasn't too bad, either, never too bad. 'I've got something for you,' he said, his lips spread thin in a grin.

I pressed the cigarette butt into the bottom of an ashtray, blowing smoke in his face again, which he never seemed to mind despite not smoking himself.

'Oh yeah?' I asked, looking down at my book, eyes scanning words bereft of meaning, a flustered concussion of letters on the page I could hold no attention to.

Apollo sprinted out of the room, which always made me smile, the way he moved, with a sprightly gait, his body moving to invisible music, film consuming his whole being. It was nice to have a body so alive and strong as his beside my own body, legs that limbered and dragged, needing the other body to remember how to move altogether.

'I forgot to tell you,' he said, striding back into the room with a book in both hands. 'I picked this up a few days ago, passing the Tate.' A thick, black-and-white hardback, distorted abstract shapes on its cover, fell to the table with a thud, its title *Great Britain in Eastern European Fragments* glaring at me in a white gothic font. 'Okay, I admit, it got me in with Eastern Europe,' he said, opening the cover, his finger sliding down the index list, 'and then I spotted Karol,' Apollo's finger paused at Karol Rosenmann: *Fragments*, Cardiff's Arts Institute, 2014. He lifted his head, his face gleaming. 'This is incredible,' he said, his voice excited, eyes sparking up. 'It gets better.' He opened the book in the middle, the pages revealing fragments of my body splayed across two A4 pages, my lips turned to the camera, parting slightly, a set of teeth sprouting forth in disproportion, eyes fuzzy, fearless.

I gasped and reached for another cigarette, my hands trembling. I put the packet back on my phone next to an empty coffee cup and lit the cigarette. I inhaled greedily and looked back at Apollo.

'Wow,' I said, inflating as much emotion as I could muster into my joyless sputter. 'This is incredible.' I echoed Apollo, my body and mind gripped in a jolt of panic. I wasn't sure what to say, suddenly hot in the attic, Karol's body sharing in the heat and the humidity, stilled above mine.

'I've always wanted to have copies of these,' he said, his face in a dreamlike daze. Apollo turned another page, my uneven breasts blown up on both with a small text in the top right corner. '*The fragments are charged with erotic tension*,' Apollo started reading the captions lodged between parts of my body. '*These intimate observations see Rosenmann look at his subject with tenderness and erotic inquisition. She surrenders and responds in a triumph of innocence and desire.*' Apollo looked up at me, corners of his lips dropping with a De Niro-like nod of approval. 'Holy shit, mate.'

I stared at the image of my spine before me, blood pounding in my head as I looked at my vertebrae meandering down the page in an uneven course, the same course tears take trickling down a cheek.

Apollo read on.

'*Rosemann's "Fragments" are seen as an attempt to dissect complexities of post-Soviet society, hopeful and innocent in its nostalgia for*—'

'What bollocks,' I said, taking a drag and lifting myself up from the chair. It made him laugh.

'I love it when you say *bollocks*.' Apollo put the book down and looked at me.

'Why?' I linked my eyes with his, tilting my head. 'Do I say it in a funny way?'

'No,' he smiled. 'There's a punch to your bollocks, though. I like that.'

There was a knock on the door.

'Pizza.' He walked towards the door. I watched him have a conversation with a delivery guy, cheerful and brief, small talk beats punched right, an impossible feat. I looked up at Apollo bearing a cardboard box the size of the table, the sweet scent of pepperoni sprawling through the room.

'Do you just want to get stoned and play FIFA today?' I asked. 'I haven't got the energy for anything else.'

'You're a full package, girl,' Apollo said, folding a slice in half and pushing it into his mouth.

I smiled and sat back down, grabbing a slice, my hands still quivering, heart pounding up to my head and squeezing it in a numbing headache, Eastern European fragments always on the brink of collapse.

15

the sea

I threw two bags of ice, two kilograms each, on the bathroom floor, glancing back at the water trail I left behind carrying them from the kitchen. I sighed and bent down, strained fingers, red and sore at the tips, digging into my jeans. I picked up both bags and placed them in the bath, tearing them open. I emptied out the ice and put the plug in the drain.

It was my fourth day off work and I didn't have a gig for another week. Apollo was away first-ADing for a friend in Scotland, and Gav's washed-up face, so white it was almost translucent, hung permanently in front of mine in a flashing slide that appeared and was gone every time I blinked. I tried to blink it away, but it hung around until I was back at work, until I was too exhausted to stay awake, to think and to remember, his lips, so alive, touching mine in a dance, my arms wrapped around him. I opened the tap and let the cold water run.

His body was washed out on the beach, flashing before my eyes now in a recurrent daydream, the day in fragments, all of them apart and slipping away from me, more and more, day by day. It was a brisk, still morning, eerily calm in the dawn. I remembered a young woman. She was soaked and shivered in the cold. She had watched Gav walk straight into the water as if he were sleepwalking.

'Amble gait,' the young woman said, and it was a strange thing to say. She said she had called after Gav but the wind dispersed her voice. He dove in. She started running towards him. She admitted she hesitated. She was drunk and the sea was rough. She didn't jump in immediately. She thought to herself that he might have just gone for a swim. She called out again. She decided to go in after a while, having lost sight of him. She was a good swimmer, she said.

He wasn't moving when she found him, waves covering both of them relentlessly, one after another. She was calling out for help, waves pulling her away from him. She couldn't get to him.

There was a guy, too. She pointed at a man trembling two metres away, his toes curling in the sand, eyes fixed on the body being pronounced dead, his gaze clouded with shock.

He caught up with her and together they wrestled him out. She couldn't say how long it took. It seemed to her she had been in the sea for hours, but it could've been minutes. He – the man – Jacob? She checked for the name with a stutter. Jacob resuscitated him, but they couldn't get the heart to beat. Neither of them had done it before. Someone else joined them, dialled 999. Jacob pressed and pressed but he couldn't get the heart to beat. The girl broke down in tears.

Jacob picked up the story from the beginning, retelling it with the details of the girl in the sea, crying out for help, the light only breaking through, he could hardly make her out.

My feet were bruised that morning, bleeding in the sand, stinging. They were curling in on themselves now, ice-cold water bending them in spasms, as I stepped into the bath, gritting my teeth. I lowered myself, shooting pain crawling up my body, distracting the mind. If I hadn't met Tallulah, if I hadn't blacked out, if I hadn't been so weak, I would've stayed with him and he would've never walked into the sea. I would've never had to see the body I would never be able to unsee or forget, ghostly white and lifeless, no air rising in his chest, lips parted without expression, concealing neither horror nor peace.

I'd run as I slept, in my jeans and Gav's white vest, a soft, warm gateway to his body, still carrying his scent from two days before, the sweet peaches he loved so much in the summer, a fragrance I still kept, afraid that if I had ever forgotten the way he smelled that night, the morning would disappear along with it, and with it, too, my Gav.

The clock stopped at four twenty that morning, murderous water seeping through the beach pebbles under the world's coarse skin. We're given the time of arrival and we're given an accurate or estimated time of departure. For Gav, it was the latter, an estimated time of death: four twenty in the morning, his last breath escaping numbers, fleeting in fragile spaces in between, between knowing anything for certain. Everyone likes a cause, the comfort of cause and effect. There was one, too: a cocktail of alcohol, mephedrone, amphetamine and cocaine.

If I hadn't been so weak, he would still be alive. I put my head underwater, turning around in the tub to face downwards, Gav's dead face finally gone. My ears started ringing in isolated beats, my skin becoming numb to all senses so that I couldn't feel its temperature anymore, my eyes stinging until they felt nothing, my lungs too heavy to hold. I stayed down until I was in too much pain to last a second longer. I opened my mouth and let the water break in, jostling through my nostrils and mouth, flooding my throat, the body receiving orders of survival, pushing me up, choking and gasping for breath, panic tearing through the deafening silence.

Eventually, there came stillness. I sat in the water, my body trembling, teeth hitting against one another. I stared down at myself through the water, single ice cubes still afloat here and there. I sat there until my mind went blank and I couldn't remember anything at all, not even where I was, desperate only for those few moments of peace.

When I crawled out, the world shimmered in a comforting haze. I smiled. I lay there on the floor, gathering the strength to clamber out of the bathroom on all fours. It took another hour before I could find my balance, my head dizzy, skin burning up, prickly. When I was able to stand, I put on Apollo's woollen jumper, his running leggings and hiking boots, and I faced the outside world for the first time in four days.

The distant winter sun hit me with aggressive blindness and unpleasant warmth that stung my whole body, burning now as if submerged in whisky. I dragged my feet forward, hands shielding my eyes from the light. I felt lightheaded and my head was pounding.

I made two stops: at a corner shop and a local Boots, one thousand two hundred sixty-seven steps there, one thousand forty-three back, my mind counting each with devotion.

I came back bearing Lambert & Butlers and a bottle of Boots' own hair bleach. I wrestled with the disposable gloves for at least half an hour, an unlit fag dangling from my mouth, waiting its turn, my fingers too stiff to spark it. When I finished, I looked at the girl in the hallway mirror. There she was, stripped of any colour. White, her skin almost translucent.

I sauntered over to the kitchen and glimpsed the shiny surface of my phone, for a moment surprised that I had ever had one. Blood slowly returned to my veins followed by calmer breath as I lit the cigarette, its warmth comforting. I looked down at my phone.

Two missed calls from Apollo.

One from Karol. First one in months.

16

One month later
'Two Strangers'
A Film by Apollo Rooney

I glanced at myself in the tall mirror on the wall in Catherine's hallway, an insect body enclosed in the safety of her black velvet dress. Catherine insisted on bodycon, I insisted on boots and thick, black tights. She offered her red lipstick, I bleached my hair back to platinum blonde after a brief flirtation with cherry red. Catherine offered a purse from her latest collection, a ridiculously tiny thing with embroidered golden lines running across the black leather. I asked her if it was real leather. She pressed her lips tighter and smiled that cold smile I was beginning to warm up to when Apollo brushed past us and said the taxi was already outside.

'You look great,' he whispered in my ear in the car. I shrugged and gave him an indifferent smile, gazing out at streets I couldn't recognise, distracted and comforted by their commotion and a restlessness only London could hold with such endurance.

When we arrived Catherine marched straight in, greeting a friend matching her height, extravagance and flamboyance, a long-haired blonde woman with a posh warbling voice. The building was how West London was imagined, grand, opulent, and carrying its age with a tinge of arrogant pride, *The Ultimate Picture Palace* arching over the white stone above the entrance. We walked in, stepping through to a surprisingly modest parqueted hallway, reminding me of a pre-war cinema in my Eastern hometown, our minds conditioned into the *before* and *after*, my hand enveloped in Apollo's small hand, my *after*, a rising film star at his film screening in Notting Hill, *before* always glinting at the back of my head, a girl without this language, then, for a brief moment; a girl in love, now, a girl that didn't belong here but persisted in her camouflage, clutching her boyfriend's hand tight.

I glimpsed this girl in the mirror, catching sight of her whenever I could to ascertain her physical realness, someone I hardly recognised. I enjoyed not having to be there as I submerged in her completely, my face floating just underneath her surface.

Apollo let go of my hand, snatched by his producer Anna, who appeared in the mirror beside me, her hands pointing in all directions and multiplying in commands, head turning left and right, questions firing at new faces as they came in through the main door behind us. Apollo once described her as a one-person production company; she was a woman in constant motion, her narrow blue eyes squinting under a heavy blonde fringe, always on the hunt for a new opportunity, hair straight and thick hanging low by her shoulders, her full lips, coloured in pastel shades, always stretched in a smile, the same smile I saw plastered on all producers' faces, part and parcel of the job.

I put on Catherine's cold smile but it was no match to Anna's powerful gleam.

'I'm proud of you,' I said in Apollo's direction, but his ear was already sealed to her lips, Anna's voice unable to lower to whisper, its shrill high howling instructions, orders and actions.

I descended deeper into purposeful inaction, staring idly at the crowd as it filed into the cinema's reception room, moving past us into the main screen in one strong current, Apollo's old school mates, university mates and workmates, everyone contained within one world, never ruptured by migration.

'We have to go,' ordered Anna, her voice sharp, small eyes not leaving Apollo's face, smiling, his eyes dazed from a steady stream of *How are yous* and *Alrights*.

Apollo nodded at her and grabbed my hand. I let go of it and said I needed the toilet, I'd see him in a minute. I walked outside when they disappeared and took a deep breath, exhaling into the sharp air, spring still looking for a place to call home, the sun distant and idle in its afternoon lull.

I tried to remember anything that I'd done in the months leading up to the screening, my mind tired and hazy after a month of running work in Leytonstone. I made coffees for actors; I fetched things production crews needed.

I fumbled a cigarette out of my bag and continued with my inventory of calming, emotionless memories, list-making comforting in its repetition, logic and structure. I printed things. I ran for things, things that were always of utmost urgency, always to be done as soon as possible. It was probably why they called us—

'It's here, isn't it? *Two Strangers*?' A male voice rang somewhere around me, but I was so focused on finding a lighter in that tiny useless bag that had nothing but my phone in it that I zoned out and continued my search, distracted by everything I wasn't doing with my life. 'Sorry. Do you know if this is the right place? *Two Strangers* directed by Apollo Rooney?'

I lifted my eyes from the bag.

The man standing right before me was studying the banner above our heads. Without answering his question, I looked up at him, then at the banner advertising Edgar Wright's *The World's End* on repeat for another week. Apollo told me once he would like to be like Edgar Wright, in his mind a complete cinematic genius, but his mouth was full of cereal and it sounded grotesque and comical when he said it. It was one of the many times I caught myself being a terrible girlfriend.

I shifted my eyes back towards the man's face. It surprised me how good that felt, to look up at someone the way I used to look up at Gav. I liked the edges of his face, angular and defined, jawline drawn with a strong, steady hand, cheekbones high, mouth broad, parted slightly just above my forehead in closeness that was charged with something else—

—something new.

The man squinted at the banner and I remembered his question.

'Yes, it is.' I paused, my eyes fixed on his lips, mouthing *The World*, 'the right place. It's in screen one, downstairs, right ahead.' I pushed the words out, waving the cigarette towards the main door. They felt heavy in my chest as if I hadn't spoken in years, every syllable a new terrain. My eyes glided down to the man's throat, quivering slightly above an unbuttoned shirt, its cornflower blue spilling out underneath a blue navy jacket that hugged his long figure. As my eyes rested on a thin, silver chain around his neck, I could sense him, too, a blend of cardamom and peppermint, and hints of lemon that drew me slightly closer, my head dizzy, my feet left grounded in a way I had never felt them before.

He thanked me, or at least I assumed so as the fragrance took over and the only list that was real and important was its compounds, the scents of something else, something new.

When I looked at him again he was by the door, looking back at me with enormous grey-blue eyes, playful as he stifled a smile, nodding in my direction.

'You look dressed for an event.' He eyed me up and down. 'I think we might be slightly late.'

I stood still, my mind blank. I whispered a quiet, '*Yeah,*' and, aware of the choked sound I had made, repeated it louder. Again I heard myself croak. My arm straightened towards the door.

'It starts in ten minutes,' I said. 'They planned a longer introduction.' I felt exhausted by the time I said it, looking down at my bag again, unsure if any of those sounds made it across to him, but he pulled my face right back in his direction when he said:

'You coming? Or do you just hang around outside cinemas looking stunning?'

I didn't respond, my brain and throat held hostage by a tight grip. I pressed my lips tighter and clenched my fists.

He chuckled and raised his arms.

'I'm sorry, I can't help myself sometimes. Embarrassingly old-school.'

'Oh, no, I,' I released both fists. 'They just do that.'

He smiled the same stifled smile, holding the door open. I waved circles in the air to signal I'd follow after him. No, after you. After you. He waited until I walked in first. I glanced at myself in the same mirror, the girl looking back at me. Was she used to this? Would she smile at him and run her fingers gently through her hair, her back straightened and gait assured, her long legs carrying her power with confidence?

'Is there a bar in this place?' He touched my back gently, glimpsing a 'bar' sign pointing upstairs. 'Great. Would you like something?' His eyes met mine.

I wanted to smile and run my fingers through my hair, but instead I shrugged and nodded, following him upstairs.

'It's always a bit sad getting a drink just for yourself,' he said and I wondered what sadness meant to him, following suit, struggling to find the right words to fill the space between us in a manner I could project as natural and confident. 'I hate these things really,' he continued, skipping every other step of the carpeted staircase.

I wanted to tell him I hated these things too, that if I could really be here, if I had it in me to be present, I would've never come. I wasn't there, the girl in the mirror was, and she followed his every word and move, not rugged and stiff like hers but fluid, every beginning spilling into the end with sense and charm. He lunged towards the small bar tucked in the corner of a square room, modest in size, old-school round wooden tables and chairs littered by its edges.

'What would you like… whisky?'

I nodded with a faint, 'That would be great.'

'Grand. Two, whatever's your favourite, mate. On the rocks?' He looked at me and I nodded again. 'Yeah, two, please. Ta, mate. Keep the change. Cheers, mate, ta!'

We tiptoed downstairs in introductory whispers, aware of being five minutes late, telling each other how bad it was of us. I couldn't catch his name, drowned in a sip. His hand leapt on the door handle. I nodded and he pressed it down. We grimaced when the door creaked open, revealing a disorientating darkness broken by a stream of stage light pouring softly on Anna holding a microphone she didn't need. We became a series of gestures: Back row? Sounds good. That one okay? Yeah, why not. Whisky good? Excellent. After you. Thanks.

We sat down in our seats, tumblers sealed to our lips, our elbows touching.

Anna was still thanking the world and the universe for this opportunity. I stuck my tongue out and decided to drink my whisky like a cat, more relaxed in the room's darkness. He tittered and did the same. Two heads in front turned towards us with a huff. Anna turned to Apollo, praising his talent and vision.

She was sure it was the first of many films they would make together.

I had no doubt.

Alcohol quieted my head a little, my throat burning in the way I liked, satisfying in its discomfort. I hung my head back on the seat, letting the blood rush up in a pleasant wave. Our eyes met in the dim light of the opening scene Apollo and I shot in Cardiff: they bump into each other on the edges of Roath Park, their eyes lock and, as the title spreads across the screen, they recognise each other.

The man smiled, his grey-blue eyes glinting at me in the darkness, inspecting my face. Something punched my stomach. Something else, something new.

The film was over in ten minutes to a loud cheer from an auditorium of Apollo's friends, rolling credits drowned in a discorded play of claps and whistles. For a second, I thought I read it wrong, but there he was, Karol Rosenmann under *Special Thanks*. I heard myself rasp, pulled back in front of a pale face hidden behind his camera and with him to a pale face lying still on the beach. I jostled out of my seat, out of breath. A buzzing swarm of cheering friends rose from their seats and surrounded Apollo and Anna in congratulations.

'Are you okay?' the man asked as we were getting shuffled out of our seats by two guys I vaguely recognised from a party in Cardiff. They scooted down towards the stage, howling. I looked up at him, dizzy, daring our knuckles to touch again, rings on our fingers clinking quietly.

'Do you smoke?' I asked, lifting my face at him.

He put his arm on my shoulder, turning his broad jaw in the direction of the door.

'Let's get out of here, this might take a while,' he said.

We staggered out, unnoticed under the slowly lifting darkness.

Our backs resting against the sandy stone of the building, shy streaks of sun piercing through thick clouds, he pulled a packet of Marlboro Lights from his inside pocket. My hand hovered above it and I took one with the tips of my fingers as if picking the best candy in a bag, which made him chuckle. I thought of the girl in the mirror, more comfortable with her now in her short, bodycon black dress and red lips that wrapped around the cigarette. His neck contracted slightly as he lit mine and looked straight into my eyes when the flame struck his.

We smoked in silence for a few peaceful exhales.

'Are you sure you're alright?'

My head jerked in his direction.

'You looked startled at the end,' he picked up again, glancing down at me.

'Oh.' I pressed my lips on the cigarette, the two faces in front of me again, real and alive, memories pressing at the thin layer of skin, ripping it open.

'You're shivering. Come on, have this.' He took his suit jacket off and draped it around my shoulders. I thanked him, my mind lost between Karol and Gav, one alive, one dead, both of them gone. It was easier that way.

'It's—' I didn't know where to begin. 'Karol Rosenmann, in thanks, in special thanks.' The words burst in honesty I couldn't afford around Apollo and Catherine, the construct of myself still too delicate to shake the past. 'He was a close friend, well, more than that,' I said, skipping between thoughts, his face still and attentive. 'Well, not more in a sense, but—' I could feel my jaw clench tighter, I needed the girl in the mirror here so badly, I was shattering to pieces with each foreign fallen sentence. 'We fell out, well, we didn't even do that. It's hard to explain. We lived in Cardiff together. He left, he went back to Poland, and I came to London.' I took a drag and exhaled slowly. 'Sorry, it's not that interesting.'

'Go on,' he said, blowing smoke away from my face, his voice soft. 'What happened?'

'I haven't seen him in a year and a half, and it's weird.' I took another drag, nervous and short. 'He called me a month ago. He's called a few times since.' I dropped the cigarette to the ground and asked for another which he lit for me, his hands steady against the tremble of my body, my tension easing under his scent that now wrapped around me, hints of cardamom and peppermint with speckled undertones of lemon calling me to safety, feet touching the ground again. 'Thanks,' I inhaled, calmer now. 'I didn't pick up. But he's in a photography book and now he's here and—' I took a beat. 'I was sure he was gone, that he would never come back.'

'It sounds like you miss him,' he said with a faint smile. His eyes met mine.

'We didn't part on good terms,' I said and frowned, recounting everything I had just shared with a complete stranger.

'Well, no, I gathered that.' He blew out smoke again and stubbed the sizzling butt under the black leather shoe. 'He's called you, a few times you said.' I nodded, smiling. 'There aren't that many people who keep on calling,' he said.

We climbed the staircase without a rush this time, at ease in each other's presence. When we got to the bar, he glanced at me and gave a smile, playful and mischievous in the way he pursed his lips together.

'Same again?' he asked.

'I'll get it,' I said but he leapt to the bar, gracefully jostling through a small group of Apollo's friends who I had never met, all a good head shorter than him. I watched him wave a victory sign at the barman.

'Thanks,' I said as we clinked glasses. I loved the sound of his voice, hoarse and warm. I wanted to ask him what his name was when Apollo's face bobbed up between us, his hand resting on my lower back, his ring and little fingers edging on my butt.

'I see you've met my father,' said Apollo. It was the only time Apollo's smile took my breath away. 'Frank,' Apollo went on, 'this is my girlfriend, Toni.' Apollo's other hand rested centimetres away from me in presentation of a prize, palm up.

Frank muttered something barely intelligible about not knowing about a girlfriend, his eyes raking the bar as if in search of something he needed to get. I pressed the glass to my lips and swallowed my drink, ice cubes hitting me in the face.

'You're Frank Moz,' I said, choking on whisky with a theatricality I detested, feeling everyone's eyes on us now. Apollo put his arm around me, tenderness shifting across his face as he pulled me closer, my body flinching under his touch, small boyish features carrying nothing of the charge surging through Frank's hand on my back just a few minutes ago. 'I'm alright,' I said, pulling Apollo's hand away from me. 'I drank it too quickly.'

Apollo smiled at me and looked at his dad. I expected hostility, but he gave out none.

'I'm glad you came, man.'

Frank looked back at his son, the horror I caught a brief sight of just moments ago gone.

'Pleasure, terrific work, lad. Cheers!'

Apollo raised his beer bottle and the glasses clinked again, the upward motion of our hands lifting our words, allowing me to breathe again. The girl in the mirror was gone and grey strands appeared in Frank's ruffled blond mess of hair, light lines cutting up his forehead like sentences of age. His angles lacked the softness of the young, slipping in between, escaping a definite answer.

'We met in Cardiff at a friend's exhibition,' said Apollo in his usual casual manner. 'Karol Rosenmann, have you heard of him?' Frank shook his head, his hand tightening on his glass, eyes wedged on his son. Apollo shot me a quick smile and went on, 'He's become quite a thing in the photography world recently. I've heard a little gallery in Brooklyn is showcasing his work next month.'

I wondered where Apollo heard that and why he'd never mentioned it. I started thinking that maybe he had, but I never listened because I was never there for those conversations between us, not really, and when I was listening and responding, my mind immediately discarded all new information, too busy listing and recounting, counting and looping.

Apollo wrapped his arm around my waist and pulled me closer, my face now falling directly under Frank's fixed gaze. Frank looked pale.

'Toni modelled for Karol,' Apollo said. 'You should go see it when you're back there.'

The corners of Frank's lips quivered slightly when he smiled at both of us and said, 'That sounds terrific, mate. I won't be back for a while, though.' Frank cleared his throat and looked away in the direction of the bar, his glass of whisky untouched. 'I'm staying in London for a few months, maybe longer.' His face strained away from mine and moved on the edges of Apollo, who kissed my forehead and told Frank he should meet his producer, Anna.

Apollo was stopping for no one today and no slow pace was tolerated. He waved at Anna furtively, pointing at Frank. She threw her hand in the air across the room and mouthed *two seconds* as a girl she was with tugged at her shoulder, pointing at something on her phone. It was their day. Apollo's and Anna's energies combusted through the night in hysterical giggles, anecdotes, and stories of set dramas, bubbling all around the rest of us.

'Mum had to leave early. Did you see her?' Apollo asked, his neck strained in Anna's direction.

Frank shook his head. It made me sick to think that we could've bumped into Catherine outside. I couldn't place this new guilt rising in my stomach, a heavy lump in my throat. I could feel Apollo's sweat on my arm and I wondered whether it was cocaine or anxiety, gripping my body so tightly. I wished he would let go of me, but I couldn't help but cling on to him, terrified of motion in this new reality, feelings lacking sense, fighting with reason, senses drunk on Frank's smell that had changed everything so quickly, filling my brain with replayed scenes, his hand on my back, coarse and firm, face held so close to mine in that very first opening line.

'Anna, you have to meet my father,' Apollo repeated as Anna appeared, lunging onto Frank with a wide hug and her professional grin. Anna's ponytail hit my cheek as she tossed her head to face Apollo and tilted her head back up to look at Frank.

'I've been dying to meet you, Frank!'

Frank's expression remained the same, as if he had somehow put on a mask that felt right for the rest of the evening.

'Nice to meet you, Anna,' he said. I noticed Anna's breasts and, for a second, I wondered whether Apollo and Frank were looking at them, too, their line running low into cups and sizes I had never dreamt of reaching. Did she ever need a girl from the mirror?

Anna shone a set of teeth so white and bright they sparkled, her eyes peeking gleefully from underneath her pressed platinum fringe.

'I see where Apollo gets his good looks from,' she said, and my lips parted. Apollo glanced down at his beer and Frank smiled the same smile.

'You look nothing alike,' I heard myself say, my voice louder than it had been all evening, looking at a man and a boy, their features in stark contrast in height and breadth, different shaped and coloured eyes glinting at me curiously, but when they bared their teeth, those very different lips stretched into an identical smile, making me gasp. 'I'll be right back, I need to say hello to someone,' I said and turned on my feet, marching away from them to the opposite corner of the room in blind hope of finding someone I remembered from the set of *Two Strangers*, the discorded voices around me buzzing in my ears.

I had never been so glad to see anyone as much as Tess in that moment, our make-up artist, sipping on a Diet Coke directly in my view. She seemed happy to see me. I tried to stir the conversation towards work, my back to Apollo, Anna, and Frank. Everyone in the film industry loved to talk work. I was ready to sponge up all the many make-up department dramas and nod enthusiastically at every detail, mouth prised at all the right moments.

It wasn't long before Georgie, our costume assistant, joined us, conspiringly pointing towards Apollo, Anna, and Frank.

'That's Frank Moz!' whispered Georgie, teeth pressing hard on her lower lip in giddy excitement.

Forced to turn around and look at them, my hands warped into fists again.

'My brother was, like, obsessed with him in the nineties. Do you know why he's here? I've got to talk to him.' Her words raced as fast as my heart, one abreast the other.

Tess narrowed her eyes at the group, opening them up with a worrying suddenness and a very loud voice.

'Holy shit, it is him.'

'He's still got it,' said Georgie, gawking at Frank, his arms crossed now as he cocked his head from one side to another, listening to Anna's story, her cacophonic warble piercing the air. In the safe space of curious girls, I dared to hold my gaze on him. I couldn't tell whether he still had it or not, but I knew I didn't want to look at anyone else in the room.

'George, he's old enough to be your dad, man,' said Tess just as Apollo laughed at something Anna said.

'You have to introduce us!' Georgie squealed, tugging at my arm as I tried to query her about her methodology behind choosing a costume, using those exact words, anything that would get us away from talking about Frank Moz.

'It would be cool to meet him,' Tess chimed in. They were both staring at him.

I excused myself to the bar, hoping I could drown myself in whisky so completely it could burn all my senses off for at least a few hours. I got to the bar and asked for a double. I shut my eyes, replaying my conversation with Frank, scanning for wrong words said at the wrong time in the wrong tense and with a wrong accent. I pulled Frank's jacket closer to my body and turned to my phone, pretending to text. I hadn't been in touch with Honey for months. Maybe tonight was as good a moment as any to check in. How was Honey doing? *How are you doing*, I typed and before I located a question mark, I decided to delete it.

When I looked up from my phone, my unreliable body calmed by the drink, I turned around and looked at Frank again, a surreal special guest arrival, giving Anna a hug and turning to Apollo. They shook hands. Father and son.

Frank was now heading towards me, shaking hands as he went. Georgie ambushed him with a phone, pointing the camera at them as she pressed her face against his. They smiled as the camera flashed and he shook her hand before smoothly moving on. I watched him glide through the crowd with a half-smile, mouthing a word or two and moving on, moving on. Towards me.

'I've got to shoot,' he said, standing a safe distance away, hesitating for a second and glancing around. 'It was really nice to meet you, Toni.'

Our eyes locked.

'It was nice to meet you, too, Frank,' I said and put my glass down, reaching for the edges of the jacket.

'Oh no, keep it. It's cold out.' He smiled. 'Anyway, it suits you.'

He raised his hand in an awkward wave as I raised mine and retraced his steps cautiously. I watched him coast down the grand staircase with a swagger, ignoring everyone's outstretched hands this time, moving on.

17

August 2014

The last time I saw Karol was the day before the funeral. I had been circling the familiar block of terraced houses for the past hour. Each time I stood in front of the blue door, my legs took a U-turn and off they went, striding confidently around the block again. They were out of control; I began to wonder if I would ever get to where I needed to go, even though I didn't feel like I needed to be anywhere anymore and could, in fact, keep on circling this block until I made a mark in the concrete staves of the pavement. It had soon become two hours and I had no way of stopping them. I hoped someone could intervene and take me somewhere where I could walk in circles, around a white room without windows, a room without past or future, until my legs couldn't carry the rest of my body any further. I could fall to my hands and scrape my knees and maybe that was the only way to rest for a little while, to fall asleep and not feel anything for some time.

'Just come in.' I froze when I heard his voice. Karol's soft-spoken Polish rang above me just as I found myself walking down the steps once again, away from the blue door and into the street. It had an authority over my body that I didn't.

I turned on my feet and looked up at him, a snow-white vest loose on his complex weave of muscles, lean and strong, his black denim jeans, clipped, as ever, by a bulky black belt with a metal buckle that could kill. Karol's face was still, black eyes motionless, an unlit cigarette dangling from his mouth. The whiteness of his skin contrasted with the world around us, a world in the full blossom of summer, a world of other bodies, alive, healthy and strong, glazed with steadied tans, thirsty for other bodies, bodies moving onwards in a dance. 'Come in, Toni.' Karol called to my body again, and it followed him inside.

'I've come to get my stuff,' I said. 'I'm going to stay with Honey.'

'And put your stuff where?' he asked.

I said I had some bags upstairs.

He was barely audible, mumbling through the unlit cigarette.

'I'll give you a ride,' he said.

I said I'd be okay.

He shrugged, sauntering down to the kitchen.

I took a step towards the stairs and noticed I'd lost all control over my legs, which were numb underneath me. The windowless white room of the police station merged with the fluffy carpeted staircase and blue walls of the corridor, collapsing time. I fell to my knees and clambered up the stairs, dragging my passive body with my hands, the most exhausting climb of my life. I gasped heavily when I got to the top and crawled into my slanted-roof bedroom, every inch of the house soaked in seawater and blood, walls closing in on my lungs and pressing on them, throat swelling up.

I leant back against the bed frame, slowing my breathing, careful to follow one with the other, willing myself to continue, one breath after the next, just as I had done since Swansea, my mind steered towards the immediate action ahead.

I eyed bin bags tucked behind the wardrobe.

I took a deep breath and pulled both legs to my chest, resting my head on my knees. My legs twitched and I managed to get myself on my knees, feeling the blood charge through them in hopeful prickling.

I launched at everything I owned like a child collecting her toys off the floor, scooping them up with my arms outstretched, pouring them into bags without pause or order, utility or sentiment, crumbled clothes and notepads, vinyl with and without sleeves, empty cigarette packets, gig tickets I never threw out, politics books I never returned to the library and never read, a half drunk bottle of gin, a quarter bottle of tequila, multiple bottles of pop, hair dye I'd bought, more clothes, two pairs of brogues, more clothes.

Seven months in two rubbish bags.

I grabbed them in both hands and stood up stronger than I had felt all day. I strode downstairs.

Quick and easy.

'Would you like to have some coffee?' Karol's voice rang before I could get to the door. My body listened.

He was hunched over the moka pot, water slowly seeping through the ground beans and spilling out as black liquid. The same cigarette was still attached to his lips, pale and chapped.

I asked him if he'd had anything to eat. I hadn't seen him since that night, the night when—

'Toast,' he said.

—he was gone before we ran, ran, ran to the beach, gone before we found Gav – and for the past week I had wanted to ask, more than anything I had ever wanted to ask anyone – what happened, what happened to him, why he wasn't there—

'For a week?' I asked.

—why he had never texted, why he hadn't called after—

'Toast,' he said.

The silence fell between us, pressing down on words that wanted to be said and questions that should've been asked, but none came out, locked in distant bodies.

'I haven't seen you wear so much colour before. It doesn't suit you,' he said without looking at me, the cigarette flapping in his mouth. Karol took the moka pot off the stove.

I needed to justify myself to him.

'I had to borrow Honey's clothes,' I said.

'That man's never had any taste,' he said, and poured coffee into two small cups, steam filling up the vacant space between us.

I cautiously agreed with 'Perhaps,' having no energy to contradict anyone or allow myself the privilege and strength of an opinion.

I sat down next to him and folded my arms. Karol didn't smell of soap but of sweat and I thought it was the nicest scent I'd ever smelled on anyone. His gelled hair was greasy and single strands peeled off here and there, breaking the gallery piece. His high cheekbones were dry, skin flaking in places. I studied his face from above my coffee cup, but it gave nothing away.

'Do you want to smoke that cigarette?' I asked.

It looked permanently attached to his lip. Karol shrugged again and took it out. It pulled his lip slightly as he did it. He lit it and handed it to me. The ashtray in front was full, short butts in a mourning mound.

'Are you going to the funeral tomorrow?' I asked.

'I wasn't invited,' he said, looking straight at the wall ahead, his voice quiet. I handed him the cigarette back.

'I could talk to his family,' I began, but he interrupted with a curt: 'Don't.' Ash falling onto his lap, he bent down and grabbed a hefty brown envelope with a newspaper folded underneath, resting on a chair. He tossed it onto the table, fingers holding the cigarette in a slight tremble. The short butt was handed back, as he pulled out a thick stash of black-and-white photographs.

Parts of Gav. A close-up of his right hand, of the mole on his lower back, his penis underneath curly light hairs, light grey in the photograph, upright and strong in the next, feet stacked next to each other, a long neck and the lower part of his pointed chin.

'If you weren't a photographer, you'd be cutting up murdered bodies,' I said.

He let out a quiet laugh, making me laugh, too. We cut it short, uncomfortable in its sound, letting it turn to silence.

Right at the bottom of the stash, the only portrait. Gav, his hair different, darker and thicker, eyes unaware of us, face brushed with a boyish softness. His mouth full of prawn.

'It was the first photograph I ever took of him. I've never managed to capture him after that.' Karol's finger quivered as he stroked the photograph gently. 'I tried for four years.' The finger curled back into his hand, which withdrew away from the table. 'You can keep them if you want to.'

I wanted to ask him why he didn't, but I stayed silent. Karol lifted the cup of lukewarm coffee he hadn't touched until now and sipped on it slowly, his eyes still locked on the wall ahead.

I stacked the photographs back into the envelope and licked it closed. I peeked down at the *South Wales Echo* underneath, pointing at us with a definite headline in bold:

WELSH JUNIOR BOXING CHAMPION,
GAVIN EVANS, DEAD AT 29.

I grazed the text with my fingers to ascertain its realness, a ruptured sigh bursting from my lungs.

'Yeah,' Karol wanted to say, but his voice broke and he cleared his throat instead. I looked at him, the smallness of him, and everything in my body longed for him in that moment.

I wanted to nestle in his arms and remain, safe and loving, pulled in by the texture of his skin, the sharpness of his vowels, the flatness of his tone that carried home, and as my body drew towards his I couldn't look at him, I couldn't look at what he'd done with the Sailor Boy that night and I couldn't fathom its consequence. It kept pushing me away from him, rendering me homeless, setting us adrift.

'See you around, Karol,' I said, not knowing what else there was, if there was anything left between us.

Karol nodded in the direction of the wall without expression. There was no around and no soon. He left Cardiff a week later.

18

One month later
December 2015

Catherine's brows furrowed over a sheet of paper with my
life broken into dates, places and titles, lips pursed as she
scanned the page, wide eyes curious and attentive. December
was closing in on us, London somehow narrower, padded
out with thicker coats and woollen scarves, umbrellas taking
up the city's scarce space. I liked our Saturday halva and
coffee mornings. There had been no rhythm and no ritual
since Sunday morning coffee at Andrew's after heavy Pulse
nights, and it felt nice to have one again, to be included in
someone else's melody of the week, in the local Greek cafe
around the corner from Catherine's place just off the filmic
Portobello Road and a fifteen-minute walk from our flat. She
had been coming here with her Greek friend Ellie for ten
years, calling it an anchor in a week's madness and noise.
When Ellie moved out of London, Catherine remained
faithful to the revarnished leather sofa the colour of caramel
tucked in the cafe's corner under the spangling orange lights
above us. She had been coming here for a year on her own,
every Saturday morning without fail, ordering a pot of Greek
coffee with a piece of spiced halva filled with almonds and
raisins. Whenever I had a free Saturday, I would sink in the
broad leather armchair with a small ceramic cup between

two fingers, sipping on the thick liquid, my world filled with hers, its turbulent fashion and turbulent relationships, stakes always high.

Today, I brought my most pressing issue. I needed to switch to a regular job, preferably one that can beat you down with lots of overtime weekend work, my days off getting too tricky to handle, Gav's dead face spilling into Frank's eyes on me, death pushed down by the new fantasy in pounding loops, my mind ripped away from the now to the point I didn't wash or eat much unless Apollo was around, the girl in the mirror seeping away through the cracks.

We drank in silence, a sweet sugary scent permeating the air, the bustle of a Saturday morning clinging in the main room behind us, Catherine always having first dibs on this small, dark corner, partitioned by a thick terracotta curtain and hidden away. My finger moved up and down the rind of a cigarette that was tucked in an inside pocket of Frank's jacket, the last of the Marlboro Lights that I had, up to this point, smoked only in solitude and only in silence, imagining Frank, his face close to mine, his breath on my forehead, the sweet scent of cardamom and peppermint almost gone. I took it out of my bag and studied it under the table.

I glanced at Catherine again. She was one of those women everyone – men and women, without exception – would turn their heads to and proclaim beautiful. Today she was laden with an ankle-long corduroy dress the colour of pine, her sleek hair brushed to the side, face bright and attended to with strokes of golden and bronze eyeshadow and delicate eyeliner, her brows arched, strong and elegant.

In 2015, she was the most beautiful of all women.

Catherine was a model in the 1990s. International career. Despite her height, despite being a child, she liked to remind me. You could do anything if you put your mind to it, she often said. I remembered my aunt stressing the importance of making something of myself and, at twenty, I felt none the wiser as to what she meant by that.

Catherine tapped the paper with her long, perfectly manicured nails.

'How about post-production?' she asked. 'I know a few people in town. You'd have to start with running, but it would be more stable.'

What was their story? Was she still in touch with Frank? How did she feel about him? How would she feel about me smoking his Marlboro Lights, thinking about his breath on my forehead?

'Toni? Hello, earth?' Catherine clicked her fingers in front of my face.

'Sorry, I didn't sleep well.' I put the cigarette back in my bag.

'You never sleep well.' She clucked her lips.

'Yeah, I guess.'

Catherine sighed and tapped at my wrist as she had just done to my CV, her lips drawn.

'I worry about you sometimes,' she said.

I shook my head and hovered over the plate of halva between us to find one with the least number of raisins I would need to pick out.

'I'm good, I'm just tired,' I said, forcing a smile.

She looked at me, chewing.

'You shouldn't be tired at twenty, that's what life after thirty is for.'

I offered a faint smile, my nails digging into crumbling halva in search of raisins.

'What did you want to do when you left Poland?' she asked after a while.

I shrugged and rested my head in both palms.

'I don't think I wanted to do anything in particular,' I said. 'I just wanted to leave.'

She gave me the same look that I imagined psychotherapists gave to their clients, attentive yet distant, compassionate yet disengaged.

'You don't start to belong by leaving,' she said, and I returned her smile, not knowing what to say. I wanted to ask her if the only way to belong was to belong with someone and I wanted to know what happened if that someone you tied all your belonging to was no longer there. What happened then? What if to leave is to start somewhere? 'Let me ask my old friend,' she said as her phone jolted through the murmuring Mediterranean soundscape. 'Oh.' A flash of surprise and irritation crossed her face. She drew her eyebrows closer together and pursed her lips, pulling the phone to her face, resting an elbow on the arm of the sofa.

'Hello, Frank?' she said in the receiver, mouthing a sorry in my direction, the palm of her other hand lifting, all fingers splayed in five minutes. 'I'm good. How are you?' My heart skipped a beat as something punched my stomach. I realised I could no longer recall Frank's scent, the cornflower blue jacket folded neatly underneath the bed next to a box with a photograph of Gav with a prawn in his mouth and a folded newspaper, announcing the drowning of the former boxing champion. 'I'm with Toni in Little Athens. Are you nearby?' My throat tightened as she said it, heat rising in my body, setting my fingertips on fire, prickling sensations shooting through each one. 'I can imagine.' Catherine lifted a cup of coffee to her perfect lips and took a sip, picking up crumbs off the table and delicately placing them onto the plate. 'I can email you their details when I get home later.' I tried to distract myself, committed to digging raisins out of the piece of halva I had just picked up, but I couldn't help but listen to every word, the distant shimmer of his voice in Catherine's ear, clear in mine, husky and low. 'No problem, Frank. Come by if you're back in the area at any point. I've just realised I missed you at Apollo's screening.' She brushed her forehead with the other hand and mouthed another *sorry*. I smiled at her, feeling the blood drain from my face. 'Take care. Yeah, you, too. *Ciao*,' she said and put the phone down on the table. 'Sorry, darling.'

'No problem,' I said and felt my own voice dwindle, my eyes linked with Catherine's. I worried she could read my every thought with her penetrating gaze, shooting at me in short sharp glimpses.

'Did you meet Frank at the screening?' she asked, filling two tall glasses with sparkling water.

'What?' I heard myself bark in a strange pitch, nails digging into my thighs under the table, head pulsating in a discordant beat.

'I can't remember what Apollo said now.' She took a sip and smiled, crossing one leg over the other. 'I had to leave straight after the film.'

'We met briefly. He had to leave early, too, I think.' I tried to sound vague, as if barely registering Frank being there. 'Apollo doesn't talk about him much.' I paused, taking a sip of water that fizzed in my throat. 'Well, at all.'

'It's complicated,' she said, tilting her head, a fleeting shadow of sadness shifting across her face. 'It's not actually,' she sighed, shoulders lifting and falling with a long exhale. 'He's just a father who was never around, the world's oldest tale.'

My throat contracted.

'Yeah, I understand,' I said, my voice faint.

Catherine smiled and placed her hand on mine with motherly tenderness.

'Apollo told me about your father,' she said. I blinked, reminded of my lie, as any other, spilling out into the world. 'I'm looking forward to our Christmas together this year.'

'Yeah, me too,' I said, squeezing her hand back.

'Let's get going, darling.' Catherine tapped my hand, her smile regaining its usual energy. 'I'm meeting some friends in town later.'

I nodded, blood rushing to my head as I stood up. I took a deep breath and put on the small black fake fur coat Catherine had presented me with the Saturday before, during an after-coffee wardrobe clear-out, now constituting the majority of my clothes. Catherine threaded her arm through mine, my hands pushed deep into the pockets of the coat, seeking warmth against the chilling gusts of wind striking our faces as soon as we stepped outside.

'When I got pregnant, I prayed every night for the baby to be a girl,' Catherine said, pulling me closer, her cheek just above my shoulder.

I smiled down at her, my mind distracted again, the girl in the mirror straightening up, her head high, her gait assured, strides longer now, matching the confidence of the legs on all the fashion magazine covers in 1990.

19

One week later
the sea

I woke up to a text from Karol.

Hey.

I blinked at my phone half asleep, pulling it closer to my face. I raised my thumb to the screen to wipe it clean, when another message appeared.

I realise you don't want to be in touch.

My body jolted up on the bed as if I could hear him speaking to me, his husky low tone edging on a whisper, his sooty eyes inspecting mine with curiosity. Another grey bubble appeared on the screen, followed by the animated three dots underneath.

I think about you, kid.

I stared at the text, wondering how many times he deleted 'kid' and put it back in there, my throat tightening in his grip, dry broad delicate hands closing in on my neck, deliberate and slow, the way they pressed the trigger on the camera at the right moment.

I hope you're alright.

My breath quickened and the phone started to shake in my hands. I closed my eyes and took a deep breath.

I'll be in London in a couple of months for an exhibition.

I scanned the text back and forth in a new bout of panic.

I'd love to see you if you're around.

I pressed the button on the side of the phone and the screen turned black, Gav's dead face in its reflection, eyes sinking in the block of darkness held in my phone. I ran to the bathroom, heart pounding in my chest, feeling the sea creeping back in underneath, my bleeding feet stinging in the salty water. I got to the bath, out of breath, as if air could only reach the very top of my lungs, the rest of their weight pulled down, water gathering at their base. I climbed into the bath and kicked the plug in the hole, yanking the cold tap open. I pressed my eyelids together as hard as I could and, propped on bony elbows wedged in the bath's hard metallic surface, I pulled my head backwards into the gush of cold water, letting the tears I couldn't cry stream down my face.

I pushed myself up in the bathtub, the colourless edges of our Notting Hill bathroom stilling, my body cold and tired, my lungs coughing up water with retching pulls, heart racing, scenes looping in my head, the Sailor Boy and his tears, the Sailor Boy's lips sealed to mine, the Sailor Boy with his pants down, his body so white, as if it was trying to erase itself, along with Cardiff and along with Karol, Karol's body bent over mine, my spine meandering like a course of tears, the pull of the camera trigger above me punctuated by Karol's warm exhales in the turgid heat of the attic.

I sauntered over to my phone, water dripping down on the floor, Gav's face still there, its blurred contours giving in to a faint flicker. I pressed the button on the side of the phone, Karol's message erasing Gav from the screen.

I'll try to be there, I typed, reading his message again, and pressed send.

Three animated dots popped up for a second and disappeared.

20

With Catherine's help, London rolled out to the bustle of Wardour Street, PAs and runners huddled in circles, filing back into basements filled with parcels and lists of deliveries; afternoon coffees, minor incidents, careers discussed, careers planned, measured in units of time endured.

Every day of the week and every other weekend, I got up at six to arrive in Soho for seven thirty. I caught the Central Line at Notting Hill Gate, the morning underground air heavy and sticky in the lungs, bodies pressed tight against bodies, bodies thrust out onto the platform at Oxford Circus in one heaving spill. I took the Argyll Street exit and turned left by the Palladium into Soho. At seven in the morning and with barely anyone else around, it carried a quiet fantasy of a different life. It spoke of status, containing its past and dreaming boldly of the future in a perpetual forward motion of new businesses and new industries steeped deep in its own tale of what was.

Every day and every other weekend, I strolled across Wardour and through St Anne's to our office on Dean Street. I opened the office, cleaned the desks, and laid out breakfast in the basement cafeteria. Fiona manned the reception desk as a head runner and arrived at eight, by which point the office had started to fill with producers, sound engineers and their assistants in a low morning commotion of quiet catch-ups and spoons clinking against mugs.

Me and Fiona reported directly to Emma, the production coordinator who was, additionally and at no pay increase, bestowed with looking after runners. She begrudged this task with a flippant attention span and a glaring disinterest in how things were done until a mistake was made and a client expressed unhappiness. Every time this happened, Emma sprang downstairs from her office and, having quickly acquainted herself with a situation, shot precise orders with specific deadlines. Emma liked to remind us how lucky we were to even see the light of day and *interact* with clients, *top* people in our industry. Where she came from, a post-production house ten times the size of ours, we would never leave the basement, washing, serving and preparing on rotation. Then came the bark as she bared her perfectly aligned teeth:

'Now, hurry up.'

Today the hurry was to get a round of coffees from Black Cat Coffee for a bunch of creatives involved in a bike insurance commercial. The four men, all identical to one another, their faces angular and shoulders broad, had heard the same jingle thousands of times now. They had decided to start ordering coffee from different places each day, to shake things up a little bit. As luck would have it, they said when I cleaned their lunch orders, they would be stuck here for another month at least. This had been going on for a week, getting more exhausting as we reached further corners of Soho, balancing the art of extra hot and still having flavour. I nodded at my challenge, pen ready against paper, staring at their bored faces.

One oat flat white, one black filter, one black Americano, one almond cappuccino. All extra hot, not burnt. I wrote everything down, smiling at them with an 'Anything else?'

Four bored shakes of heads.

'Oh, actually,' said the man with an LA baseball cap, his jawline not far from that of an actor in a commercial, 'throw a round of pastries in there.' I was beginning to be trusted with something.

I tucked my notepad and pen in my back pocket, on the high of a new mission. As soon I'd completed it, I could throw myself into stock calculations and cleaning schedules with specific instructions on what items to clean, how and when; pleasant mundanity dulling my brain with the satisfaction of things crossed off a list, tasks accomplished, life a bit more measured.

It was four in the afternoon and The Black Cat was almost empty. A tall woman behind the counter glanced at me with polite indifference, a short brown bob enveloping her round face with its beady brown eyes. I smiled and walked over, placing my order.

Eastern Europe had a way of weaving herself around syllables, sitting on diction, tilting and pushing vowels in her direction; language always the migrant's traitor, whichever direction we looked.

'Are you Polish?' the girl asked in English. I flinched in surprise and met her smile.

'Yes,' I said, grappling at the words left behind, abandoned with Karol's departure. The girl's small lips widened in a grin.

'How long have you been in the UK?' she asked me, the standard foreigner to foreigner. It made me smile.

'Two years,' I said. I hesitated and looked at her, catching the edges of her face with caution. 'How about you?' I asked. We continued with further migrating foundations of where in Poland we were from. We politely acknowledged tenuous links with that place and the other, some friends studying here, distant relatives living there, a vague school trip or two, driving past a place once; however, maybe it was a different place entirely. The girl's name was Magda and she had come to the UK five years ago, after finishing university. She found a cleaning job in one of the hotels north of Russell Square and managed to get a barista position in Shoreditch. Three years ago, she got a dream gig in The Black Cat and last month she became general manager. There was a rigidity to Magda, the angles of her face were uninteresting, squared with blandness. There was something in the way the synthetic fabric fell flat and safe on her proportioned features, her straight hair layered and thinned at the ends, a face I could spot a mile off as one of ours, her cat eyes brown and inquisitive, her narrow lips parted as she sighed.

'What I really want to do is get into advertising. How did you get to be a runner?'

I paused, imagining Catherine making a call to Lauren Howells-White, the co-founder of our studio.

'I've run before,' I said. 'I've done some set work.'

She smiled and placed two drinks in a takeaway holder, disappearing back behind the coffee machine, the scent of cardamom filtering through the air, whirling and dancing with the sweet and heavy coffee aroma.

'How far do you live from here?' she asked out of the blue, fitting two other drinks in the same holder. 'I'm down in Catford and the commute is a nightmare. I wonder where else is cheap and more straightforward.'

My lips parted, my throat making a barely audible sound. I had never had to pay rent in London, and I felt my face flush hot.

'I've only lived in Notting Hill,' I said, my voice as quiet as I could lower it, edging on a whisper.

She looked up at me with a different glint in her narrowed eyes, but before she could say anything a male voice rang behind me, a familiar husky tone leaving its warm breath on the nape of my neck.

'When you're ready, love.'

I stood still, my fingers clawing the counter, afraid to move.

'I'm so sorry.' Magda switched to English, throwing an apologetic glance at the man behind me, her accent now very British, her voice rising and falling appropriately. 'Anything else?' She smiled the English smile at me.

'Four plain croissants, please,' I said, panic rising in my voice. I pointed at a heap of chocolate and cream brioches, feeling my finger quiver. 'Two of those, too,' I added, as if only to ascertain that I was still there in my body, that it could still do the things bodies did. 'Please.'

'What a feast,' rang the familiar voice behind me, morphing the ordinary into a dream, numbing me from head to toe.

'Is that everything?' asked Magda with a new degree of cold politeness. I nodded, my heart pounding, the cool runner girl gone. 'Twenty fifty-two, please.'

Twenty fifty-two, twenty fifty-two. I scrambled the loose change out of my work wallet and asked for a receipt.

'It's been a while.' Frank stepped forward to the counter. I looked down, his little finger edging close to mine.

'Yeah,' I gasped and looked up at Magda, who was endowing Frank with a generous smile, so foreign to her face only seconds earlier.

'Black filter, please, love.' A crumpled five-pound note fell between us. I looked for cardamom and peppermint with hints of lemon but all that hung heavy in the air were sharp strokes of coffee and sugar. 'Thanks, darling.' He popped the change into the tip jar, stretching the barista's smile to capacity.

The memory of Frank, dashing in every detail of pattern and colour, whirred into this new man I would not have recognised but for his voice, hoarse and soothing, the one that echoed in my mind through all long inhales and exhales of the finite packet of Marlboro Lights. He was hooded up in black, a silver zip brushing against his stubbly chin, round shades hanging on golden wires despite the greyness of the new year, obscuring his high cheekbones. We stepped away from the counter, my left arm wrapped around the package of coffees and pastries, my right hand pinching the notepad in my back pocket.

I had imagined this moment a thousand times over and in none of them were we here, caught by the casualness of the day, off guard, the ground treaded with caution.

'It's nice to see you,' I said, resenting how little I could reach in his face, hidden from the world.

'Yeah, you too.' He smiled. 'Do you work around here?'

I nodded, pointing vaguely at the door.

'Down the road,' my voice quaint again. Magda shouted a black filter, beaming at Frank from across the counter.

'One second.' He drifted off, the jaunty swagger bringing him back to Frank at the screening and Frank moulded and morphed in my faded memory.

I cleared my throat a couple of times to regain its trained volume, the voice that had learnt what to say, when, and in what tone, so no one took offence at its Eastern European flatness.

'I have to get back,' I said. 'Bringing in cold coffee is a serious offence among runners.'

'Yeah, of course.' He smiled.

We stood still for a moment and I didn't know how to say goodbye. My free hand jutted forward in offer of a handshake which made us both laugh in relief.

'Alright.' I withdrew it and pinned it in my back pocket. I turned on my feet slowly and he said:

'Listen, Toni, what are you doing tonight?'

And I should've said that I was busy doing absolutely anything, but even though I had already made plans with Apollo, I said:

'Nothing, why?'

I imagined his throat quivering as he said it, but I couldn't be sure, I couldn't detect anything in his face.

'I'm seeing this band in New Cross Inn.'

The information hung between us as I hugged the package closer to my chest, aware of the fleeting heat, the vanishing chance.

'I'm done around seven,' I said, my hand finding its way to my hair, seeping through it gently as I looked at him. 'I can meet you there after.'

'Grand.' He smiled. 'Can I grab your notebook and pen for a second?' I nodded and pulled it out of my back pocket. 'Ta.' He scribbled something down and handed it back to me. 'Let's not push our luck with chance encounters. Pop me a text if you can't find me.' He smiled and held the door open. 'After you.' I obliged.

I walked back to the office, my mind whirring around what had just happened. It was the first time in a year and a half when Gav's face wasn't piercing through my every thought, stopping any attempt at forward motion, the distance between the coffee shop and our office filled with the bombastic fantasy of Frank. He came with no future, but the present was opulent and dazzling.

Tonight came with a release from the waves, from the sea, from me.

Before I pressed the buzzer for the office, I pulled out my phone and opened a message thread with Apollo. With a lump in my throat, my fingers clammy and stiff, I started typing:

Can't make dinner tonight. I paused, biting my lip. *One of the producers' birthdays. We're all going out xx*

Apollo replied straight away. He always did.

No problem. I'll rebook for tomorrow. Have fun! Xxx

I hesitated for a moment before texting back.

Thanks, I said. *See you later.*

21

It was easy to spot him despite his camouflage, his head nodding along to the rhythm of jangling guitars.

I walked over to the bar, trying to catch a glimpse of any poster suggesting the name of the band. I glanced over to check that he didn't have a drink and ordered two pints of lager and a double shot of vodka, which I quickly downed before wrapping my hands around the pints, cold glass cooling my hands.

The scattered crowd cheered as the song fizzled out. There were not many there and Frank huddled at the back behind everyone else.

'Hey,' he said, smiling at me as I bobbed up in front of him with a wobble, handing him his pint, his eyes still locked away behind his shades despite the darkness, his face lit by haphazard strokes flashing at us from the stage. 'Oh, cheers, very kind of you.'

We clinked glasses.

'Who are they?' I asked and stood beside him, taking a sip of my pint.

He leant down, his lips grazing my left ear.

'Veronica Falls.'

I shook my head at never having heard of them.

'A firecracker of a band,' he said, his lips still sealed to my ear, the rolling drums introducing the next song, beats punctuating the air.

The drums carried their sound through the songs as our bodies swayed, pulled by their dictation. They weaved in the punchy guitars in a sweeping pop romance, catapulting me out of space for a little while, and back to Cardiff, standing by Karol, a barely detectable beat moving through his body, his long, slender neck vibrating in broken lyrics, both of us safe in the melody.

With gentle strums, the band announced the last song of the evening and thanked everyone for coming.

'Come on over,' muffled the lead guitarist, electric sounds stitched together in an ebb that anticipated something bigger, pop so powerful it would send hearts reeling for hours.

'Now, listen to this.' Frank's lips stretched with joy as the drums fell on us so unexpectedly my heart skipped a beat, running, running, running ahead, and taking all our senses with them. 'Fucking brilliant,' he said, voice drowned in their sound as the sweet, lucid vocals lapped against the guitars crashing in, sprinting to the end of the night.

Our pints dry, we pressed them against our chests as we howled and cheered the band off stage.

'There's a little beer garden at the back, through there.' Frank pointed at the narrow hallway snaking around the back of the bar, his other hand momentarily resting on my shoulder. 'Same again? I'll get it.'

I nodded and made my way through to the back, finding us a place in the far corner, barely reached by the heating lamp in the centre, its glow fading where I sat down.

Frank's long, slender shadow meandered slowly past old picnic tables scattered chaotically in the long narrow space.

'Same again.' He placed a pint and a shot each between us, straddling the low bench opposite me. I let out a stifled sigh, looking up at him.

'Busted,' I said, laughing. 'Cheers.'

'Cheers.' He clinked his pint with mine and took off his glasses. I could just about make out the forgotten details of his face, deep grey eyes glinting in the night, reflecting faint sparks of the fairy lights behind me, the blond mop of his hair trailing off in all directions.

'They were great,' I said. 'How did you hear about them?'

'Oh, I forget now. Someone sent me their album a while back, I thought they were ace.' He took a beat and looked at me. 'It was really great to bump into you and your many coffees today.'

I wanted to say how random that was, how random we were, drawn into something neither of us was willing to acknowledge tonight; was it only a matter of time? What was the probability here?

'It was good to bump into you, too.' I smiled. 'Sorry, I haven't got your jacket.'

'Don't worry about it. You can get it back to me some other time,' he said, his voice hoarse and warm, soothing.

'I've also smoked all your Marlboro Lights.'

Frank gave a short laugh.

'Thought you might.'

The girl in the mirror tilted her head, letting strands of hair fall on her cheek, laughing along, finding it so easy to be around him.

'Your hair's got long since I last saw you,' he said, his voice softer now.

'That's what usually happens to hair,' I said, which made him chuckle.

'What I meant to say…' He hesitated but took a sip of his beer instead. 'How long have you worked in Soho?'

'Not long, maybe a month,' I said, unsure how to navigate myself away from Apollo and Catherine, their presence permeating all my choices in the last few months. We took a beat and eyed the shots.

'Cheers,' he said, and I echoed, clinking my glass with his, vodka tearing through my throat in one thirsty stream. We took to our lager and quenched the burning in quick sips. 'How's your friend?' he asked. I narrowed my eyes at him, mind dizzying with having him in front of me. 'The one who kept calling.'

'Oh.' I smiled, surprised he remembered. 'He's coming to London soon with an exhibition. He's a photographer.'

'Are you going to see him?'

'I don't know,' I said. What I didn't say to either of them was that there was no one else I wanted to see more, and no one I was more afraid to see. 'Are you hungry?' I asked, my hand landing on my stomach. 'I haven't had anything since lunch.'

'Ravenous,' he said. 'Do you want to get some chips and have a stroll?'

He tucked his shades into the pocket of his denim jacket, safe in the night.

'It was nice to see you, you know, see you see you,' I said, the girl in the mirror confident and deliberate in her smile.

Frank stifled a grin in the same mischievous way that was etched in my memory of him.

'Come on then,' he said softly. 'Careful now.' He grabbed me by the elbow, nudging me gently around the table. 'Let's get some grub.' He grabbed my hand and pulled me forward, through the whirring maze of tables and down the meandering hallway of the pub, out onto the street.

+

'Oh god, this is so good,' I said with an audible gasp, dunking my chips in a polystyrene cup of watered-down curry sauce while Frank bit into his second chicken leg.

'Oh yeah.'

We were good now, alcohol flushing out things unsaid, the starry sharp sky steadying our heads in pleasant intoxication.

'I was born not far from here,' he said through a mouthful of chicken. 'Just up the quays.'

'What was that like?' I asked.

'Rough as fuck back then,' he said, laughing. 'Fun though. Do you want to take a walk up there? I haven't been in ages.' He stood up with a slight groan and offered me his hand, pulling me up closer to him. 'There's one gorgeous spot, I wonder what it looks like now.'

'That sounds great,' I said, aware of our hands enclosed in each other. 'Do you want another drink?' I pointed at the red and yellow corner shop illuminated by harsh light pouring from the inside.

'Tell you what, I'll get us a couple of cans each and you find a bin for these.' Frank handed me his box of rattling bones.

I watched his figure disappear into the shop, London expanding eastwards, stretching to a new feeling, pulling me closer to him, how unreal we were, without context, in a London that was new and borderless in its nighttime mass.

He emerged, grinning, cans raised in victory. He popped one open and handed it to me. We touched cans with a smile. It should've felt cold that January night, but the air lay light in its sharpness, a rare friend, engulfing us in the moment with pleasant softness, the forgotten lightness of being.

'Where's home for you?' he asked as we strolled on, my hand back in his, following in his steps.

I wanted to tell him that I didn't know, yet, but instead I told him of the hills and the square houses, each in a different colour, and of the multitude of churches and pharmacies lining the streets, recreated in a country that had always wanted to be someone else, someone more western and wealthy.

Frank listened to my stories of the sprawling spaces, the mountains nudging at the sky, the best potatoes in the world, especially when you poured kefir over them in the summer and sprinkled spring onion on top. I rubbed my thumb against all four fingers and sprinkled the air in front of him.

I told him about my grandfather and how much he loved his herring, and of my grandmother, how much she hated the sea, and how much she fancied Stalin, and how Jan's moustache looked like Stalin's which brought them together, and I realised I hadn't told anyone about this since Gav and I wasn't sure why and he wasn't sure why he hadn't been back to Surrey Quays in so long, maybe as long as fifteen years.

'How about your mother?' I asked, the past hardly ever adding up for anyone, least of all for migrants, the narrative retold too many times to stick to the original.

Frank glanced at me, his eyes darting across my face in question.

"Genevieve,' I pressed on. 'What about her Notting Hill apartment and her four-pillar bed?'

Something shot across his face, a reminder, a context.

'I forget that you live there.' He cleared his throat and forced a smile. 'Her name was Jean, Jean Rooney. She always wanted to get out, a fantastic character, full of life my mother was, with a huge heart and big ideas which are reflected in her choice of furniture.' He paused for a moment of half laughter. 'When my father died, I moved her in. She insisted on being called Genevieve from then on, the most foul-mouthed Genevieve in the whole of west London.'

I wondered if Apollo knew this, but I didn't dare drop his name in the air that hung so silky, so soft and warm between us.

'That's incredible,' I said after a while. For the first time in months, I couldn't wait to fall asleep within her four pillars, in her new world Frank had created.

'We all want to erase something,' he smiled.

We walked on into my London unknown and his London erased, equipped with a small bottle of vodka between us, coating our bodies as our hearts beat faster to the music long forgotten and long not discussed. I let myself delve back into the familiar abandoned sounds, scraping for names first as if unfurling a new tongue, but soon they all came, pouring out, out of breath, cut up by memories of parties, of dancing so long your body could barely carry you, of the bands scribbled down in Karol's red notebook, Sunset Rubdown and Wolf Parade and Fang Island and WHY? and Animal Collective and The Magnetic Fields, all the bands we had seen together and got excited by, the kitchen filled with their sounds when Gav wasn't around with his devout love of pop and disco, the memory of a serpentine body pulled and pushed by faded melodies.

'I love how alive you are when you talk about music.' Frank stifled a grin in the coy, boyish way I began to recognise. He meandered through bands emerging on local scenes and in my consciousness, taking me through the excitement of discovery of something else, something new.

It felt romantic in its chaotic recollections and lapses of misunderstanding, all things about us wrong and therefore befitting, the fantastical realm of physical attraction and romance, of pure pop.

Being with Frank was belonging in our movie, figures drifting towards each other in the way I heard of others drifting, smiles exchanged and laughs synchronised, excitement knotted deep in the stomach. In the movie, we collide with intention, Frank extricated from Frank Moz, me released from myself just for tonight, enjoying the relief of laughter, the way only laughter can float and dive in your body, so light, enjoying feeling sexy under his gaze, mustering the courage to direct mine back at him.

My heart beat faster, swung in the rhythm of our bodies drifting forward, plunged out of the sea onto the shore where it had no right to survive; but it was not playing to live, it wanted to be devoured.

We reached the edges of the looping lump of Surrey Quays, sauntering through the cobbled Rotherhithe Street, bricked limbs curving above our heads. Frank smiled, pointing at the heavy pub banner of The Mayflower, tucked underneath the arches.

'I had my first pub drink here,' he said, looking up at the painted ship, motionless in the winter night. 'Tried to impress my first girlfriend.' His face stretched in a grin and he shot me a quick glance. 'Stella, her name was. We were both twelve.' Frank shook his head as if surprised by the distant memory. 'The barman gave us half a pint each, good lad.' He laughed and tiptoed around the pub with caution even though there was no one in sight, Rotherhithe laying still in the night. 'There used to be three steps down onto the river, just on the side.' Frank stopped by the pub door, looking down as I stooped behind him. 'There they are.' He pointed at some small stone slabs skirting down underneath the pub's decked out beer garden, its four pillars pushed deep into the river, resisting its flow.

I followed him down, ebbing myself closer, my hands resting on his shoulders for balance.

I could just about make out the receding river, baring the jagged shore, washed-out bottles and crackling crisp wrappers, an unwelcome reminder of the city, otherwise barely discernible in the dark. It must've been somewhere here, in the old docks, where Marlowe set off east.

'Have you read any Joseph Conrad?' I asked, my voice ringing clear in the quiet night, standing next to him, our eyes distracted from each other for a moment and wedged in the impenetrable black coat of the river.

'Not much,' he said, his voice soft, his shoulder touching mine. 'I've always loved *Victory*, though. I must've read it half a dozen times over the years.'

'I've been meaning to read it for a while,' I said, my body inching closer to his. 'I'm just making my way through *Lord Jim* in Polish translation.'

'Oh, the irony,' said Frank, a quiet voice edging on whisper.

'Indeed,' I gasped, my restless heart thudding against my chest, hands furling into fists.

'Interesting, though.' His breath brushed my forehead, his throat quivered just before my face.

We fizzled out, our mouths dry, thirsty for a drink.

We fell silent. The unfamiliar comfort, uninterrupted by chasing thoughts, uninterested in pleasing; at ease, stilling every muscle in my body, even my heart. My lips curved a smile as I looked at him, feeling his breath now moving down my face.

And then, he leant over and kissed me.

22

Three weeks later
February 2016

A rock star father and a fashion designer mother, Apollo's pursuit needed to be different from the glamorous and the popular if he could call it his own, his art unburdened by popularity and money, girlfriends unburdened by glamour and grace.

Apollo once told me that I was nothing like the women his dad had dated in the past, conceit slipping through the cracks in his smile. When I asked him about the women, he said they all blended into one, indiscernible from one another, his voice tinged with sad smugness that always concealed rejection. His timeline was running against the inherited current, but so was mine, within his, defying the Eastern European chronology, caught in ambiguous glimpses and mouths opening in surprise at age, a number of rooms and square metres, and above all, at Notting Hill.

I lay by Apollo's side in a waking sleep paralysis, unable to move or relax a single muscle in my body as he drifted off to sleep, calm and free, my frazzled mind wandering out to Frank's lips sealed to mine, his eyes wandering my body, now trapping me in a fixed half-conscious stare at the ceiling until it gave in to an exhausted, restless sleep hours later, a different scene looping in my head, different from the cold pale body washed out by the sea, lips, warm and alive, pulling away from lips and my own voice reverberating a quiet 'I should head home', words spoken against the pulls of the body, against the cold hands knotted at the nape of his neck. I replayed the glimmer in Frank's dark eyes, treading with caution, a smile shooting across his face in understanding, but of what I didn't know, since neither of us could've understood anything of that moment, now a part of every sleepless night, of the wrong words said at the wrong time, prompting an agreement from Frank's lips, words against his body, still pulling me closer, still holding me in his arms.

I lay my hand on Apollo's, giving in to small trembles of deep sleep. He'd been absent by my side lately, to my relief, pushing forth fast in exact knowing and understanding, film set hours keeping us apart, Jean-Genevieve's bed rarely cradling two bodies, Apollo away most nights, wanting more, me needing his dreams to fill the lack of mine.

My oversized jumper hung loose over boy jeans, feet wrapped in shabby-looking Converse, skin uncorrected, lips dabbed in deep red. I was ready. Apollo looked at me with a smile, his boyish frame sunk in a black hoodie, light brown ringlets tucked behind the ears, black jeans rolled up at the ankles above woollen green socks in weathered brown brogues. The moment of our days off finally colliding was only a matter of time and here it was, its penetrating winter breath piercing our bodies laden with impractical vintage coats flailing about in sudden gusts.

'Jesus.' Apollo squeezed my hand tighter and put his hood on. 'The one time we try and have a date night.' I followed by his side in silence, lips pursed in defiance against the unfaltering storm.

When we reached the Ultimate Picture Palace, my lungs contracted with a whip of the wind. I looked up at the cinema's banner, lit up in the night, and my throat tightened as if at the possibility of Frank underneath it. I shook my head and gripped Apollo's hand, comforted by its familiar soft texture, small bones knowing mine, no danger surging through our touch. We walked through the door, the dry heat nibbling on our skin with pleasant prickling.

'God, that was nasty,' I said, maybe finally understanding the safety of weather in any British conversation. 'Did you say you had tickets?' I turned to Apollo, pulling the hood over his head, the wavy locks he inherited from neither of his parents flapping about his face.

'Yeah, we just need to pick them up,' he said, his hand still enveloping mine, pushing forward to the box office in the opposite corner to the winding staircase that climbed up to the bar, hidden behind elegant wooden panels, purposeful and graceful in its art deco, glinting in the subtle oranges of the evening lights.

A man with a golden nose ring and olive skin met our smiles.

'How can I help you, guys?' he asked, Italian tones entwined in syllables, making them sing.

'We've booked two tickets for *She's Gotta Have It* at six,' said Apollo. 'Apollo Rooney.'

The man, in his early thirties at a first glance, narrowed his eyes at Apollo.

'Didn't we show your film a while back?'

Apollo's lips spread in a smile.

'Yeah, I was screening my short here,' he nodded.

'Yeah, yeah, that's right,' rang the man's voice. 'I missed it, man, had to work. My colleague Marta said it was really good.'

There it was, the necessary addition to our date, my body relaxing in a familiar pattern, Apollo and I existing only within Genevieve's walls, everywhere outside, surrounded by the incessant flow of a filmic world, actors and crews Apollo had worked with, close and distant friends, his introverted nature dissipating at the sound of cinema, thwarting everything else. He smiled again, cocking his head to the right in a terrifying resemblance to Frank.

'Thanks, man, that's really nice of you to say,' said Apollo. 'What's your name?'

'Luca.' The man stretched out his arm from across the counter.

'Nice to meet you, man.' There it was, Apollo's calm demeanour charming, pulling everyone close. 'That's my girl, Toni.' We shook hands.

'Do you guys have a minute?' asked Luca. 'We are curating a very small giallo film poster exhibition upstairs in the bar. Do you want to take a look?'

I looked around at the foyer, a dance of grand elegance with boutique cosiness, empty on a Monday night.

'Yeah, sure, man,' said Apollo, shooting me a slide glance to check if it was okay.

'Sounds great,' I said, smiling, my eyes wandering away towards the staircase, remembering Frank's long figure skipping the steps with a swagger.

'Anette!' Luca's baritone shot through the air in an indistinct direction. 'Can you jump on the till for a sec for me, please?' he said, and without waiting for her, a short girl with a fizz of purple hair, to reach the counter, he sprinted towards the stairs, showing us the way.

The bar looked different to how I remembered it, tables and chairs arranged neatly at the back, parquet floor shimmering in the dulled ceiling pin lights, the walls, repainted white, laden with film posters bearing Italian titles stretching on either side of the bar.

'Hey, Margot.' Luca addressed a woman behind the bar, noting stuff down in a large notepad, bottles of wine in different sleeves lining the bar next to her. 'There's no one downstairs so I'm showing these guys around.' The woman smiled at us and returned to counting bottles, her beautiful jasmine eyes shooting us curious glances. She had the figure of a ballerina, petite and toned, dark hair engulfing a small, pointed face.

'I've brought them all from Italy,' he said, standing at the centre of the room, muscles under the tattoo sleeve on his arm tensing in presentation. 'They're all originals, first print,' he said with the same pride and love Apollo held only for films.

'They're wonderful, man,' Apollo said, his head shifting from one poster to another, multiple female figures weaving through the modest space in erotic displays of desire and murder. I clung to Apollo, my eyes darting to Margot, rose lips pursed in confusion above the scribbled pages. 'Where did you get these?' Apollo turned to Luca, each of them basking in mutual adoration.

'My aunt, she was a collector, drove all around Italy to get them,' said Luca, his voice animated and beautifully melodic, like a dramatic pop song. 'I brought a lot, some original Antonionis, Pasolinis, Fellinis, De Sicas, Viscontis…' Names rolled off Luca's tongue with a different song, each name contracting Apollo's hand still holding mine, his eyes sparking up to the melody of the only love language he understood.

'Oh man,' Apollo said, his mouth open, speechless.

'She put them all dying in the attic, man, dying!' This tragic statement came delivered with a clasp of the hand on his forehead and a quiet sigh from behind the bar. I imagined the posters decaying in the heat of the attic, now able to breathe, thousands of kilometres away. I followed Luca's outstretched hand, his finger pointing to the first poster in the collection.

IL GATTO A NOVE CODE: a woman being strangled set against a black cat with its fangs dipped in blood, its eyes intense yellow, hers closed, mouth open in agony, or maybe pleasure.

Margot joined in behind us with a glass of red wine.

'They're quite incredible, aren't they?' she said. 'I never liked giallo, but I've always loved these posters.' She was shorter than me, her sweet flowery perfume tingled my nostrils.

I nodded, putting my free arm around my waist, Apollo drawing me closer to the poster in step with Luca.

COSÌ DOLCE COSÌ PERVERSA: a multicoloured square collage above the title and credits showed a man, tinted blue against a blotch of red, glancing to his left. He was wearing a black suit, a white shirt and a tie. His gaze should have been directed at two women but instead lurked in between them. The brunette had her hands on the blonde's neck. The blonde's mouth was open, neither in a shriek nor pleasure, as if she had been merely discomfited.

Margot's head bobbed just above my shoulder as Luca pointed at another poster. My lips drew closer, imitating Margot's.

'Looks like the brunette's going to get it,' said Margot, her lips tainted light burgundy.

'Did she?' I asked but none of them had seen *Così Dolce Così Perversa*. A different blonde appeared in the top right corner, too, facing downwards, mouth open in pleasure. The giver of pleasure wasn't disclosed, her body cut by the poster's edge at the torso.

'Brilliant, aren't they?' said Margot, our bodies turned to the posters in admiration. 'We're having a giallo night here this weekend. Showing this one.' Margot skipped a poster in the middle and pointed at the biggest one of all, the fourth in line on the wall, the background halved in black and white, the title spelling out *FEMINA RIDENS* in red. A man's head was hiding behind the title above a headless woman with two strips of see-through material revealing her breasts, running up her chest and behind her neck, its belt forming a thicker layer underneath her bust. The woman's four arms spread in a fanning motion, two arms on each side of her body, the index finger touching the thumb in peace and control. Did her body possess it irrespective of her mind?

'Like a goddess, isn't she?' said Margot, finishing off her glass. 'Despite being exposed, despite fragmentation of the body, she stands fierce, she is divine.'

'She looks like a Hindu goddess,' said Luca and Apollo hummed an affirmative 'Hmm.'

'What does the title mean?' I asked Luca.

'It has been translated to both *The Frightened Woman* and *The Laughing Woman*,' he said and gave a short laugh.

I looked at the woman, her head decapitated, the gaze erased.

'Which one is she?' I asked.

'You have to decide.' Luca smiled and led us to the middle. 'Our little wall of fame,' he chuckled. 'Frank Moz popped in not so long ago, actually. Now that I think of it, it might've been your screening,' Luca said to Apollo and pointed to a small photograph in a black frame, Frank and Luca by the box office, Frank's arm around Luca's shoulder, a cornflower blue shirt without a jacket, still folded neatly underneath our bed. I glanced at Apollo, his face pale, lips giving into a tremble, just like mine, my head spinning in an exhausting regret of pulling away too soon, of saying the wrong thing at the wrong time. 'If you don't mind me asking, how come he came to your film, man? Do you know him?'

Apollo wrapped his arm around my waist and smiled a smile identical to his father's, the smile they both gave when neither of them wanted to reveal too much, eyes glazed with rehearsed confidence.

'Not well, man, no,' he said, his voice composed. 'He knows a friend of my mother's, I think.' Apollo pulled me closer to him, his fingers kneading at my jumper, my eyes on Frank in the photo, paralyzed by his gaze, just like I was two weeks ago underneath the Mayflower, the freezing Thames grazing at our feet.

'God.' Luca sealed his lips with tips of his fingers, which sprung open towards Frank in a bow. 'Such a gentleman, too.' Apollo concealed a snigger with a wide smile and exasperated nod neither Luca nor Margot paid any attention to. 'He kept punk rock alive. Fuck, he kept me alive for a while.' Luca clucked his tongue, his hands folded into each other on his broad chest, staring at Frank along with the rest of us.

'He's a bit trad now.' Margot's voice rose between us, eyes narrowing on the photograph in inquisition. 'One of those dad rockers. I mean, what has he done in the last twenty years? Anything good?'

Luca's eyes dilated in shock and Apollo shook his head, laughing.

'He was pretty iconic in his day,' Apollo said after a while, sending a hot wave flushing through my body.

'Iconic,' repeated Luca and clasped his hips with both hands, shaking his head. 'It doesn't matter what he has or hasn't done in the last twenty years. He did everything before.'

This didn't entirely make sense, but was tinged with enough passion for Margot to roll her eyes and walk back to the bar. I looked at my phone, the absurd temptation to text Frank every time I glanced at the screen.

'We're late for the film,' I said, turning to Apollo. I knew he had to be in his seat at the start of the adverts and trailers or he would leave the cinema.

'Oh shit, yeah.' Apollo looked at his phone and back at Luca. 'Thanks for the tour, man, these are great.' He glanced around the room in a quick sweeping motion.

'No problem, friend.' Luca patted him on the back and raised a hand in my direction. 'Nice to meet you both. Enjoy the film!' He walked towards Margot, who rose from behind the inventory with a friendly goodbye.

We walked past the tortured, pleasured women and followed the steps down.

'Oh, I forgot to tell you,' Apollo said, as we reached the bottom of the stairs. 'I've seen Karol's post about being back in town at the end of the month with a new exhibition.'

My heart skidded forth at the sound of his name the way it always did.

'You're a bit of a fanboy,' I said, concealing the anxiety rising in my chest.

'Yeah, I guess,' he laughed. 'We should go if we're both free.'

'Yeah, definitely,' I said as we slipped into the dark room, the black screen pulling me away from Karol, from Frank, from Gav, skipping heart stilling in the brash sounds of adverts, their colourful fantasy worlds wrestling for my attention.

23

One month later
March 2016

My phone vibrated in my back pocket. A number I had saved as 'Veronica F' popped up on my screen with a text:

I'm seeing this band tonight… ;-)

Something punched my stomach, making my body that bit more alive – usually there wasn't much, a day-to-day rehearsal, swelling in the head, numbness crawling down that I needed to walk out, work out, smile out, but it never completely went away.

This punch was different, physical, sharp, exciting. I'd only felt it once before, on the blunt edges of unravelled rocks beneath the Mayflower, when Frank leant over and kissed me and it was the only kiss I ever surrendered to, so unlike those reserved for sleazy boys and drunk girls, their tongues pushing too deep, their hands too greedy.

Now, here he was, in my phone, a different form of abstract to a hazy, unreliable cloud of memory.

I asked him what band.

He gave a name, location and time.

I said I'd be there.

I wanted him to erase what was left of me. Frank held that power, he helped erase Jean and created Genevieve and he could erase me and create me anew, differently, in gentle strokes running down the edges of my body and maybe in harder pulls, too. He held the promise of the world after Frank and with him the world after myself, too.

Frank wore the same leather jacket and shades, hovering at the back of the bar like last time. I ordered two pints and two shots of vodka and I sauntered over to him in confidence, the girl in the mirror clad in a short black bodycon dress she had bought today just for him. The dress would have never belonged to her before, but it fit that space and time, where she could be what he wanted her to be, and it made everything so much easier.

I wanted to be whatever he wanted me to be.

Guitars strummed harder that night in an abandon of punk, beats thumping our hearts that had already been set on fire as we talked, smoked, and drank more in blurred cycles of a good night out. When the night was shifting to nightclubs and house parties, he pressed his lips against my ear and, with an electric shock that vaulted down my back, he asked if I fancied going back to his.

My throat dry, I nodded, to which he gave a wide smile, a smile no one had ever offered at the prospect of having sex with me.

Enclosed by the anonymity of the cab, our lips could finally meet and limbs intertwine, his hardness exciting, the warmth of his touch safe.

'Fuck, I've been thinking about this ever since I saw you in the cinema that day,' he said.

The night broke into images and ran out of sequence, remembered in the feeling of skin burning skin, in his scent grazing my neck, his tongue in an awkward dance with mine, fingers sliding down my chest, the weight of his body pressing on mine, our breath interrupted, my lungs constricting under his chest.

I was the girl in the mirror, wanting my man, for a little while existing in wanting, and what is desire if not the hope in the existence of a future. I wanted his hands to define me, tell me who I was and who I desired, mine splayed palms up above my head. My body wanted to be devoured and I wanted him to fuck me.

Frank's breath quickened under the directness of my request, a desperate cry to feel. He pushed me down onto the floor, pain jolting through my body when he entered me, but I remained still in resistance, knees and elbows digging into the hard wooden floor, scraping the skin.

This is how he did it, erased me when I surrendered under him, taking in all his hunger, and I felt alive within his desire, in the strength of that impulse. Pushing away from the floor, her mind empty of the murdering sea, the girl in the mirror asked:

'Can you hit me?'

Frank stilled, the sweaty palms of his hands resting gently on my butt, his voice faltering when he repeated:

'Can I hit you?'

I twisted my head backwards and up, glancing at his face, thrown off, caught in a moment between fear and fantasy, the unknown territory we tried to find a language for.

'Do you want me to spank you?' he asked, words treading cautiously, breaking in places.

'Yes,' I demanded, safe in us, in what we were not, never to exist outside of that small Soho flat.

Frank's eyes glazed again under the firmness of my voice and a sharp, piercing pain shot across my right butt cheek, his chest touching my back when he pushed deeper inside me, the other hand wrapped around my waist.

With a second strike I came, letting tears sling down my cheeks silently, relieved to feel them on my face, a salty taste slipping into my mouth, a silent cue I was still alive.

I smiled to myself and, hearing his panting quicken in my ear, I turned my lips to him and moaned quietly, cheek to cheek now. I groaned louder and louder, synching myself up with his rhythm, quicker and quicker, until he came, too.

Frank slid off me and fell on his back, his arms outstretched, chest rising and falling out of breath. I lowered myself onto my stomach, putting my head on my arms, and watched him catch his breath.

'Fuck.' He glanced at my butt and touched it softly. 'I didn't hurt you, darling?'

He looked at my face, but I turned away and wiped my cheeks dry discreetly, shaking my head no.

I smiled at him, unable to tell him the truth, that all of him hurt me that first night and that I wanted him to hurt me, I wanted to feel hurt. The pain prevented me fleeing, it held the promise of rooting me in something that felt like the beginning.

'I would never want to hurt you.' He said that a few times that night, and each time I shook my head and reassured him that he didn't.

I wanted to tell him that those were the first tears since the night of Gav's death, when the Sailor Boy's tears rained down his face and I didn't shed one.

Instead, I told him this was great, he was great, the orgasm was great.

I nuzzled up to his armpit, where I could nestle in his warmth.

'Well, thank you for a great orgasm, too,' he said and kissed my forehead, fingers grazing my face, eyes locked with mine.

That night he called me extraordinary. He called me sexy. He called me beautiful.

That night, in his shadow, I was all the things he said I was.

24

With Frank's arrival, with a new feeling prickling at my limbs, with the excitement and fun of him, with the music he put on, melodies pulling at my heartstrings again, Gav returned, too. Alive this time, in glimpses of happy memories, pushing the sea away, its killing waves quieter in my head. These good times would catch me off guard and happened only on morning walks from Frank's apartment. In those moments, Soho was mine and Gav was mine too. The waves had never existed and this became my home, between Frank's sheets in the shifting heart of London. I walked, turning fantastical corners to meet him, finding him in a red silk jumpsuit that came up to his chin in a rolled-up turtleneck, a black vintage padded suit jacket draped over it. Gav, an otherworldly goddess.

In those moments, and only in those moments, with my skin tingling under Frank's touch, the body on the beach opened its eyes and shook off the water, like a wet dog clambering out of the sea. There he was. There we both were. Getting ready for another night out.

I turned Soho's corners, my shoulders brushing past hurried shoulders, my mind in Cardiff, the Welsh days short and sunless. Second month in a row. Maybe fourth. This was why we drank the way we did in Wales, and why our hearts had to rise louder in song. We were standing in my room behind the safety of the blue door and I could touch him, he was this close again. Then one morning, leaving Frank's flat, I heard his voice, loud and booming in my ear, an exclamation.

The queen Madonna of the eighties herself!
In the name of Cher's number one records!

He called himself a caricature. I longed to be one, clear and defined.

Gav was looking around at the mess in my room, covered in unfamiliar piles of unwashed clothes and plates, cold chips sprawled underneath the duvet, blotches of vinegar on the sheets.

'You smell incredible,' I said, the scent powerful and extravagant, warm and spicy and opulent, the memory of that smell so strong, my lungs contracted sharply, my whole body ready to cry. I sat down on the kerb and took a deep breath. No tears came. They never did.

'And you really, *really* don't. I beg you, please, use some soap.' Gav winced, putting his hands together in prayer, lips giving in to laughter. My own lips wide in a smile remembering the two of us, effortless and light in our banter, as I sat there, looking through a window at Pret on Broadwick, the street snoozing in a pre-lunch lull.

'Which dress?' I always asked him. Gav had my entire wardrobe memorised and I knew his by heart, too.

'Your green jumpsuit, the long-sleeved velvet one with those funky puffy shoulders,' he would fire under a shallow breath, his outstretched index finger pointing in different directions in the wardrobe as he listed everything. 'Your white brogues, golden socks, those cute, sparkly ones, your gold necklace and you're done.'

One morning walk through Soho, my thoughts back in that room in Cardiff, I leant over and gave him a kiss and I could feel him now, the texture of his lips, soft and thin.

'Oh, thank god you've brushed your teeth,' he said, his face before mine. I could stretch out my hands and run my fingers down the pointed cheek and sharp jawline. Give in to the current of shallow creases around his laughing eyes. 'Come on, darling, all that gin won't drink itself now.'

I stepped onto the platform at Tottenham Court Road and let the escalator carry me down, away from the dream of Soho, and away from the dream of Frank. When I walked out at the platform at Notting Hill Gate, that smell of lemongrass and bergamot was gone, and so was Gav, his edges impossible to trace.

25

One month later
March 2016
Warszawa

I met Honey at London Victoria. We threw ourselves into each other's arms with disbelief at this clash of worlds, the last time we saw each other batted away from our lips with questions of now – How are you now? Show me where you're living *now* – the present feeling safe, keeping us at bay from dying.

Notting Hill was a gasp I heard him make all the way back west, London dreamlike, its romantic vision etched in minds across the globe, reaching even the far corners of Eastern Europe. There was sweetness to his excitement, a distraction from the time that had lapsed since I last saw him, a comforting diversion from Cardiff. When I told Honey I'd heard that Karol was back in the country for a couple of days with a new exhibition, he decided he couldn't miss it. I told him Notting Hill would be the exact opposite direction to where we needed to be only a few hours later but he didn't seem to mind, determined to set foot on the same ground as Julia Roberts.

'Notting Hill!' I watched Honey's mouth open at the view from our kitchen window, his face pressed against the hot glass. I'd missed him, the spectrum and rage of his pouts and the overly drawn arches of his brows, bronze cheeks shining beautifully. Honey took a phone out of the pocket of his white skinny jeans, thin pale ankles spilling into a pair of white trainers, and lifted it high above his head, now jutting sideways in controlled, seductive tilts as he caught the spring rays in an elaborate pirouette of poses and pouts.

'You're living in a sodding palace, princess!' he shouted from across the room, his face still focused on the screen raised above his head.

Apollo watched with suspicion, finishing off a cup of tea, his shoulder a safe distance away from mine across the kitchen counter. His eyes narrowing at Honey, I knew he was trying to connect the dots between Honey, myself and Karol, make sense of the foreign presence in his home. I knew he could never succeed. He never knew the connector.

'I've got to get ready.' Apollo took one more slurp of the tea and plonked it down on the stained surface behind him that we probably hadn't cleaned for weeks. 'I need to pop over to Soho quickly to check on the grade.'

I watched Apollo walk to the bedroom, his body tense around Honey, who continued to ignore him. I opened the fridge and pulled out a plate of various cheeses that Catherine had told us not to store in the fridge for a number of posh-sounding reasons, and put it next to the bottle of wine Apollo had nicked from his mother the last time we went over. I tried to remember what Honey drank, glimpses of parties whooshing through my head in a haze, clouded by a long lanky figure with blond strands across his erased face, washing everything else away with him, all of my Cardiff.

'Do you just maybe have toast and some brown sauce, darling?' Honey winced as he leant over the table, eyeing the mound of cheese with suspicion, his skin pink from the sun, tight shirt creased on curves he didn't have the last time I saw him, his face the colour of what he described as Californian tan, hair dyed chestnut brown and gelled back. He was delighted with toast, disappointed at our lack of brown sauce, worried about me losing the last bits of Welshness that had been planted in me, and finally, he reminded me that he hated wine and any cheap cider would be great.

I smiled and fished out a four-pack of White Ace cans from the back of the fridge. Honey started telling me about two guys he was currently dating. One of them was in his early twenties, the other in his late fifties.

'The best of both worlds, darling,' he said, his eyes glazed, lips curved up in a smug pout, my Welsh world in my London film, intercepted in a confusing twist, pushing at the seams that wanted to burst with the things we didn't want to talk about. 'The younger one, Phil, is milking me out of my savings but has a cock to die for.' Honey grinned at me with a mouthful of toast. 'George has a gorgeous house down the bay.' Honey took a beat, chewing. 'A very generous lover, Georgie.' I grit my teeth and didn't say anything. 'A real hot sugar daddy, darling, I can't believe my luck sometimes.'

Apollo walked back into the kitchen, eyeing Honey cracking open his can.

'I've got to shoot, babe,' he said, and came over to give me a kiss, his lips foreign and clumsy on mine, which were used to the texture and taste of other lips now, pressing and pulling at mine every night Apollo had been away on location this past week.

'Cool,' I said and forced a smile. 'We'll see you at the exhibition.'

'I *might* be late.' Apollo's voice broke into an exasperated sigh. 'Frank reached out, I said I'd meet him at his flat while I'm in town.'

I felt a spike in my chest as he said it, having never thought about the possibility of Frank and Apollo meeting up, even existing without me at the centre between them, but of course I knew I was the only superfluous part.

'Why?' The question blurted out, loud and panicked and I had nothing to bury it under, no smiles and no more words, all knotted in my throat now, my imagination let loose, scanning Frank's flat in search of my underwear or my scent, if there was one, for any catastrophic traces of me.

Apollo kneeled down to tie his shoelaces, no heed paid to my shattered tone or the colour draining from my face. Honey was back on his phone, the can pressed to his cheek.

'I don't know.' Apollo shrugged and sprung up on his feet. 'He likes playing a good dad sometimes when he's not being the great Frank Moz.' Apollo stopped by the door and lifted his hand at us in a wave. 'See you guys later.'

I smiled back, relieved to see him gone, able to relax into who I remembered being around Honey, playful and brash, louder than I let myself be around Apollo and his friends, Catherine or Frank.

I looked at Honey, his phone screen-down on the counter, his mouth open, eyes bulging in excitement.

'What did he say?'

'What did he say when?' I said, draining the rest of his cider.

'Frank Moz is your baby face's dad?' I nearly choked, drink fizzy and warm in my mouth.

'Yeah,' I cautioned, my hands curling into fists again, my voice on a tightrope, willing all my senses to sound completely uninterested.

'Have you met him?' Honey whispered this, his clammy broad hands on my shoulders, eyes locked with mine.

'Have I met him?' I said, flustered, feeling Honey's gnawing curiosity crawling up my back. 'Well, yeah, he's Apollo's dad.' I stuttered my way under Honey's prying eyes and looked down at the counter between us, conscious of his innate ability to extricate any piece of gossip or hot facts from anyone.

Honey released a squeal and thumped the table with open palms, his manicured pink fingers splayed wide.

'You know how huge he is, right?' he asked, and I shook my head. I never googled a thing about Frank, not wanting to know anything about his past beyond what he wanted to share. Part of me feared that if I ever did, I'd lose the fraction I had of him to Frank Moz, and without Frank, I would only have the sea, freezing water filling my lungs.

'You don't know?' Honey repeated, his voice rising to a whole new realm of high-pitched.

I shook my head again, clenching my whole body, my lips pursed tight, everything physically unbearable.

'The entire country above thirty knows him,' Honey said, the flash of an unpleasant realisation on his face, 'and I am,' he sighed, 'thirty-one.'

'Well,' I said and lost a beat, imagining the horror on Frank and Apollo's faces, glimpsing something undeniably mine on the floor between them, horror brushing the tips of my fingers, my fantastical worlds so close to collapsing.

'Right!' Honey battled with his phone tucked back deep in the pocket of his tight skinny jeans. It flew out eventually and landed on the floor with a thud. 'Christ!' He bent down to grab it from the floor with a heavy huff and straightened up in a spring-like motion, clearing his throat. Honey ran his fingers through the gelled spikes of his hair, puffing up his quiff with care, and began typing fervently, mouthing Frank Moz in slow motion.

'I can't believe you don't know him, his Wikipedia page is like five hundred pages long.'

I shook my head slowly, chewing on a cold piece of toast. Was there even such a thing? Something undeniably mine? Could I be identified by anything when all my life was borrowed, my clothes, my flat, my job, the girl in the mirror composed of everyone else's ideas?

'Oh my.' Honey made a squawking sound and slapped his left cheek, throwing his arm forward and almost hitting me in the face with his phone. 'Just look at that photo, he was pretty fucking gorgeous, wasn't he?'

Frank's pixelated face whirred blurred in front of mine. I steadied Honey's hand and held it away to make out the full features of the man I never knew, leaping out of a bar in Manhattan, New York, in 1998. I read the caption underneath, the lines of his face much lighter than those I ran my fingertips down only two nights ago, this body leaner but less sinewy, his smile glazed, his jeans ripped, his golden shirt tight underneath a black velvet jacket. Frank Moz's eyes flickered in the flashes of the cameras surrounding him in the photo. He looked happy and high.

I felt a twinge deep in my stomach.

'Can you just dump baby face and get with the daddy, love?' purred Honey, scrolling, the rolling text glistening in his eyes. This was the epitome of Honey's playground.

'It'd be a bit awkward,' I said, my voice quiet, hanging on, drowned in Honey's shrill excitement, no place for company.

'Forty-seven? Now, I would never.' Honey leapt over with his phone but I ducked down, busying myself with looking for some white wine I was sure we had somewhere.

'Oh yeah, two Brit Awards, I remember those.' With Honey in full investigative mode, I clanked the bottles as loudly as I could to distract myself from Frank Moz, but Honey's voice boomed loud and clear above me, 'I am *living* for Wikipedia's personal life section, darling.'

I stood up, excavating a half-drunk bottle of white from behind some cans of lager.

'He was with *her*! No way.' Honey pressed his hand to his chest, mouth open in disbelief. 'There's a photo of him and your baby face, three years ago at the BAFTAs. Do you want to see?'

'No,' I said, grappling with the wine opener.

'Talking about my daddy issues, I'm surprised you haven't got any.' Honey jumped to his feet and helped himself to another can of White Ace, plonking back on the seat in front of me, my face flushed hot, my whole body swelling up, Frank setting everything on fire.

'Honey,' I whispered, shaking my head.

'I would call Frank Moz "daddy" all night long.' He took a swig of cider and laughed, looking at my face, eyes narrow, inspecting. 'You have thought about it, haven't you?' Honey's finger flew before my face. 'You naughty girl.' He winked at me and started laughing, relieving the tension, laughter a cooling wave coating our bodies, released free and at ease.

'Do you know what?' Honey tilted his phone left and right, sliding his head in the opposite direction as he did that. 'They look nothing like each other.'

I could tell him they had the same smile and cocked their heads in the same way when they listened to you, their voices falling in related husky tones, but I agreed instead.

'Who's Catherine de Palma?' Honey pronounced Catherine's name terribly and waved her pixelated photo in my face before I could turn away. 'She looks like our own Catherine Zeta-Jones, don't you think?'

'That's Apollo's mother,' I said, tired of the red-carpet investigation, the opening credits of my strange London life flashing before my eyes.

'She's bloody gorgeous. Was she a model?' Honey's face buried in the phone filled with Wikipedia's hot juicy facts, he needed nothing else. His index finger tapped on the phone. '*Oh, yes*, yes she was.'

I pulled the cork out and took a swig from the bottle, white wine dripping down my chin and onto the table. I wiped it up with my elbow, holding on to the bottle, to Honey's horror.

'Classy as ever, Ton.'

I let out a loud burp and thanked him. Honey somehow managed to turn paler.

'How did Karol let you live with him?' He pointed a finger at me and moved it towards a tired square clock in the corner of the kitchen. 'Speaking of whom...' He clucked his tongue.

Our eyes met. I looked at my phone to check the time. It was five to five. We were going to be late.

'You're not going looking like this, are you?' Honey eyed me up and down, his finger pressed firmly against his lips in open judgement, his eyes hovering over my baggy leggings and the Chelsea football shirt I'd borrowed from Apollo.

'I'll be ready in ten minutes,' I said.

To another gasp from Honey, I slid out of the pants and peeled the shirt off, leaving it on the kitchen counter next to crumbs of pizza from yesterday's dinner. In just underwear, I walked across to the hallway mirror. I glanced at the girl looking back and came closer to her, picking up the can of deodorant I'd left in the same spot on the floor the previous morning, and sprayed my armpits generously, white foam gathering on spiky hair. I took my fake lenses out, leaving my eyes to mismatch, hints of brown betraying the union. I padded my bleached blonde hair back and dabbed at it for a bit until it all lay flat and tamed against my skull. I drew thick black lines on my eyelids and two red lines hard against my lips, pressing them against each other, levelling the curves.

The girl in the mirror smiled in confidence.

The only wardrobe in the flat, a new addition to the pieces of furniture we'd found on street corners of West London, rebelliously putting Genevieve back to Jean, was a disposed-of antique without a leg and only one door. It housed the few items that had any value to me, and among them a white velour playsuit I picked up in a charity shop with Catherine on our walk back from halva and coffee. The playsuit had square, golden buttons running along its side in a curve, playfully imitating a uniform.

'Three minutes, love,' Honey's voice rang out as I walked back into the kitchen, his head lifted from his phone. We matched in white head to toe, my golden buttons twinning with the golden lines running down his shirt and wrapped around the bulk of his stomach, which was slipping out of his tight jeans. 'London has indeed changed you,' he said. 'Very glam, darling.'

A compliment from Honey was a rare thing.

I snapped a quick photo and sent it to Frank.

The underground spat us out at Piccadilly Circus. We gasped for air greedily, a small respite in the undying stream of people that made up London's heartbeat. I held onto Honey's hand, readying for a final push through the swathes of tourists and weekend shoppers, past the statue and towards Green Park. My phone flashed with multiple texts at once. I glanced at the screen, momentarily losing Honey to more selfies with the barely visible Eros and some lipstick commercial on the world-famous animated billboard.

APOLLO: *I'm going inside.*
APOLLO: *Where are u? Tried to call you.*
VERONICA F: *You look stunning. I'll see you this Sat? X*
APOLLO: *Here. Where are you? Xx*
KAROL: *Hey. Are you coming? Your boyfriend's here.*

The physicality of Karol's reality dawned on me. The realisation felt absurd; that Karol would soon transform from curt, lifeless lines of text on my phone into a body once so familiar, holding mine in the heat of the attic.

'Right, I'm done. Let's go, girl!' Honey tugged at my shoulder but I stayed rooted to the spot, swayed under excited hands and elbows, nudging me as they brushed past me.

'I'm not ready to see him, Honey,' I said, my voice breaking under shallow breaths, struggling to fill my lungs. 'Maybe I could see him next time he comes.' The square was filled with people, foreign voices ringing in my ears in brash tones, my heart speeding up in warning. Honey took my hand in his this time, and led me slowly across the street to a slightly quieter corner.

'Listen,' he articulated calmly, his chubby index finger landing right on my nose, pressing hard into it, getting my attention. With a hardened voice he said, 'Queen. Snap the fuck out of it.'

Bizarrely, it worked. I gave a faint chuckle.

'I'm good,' I said.

'Karol's called me three times to make sure you were going to be there today,' said Honey, his voice quieter but unyielding. 'He's even texted your, whatever his name is, Albert.'

I nodded, not losing sight of his face.

'He really wants to see you. Sometimes I think he's only stayed in touch with me to ask about you, Toni.' Honey placed both hands on my shoulders and shook them lightly in reassurance. 'You can do this.'

I took a deep belly breath and exhaled slowly.

'I'm good,' I said, looking back at him.

We located a concrete slab of a building at the back of Pall Mall without as much as a name, only a number eight above the black steel door, its bare walls at war with the opulent displays of wealth in the windows of Piccadilly. I bit my lip and looked at the black number eight. I glanced at Honey, who seemed similarly clueless as to our whereabouts.

We walked in, the air thickening in the all-white space, our chests rising and falling in the heat.

'Jesus.' Honey ran a hand across his forehead, beads of sweat gathering at his temples.

I eyed a stack of leaflets on a marble shelf to our right. I took one, examining the gallery's programme for the week ahead, Karol's name introducing a third paragraph in red spaced-out letters. Underneath Karol Rosenmann: *Warszawa, a city pretending to be someone else, its many faces erased and created anew*. Who was she now? I thought. The lines were too scuppered.

I put the leaflet down and followed Honey down some white concrete steps that led to a long white basement, filled with enormous photographs of socialist blocks, decaying in their own rhythm, out of sync with the beat of the twenty-first century. There were a few socialist farm buildings too, creating the illusion of being caught before the West and after the East, still inhabited by those who had once worked on the newly created agricultural dreamscapes that had, in turn, replaced synagogues that'd been burnt to the ground, now obstructed by posh English people drinking free red wine. I couldn't take my eyes off the stretches of fragmented housing blocks, Honey leading me forward, his wet hand squeezing mine, navigating the crowd of black turtlenecks, velvet jackets and concrete-textured jewellery half concealed by locks of silver hair.

'There they are.' Honey pointed at the very end of the long room. I followed his finger but couldn't spot either of them between the many long, snooty postures, all dressed in black. 'By there,' said Honey, pulling me forward.

Karol was standing at the back of the room, a white T-shirt tucked into black cotton trousers, pulled up by a set of black leather suspenders, crossed on his back, his dark hair pulled back and gelled down like mine, his eyes concealed by shades, his lips drawn together in a vacant, slightly bored expression. He was nodding at a very animated Apollo, whose body was restless and almost jittery next to Karol's stillness. Apollo spotted us wading towards them and gave a sweeping wave, nearly knocking a glass of wine out of the hand of the long-bearded man standing next to him. Luckily, no wine was spilled, and profuse apologies poured out of Apollo with his most sophisticated accent, the one Catherine used every time she ordered anything in Mayfair. It always worked. The bearded gentleman brushed the accident off with a nonchalant wave of his hand. He called Apollo a young man and returned to the conversation about communism.

Honey threw himself on Karol with a pouty kiss on the cheek.

'Hey darling.' Honey's trill waned as he realised the inappropriateness of any volume in this suffocating room, the spare oxygen not to be wasted on exaggeration of any kind. 'It's been ages,' he finished with a whisper.

Karol smiled the same barely detectable smile and gave Honey a gentle pat on the arm.

'Indeed,' he said, and I felt struck under the sound of that voice, broken and grating the last time I heard it in the kitchen of the blue door house, now back to what it was before–

'Hey,' I said, standing back and raised my hand in a faint wave.

'I'm glad you could make it, kid,' Karol said with the same smile. Honey offered to get wine, suddenly okay with it contrary to the previous allegiance. It made me so sad to see Karol and I couldn't pinpoint this sharp, overwhelming sadness, its evasive centre. There he was in the flesh, I could no longer deny his existence. And when I stopped, everything else stopped along with me and I missed him with my whole body as he went beyond the constitution of a person and became a world I had once inhabited, the only time I felt part of something.

I took a breath and exhaled abruptly.

'Congratulations,' I said to Karol, words swelling up in my throat. Up close, he looked paler and thinner than when I saw him last, aged somewhat.

'Thanks,' Karol said when someone tapped him on the shoulder and took a step between us. The man was taller than me, his voice deep and booming, shoulders broad and brawny, obscuring Karol from my view. He also started with congratulations and proceeded with Polish communism with intriguing confidence.

Apollo pulled me closer to him, warbling on about how amazing all this was, what a success, to get this whole space in Green Park. His voice rose and dropped as we spoke. He used 'extraordinary' at least five times, even his wavy strands were excited, flapping in the air as he spoke, stirring me back towards Polish communism in a manner of introduction. I listened, absently agreeing with him on all points; yes, the historic shame and the guilt, so much guilt, wherever you looked, there it lay and simmered, the unbidden inheritance of communism, the past erased from schools and public debate, the past erected and triumphant in the centre of the capital, its presence unhindered by modern glass climbing higher all around it.

'I can't wait to visit Poland with you one day,' Apollo concluded with a smile. I couldn't think of anything I wanted to do less.

'It'd be great,' I said.

Honey appeared with four reds and squeezed one into Karol's hand with a rasped 'Christ', pulling him away from the brawny man talking about *Lek Valaza* much louder than seemed warranted.

'Cheers.' Honey raised his glass, a smile tired against a face glistening in sweat.

We clinked our glasses in silence.

'I met Toni at your exhibition, man, back in Cardiff.' Apollo flashed Karol with the full breadth of the friendliness of his smile. 'I spotted her outside with…' He turned to Honey, his eyes narrowing, Honey's brows arching slowly. 'Hang on, was that you?' Apollo asked.

Honey shot me a confused glance and looked back at Apollo, words wedged in his throat as deep as in mine, both of us speechless, all around us the washed-out prairies of Eastern Europe closing in on us, blood pounding in my head, no air left between us.

'It was my boyfriend, Gav,' said Karol and drained his glass of wine with a steady hand and without as much as a quiver in his face.

'Oh, yes, I remember now,' Apollo laughed, his countenance nervous, eyes shifting between our dumbstruck faces. 'Is he here today?'

Honey let out a gasp and pressed the glass of wine to his lips, his eyes bulging out at me, but I said nothing, looking down at my feet blurring from the heat and the warmth of wine, my head dizzy.

'He couldn't make it,' said Karol and smiled at Apollo.

'Are you in London long?' asked Apollo, his socialite upbringing coming out in the skill of keeping any conversation going with the same degree of composure and interest.

'Until tomorrow evening,' said Karol, his face locked somewhere behind us now. 'Sorry,' he raised a hand at someone, 'if you could excuse me for a few minutes. I have to talk to my manager.' He stepped forward and turned back towards us. 'Truth be told, it might be a while. How long are you staying?'

Before Apollo and Honey could say anything, I said, 'I'm not feeling well.' I squeezed Apollo's hand. 'We're going to have a wander and probably shoot off.'

'I can stay,' Honey chirped by my side, edging his way under Karol's concealed gaze. 'My coach doesn't leave until eight,' he said and added under his breath, 'and it can leave much later.'

Karol's head jerked in his direction for a second and returned to me.

'Are you free tomorrow afternoon?' he asked. 'Do you want to have a drink?'

'That would be great,' said Apollo, putting his arm around my shoulder.

'I meant just me and Toni.' Karol turned to Apollo in the same monotone, making him stutter under this demonstration of Polish directness.

'Sure,' I said, feeling the corners of my lips lift. 'Let's do that.'

'Great,' Karol's lips stretched in a smile for the first time this evening, distorting the face that no joy looked natural on. He leant forward and kissed my cheek, sending a long forgotten electric current through the corners of a fading memory. 'See you tomorrow, then. I'll text you.'

I watched him saunter towards a group of men, his gait as stiff and straight I remembered it, leaving a new trace behind him, an unfamiliar blend of bergamot, caramel and vanilla.

26

One day later

When he texted, I gave him the address of a small bar at the back of Waterloo and poured myself half a glass of vodka. When it settled in my stomach, I put the other half of the pocket bottle in my bag.

Waterloo meant a little bit more time, he could grab a train down to Gatwick from there without any changes. Karol wanted more time. I was afraid of any time, the time lapsed between us in unanswered calls, the time we didn't speak about, the time I hadn't mentioned to Apollo, the time that didn't exist outside of us. I was afraid of the time in the attic, afraid of his body hanging over mine, the pull of the trigger, the time drowned in the beats of music and hours of silent reading. I was afraid of the brevity of yesterday's encounter, the kiss on my cheek and his smile. More than anything in the world, I was afraid of the possibility of us.

When I got to the bar, I downed the rest of the vodka at the door and ordered an espresso martini as soon as I walked in, the steady flow of alcohol keeping me calm, caffeine setting my mind alive and sharp for a little while, otherwise drifting in broken syntaxes of half-imagined memories and forgotten daydreams.

When Karol came through the door, I straightened and stood up with a curt wave in his direction. He looked different today, his hair was rumpled and falling to the side of his face, a white T-shirt falling loose over black jeans. He was smaller and more frail than the day before somehow. When he came nearer, I glimpsed bags under his eyes, light lines arching above his eyebrows.

'You've never looked worse,' I said by way of hello, which made him chuckle.

'I don't sleep much.' Polish rang foreign to my ears, the familiar soft baritone shooting a pang through my heart.

'No, me neither,' I said and watched him park a small black suitcase next to his chair. 'What are you having?' I asked. He asked for a bottle of any ale, and when I came back with it and another espresso martini, he was hunched over his phone, typing.

'This might be why you don't sleep much,' he said, looking at my drink. I smiled and downed the first glass as he took a sip from his pint.

'Did you sleep with Honey last night?' I asked, alcohol surging through my veins in transient confidence, keeping us at the surface for a little while.

'What?' Karol winced at my question. 'No,' he shook his head, 'definitely, definitely not.'

'Okay, a simple 'no' would suffice,' I said.

'What made you even think that?'

'Honey was still in London this morning when I texted him,' I said and forced a laugh, so well performed lately, but I couldn't make it ring and I couldn't look up at him, my eyes wandering up and down my fingers as I spoke.

'Well, whoever he slept with wasn't me,' said Karol, words tentative, syllables slow to rise.

'You're a bit of a heartbreaker,' I said, a tinge of sadness at the back of my throat, a drop of blood in a pool of water, tainting everything. My mother used to tell me my sadness was all in my head, and I hoped that was true, that Karol couldn't detect any of it.

'You're a bit drunk,' he said, and here it was too, a tinge of sadness, and maybe it was enough, maybe it was all we needed.

'You broke my boyfriend's heart last night,' I said.

I glanced at Karol, his new slight frame still, sooty eyes locked on me without expression.

'I'm sure he'll be fine.'

I spent hours daydreaming about this meet-up. *Why did you leave?* I would always ask. *You know why, you know*, he would say.

'Congratulations,' I said, forcing a smile that worked this time. 'The exhibition seemed very popular.'

In the daydream I would hang my head low and tell him that I understood why he left. I knew that it was impossible to become otherwise, it was impossible to live unbecome.

'I'm selling a nice story,' he said with a vacant shrug. 'Communism sells under the Tories. Nostalgia for a fantasy.' He smiled. 'Something like that.'

I thought of his lonely concrete buildings and remembered my grandmother in the window of a copy of the blocks on display in Green Park, a fag tucked inside a cheap and yellowing cigarette holder, her kitchen always smelling of smoke and burnt butter.

'Apollo thought it was a big deal,' I said, 'and a great turnout for an opening.'

It surprised me how quickly we fell in between the cracks of Polish and English we had mastered intertwining, homeless words always running loose, breaking syntaxes, patched like wounds between two worlds.

'What did you think?' he asked.

I took a sip of my drink, alcohol already starting to lose its grip today.

'I don't know,' I said. 'I felt proud of you.'

Karol smiled.

'You can't always get twisted spines and beautifully spiralling teeth,' he said. 'Or men with prawns in their mouths.' Fresh warmth shot across the greyness of his face, brightening it up. We looked at each other, a spark in his eye giving way to a new glint: fear, perhaps. I couldn't tell, but I knew I was afraid, and I thought he was afraid, too. Karol's body twisted towards the bar, and without raising his voice or changing his inflection he called for a double shot of vodka. 'Do you want one, too?'

I shook my head.

'I don't think they do table service,' I said, watching a barman spring to our table with a smile dedicated only to Karol.

'Who wouldn't fuck Karol,' I whispered watching the barman walk away, his hips swaying, his eyes darting back at Karol.

'What?'

'Something Honey used to say,' I said.

'Oh god.' Karol downed his shot in one gulp and chased it with a swig of ale.

In my daydream, we would be back in Cardiff, sitting on the steps of Cardiff Arts Institute, a dappled streak of sunshine peeking through the wide branches of an oak tree arching above. We would see each other tomorrow, we would say, at the same time.

I watched a group of girls at the opposite corner of the bar break into loud peals of laughter.

'If campness is a way of belonging,' I turned to him, 'could femininity be performed too? Can you get good at it?' I pursed my lips, my eyes pinned to no particular point behind him.

'Isn't it always a group exercise?' he said and waved at the barman for another shot, asking me if I wanted one this time. I nodded.

'I was never good at group exercise,' I said. My voice trailed off, my mind wandering to Cardiff and its fleeting semblance of belonging. There was nothing in its place. The barman placed two shots between us, his hand brushing Karol's shoulder as he pirouetted back to the bar. We clinked glasses with quiet cheers.

'I haven't told my boyfriend about Gav, either,' Karol said after a moment of silence, a liminal space for the comforting burning in our throats.

'What's his name?' I asked.

'Igor.'

I said nothing, an unfamiliar feeling rising in my chest, falling somewhere between jealousy and longing.

'Are you in love with him?' I asked.

'No,' he said without as much as a flinch. 'No, I'm not.'

'I'm sleeping with Apollo's father,' I said, my voice weaning off with my confession. I couldn't tell why I needed him to know this, but I wanted him to know everything about me, all there was to know about the girl in the mirror, but the words were too few and so many of them forgotten, the language pulled apart, skin tearing at like it did growing up, leaving its marks.

Karol shot me a glance and said nothing for a while. When he pulled out a packet of cigarettes from the pocket of his jeans, he stuck one in his mouth and jutted his head in the direction of the door. I nodded.

We stepped outside, the lightness of the day catching us both by surprise.

'What's his name?' He took a drag and smiled at me, smoke escaping his mouth.

'Frank,' I said, lighting mine.

'Frank,' he echoed.

'Have you heard about Frank Moz?'

Karol shook his head.

'Is he famous?'

'Something like that.'

'Are you in love with him?' he asked.

'I don't know.' I hesitated. I'd never thought about it. 'Maybe. I think about him when I'm not with him and when I'm with him, it's easy. It's easy to be with him.'

We smoked in silence for a while until the short butts of the cigarettes burnt our fingertips. Karol stamped his out with the heel of his black leather boot.

'Did I ever tell you that I'm Jewish?'

I held onto mine, savouring the last short inhales.

'You're telling me,' I said, my eyes leaving the sizzling cigarette at my feet and wandering up his body to his face, coated by falling rays of sun, tiptoeing away from us into the evening, 'that you're a gay Polish Jew?' I felt my face stretch in a wide grin.

'Imagine that,' he said, smiling back, his eyes sparking up.

'You should be a communist, too,' I said. 'You could make the whole country implode.'

'I would like that,' he said and started laughing, the laughter infectious and light in my chest now, too, its lightness bursting the banks of the months that lacked relief, our foreign voices attracting the attention of two passers-by in suspicious glances.

'I started this book the other day,' he picked up as we walked back inside. '*The Night of the Living Jews*. Have you heard about it?' he asked, reaching the bar and raising his hand for two more shots of vodka.

'No,' I said. I had never seen him drink vodka before.

'You've got the idea,' he said, thanking the barman and walking back to our table, my body following suit behind him like it used to. 'The Polish Jews, erased, undead and feared.' He sat down and raised his glass, waiting for me to join him. 'I was never here in the first place, how could I know how to be alive?' he said and downed his shot. I only managed half of mine. 'Cheers.'

'Did you ever want to photograph what's remained, to preserve it?' I asked, even though I knew, we all knew, that there was nothing but shells and graves, curated in a tourist showcase of survival.

In my daydream, we would be walking past the town hall and through Roath Park to Pontcanna. We would be heading home despite knowing there wasn't one behind the blue door anymore. I would hold his hand and tell him that sometimes I felt I drowned in the sea with Gav, something I was becoming died that day. I would tell him that when I'm with Frank, I have an odd sense that something of myself has survived, but once I'm out of his Soho flat, this girl is gone and I don't know how to get her back.

'If I don't know how to be alive either,' I started wading through this new silence between us, 'does it make me undead, too?' The churning sea flashed in front of my eyes, as it often did, in and out, tugging at my bloodied feet in pulls and pushes.

'I hope not,' he said and looked at me with cold ash eyes, wherein lay the outside space where we scuttled, safe, having let go of belonging, being with each other in silent understanding. It was that disruption that glinted in Karol's eyes now, the space that somehow and somewhere was created for us only, in the wishful *us* against everyone else. I reciprocated his smile, recognising this strange cosmic union

I couldn't fully understand. 'Will you answer my calls from now on?' he asked.

'I will,' I said, a smile choked, our faces turning away from each other.

'I have to go, Toni,' he said with the same tinge of sadness.

'I know,' I said.

'Do you want to walk me to the station?' he asked, rising to his feet. 'You could tell me more about that man you might be in love with.'

We walked side by side, our feet dragging, hands in our pockets, the trotting sound of his suitcase skidding behind us, no space for Frank or anyone else in the words that were always too few, so many lost in the cracks between Polish and English.

When he disappeared behind the barriers at Waterloo Station I wanted to run after him, but my body kept still, heart pounding in the new sadness of losing him again, so much worse this time.

When I jumped on the Tube, I glimpsed the girl in the door's reflection, a jagged creature, gluing her wounds, becoming a new thing. Who was she now? The lines were too scuppered.

27

One month later
April 2016

Karol called me every day after the exhibition, his voice alert and brisk in the mornings, wavering energy occasionally piercing through his deadpan monotone. It felt like we never talked about anything in particular and yet the words never dried out, those forgotten and others well remembered, pushing at our lips, thirsty, pouring over the last two years and spilling past Cardiff into Eastern Europe, flooding everything else along with it. I had spoken more those mornings than with anyone else for the rest of the day and night, contrary to our silent mornings over coffee in Cardiff, this longing never satiated.

'You're doing much later?' asked Karol on the other end of the phone, our usual way of winding the conversation towards an end, to anchor it in each other's present as if to carry it away with us once we stopped talking, always knowing what the other one was up to.

'Might see some friends from work,' I said. 'They're always out somewhere in Soho. It's just a case of going along.'

'Sounds fun,' he said, and I knew he didn't mean it.

'It isn't,' I said, spilling sugar all over my coffee cup, only scarce particles landing on the surface of the black liquid. 'It's something to do.'

'You're very dramatic,' Karol said, stifling a yawn on the other end of the phone.

'You want to say that I'm being very dramatic,' I corrected him.

'No. No, I don't,' he replied slowly, and paused. It made me smile.

'Are you doing anything fun?' I asked.

'What's that?' he asked, snorting into the receiver. 'I'm meeting some photographers to talk about photography later.'

'Sounds thrilling,' I said, laughing.

'It is,' he said in his cold monotone, but I knew he was smiling.

Those were the only times I laughed and the only thing in the day I looked forward to, grounding me in something I couldn't understand. Perhaps because I felt present somewhere, and he was present too, and I couldn't say that about anything else in my life.

I asked Karol if he'd changed his mind about going to Scotland to follow his communist buildings on a tour of small galleries around Glasgow. He said he had recently developed a fear of leaving Warsaw and was not going anywhere anytime soon.

'You shouldn't laugh, I'm absolutely serious,' he said.

'I'll have to come to you someday, then,' I said.

'That would be nice,' he said. He sighed into the receiver and I heard a muffled male voice say hello.

'Is that—' I began to ask, but he cut in with a curt 'No.'

'You're having some fun,' I said.

'I'll call you tomorrow.'

28

One week later

My eyes still closed, I turned over to find Frank gone, his scent escaping sheets still warm from his body. I rolled over to his side and buried myself in his smell, the shimmer of the shower echoing through the flat. I kept my eyes closed, listening to his heavy steps, the muffled thudding of wet feet on the creaking old floor, the shuffle of clothes, a dull clasp from a leather belt buckle. Frank cleared his throat and I glimpsed his long body standing in the hallway, half dressed. I buried myself deeper under the sheets and observed him turn sideways to the full-length mirror, breathing in and out, straightening up and slouching. I squinted my eyes, my view a peeping tom, and watched him draw closer to the mirror and run his hand through ruffled wet strands of hair, pulling at some in inspection. He shook his head with a sigh and I shut my eyes when he walked back into the bedroom.

I felt him stand above me, but he didn't say anything.

Instead, he bent down by the bed. He kissed my forehead and picked up something from the floor. When I opened my eyes again, he had his black hoodie on, his back to me. He shut the door quietly when he left the flat. I perched myself up on my elbows and looked around, as if surrounded by a completely new environment. In a way I was, the corners of the flat finding new edges in the gleams of the late morning light, its colours, subdued greys and browns, carrying a different energy to that of swollen nights dominated by bodies in their space. Frank would always wake me up first, his hand crawling up my thigh half asleep. With the gradual stillness of hot, quickened breaths, he would tell me he had to go to a studio, or he had an important meeting. He would always apologise and tell me he would sort me out with some breakfast and a cab. He would never kick me out, but I would know not to stay.

I slid off the bed and walked across to the mirror, tracing his steps.

The girl smiled back, thin blonde hair reaching bony shoulders, eyeliner smudged under her eyes. My hands wandered down her wanted body, fingertips reaching butt cheeks, red and sore to touch, an old purple bruise in a streak on top of her thigh. I turned around and walked through to the main room, careful of my steps on the unknown terrain, my feet treacherous and curious, now basking in the streams of sunlight coming through three enormous sash windows on both sides. The room I had hardly spent any time in, concealed under layers of alcohol and unreliable lights, my eyes only on him, uninterested in anything else, had now come alive as if under a spell; stacks of records spangled all around on the floor, silver and golden plates nailed to the walls in heavy frames. I came close to one of them, the platinum and gold records, dating back to my childhood years, reaching beyond my beginning. I rested my hand on the old record player, a Jonathan Richman record still in, echoing the sounds we fell asleep to the night before. I walked past the small, threadbare sofa in the middle of the room where I had once wrapped myself around Frank and he picked me up and carried me out to the bedroom, his lips not parting from mine. I circled the sofa and stood by the old desk, everything in this room a long-forgotten artefact of his rock'n'roll days. I looked at the music magazine he had open and flicked through the pages. There he was, looking back at me, Frank Moz, about fifteen years younger than Frank leaving the bed this morning, his tongue stuck out in a sly smile, eyes glinting with mischief. The caption to the left read: *Can we finally agree that Frank Moz is dead?* The title startled me, something pinching at my throat at the directness of this death sentence. The text in bold underneath continued with the question:

Eighteen years and two Best of *albums later, is there any chance of Frank Moz returning to the success of his last triumph, the extraordinary* The Beginning of an Interminable Waterway *from 1998?*

I glanced at the magazine next to it, its pages open to a column listing of the New British Talent Under Twenty-Five, Apollo Rooney third in line, *Two Strangers* premiering at Berlinale and a strong contestant for a BAFTA nomination.

My finger touched Apollo's name, feeling his dry lips on mine yesterday morning in a quick goodbye before he left for a weeklong shoot somewhere in Croatia. My back was burning from a pointed streak of sunlight. I turned around and faced a corkboard, hung between two windows, disappearing between beguiling views of the heart of London. I drew closer, different headlines peeking at me through a thin layer of dust, coating celebrations of number one hits and sold-out tours, all circulating back to the nineties. At its bottom right corner I spotted two photographs, their rugged edges peeling away from the cork. I bent over to look at them closer. One was a polaroid, washed out now: Frank, probably only a few years older than me there, cradling a newborn baby, Apollo's tiny body enveloped in arms laden with black leather, Frank's face stretched in a grin, looking up at the camera. Next to it, a more glossy photo, its colours vivid, bodies illuminated in the harsh flash light, Frank's tongue out in a comical headlock executed by a primary school age Apollo, laughing at the camera.

I straightened up at a turn of the key in the door and turned around, Frank taking his shades off as he walked into the flat.

'I've brought us some grub,' he said, a slight hesitation shifting across his face as he found me behind the desk. 'Hope you're hungry, gorgeous naked girl.' A smile slid across his face now as he meandered around the record towards me and put a paper bag and a paper tray holding two coffees on the desk in front of me. 'The best thing in all of Soho, bacon egg sarnies.'

I smiled at him and rustled out a big bap wrapped up in more paper.

'Thanks,' I said, sitting down next to him on the sofa, sun rays escaping the room now, falling on our faces in single stranded streaks. 'Does it bother you?' I asked. 'The stuff they write about you?' I bit into my sandwich, feeling a squirt of ketchup trickling down my chin.

'Frank Moz being dead and stuff?' He glanced at the magazine spread on the desk and back at me. I nodded, suddenly ravenous. 'It's just journos at the end of the day.' He bit off a quarter of a sandwich and chewed slowly, looking away from me and at the desk. I smiled, not knowing what to say, not knowing anything about Frank Moz.

'If they're right,' I said, cautious, encouraged by this new closeness, our knees touching, cross legged, 'would you be okay if he died?'

'It's always surprised me that I've got this far,' he said, taking another bite. I wiped my face with the back of my hand, reached for my coffee and took a small sip.

We finished our sandwiches in silence, glancing at each other with half smiles.

'Why did you and Catherine break up?' I heard myself ask. I never asked him about any women, accepting us as we were, existing only here in this flat, our conversations always an escape from ourselves. I could see it in his face that I'd surprised him with my question, his fair brows rising for a second with a rushed sip of coffee.

He put the cup down and cleared his throat, smiling.

'Well,' he paused. 'I took a lot of drugs and slept with other women.'

I nodded, my body heating up in regret at asking him anything, dead Frank Moz tearing into the erased place between us.

'That'll do it,' I said, attempting a smile. He laughed at that, relieving me from the burning guilt prickling under my skin.

'Easily,' he said and gave out a quiet chuckle. I crumpled the wrapping in my hands and finished my coffee in one gulp. 'I'll have to shoot off in a few minutes, darling,' he said as we lifted ourselves from the sofa. 'I've got a meeting down in London Bridge in an hour.' He squeezed the bridge of his nose and rubbed his eyes with his knuckles.

'How's the album coming along?' I asked, putting all the wrapping in the bin as he sauntered towards the window and rested both hands on its frame, face pulled between half a smile and a wince. 'I'd better put some clothes on,' I said, the girl in the mirror regaining control as she brushed past him, leaving a soft kiss on his back.

I always left half an hour before he did, the block of flats big enough for no one to make the connection.

'See you around, Frank,' I said, my hand on the door handle. His cheek was pressed against the window, sunlight sparkling up at the tips of his blond strands. He smiled at me as I turned the door handle , and said:

'See you soon, beautiful.'

29

Today was Apollo's twenty-first birthday. I would have never thought to gift him anything beyond dinner in a pub, but I had also never slept with his father before. I had saved up and presented him with a Super 8 and two rolls of film, one in colour, one black-and-white, and the original poster for *I Vitelloni*, Apollo's favourite Fellini, that I managed to haggle off Luca at the Ultimate Picture Palace. It took me half an hour to write his birthday card. I stared at an empty page, having nothing to say to my boyfriend. I drew a little dinosaur first and things picked up from there.

Happy birthday, mate! I wrote. *LOVE, Toni.*

Apollo welled up a bit and kissed me. I thought it must've been the dinosaur that did it. It felt like the right moment to go down on him, like the right thing to do.

Apollo's birthday weekend was packed with plans and people, the spectrum of personalities and activities ranging from board games in a pub and a mini film festival in Hackney to a rave the drugs had already been bought for, various guest lists combusting at over a hundred people. I wondered what it felt like to keep this many people in your life, whether it was down to Apollo's ease around people, the ability to make them feel listened to and appreciated, or no one getting too close to devour your heart completely, everyone a good acquaintance.

Tonight was a prequel to Apollo's big weekend. Catherine asked us to have dinner together, making tonight the inevitable night when Frank returned as father.

'I've already seen Frank for a birthday drink.' Apollo rolled his eyes, squeezing my hand tight as we stepped into the warm night, eerily calm, air congealing in the anticipation of this bizarre reunion.

'How was it?' I asked, my palm sweating in his, trying my hardest to sound indifferent, desperate curiosity pushing at my throat.

'Alright, I don't know, weird.' Apollo shrugged again as we wound our way through familiar corners of half-illuminated restaurant lights and small boutiques gleaming in the dark. 'Oh well,' Apollo let out an exaggerated exhale, 'let's just get tonight over with and have fun this weekend.'

In the commotion of the birthday morning, I had only now realised I'd put on a dress borrowed from Catherine a while back. It had puffed shoulders and seventies flared sleeves, drawing short just below the line of my thighs in a wavy hem, its mauve velvet soft on my skin, all of it so deeply unfortunate in the combination of the four of us.

'I need to change,' I said. 'I look so stupid in this dress.' I scrambled to find a good reason, beads of panic trickling through my body. 'Can we go back? I won't take long.'

Apollo stuttered and looked at me, his small eyes glinting in question underneath raised eyebrows.

'We're already late, Ton,' he said and broke into a nervous smile. 'Come on. You look great in this dress.' He grabbed my hand and nudged me forward. We were only a corner away from Catherine's. 'You're beautiful.' I bit my lip at the statement always ringing false, like a trap. I pressed my teeth hard into my lower lip, wanting to fight on but having no further argument to support my case.

'Okay,' I whispered back and slid my hand out of his, following him around the corner and up the chequered steps.

Catherine answered the door. She looked radiant in a long red tunic dress accentuating the waist and heavy black stones resting softly on her chest, woven with a golden chain. She was so beautiful, I kept thinking whenever I saw her.

'Hi Mum.' Apollo leant in for a kiss, her long manicured fingers laden with large ruby stones entwining around his head as she cupped it in her hands, a grin fighting the tears that were gathering at the sidelines of her eyes. 'Mum, don't cry, man.'

'Happy birthday, darling,' she whispered in his ear, pulling him closer. When she let him go, she clutched my hand in hers. 'Hello, sweetheart.' She let go of Apollo and stepped forward to give me a kiss on the cheek, marking it with lipstick the colour of cherry liqueur.

'Hey Catherine,' I said, falling into a tight embrace. 'Thanks for having us. It's so nice to do this.' I strained my neck to look at Apollo, now shuffling through the hallway towards Frank. I looked down at my feet, as if seeing him here would erase completely what we were, the reality tearing into the fantasy, just like the dead Frank Moz was ripping into us that morning in Soho. 'How are you doing?'

'I'm on a mission to be the most embarrassing mother tonight,' she said, holding me in her embrace as Frank wrapped his arms around Apollo, his voice so out of place I shivered at the sound of it.

'Happy birthday, mate. Good to see you.'

'Yeah, good to see you, too, man,' I heard Apollo say.

'Oh my.' Catherine glanced down at me, her hand over her mouth. 'It's the dress I gave you.' I nodded, feeling my hands bunch into fists and splay open. 'You look stunning. I knew it would be perfect on you.' She jerked her head at Frank. 'Frank, do you remember?'

Frank looked pale. I could no longer ignore his presence, my body still feeling his from two nights before, hurt and pleasured. Apollo scanned the room, confused.

'What's that about?' he asked, glancing from one parent to another, Catherine's face gleaming, Frank's struck in shock that lasted only a few seconds but froze on me, paralysed me for that moment, both our bodies breathless, the eyes of the family all on me, transfixed in transient states of nostalgia, horror and confusion.

'I was wearing this dress when I met your dad.' Catherine's eyes dilated at Frank, words falling slowly when she said, 'Nineteen-ninety-three,' as if in disbelief that her own time could stretch that long into the past. Frank hadn't made a sound or twitched his face. 'Frank? You're alright? You've gone pale.'

Frank shot her the smile I had seen a few times before, neutral and charming, masking everything else.

'Have I now? Christ, sorry love.' He gave a short, rasped laugh and looked at her. 'My mind's been all over the place today, I'm sorry.'

'You've been busy, man?' Apollo looked at his father with a short courteous smile. My legs gave in to a sudden tremble. I felt a pang of pain shooting deep in my bladder. Second time this month, I padded my bag for a box of antibiotics I had a regular subscription for. Frank wasn't looking at me. I wanted to be empowered within our elaborate act of romance and deception, but his committed persistence in omitting me entirely from his field of vision as he panned between Apollo and Catherine made me feel like one thing only: a worthless piece of shit.

'Are you alright, darling?' Catherine squeezed my hand, her face close to mine now with intent worry.

'Yeah, I'm good.' I pulled away, feeling my face quiver, my hand clutching the strip of pills inside the bag. 'If you'll excuse me for a second.'

'We just had a bit of a nightmare at the studio this morning,' I heard Frank tell Apollo as they sauntered away to the dining room at the end of the hallway.

'Give me a shout if you need anything.' Catherine rubbed my shoulder and glided down the hall towards them, Frank's voice dwindling with every step of the stairs. I shut the door of the bathroom behind me, the conversation downstairs muffled, intercepted with spikes of sharp laughter. I gritted my teeth and pressed my hand against my bladder in hope a bit of pressure would relieve some pain. My mind whirred around Catherine, the size of her in Frank's life, the intricate sea of connections I had never heard about and memories running back through the timeline of my entire existence, through the love and the loss and whatever it was at the moment, a bond I hadn't known in life yet. If I ever was powerful, I wondered where all that power was now. I pulled down my pants and jolted down on the toilet seat, but not one bit of pee came out despite the pain. I threw my head on my knees, tucking my nose between them, and growled. I reminded myself to breathe in Honey's voice, as he once took me through ways to relieve anxiety, methods his therapist had introduced him to.

'I'm not in real pain, I'm not in real pain,' I kept whispering, trying to gather as much oxygen in my belly as I could and releasing it through my mouth in a gentle count to ten. I reached down to my purse and scooped out two pills I swallowed, shutting my eyes and keeping still for a second. I glanced at the bath, holding my breath to the point my chest started to ache, and I felt a little bit calmer. I got up and touched the taps, comforted by their coldness, and thought that maybe I could get in, if I didn't wet my hair, no one would notice.

Someone knocked on the door gently. Completely irrationally, I hoped it was Frank. It must've been Catherine.

'You're alright there, Ton?' Apollo's voice rang behind the door. 'You've been gone for like fifteen minutes.'

'Yeah, thanks,' I said, breathing slowly. The pain was slowly subsiding.

'Can I come in?'

I opened the door.

Apollo came in and closed it behind him quietly.

I put my arms around his neck and drew myself closer. His arms intertwined on my back, he rested his head on my shoulder.

'You're sure you're alright?'

'It's the UTI. It's taking forever to clear.' I sighed, nuzzling up against his neck, holding him close, needing to hold on to someone. 'I've taken some antibiotics.' I pulled away and looked around the bathroom, slightly dizzy. 'It's already a little better.'

'I'm sorry,' he said softly and looked me in the eye. He had beautiful hazel-green eyes, narrow and long, so unlike Frank's. He cupped my cheek and I let my head hang there for a second.

'How are you feeling?'

'It's a bit of a circus,' Apollo laughed. 'I'm sorry we have to do this. I wish they just gave it a rest, you know. Frank's excruciating. I'm sorry about the dress, too. She can be so embarrassing sometimes.'

I shook my head and smiled.

'No, it's alright.'

Apollo took my hand and kissed the edge of my palm. We let out a tinkle of laughter, all we needed in that moment.

I was fine, I thought. I was just about fine enough to do this, to get to the end of tonight.

'Hey ho,' he said, rolling his eyes. I liked a British 'Hey ho', so light compared to Polish 'That's life' usually accompanied with a heavy sigh and weary eyes, drooping low and causing all conversation to cease; unlike 'Hey ho', upbeat, awaiting the follow-up to life. 'Let's get drunk and leave early.'

I nodded.

'Sounds like a good idea,' I said.

As soon as I arrived at the table, I had to reassure Catherine that I was okay.

'Sorry, darling, I forget. Have you actually met Frank?' She pointed at the man in question, who had acknowledged me with curious politeness. I had always underrated good acting as a life skill.

I inhaled slowly, gentle hints of lemon brushing my nostrils, the scent in Catherine's space feeling like betrayal. I narrowed my eyes at him and mustered my best attempt at a Gav kind of smile, wide and joyful. I wasn't even sure whether we were supposed to know each other at that moment, all memories tangled up in an indecipherable screaming knot.

'Toni,' I said, reaching my hand across the table towards him. Frank took it in his gently, pleasantly burning my skin like he always did, smiling as he said:

'I think we met at Apollo's screening last year, if I remember correctly? Frank.' We shook hands.

'Was it last year? My god,' said Catherine and Frank nodded in agreement, relieving us of any further elaboration on the matter, as he turned his attention to Apollo, asking him how everything was going with the festival submissions, navigating the topic with general compliments, *Two Strangers* a safety net for the evening, something to cling onto for us all when confused or caught out by the details, the only space other than Apollo himself we all shared.

It was a different kind of dinner tonight, Catherine's go-to tapas and mezes replaced by a huge bowl of roast rosemary potatoes drenched in butter and a long slab of the largest salmon I had ever seen, surrounded by small bowls of Mediterranean salad, laid neatly in colourful terracotta pots, Spain amicably shaking hands with the British Isles.

'Very on trend, Mum,' Apollo chuckled at the spread.

'What do you mean?' Catherine's beautifully drawn eyebrows flung up in surprise.

'The referendum next month,' said Apollo, taking a plate of potatoes from his mum and digging into the salmon laid directly in front of him.

'Oh, that.' She gave an exasperated gasp.

'It's just noise.' Frank pinned slabs of salmon with his fork in swift movements, sliding them onto his plate. 'They like to talk the talk. Nothing will come of it.'

'No politics, guys, please,' she said, and it sounded like a reminder.

'It's a big one, though,' Apollo trudged on, swallowing the bites as if already on a race through the evening. 'May I remind you that you're Spanish, Mother.'

'May I remind you that I have dual citizenship. Anyway—'

'I don't,' I said, helping myself to a green leaf salad. They all looked at me; the mother, the father, and the son.

The son spoke first.

'It'll be alright, Ton.'

'Darling, you really don't need to worry,' said the mother.

The last words belonging to fathers. Frank's eyes darted around the table as he said, 'Of course it'll be alright.'

I smiled, feeling my skin flush under everyone's attention. I anchored my eyes in the bowl of buttered potatoes, probably the most Polish of helplines.

'These are really good,' I said, pushing the right words out.

'Frank's mother's best recipe.' Catherine said and smiled at me and Apollo, and I couldn't tell whether she was being ironic or not. I wondered who she knew: Jean or Genevieve?

I slid one of the salad bowls towards me and poked a vinegared rocket with a fork. Apollo was facing Frank, and Catherine sat opposite me, now enquiring in detail how the job was going. I kept glancing at Frank to see if he was listening to anything we were talking about, but his attention was devoutly on Apollo and his next film project, that his son was trying to give away as little as possible on. Frank ploughed on tirelessly, question after question. It was either nice of him or it was pure survival.

When wine was poured and we clinked glasses to Apollo, our eyes locked for a split second and my stomach contracted in sharp pain again. I forced a smile to cover the wince and looked away at Catherine. I thought to myself that he looked worried, which seemed enough, but maybe he was scared, maybe we both were. When Catherine put her hand on his shoulder, asking if he wanted to do the honours and light the candles, I placed mine on the back of Apollo's neck and leant over to kiss him, wishing him a happy birthday.

I wanted Frank's stomach to contract, too, twist in knots so tight it would hold his entire body in a stifling grip.

Apollo smiled as I pulled away and his eyes flickered.

'You make it a happy one, Ton,' he said, as I froze, aware that no matter what I did that evening, the night could only get worse.

I glanced at Frank, but he wasn't looking at us, double checking with Catherine where the candles were, his face glazed with the same impartial character he'd invented at the beginning of the evening and clung tight to.

I was starving but too sick to eat anything, dabbing at a piece of chocolate birthday cake that Frank had managed to get from a patisserie in Portobello, 'The very same,' he said, awarding him the first smile from his son tonight.

When Apollo's lips parted slightly and a generous slice hovered below his chin, his tongue hanging out ever so slightly, it was a moment I thought he would say something. There were so many things, so much to break and release. If he made a start, maybe everyone else would follow. Maybe I could say something, too. But he didn't say a thing, the cake slowly landing in his mouth. I looked at Catherine, leaning back on her chair, red wine touching red lips, eyes tinged with an inebriated sheen, looking at her men, streaks of amusement and curiosity shooting in the corners of her dark amber eyes. I always insisted on refusing biology the rights it demanded, but it ruled over tonight. I had nothing to fight it with.

The family photograph followed. It was something they used to do, said Frank; sometimes, said Apollo; a long time ago, said Catherine. I offered to take a photo of the three of them, but all three dismissed it in discordant waves of hands. Frank and I, in our only unison that evening, offered to hug the edges of our foursome. No further act got broken that night.

My head buzzing, I craved a cigarette. I knew that Frank wanted one, too; I didn't understand why he hadn't had one yet, and I didn't dare have one in case he followed me outside and I would no longer know what to be and what to say to any one of them.

When we sat down, the final act of the happy family party came with the announcement of departure.

'Your dad's going back to New York next month,' said Catherine, lips quickly sealing the glass she promptly drained and started refilling.

I looked at Frank instinctively and he looked away.

'Oh,' said Apollo without a change in expression. 'Cool. You're all done with your album, then?'

Catherine looked at me, a pointed piercing look I couldn't place. It would have sent a dart of panic through me in any other given moment, but not now, when my Frank was ending, the news mediated by Catherine over the goddamn family cake.

'I'm sorry, I didn't want to tell you tonight,' said Frank, glancing at Catherine, and in a sweeping turn of the head, catching only the side of my face, he paused at Apollo. 'I guess I should've told you earlier, but yeah, it's all done, pretty much.' His voice crackled now, as if all out of fuel. Everyone reached for wine, but for Apollo, who stared vacantly at his dad, finishing off his cake.

'No worries, man,' he said. 'Wasn't that always the plan?'

'Was it?' I heard myself say in a much too high a pitch, my nails taking to my thighs in hope of some blood relief. There it was, something in the way Catherine looked at me again that made me sick to my stomach, a question, a betrayal, *why*, weighing me down, all in my head, all the sadness and paranoia, just like my mother said, all of it my fault. I looked down at my plate of unfinished cake that was now rising slowly in my throat.

I heard Frank stutter when Apollo asked calmly:

'Are you happy with the album?' Apollo's tired eyes trawled their way back to me and shifted our faces to glance at the clock on the cabinet behind Catherine in a non-verbal agreement that it was time to leave.

Frank looked taken aback by the question.

'Yeah.' He cleared his throat. 'No, yeah, it's good.' The dregs of the rehearsed smile grated the sides of his lips, broken now as if unsure what to express and how.

'Cool,' Apollo said, placing his hand on my thigh and massaging it lightly until he reached my hand, that slid into his in a desperate grasp of something tangible. 'Well, that's the most important.'

Catherine smiled and took another sip of wine, her long elegant fingers splayed on the table in front of her, head tilted, watching the evening play out. I had never seen her say so little.

I looked up at Apollo, feeling my stomach pain slowly wean off, as if it was being numbed out, joining the rest of my body in feeling less and less attached to me as the family tiptoeing continued around me.

'No hard feelings, man,' said Apollo, looking at Frank, his act cracking too, the laddish banter giving in to a face I hadn't seen on him before, too drawn and tired to keep fighting to stay young. 'Mum.' Apollo looked at Catherine as he stood up with my hand still in his, raising me with him like his puppet. 'We've got to go, but I'll see you next week at some point.' Apollo turned to his father. 'Frank, thanks for coming, man.' He reached out his hand to Frank, who shook it meekly, smiling at both of us with the same crumbling smile.

'It was lovely to meet you properly, Frank,' I said, gathering the rest of the volume I could find within my lungs. He smiled a smile I couldn't distinguish from the ones he'd bestowed on me earlier that night. I could only hope my face betrayed as little as his.

'It was great to see you, Toni.' We shook hands.

Apollo kissed his mother good night and thanked her for everything. I linked my arm with Apollo's and put my hand in his pocket. I wasn't sure if I could feel my body at all anymore, legs like corroded pieces of screeching metal lumbering on with a stiffness that I couldn't shake. If I could just even my stride with Apollo's and let him lead us out, I'd just about make it.

I hugged Catherine goodbye, not letting go of Apollo, and our cheeks clashed violently which we both ignored, saying another goodbye with a polite smile.

I kept my eyes on Apollo with obsessive attention to every detail of his face, each wave of his dark hair and the slight crease under his eyes pulling me away from the face I wanted to look at and be seen by, but no exchange was happening as we left, no one was looking or being seen, eyes resting with a distracted lack of focus, others, like mine, shooting desperate anchors. Stepping out of Catherine's that evening, I thought I would never see either of them again, and the thought surprised me with relief. I had always found it easy to migrate. Wasn't the only way to stay afloat to leave everything behind?

When Apollo asked me if I wanted to head to town, I told him the truth, so rare between us, that I was exhausted and needed a bath. When Frank texted later that night, my body floated calmly, knees bent downwards, feet raised behind me, eyes stinging in ice-cold water, mouth open, waiting to let go. When I did, water burst in greedily, tearing through my throat and nostrils, reaching my lungs that thrust me upwards in a panic that had me choking, skin pink and burning. When I clambered out of the bath my body shrivelled and turned a shade of blue, jolting in pangs of violent shudder.

I looked at my phone, gasping for breath. The message read:

What a shitshow, darling, I'm sorry. Pop round tomorrow if you're free x

30

One month later
Out

There are two certainties in migration: the moment of departure and the one of arrival. There's the looking behind at what you're leaving and the looking ahead at what you're entering, the ceasing of *Ja* and the birth of *I*, apart in every word going forward, *Ja* and *I* pulling in opposing directions, offering the comforting illusion of synchronisation and translation, of keeping *Ja* and *I* looking at each other, assured of the other's existence yet elusive, too distant from one another to really know what they are.

The moment has its ripple effect, diluting *Ja* and *I* into particles lost in the now indiscernible moments of departure and arrival, into the constant movement of leaving and becoming with each sentence, with each memorised piece of vocabulary, *Ja* fabricated into *I*.

Can you hear music underwater? It vibrates deep into your body, expanding your lungs into the best of you, the you that you like, the story of yourself you like telling both yourself and others, of the past lived with the music and the past danced through.

I kept our morning conversations short those early summer days, Karol's frantic obsession with Brexit weary.

'It might not even happen,' I kept saying to his generalised dread in varied iterations. 'There is no way they're going to go ahead with it, even the Tories.' I said that as a thing to say.

'It was my home, too, you know,' Karol reminded me daily, 'and now they're dragging Wales down with them. It will happen, Toni, and I never even got round to, I have no papers, I never applied for a citizenship, I've been away for too long now, essentially, I will never be able to get back, I'll always be a tourist in *my* country, these fuckers, they'll never let me get back, and with these mother— we're under fire *here*, Toni, it'll only get worse now they've got a government majority, a queer hating government majority, what are the chances of our survival?'

It was all he ever said those weeks, words tugged and tweaked each day to fall into the same sentiment and fear, his speech rapid and muffled, sentences interrupted, spilling into lengthy monologues, thoughts derailed and picked up again.

I wanted to tell him that it was all going to be fine, as long as little worlds pushed through, but I was never sure of those myself, days completely numb now, mechanical in daily tasks, lists fulfilled, lunches delivered and suites cleared out, Frank's calls ringing out and texts left unanswered, nights aided with pills.

'Don't worry about it. Go cuddle your boyfriend or something,' I said the morning of the referendum, impatient, worn out, my head weighed down by a permanent clasping headache I had grown accustomed to, even felt accompanied by. I pressed the butt of a cigarette against the windowsill, my eyes squinting in the rising sun.

'We don't cuddle,' he said dryly and sighed into the receiver. 'When one of us is on fire, we're all set alight.'

'I have to go to work,' I said. 'I'll speak to you tomorrow.'

+

When Karol called me the morning after, the referendum results tore through the walls and windows, hailed and howled, the crack only starting to show. I let his call ring out, his name in red above Veronica F and three missed calls in brackets. I called in sick to work, too sick at the thought of playing a token Eastern European at a company full of worried liberals. My phone buzzed soon after, Apollo's name flashing the screen.

'Shit man,' he said when I picked up and a long sigh crackled on the line. Neither of us spoke for a while.

I bit my lip, resting my head against the carved oak headboard.

'Are we still going to that wrap party tonight?' I asked him, shutting my eyes.

'We don't have to,' he said.

'Where is it?'

'I'll text you the address now.' Apollo's voice waned and the phone buzzed in my ear. 'My train pulls in at about half seven and I could head straight there.'

'Sounds good,' I said. 'I'm going to be late for work. I'll see you there, okay?' I hung up before he could say anything. I rolled onto my side, pangs of panic rising and falling in my chest, familiar now, its intermittent presence predictable in the fright, and I pressed my eyes tighter, waiting for the sleeping pills I had nicked from Catherine's bathroom cabinet a few nights ago to kick in, relaxing my eyelids, my muscles tensing underneath the duvet, stilling the head and parting my lips in restless dreams.

When I woke up, the day was still today, one of those conceited days etching themselves in the memory as more important than others, forgotten as soon as they passed. I pushed my body upwards, face shredded in the orange streaks of falling light, the sun crawling behind the dreaming Notting Hill skyline.

The address for the party was in Catford. I rubbed my eyes with my knuckles and yawned at my phone, TFL website frozen in a loading wheel before it showed me the one-hour route, taking me eastward into the opposite corner of London.

Something to do, I thought, and pulled out a black dress I had got for Frank. I wondered if he had left town already. I'd wanted to see him every night since the night of Apollo's birthday, but my legs had grown heavy since and my mind went blank every time I heard the phone ring. I watched it flash in my hand, his concealed name before my face, so close, and there were no words and there was no *what next* other than the daily act of keeping everything going, and there were still places to go and things to do. I clucked my red lips, spreading the lipstick evenly, and wiped off two puckered splodges on my front teeth. I slid my feet into black DM boots and glanced at the girl in the mirror, her eyes glazed over, face still.

'Pull yourself together,' I ordered her, but I wasn't sure if she took any notice, her face exactly as it always was, indifferent.

When I arrived in Catford, I put the address into the maps app on my phone and, with my face glued to the screen, I followed the blue dot down the street, meandering around headlines proclaiming British independence, union flags peering through the day-old pages, some still in their holders outside the station, others fluttering about the street in the summer wind. I tried to remember if I knew anyone from the shoot we were wrapping up and celebrating tonight, but no thoughts seemed to stick in my addled memory, all pausing for a second and taking off again before being understood.

I rang a small plastic buzzer next to the bright yellow door of the threadbare terrace. I looked up from my phone and glanced around the street, brick greying on opposing rows of houses, so different to west London. A woman slightly older than me, wearing a dark purple playsuit pulled at the waist with a red belt, answered the door, her face framed by gentle waves of auburn hair reaching her shoulders.

'Hello,' she said in a low voice, a melody, soft and sweet, woven through. 'I'm Jo.'

'Hi,' I said, something in her face making it impossible to look away. 'I'm Toni,' I heard my voice drop under her enormous brown eyes, which curved upwards in a thick eyeliner.

'Come on in,' she smiled, the arches of her lips full in a perfect red lip contour. I followed her down the corridor into a long room filled with Diana Ross and laughing, loud bodies shifting through a low-lying cloud of smoke in interrupted swirls of a dance, lips pressed to ears, hands touching hips. I circled around them towards the back of the room, a tired old kitchenette lined with cans and bottles. Jo rested her hand on the kitchen counter and lifted a bottle of gin in the air.

'Do you want a drink?' Jo asked.

I nodded. She poured half a glass of gin and glanced at me.

'You can keep going,' I said, feeling the panic rise in my throat, its numb thudding pushing at its side. 'Just top it with tonic.'

She laughed and squeezed the glass in my hand.

'We all drink tonight,' she said, the corners of those beautiful lips dropping slightly. I took a swig of my gin and glanced around the room for Apollo but couldn't spot him anywhere.

'Yeah,' I said and drained my glass in a few more gulps.

She took the glass from me, smiling as she pressed her red lip with her teeth and poured two more gins, filling them halfway and topping them up with tonic.

'Cheers,' she said, handing me my glass.

'Cheers.' We clinked glasses and took a sip, our eyes locked.

'I can't remember you from the set,' she said, sitting up on the counter now, her lips at my forehead. I glanced down her black top, noticing her breasts filling out a laced black bra, and I wondered, for a strangely pleasant second, what it would feel like to hold them in my hands.

'I work in post,' I said, looking up at her face, teeth still pressing her lip. She smiled and touched the tips of my fingers, making my skin burn with a sensation I hadn't felt before, disarmed and confused. She stroked my hand lightly and I didn't dare make a move or take a fuller breath, her skin brushing mine with intention, so soft, so different to Frank's, the gentleness of her touch unexpectedly soothing, simple, nice.

'Do you want to have a cigarette?' When the words eventually left my mouth, they spilled into a stifled croak. She tilted her head and nodded, jumping off the counter and taking the bottle of gin with her. She walked to the door behind the kitchenette and pulled the door open. I followed her out onto a small patio filled with smoking faces I didn't recognise, the conversations shifting from film to the referendum, exasperated sighs lingering in the crisp summer evening.

'Did you vote?' Jo asked, sliding a lit cigarette between my fingers and looking up at me.

'I couldn't,' I said, another gulp of gin quieting the heart to a pleasant murmur, unconcerned with meaning. 'I'm not a citizen.'

'I understand,' she said, turning to face the garden, her shoulder brushing mine, features sharpening. 'My dad is Danish. He couldn't vote either.' She exhaled, eyes squinting at the befalling darkness, coating talking heads before us in a pleasant haze. 'Neither could my Greek mum.'

I wanted to hear all the histories of bloods merging into her pronounced cheekbones, black eyes set against white skin, everything in her face a trace of the fragmented world.

'They've both lived here for thirty years.' Her face was speckled with a rage I envied, only able to acknowledge everything she was saying with silent understanding, knowing that it was never enough.

My phone buzzed in my bag. I took it out and glimpsed a text from Apollo, telling me his train was delayed and he wasn't going to be back in London until after ten, by which point he might head straight home.

Cool, I texted back.

Are you already there? he replied immediately. I took a drag of my cigarette, annoyed at his presence between us. I was relieved, too, freed among no one that knew me.

Yeah. It's good fun. I'll see you later, I typed and pressed send, putting the phone back in my bag. I glanced at Jo next to me, my eyes crawling down her figure, gleaming purples and navies in the house now merging with the descending darkness of the evening. Smoke was weaving out of my mouth between us, setting fire to breath for a moment, then turning to ash.

'Did you know that whales are conscious breathers?' I said. I wanted to kiss her, surprised by the impulse, but I pulled myself back and dropped the cigarette on the pavement slab, stamping it with the heel of my boot.

She smiled at me, her eyes glimmering in the dark.

'How do they sleep?' she asked, her voice soft.

I inched myself a bit closer, lifting my half-drunk glass of gin in an old man's story I was imagining I was telling.

'They can sort of shut down one side of their brain at a time as they rest at the surface. The other side is keeping them alert and breathing. They're able to switch between the two sides, resting for just a few hours at a time.' I drained my glass. 'They're half alive all the time,' I said.

'They can never dream,' said Jo, her eyes sparking up in the night, not leaving my face. I studied hers in search of something that would make me walk away, but the closer I looked, the faster my heart beat. Her eyebrows were crafted in thick, perfectly drawn lines now raised in unconstrained passion as she recounted a near encounter with a whale on the cruise in Iceland she went on last year with her dad, full and beautiful red lips pressed tight together at the disappointing conclusion to the trip. 'I've seen one once, the rupture of water at the surface, the conscious breath before submerging, but it was too far away. I often thought that maybe all I saw was only its trace.'

I let her hand touch mine now, as she sipped on her drink, her eyes still on my face.

'When I was little, my father told me he saw one once as it leapt above the water,' I said, my voice quieting with her touch. 'He said he had never seen a creature this godlike.'

'Where was he from?' she asked.

'Oh.' I blinked, surprised by the possibility of originating from multiple places. 'Poland. My entire family is,' I took a beat, 'from there,' I said, hearing myself stutter, never able to speak of Eastern Europe without tripping. 'No one made it out, but my mother, my father, and now me. He was a sailor. That helps, I guess.' I glanced down, conscious of my words stitched together, my accent ringing east today louder than it had ever sounded before. 'A bit dull,' I said and forced a smile, but she shook her head.

'It isn't,' she said. 'What's your full name?' My lips prised open under the question, never asked. 'Sorry, I'm just curious.' She bobbed her head and smiled at me again. 'I bet it's beautiful.'

'Romanowska,' I said.

'Romanowska,' she repeated. 'It is beautiful.'

'Yours?'

'Lindhardt.' She smiled as I echoed her name, its syllables ringing out low under my tongue.

'You know, coming from all these places can be lonely, too,' she said. 'You're foreign whichever way you turn.'

I agreed and glanced down at her long neck and bare shoulders, toned arms with a tattoo on each forearm that I only managed to catch a glimpse of.

'Sometimes I think,' I said, breathing in deeply in an attempt to stop my head from spinning, thoughts lucid and bleary, easy to come by and let go of, 'I worry, I constantly worry about expressing myself in the correct way, mispronouncing words, saying them wrong.' I leant back against the wall, steadying my head, knowing it would pass in a few minutes. 'Today, it feels like I'm more foreign than I've ever been.' I shut my eyes and opened them again, the ground already more stable under my feet. 'Maybe living here as an immigrant has made everything easier, though. Maybe I wouldn't know how to belong if I wasn't foreign either?' I looked at her, her face illuminated in golden streaks by the light from the kitchen. She was looking at me, fear pushing in through the cracks between us, everything broken today, neither of us knowing how to put the pieces of ourselves back together. My eyes closed, my body outside of me, attuning to her rhythm and no one else's, not even mine. My lips parted and her tongue slipped into my mouth, her lips encasing mine, juicy and soft, orange flower pushing through my nostrils. Something in me wanted to push back, to entwine and belong to her, angles fitting into mine with such ease, our hands on each other's face in gentle caress.

'I'll be right back,' I said. The familiar thudding sounded loud in my chest again, tightening my throat.

'Are you okay?' I heard her ask behind me, but my hand was on the handle already, pushing it down, my lungs filling with other people's smoke as I walked into the kitchen, its hazy colours splodgy, frames jittery and distorted. I walked across the kitchen to the sink, the most beautiful sink I had ever seen. I bent over it, turned on the cold water tap and put my head underneath it in relief, a cold stream running down my head and face, trickling down my neck and chest, prickling it in surprise, senses back sharper. I laughed, my breath loud and clear under a running stream of water, my thoughts stilled to momentary silence.

Someone turned off the tap and asked me if I was okay. It was Jo. My body flinched when she put her hand on my back.

'I'm fine,' I said, pulling myself out from underneath the sink, squeezing the ends of my hair lightly. It reached my shoulders, just like it did when I met Frank. Platinum blonde, coldest of them all, reaching down the black puffy shoulders of my dress in waves.

'I'll get you some food.' Jo's hand moved down my shoulder, setting it alight, my skin throbbing under her touch. I nodded, drawing deep breaths, water snaking down my neck. I grabbed my phone and, relieved to be able to see only one screen, I texted Frank, asking him if he was still in London. A sharp pang shot through my body at the thought that he could have already gone. A single drop fell from my face and splashed against the screen when he replied, seconds later:

Still here, darlin'. All okay?

I asked him if I could come over, thinking about all the times I could've seen him in the last month and a half, all the times he'd checked in since dinner at Catherine's and asked to meet, and I'd stayed with Apollo and had bad sex or no sex at all, despite wanting nothing but to be next to Frank, to be away from myself for a little while, just being whatever he wanted me to be.

I'll be home in half an hour. Pop over x

I told him I was drunk in Catford and had no idea how to find London.

Frank texted back, telling me to get a cab and put two kisses at the end. I threw my phone in my bag and looked around the room. It shifted away from what I comprehended as English, a mess of sounds that carried no meaning at all. I felt too tired to tune in to the foreign voices and their accents, to how the sentences were formed, to fit myself around the codes I could never crack, none of them mine. My heart raced as thoughts bounded back to work, anxiety twisting itself around the possibility of not knowing what was of interest to me beyond Frank's cock – the cock that was on its way to New York anyway, only the second cock I had sucked in my life and I wasn't sure if I wanted to suck any others – but there must've been something else, and I couldn't remember if there ever was a thing before Apollo and before Gav and before Toni. All the words that I had ever repeated and echoed and I had nothing constructive to say about global capitalism and had no knowledge of feminism or its history, no real knowledge or education of anything, and that shame ran as deep as the symmetrical lines on the face of Catherine Zeta-Jones, and when Jo looked me in the eyes, her gaze long and kind, I froze. I couldn't say a word.

'That's the only thing I've found,' she said, bearing half a pepperoni pizza on a paper tray cradled in her open arms.

She looked worried, her big eyes scanning my face. 'Look, Toni, can we talk?'

I took it in my hand and thanked her, looking away from her face, and excused myself, squeezing past new conversations, all inebriated, half engaged, high and animated. I heard her call my name when I reached the door and pulled it open. I took a bite of pizza, and with water still dripping onto my shoulders, I stepped out onto the cracked chequered tiles, closing the door behind me.

London hid behind the lines just like Catherine's face but there was no symmetry where I was, no precision in the zigzagged streetlights, thin strokes spilling one into another, Catford lights dipping in darkness above a loose chain of chicken shops, a scattered string of customers sucking on juicy bones in eruptions of laughter, their backs against the charcoaled brick walls. Scary south in its unknown, one of London's many worlds, distinct and demarcated. A bizarre Cheshire cat hung above me but I could've imagined it, its cartoon body splayed between buildings.

I stood at the bus stop, my head cold, hoping for a passing taxi, but only two buses came and both were heading in directions I had never heard of. The cat's eyes were huge, so big, yellow and menacing. He was ready to pounce and eat me alive in this sad wonderland. I convinced myself I would die of a heart failure under the cat and its gaze, my heart would stop and they would misspell my name on my death certificate and I would never exist, not in a theoretical or philosophical sense, but the only one that mattered to anyone, the factual.

Faces filing out of buses looked familiar, cheekbones aligning with mine in structure, eyes narrower and longer like mine, like the cat's eyes above us, commuters' hands thick and strong, voices hardened and low, determined as they pushed through the night, spilling into Catford, glancing at me with passing curiosity. London had seen stranger things than wet white girls, looking like Notting Hill, Cardiff still sitting on some syllables, but fewer and fewer, day by day, and always foreign, Eastern European through and through, they could see it, we could always recognise ourselves in others, our cat eyes blinking yellow at one another in the darkness.

Frank texted, asking if I was okay.

I didn't reply, looking around.

There was no Gav to hold my hand, and there was no Uber to click a button for, and the times were different before and after Uber, it was impossible to recreate the many night scenes in which we'd got cabs, and the times before Gav and after Gav, myself before Gav and after Gav, and that self – within Gav – those were the toughest times, that limbo before Uber and after Gav when nothing made sense, when wet hair froze and pricked my skin in the night and danced with gin long enough to get me to the time when Uber came and made that one thing easier. Just one thing easier.

My jaw clenched, the phone's battery on ten per cent. I felt sober but knew I couldn't have been. I looked at my phone; two missed calls from Frank and another text: *Where are you, darl?* The phone was shaking in my hand, water dripping on the screen, my ungainly fingers sliding across. Water fell harder, splashing against the screen, dissolving my reply that burst into thousands of black dots for a second before morphing into a scrambled *IM ok*, and as my index finger hovered over the send button, the screen went black and Toni looked back at me, her eyes dissolving in water, dripping into her mouth, smudging away at the cheekbones.

'Toni!' I blinked away the voice ringing in my head, but the name rang closer and closer. I turned around. 'Are you okay?

I was worried about you leaving on your own this late.' It was Jo, wisps of her hair glued to her face, flushed, her lips parted, panting, chest rising and falling in sharp breaths. I started to believe that it was the only question anyone ever asked me, and maybe if I'd taken the hint early enough, I wouldn't hear it just now, I could just about keep moving without grabbing onto helping hands.

'Yeah.' I hesitated, my eyes darting between the dwindling streetlights above us. 'No, I don't know,' I said. 'I don't think I am.' She came closer, the touch of her hands sending a jolt through mine with the same burn, different to Frank's, lacking escape, setting me alight, painful. I weaved my hands in hers, biting my lower lip, harder this time, teeth piercing through the skin, blood salty under my tongue. 'I don't know what I'm doing,' I said. She looked at me the way she'd looked at me outside the house before our kiss, as if I was the only person in the world in that second, the way only Gav looked at me before he even knew me, when he saw me in Pulse the night we met and never let me go. 'Can I stay with you tonight?' I asked.

'Sure,' she said, her voice sweet and soft, calming everything within me. 'I'm up the road in Brockley. Are you okay walking?'

I nodded, entwining my fingers in hers, steadied by her pace. I didn't register any details of the walk, mind battling mind, silent residential streets blurring into the background, the conversation circling around what we did and how long we had both lived in London, her east and my west intersecting in the centre in places known to us both.

Jo's flat in Brockley was perched on the very top of a hill and looked down on London far away, the passage of darkness in between marking many Londons and many histories, all of them strange and unknown. Jo's flat was in a mid-century ex-council estate that climbed high above the surrounding Edwardian terraces, a forgotten victory of inclusivity as up until its erection the views afforded by these heights had only been granted to the neighbouring Victorian detached houses. We climbed the patterned tiles all the way up to the top floor and the door creaked open into a wide, dark corridor. Jo pressed a finger to her lips and, not letting go of my hand, led me through to her room. It was pastel green and filled with plants that were dotted around the bed on the dark oak floor. Two floor lamps stood on either side of the bed, glowing an orange yellow, soothing and warm.

'You've had a long night, we don't have to,' she said when it was my tongue pushing into her mouth this time, tender and wet, my hands grazing her small waist, unbuttoning her dress, orange flower and bergamot sharpening my nostrils, the waking sun seeping through the half-opened curtains etching her luminous pale skin. I wanted to tell her that I hadn't slept with a woman before but felt I didn't need to, my hands knowing the way around her body without will or direction, my lips sinking into hers, the softest lips I had ever kissed. She was just that little bit shorter than me without her boots and soon height or any other numbers stopped making sense and disappeared when she started taking off my striped top and slid my pants down to my ankles. When she pulled up from between my thighs, her lips still tasted of me. She smiled and kissed me. I cupped her breasts in my palms gently, delicate and soft, hard nipples slipping through my fingers as I stroked them. She pulled away and sat on me. Her left nipple was slightly smaller than the other, so was her breast, above a birthmark spread underneath it, thin and long, like a stroke of ash in half-moon. My hands slid down her stomach and moved softly down the creases of the endings of her thighs.

'You're so beautiful,' I heard myself say over and over that night. I kept saying it, feeling her wetness with my fingers, moving up and down inside her. I kept saying it as I came, her tongue snaking down my body and pushing inside me. I kept saying it as I lay my head in her lap and she stroked my face, her body safe and calm, away from the sea, in that brief moment the only place I wanted to be, the place where my eyelids shut eventually and I fell asleep, without fear or pills, her hand grazing the back of my neck.

When I woke up, Jo was still asleep, her long back curled against me. I peeled myself off and sat up. The sun was in full beam, pouring through the window and flooding a long triangular streak on the bed between our bodies. I put on my dress and picked up my bag from the floor. I unplugged her phone and pulled the charger out of the socket. All of it felt so normal, as if I was in my house and this was my girlfriend and it had always been this way, us, in this room, out of any geographical context. I had never heard of Brockley until she mentioned it last night, and my only point of reference was that it was really far away from Notting Hill. I tiptoed out of the room, glancing left to right. The room opposite was shut, the bathroom to my left was open. I looked right, the midday light streaming through another door. I careened towards it as quietly as I could and found a small square lounge, four two-seater sofas hugging each wall in a circle around a round table, its sheen glimmering in the light falling through the glass balcony door. I located a plug next to one of the sofas and left my phone to charge. I scooped a cigarette packet out of my bag and stepped onto the hot concrete of a robust brick balcony, baked in the southern sun, north-east London scintillating in the distance. I smoked in silence, my throat dry, itchy as I swallowed, the sun burning my skin, too present and powerful to feel anything else. I walked back into the lounge and looked at my phone, the screen flashing with two messages, Frank asking what had happened and Apollo wondering where I was. I ignored Frank and started typing a reply to Apollo.

Met a friend and stayed over at her place in Catford. Will be over soon. I pressed send and flicked the news on, tired and hungover enough to finally face it. My heart skidded at the morning headline – *Polish Cultural Centre in Hammersmith vandalised*, with one word, *Out*, sprayed on its walls. I stared at the three letters in front of me but there was nothing to feel, another punch against a body that wasn't real, a numb dummy.

'Morning.' Jo's soft melody rang above me. I looked up at her, bleary eyes gazing down at me with a playful flicker. She was wearing a two-piece bathing suit, weaves and knots of ferns and roses etched across her body in black ink. 'I thought you might want some water.' She placed a glass in front of me on the table and leant in with a kiss, our lips dry, rubbery against each other.

I switched the screen off, ashamed of her seeing the headline, exerting more pity, seeing me as just one thing, an immigrant.

'Thanks,' I said, pulling away and taking a greedy sip of water and then, as if hit by thirst, I drained the glass in breathless gulps, which made her laugh.

'You needed that,' she said and took a sip from her glass, the corners of my lips lifting, feeling my phone vibrate in my hand, Karol's name flashing on the screen.

'Sorry,' I said and rejected the call, switching the phone to silent.

She glanced down at it and let out a nervous laugh.

'Your boyfriend?'

I shook my head.

'No,' I said, 'but I have to go.'

'Can I have your number?' She tilted her head, baring her teeth in a smile, stirring my heart in a new motion.

'Yeah, of course,' I said, feeling out of breath, her big eyes peering right through me. I took her phone in my hand and typed my number. I glimpsed her saving it as Toni Romanovska.

31

Two months later
August 2016

Frank texted that morning. *Are you okay?*

I am okay, thanks, I texted back, my eyes inspecting the loose threads peeling away at the edges of the canopy of the bed. I was too tired to see him. The summer heat was difficult, sunglazed bodies and laughter bringing back the sea, bringing me back to that day, to Gav. My body felt sick and weak. *Are you okay?* No, I wanted to say to Frank, come, I wanted to tell him, but I lay still instead, his calls ringing out.

Jo messaged a couple of days after. *Do you fancy a drink this weekend?*

Her message rang with the possibility of a new curve, a new escape, reminding me of the sensation of her on my skin, how right she felt under my fingertips and how wrong, too, in this doomed timeline.

When I was too sick to lie down, I stood up on the bed and pulled on the canopy threads, ripping the fake world of the fake Genevieve piece by piece, weaving the threads around the pillars like a black widow, but I lacked her persistence and precision and in the end it exhausted me, the threads untangling.

Sorry, it's not the best time, I texted back, my fingers stiff, curling and straightening above the keyboard with difficulty.

I thought about her often, daydreaming an alternative life where I stayed in the flat with Jo. After work I would head east, into her arms instead of lying here sick in the west, surrounded by the very literal mess of my life with Apollo, among unwashed clothes piling up next to crumpled pizza boxes, the two of us never under Genevieve's canopy together anymore. On hot, impossible days when I felt marginally better, I disappeared into overtime at work until I felt worse again. I watched as Apollo climbed higher and higher into bigger budgets and bigger names, his attention fleeting. Gav only occasionally flashed in screens and mirrors now, my weary eyes shutting at the fall of night, too busy in the day to wander.

Karol called every morning, more agitated and paranoid since the vote, his sentences broken and under attack, my syllables too clumsy and cumbersome to gather and form words, let alone sentences. I rushed goodbyes, too tired to talk to him. I longed for Karol to stay on the phone longer, to be without being, but I didn't believe conversations could happen that way, the silences between us too dangerous, leaving room for the forgotten Welsh melody neither of us was ready to hear.

I was halfway through my dinner, a packet of Doritos and a warm can of lager in bed with an episode of *Silent Witness*, when I heard a knock on the door, hard and purposeful, repeated, and again. I looked at the time in the screen's corner. It was getting close to eleven, numbers flickering next to 'Tue 2nd August'. I closed my laptop and put aside the Doritos, leaving both on the bed. I tiptoed to the front door and looked through the peephole, spotting a familiar tangle of blond hair, suppressing any airflow.

'Toni?' Frank's voice rang long and low, ring-clad knuckles clinging in my ear pressed to the door.

My mind froze under this collapse in the routine, most precarious showcase of unpredictability – Frank, and before I knew what to do, before I felt what the right thing to do was, my body jolted out a response.

'Give me two minutes,' I said, my foreign voice ringing notes only Frank had ever heard, my limbs prickling at the possibility of his touch. I took a step back and a deep breath, my head turned towards the mirror, looking for the girl who had always showed up when I needed her, but I couldn't make sense of her. I saw a long-framed figure as if pinned and stretched, wearing only pants and Apollo's *Hot Fuzz* T-shirt, brown roots crawling down washed-out blonde hair in ugly streaks, lips hardened, eyes laden with a day's make-up, black lines of eyeliner smudged at the corners, my mind frazzled at the request of such sudden reinvention. I pulled up the T-shirt and tied it into a knot, revealing the line of my stomach above my pants, black and laced, good enough, maybe. I smiled at the mirror, lips pulled by this long-unexercised stretch. The girl smiled back, her chin up.

I pulled the door open.

Frank looked different than usual, all suited up, spikes of his hair still holding themselves in order of a sophisticated night out, his face glazed with an approaching hangover. He must've been at some important event. In my mind all events in his life were important. It was me, I hoped, that wasn't. I wanted to believe that I was urgent in his eyes. That's what lovers were. I wasn't sure if I was either urgent or a lover, but here we both were, his left eye bloodshot around the edges, lips stained purple-red. We didn't kiss hello this time as he stepped into the flat, his lips occupied with the unlit cigarette he liked to suck on late at night, when we lay still, sharing the loneliness of sleeplessness. His suit was purple, its body-hugging jacket open, a white shirt unbuttoned at the top, stubble climbing his jawline, a shave missed only by a day or so.

'Are you here to see your son?' I asked, surprised at the possibility of anger directed at him, anger I didn't feel entitled to have.

'No.' Frank lost a beat before he said, 'He's in Wales filming, isn't he?'

I bit my lip, trying to comprehend the time that had lapsed between us, to extricate him from what he was the last time I saw him, Catherine's ex-husband, Apollo's father, a stranger to me.

'Oh, so you're in touch now?' I said, hearing myself croak.

'Yeah,' he said, eyes narrowing at me as his lips drew closer into a confused pout. 'Sort of.' He looked around the hallway and craned his neck past me into the kitchen. 'It's so strange being here,' he said, and I knew he didn't mean because of his son, he meant because of his mother.

'Do you want something to drink?' I said, my memory clinging to standard questions before, if ever, I would know what it was that I wanted to happen.

'Do you have any red?' he asked, walking into the kitchen, uneasiness in his swagger, geranium and cedar only now hitting me with full force, as if my body had just relented and come alive.

I brushed past him and careened towards the kitchen cabinet, aware of every step, feeling him watching me, my body stiffening under his gaze when I bent down to reach a bottle of red from the bottom shelf of the kitchen cupboard.

'I worried something happened to you that night,' Frank said as I lifted myself up, hands aware of their intricate attachments as if they weren't mine, rummaging through a drawer, looking for a corkscrew. 'I stayed up all night thinking about you.'

I wondered if that was the only time he stayed up thinking about me, if I etched myself in his thoughts as much as he incised into mine, taking every last bit of space left, gouging into the imagination, gushing in a myriad of scenarios, his touch different each time, his scent always the same. I took out two short whisky glasses and filled them to the brim with Merlot, awaiting an accusation, a line of questioning. I could've let him know that I was okay, I could've said something, anything, but the silence stretched as I walked back towards the table, his face cupped by the palm of his hand, three rings glimmering in the fuzzy kitchen light, all silver with black and purple stones.

'I'm off to New York tomorrow,' he said, looking down at the wine spilling out of glasses between us as I put them down, sitting opposite him. 'I wanted to say goodbye.'

'Wasn't that always the plan?' I said.

His eyes lit up with familiar playfulness. He took out a cigarette, tucked it behind his ear.

'You were never the plan,' he said. My lips quivered, their corners lifting against my intention of staying distant tonight.

'No,' I said. None of it was, nothing since Gav died. Sitting opposite Frank, Catherine's warm red lapping softly at our lips, I missed Karol, the one thing that had made sense since—

'Are you all packed?' I asked and realised there were never any things in the Soho flat, none of them anchored in any idea of the present, only artefacts of the past and an empty bedroom. 'You don't even live in that flat, of course you don't,' I said, my face flushed with the naivety of realising only now that a place I had run to for safety wasn't even a real place in the world.

'No,' he said calmly, putting down the glass of wine and taking off his jacket, his foot brushing against mine under the table. 'I have a house in Camden.'

I downed my glass and topped both tumblers to the brim, watching the wine spill at any slight movement as we took them in both hands, slurping.

'Was it your hook-up place?' I asked.

Frank looked amused as he took a swig.

'I don't need a hook-up place, darling,' he said.

'Clearly.' I lifted my glass in the air.

'Touché,' he said, gleaming, clinking his glass against mine, the edges of his face blurring in laughter as he split into two and morphed back into one person again. I made myself blink to keep the contours of the world straight, but everything felt fuzzy. 'I squatted there in the nineties. Call it a sentiment.' His phantom face became clear again, Frank, all of him as fantastical as his sentimental property buying. 'I'm sorry I didn't tell you about going back to New York. I liked to not think about it when I was with you,' he said after a while.

'It's okay,' I said, looking down at my glass, wine turning to blood, a single drop in water. I wanted to ask him if he *had to* leave, but I knew the answer and didn't want to hear it. 'I'm starving.'

'I could get us a takeaway.' He said this in the voice of someone who could get anything he wanted at any time he wanted it, and I wondered if he practised that voice like I exercised the smiles of the girl in the mirror and the way she was able to walk in front of him, straight and tall, desired.

We never did, my foot in a dance with his, moving up his thigh, the air congealing into a still mass, coarse in my throat, my lungs drawing short breaths, hungry and impatient, our eyes locked in silence.

When we had sex that night it was a perfectly synchronised dance of two bodies that had studied each other and knew exactly how to get their fix, all done in ten minutes, an understated ability of pleasure that few pairs of bodies master. Mine and Apollo's never did.

Frank fell asleep on his front, his face turned towards mine as I lay awake on my back, his breath brushing my chin softly, his arm resting heavy on my stomach. More than anything, I knew I would miss the weight of his body pressing down on mine, as if he ever let go, I'd resurface floating without any ground to stand on.

Before he left, he hid his beautiful green alcoholic bloodshot eyes behind his shades. Someone told me once that we share a piece of everyone we choose in our lives, we connect with a deeper, unconscious part of ourselves in others and I wondered if that was it between us, the sad bloodshot eyes. We hugged goodbye with multiple and hushed thanks for a great time, intertwined with smiles, stumbling upon sighs. We both instinctively knew there should never have been a goodbye and we didn't know how to have one. I wished him a safe flight and he hoped everything would work out well. Neither of us said we should see each other again when he gets back, there was no future tense in what we were saying, just the mundanity of the flight duration and London traffic being awful, his cab being late, both of us feeling hungover and exhausted, my favourite state to be in, free of anxious alertness, terrifying energy to experience things as they happened to us.

When he left, I took three sleeping pills. I weighed them in my hand, the last three. I put all of them in my mouth and washed them down with watered-down wine, a struck balance of hydration and not wanting to sober up. I went back to bed and gently lowered myself onto his side of the sheets. I closed my eyes. I wondered if his scent would still be there when I woke up, how long it would linger.

+

It was early evening when I woke up, the corner of my mouth glued to the pillow in a steady drip of saliva, the setting sun shooting through the blinds in sharp streaks, striking the white empty walls. I lifted myself up, my body weighing more than I had ever carried, every inch of it sinking into the sheets with weariness. I glimpsed one of Frank's cigarettes between the pillows, crumpled, half broken and limp. I put it in my mouth and reached for a lighter, my tongue weaving around the rim, its bitterness sharp and tingling. I looked at my phone, disappointed in one message from Apollo and no calls from Karol for the second day in a row. My brows furrowed over the date of the last call. I opened a text from Apollo, sent three hours ago. It said he couldn't wait to see me this evening. We should do something, it said, just the two of us. Frank's cigarette burnt my hand, the top half brushing my knuckles. Swearing, I dropped it to the floor and stubbed it out with the back of my heel, which was burning now too, sharp pain jolting me upwards. Sucking on the burnt knuckle, the skin of my lips throbbing, I pulled the cover off the duvet and dragged it across the kitchen to the washing machine. Two half-empty glasses of red were still on the table, their spilled blood soaked in the crevices of the second-hand oak, dry, all done. I pushed the duvet cover into the machine and threw my hand under a stream of cold water in the sink, a brief moment of comfort. I wanted to push my whole self under the lash of the stream, but I was out of time. I considered rinsing the glasses, weighing the evidence stacked against me, patches of red inked across the table in uneven blotches, marking the journey of Frank's body reaching for mine, his hand pulling my head to his. I walked back to the bedroom. I looked at the sheets and felt I never wanted to wash them of

Frank's body, wondering if I could hold on to him in that way, through the decaying cotton threads. I looked at the small plastic bin next to the bed Apollo and I had never used, one of the things found and picked, my heart skipping a beat at a used condom splayed at the bottom of the bin, the only item there, the only evidence that mattered, my lungs constricting under its weight. I took it out of the bin and sprinted across to the bathroom, my steps punctuated by the intermittent throbbing of burnt hand and foot. I wrapped the condom in multiple layers of toilet paper and marched back to the kitchen, burying it under all the other rubbish in the bin. I washed my hands, lime washing-up liquid foaming at my fingers, and padded them dry against my thighs. I marched back to the bedroom and put on a loose linen dress that came in a long line of items gifted by Catherine. My phone pinged. It was Apollo, asking me if I was hungry. He was half an hour away. I took a deep breath and dialled a number for my colleague Fiona. I couldn't remember if I had ever called her before.

'I've had to cover for you today, shithead,' said as a hello, Fiona's voice having a rasped ring to it, a croaky kind of wisdom of someone who couldn't be twenty-three.

'I know. I'm sorry,' I said, my heart pounding. 'Thanks.'

'What's happening?'

'I need to crash at yours for the next few days, is that alright?' I asked, my thoughts released into the wild and now racing ahead of one another, tumbling down.

'Did you and Apollo break up?' she asked, sweet spikes of drama tinting her voice.

'No,' I said, 'but we will. In half an hour.'

There was silence on the other end of the line, followed by a crackling sigh.

'I'm sorry, babe.'

'Is that okay?' I asked, impatiently eyeing up piles of clothes I needed to pack in twenty minutes of the rest of my life in Notting Hill.

'Of course,' she said. 'Of course it is.'

'Thanks,' I said and hung up. I texted Karol and apologised about being a shit friend lately. I told him that Frank had left and I was breaking up with Apollo and said we should talk. I pulled out a suitcase with all Catherine's clothes and started shoving them into hasty crumpled bundles. When I finished, I had five minutes left. I lowered myself to the floor and tugged out a small wooden box that carried only two items, out of proportion to the size of the box: the photograph of Gav with a prawn in his mouth and my Polish passport. There was one more thing, tucked away and hidden from Apollo: Frank's cornflower-blue jacket, neatly folded at the top corner of the bed and gathering a layer of dust. I pulled it to me and gave it a shake, cedar, geranium and hints of lemongrass gone, there was only dust, its particles flying into my nose, making me sneeze. Evidence number two. I returned to the bin and buried it under scraps of food and non-recyclable containers together with the condom, my mind practised under small tasks. I was washing my hands when the key turned in the lock and the door clicked open, the voice so familiar and always so grounding, making me shudder, uncontrollable shakes spilling into burnt throbbing that spread through my body.

'Hey Ton,' Apollo said, standing in the doorway, his smile spread across his tanned face. I couldn't help but notice how much that face had changed since the time of Karol's exhibition in Cardiff. It was the face of someone who was confident in the future, and maybe that was the ultimate rift between us, me looking only at the past, Gav taking all my future with him. The past had lapped at every day, rippled and covered me completely, water filling my lungs with exhausting repetition, no hope of stopping.

'I'm leaving, Apollo.' I pushed the words out, or rather, they pushed through my clenched jaw, rising in my throat like stinging bile.

'What?' The smile hadn't left his face. It lingered on, unchanged.

'I'm leaving. I'm packed. I'm going.' Everything in my body told me to run, but I stood so still, my hands clawing the counter, arms bent at the elbow, needing to hold on to something.

'Are you breaking up with me?' Apollo's friendly countenance switched off into an expression I had never seen him wear, one devoid of any discernible emotion. 'What is this? Has something happened?'

'I need to go,' I said, feeling the skin break at the place of my burns, the tissue falling apart under the weight of words.

'What, like, are you coming back?'

'I don't want to be with you, Apollo,' I said.

'What the fuck, Ton? Are you for real?' Apollo stood still, squinting at me now, his eyes forming tears I was incapable of responding to. 'I know I've been a fucking terrible boyfriend lately,' here the words broke and two streaks glistened on his face, 'but that's not how it's done, that's not how…' The words waned into a dull silence. This was exactly how it was done, I wanted to say, loud and angry, this was how people are gone, jostled out of your embrace, the ground shifting underneath feet, they drown and they leave the country without a word, and that is it sometimes, that is exactly how you lose them.

I pushed myself away from the counter as if unable to walk without any assistance and lunged myself into his arms.

'I have to go,' I said, my cheek brushing his, delicate and soft.

'Fuck you, Toni,' he said, his voice small and cold, his body still, frozen in the doorframe.

'I have to go,' I said. I walked back to the bedroom and picked up the suitcase. When I walked back into the hallway, I glimpsed a girl in the mirror. She looked so tired. Apollo was leaning against the kitchen doorframe, his arms folded in resigned acceptance, his teeth biting his lower lip, cheeks wet now.

'Get out,' he said without raising his voice.

'I'm sorry, Apollo,' I said. I knew there was nothing else, nothing to it. It surprised me how easily it began and how easily it ended, my own Hollywood film. I closed the door behind me. I looked around, making sure no one was looking, and did a thing I hadn't done in a long, long time, a thing I watched everyone around me do growing up, every morning and every night, the thing that some of us lapsed Catholics catch ourselves doing sometimes, out of habit perhaps, when there is nothing else, no gesture to cling on to, all words dried in the throat. I crossed my face in the name of the Father, and the Son, and—

I always wondered why the mother was missing, and with that thought I knew I needed to say one more goodbye.

The door flung open as soon as I pressed the buzzer, Catherine draped in jungle patterns on silk-like fabric, the equations of her face defying time, thick dark strands combed to the side, black eyes inspecting me with surprise.

'Toni?' she said, 'Everything okay?' She glanced down at the suitcase gripped in my hand. I knew I would miss the warmth of Catherine's voice, her distant yet insistent motherliness.

'Yeah,' I said. 'Well, not exactly. Can I talk to you for a second?'

'Of course,' she said and turned towards the dining room then straight past it into the kitchen. I followed obediently, examining this new terrain. Catherine had a very graceful way of eliciting complete submission. 'Oh, this is just for show.' She waved vaguely in the direction of the dining room I had spent all my previous life with her in. 'Let's sit down in the snug. Are you hungry?'

I gave out a faint yes, my steps more cautious now, as if I was slowly lowering myself deeper into a den I might never find a way out of. She pointed at a gigantic corner sofa and a scatter of boho-type armchairs that faced it, an octagonal mid-century coffee table between them.

'Make yourself comfortable. I have pizza.'

I took my shoes off and climbed the orange sofa, plush and soft, resisting the urge to sink into it and collapse.

She returned bearing a Papa John's pizza and a very expensive-looking ceramic pot of something she spent five minutes describing as a green tea blend of something or other imported from Japan.

'Oh, and coffee.' She rushed out of the room before I gathered any vocal power to say thanks. 'How are things, darling?' Catherine asked as I shoved the slice of a margarita into my mouth. I started chewing as fast as I could, watching her pour us a full mug of coffee each. 'I hope you're enjoying head running. I'm sure you'll be promoted to an assistant in no time.'

My head nodded involuntarily and I looked down, comforted by the bitterness of the coffee.

'Me and Apollo broke up,' I said, afraid of those swollen, heavy words, always sparse, pushing against silence.

Catherine looked at me, nibbling on her slice with elegance, baring her teeth slightly to protect her lipstick. My words fell apart under her scrutiny; maybe it was just a mirror of myself looking at me around her, watching my every move. 'I'm sorry,' she said after a while and eyed my suitcase again. 'What happened?' she asked, words hanging in the air, hesitant. 'If you don't mind me asking.'

'We were never right together,' I cautioned. Sometimes I wondered why we ever got together, what made us stay, afraid of the answer. I knew it was fear.

I looked up at her, Catherine, stoic and warm in her composure, powerful and elegant, a mother and a wife. My words ceased, my throat shrank and my chest tightened, my body held up in a clutch, seeking escape, but there would never be another opportunity to confess, at least to her, to apologise, to be granted redemption, because if there ever was a human that could wave away my sins with nonchalance and prowess it would be her.

'Toni, will I make it easier if I tell you that I know about Frank?'

She said this quietly and slurped on her coffee. There was no air in that moment and no motion, only prickling pain that had increased in its intensity to fire: it jostled me upwards, spilling lukewarm coffee all over my hands, dripping down on the sunset orange of the sofa.

'Oh god, I'm sorry.' I started rubbing the sofa with the back of my hand, dilating the black splodge further. 'I'm sorry. I should never have come, I'm sorry.'

'Toni, stop and sit down,' she said gently with unwarranted softness. 'Please,' she pressed as I stared at the stain in horror. I glanced at her and noticed she hadn't moved from her chair, her coffee still cupped in her gold-and-black-stone-clad hands.

'I know I'm sick, I know,' I sputtered, but she raised her hand as if to wave me away.

'Stop,' her voice now firm. 'Sit back down, please. I think I knew the entire time.'

I felt nauseous, coffee irritating my senses, its overwhelming aroma inescapable, too. I clambered back onto the sofa as told, exhausted. My eyes pricked and fuzzed the reality of her.

'You're a kid, Toni. Frank's a grown man with a kid,' she said, in a manner of explaining the basics of living a life.

I said nothing, grappling with my cold coffee cup again, needing to hold something. I wanted her to hate me. She needed to hate me.

'He didn't make me do anything,' I said quietly, looking down at the cup, following the woven pattern on the thin ceramic, conscious of its frailty, how easily it could break.

'How old are you again?'

'I'll be twenty-two in December,' I said and leant back on the sofa, my body imitating hers with an increasing unease surging through me, as if it only caught up on the geography and history of the place.

'Good god.' Her face crumbled into exacerbated weariness. 'I can't believe I was married to that man sometimes.' She looked away for a second, padding her cheeks with the back of her hand. She cleared her throat and looked back at me. 'Listen, darling, I've worked in fashion for thirty-five years. I was very young when I started and infatuated with a lot of men I shouldn't have been, a lot of these men taking advantage they should've never taken given their position of power and, often, their marital status.'

I looked at her with disbelief. Can forgiveness be this easy? Was I asking for some?

'I'm sorry,' I said.

She stood up from her chair and disappeared into the kitchen, filling the silence with fervent rustling through the shelves.

'Some idiot sent me a box of amazing truffles.' She shuffled back into the snug, holding a small brown box. 'Do you want one?' I shook my head and thanked her. Catherine threw a truffle into her mouth and grimaced in pleasure. 'I'm just glad Apollo's never found out.' She paused and looked at me.

'Of course not,' I said, feeling my face flush. 'I'm sorry, I never wanted to—'

'Toni, you have to stop with the sorries now. I'm not saying any of this to make you feel more guilty.' She shot me a warm smile and reached for another truffle.

I smiled back, my hand circling the coffee splotch.

'I'll miss our halva and coffee Saturdays,' I said.

Catherine bobbed her head to the side.

'Me too,' she said with a sad smile.

I took a beat before I asked, 'How did you find out about Frank?'

There came the wave of hand.

'Soho is a very small place,' she said. 'Frank's very predictable like that. He's a compulsive liar, but not a very imaginative one, bless him. Whoever he was with, he always had an affair. I'm actually,' she clucked her lips, 'funnily enough, good friends with a couple of his ex-girlfriends, so it's not all that bad. They're, for the most part, brilliant women.' She threw another truffle into her mouth, chewing slowly. 'You know, I confronted him about you after Apollo's birthday dinner but he denied it was you.'

I threw my head on my knees and rubbed it against them. 'Oh god, I'm so embarrassed.'

Catherine smiled at me, a lighter glint in her eye.

'Well that you can be. It's not too unhealthy.'

'I should've broken up with Apollo a long, long time ago,' I said, my voice waning to a faint groan. I wanted to tell her that I should've never got with Frank but it wouldn't have been true, Frank holding my head above water, Gav alive in my dreams when I was with him, a knot in my stomach stirring at the dull pain, in excitement, and longing that could be satisfied, the fantasy of Frank within reach when everything else was gone, all of Cardiff under the sea.

'We all cling on to something until we learn how not to. I hope that one day you won't need to, Toni. You'll feel safe within yourself,' she said, her slender hand reaching to my knee and patting it with a reassuring smile. 'You need to let yourself fall in between the cracks and drown for a little bit. Isn't that the way everyone learns to swim? Your instinct will keep you afloat.'

I stifled a croak, the noise of waves lapping against the shore suddenly between us, menacing and cold.

'I'm tired,' I said, thinking about the night-time commute to Fiona's in Walthamstow. 'Would you mind if I stayed tonight? I'll be gone by the morning.'

'Of course you can,' she said.

She stood up and grabbed both cups. I offered to help but she said she would clean up tomorrow and not to worry. I obliged with a smile and thanked her.

'Toni, I know things might not seem this way, but you'll be alright,' she said, turning at the door as we said good night. 'Things have a weird way of continuing, you know. When you let them.' She smiled and walked away, large green leaves on silk grazing her calves.

A phone call ruptured the stillness of the night, tearing through the safety of Catherine's spare room with the harsh white light of a police chase flooding in, no distance left to run.

'Karol?' I groaned into the phone, pressing it into my ear, eyes closed.

I could hear his breath, elongated and heavy.

'Karol, are you okay?'

Then a hissing noise.

'Karol?' I said again, lifting myself up, pressing the phone harder into my face.

When he spoke, he didn't sound like himself, his voice very small and faint, fractured by punctuated gasps.

'Can you come? Toni, can you come to Warsaw, please? Please, come tomorrow. Please come. Can you promise me you'll come?'

I asked questions but none were answered, met with muffled hissing, a gnawing fear crawling on the surface of my skin, the possibility I wouldn't make it no matter how fast I ran, I would run and run and run, and, against all logic, in every scenario shooting through my head, thoughts lodging themselves deep like bullets, the sea would take him too.

'Can you breathe okay?' I tried again, out of breath myself, my lungs constricting in ruptured pangs, anxiety's grip stifling my throat.

'Can you promise?' he asked, heaving into the receiver like a wounded animal.

I told him I would, of course I would. I would be there as soon as I could.

Karol said he would send me his address and hung up, fizzling the night into sentences strung out of sequence, scenes of my life falling apart from one another. I ran upstairs to Catherine's bedroom, the otherworldly palace of a place she called home sprawling away at my feet into luscious wallpaper patterns and photographs of people I had fallen in love with, and paintings, fantastical and strange, even though familiar to me before, as if they were part of a once-loved television show.

The night fragmented into chunks of advice, Catherine's lips drawing into pouts, considering best options, our faces illuminated by the cold light of her laptop screen.

'No, you're not flying to Modlin, good god, darling. Let's get you to Chopin Airport, it'll be much quicker this way,' and, 'No, I'm not letting you fly from Stansted, good god. There's one from Heathrow at eight,' with crumbs of motherly reassurance: 'I'm sure he's fine, darling,' and, 'If he was in real danger, he wouldn't call *you* in *London*.' Catherine put her arm around me as she said it but she didn't understand that you could run and run and run and not make it, that real danger defied sense.

When the cab pulled up outside the Notting Hill dream, she pulled me close to her chest and told me to take care of myself, her voice breaking in the permanence of our parting, her warmth and softness soothing my sleepless senses into the dawn of the new day, brushing the sky behind us with gentle strokes.

I felt my body run forth and out of breath, out of blood in my veins and feeling at the tips of my toes and fingers, my limbs cold and still, carried away to Heathrow and Chopin, all directions now pointing east.

Everything in me ran towards him, urgently, and as the machine's feet touched the ground, a long-forgotten thought crossed my mind: maybe I needed to rescue something, and here he was, everything I'd been waiting for.

III

Karol

32

One day later
August 2016

I'd forgotten how sharp the air was in Eastern Europe, its fragrance like no other scent in the world, but anchored nowhere, in no particular memories, basked in the sun that fell harder on the flatlands around here, lacking the humidity of the island I had flown from.

I never considered my moment of return and, confronted with it, my mind whizzed empty, my hands clutching the phone with Karol's address, as if we were extricated from the geography around us, beginnings and endings and foreign sounds, now familiar, the only sounds that carried home, the sounds clumsy in my mouth as I asked for directions to the taxi rank, wrong suffixes falling at my feet, foreign English words weaving themselves between me and everyone around me.

The odd Polish person I had failed to avoid in London joked about a life in London being not far from a life in Poland; surrounded by familiar sounds, compounded consonants flurrying, our ears able to pick them up and pull them apart in meaning, stacks of *pasztets*, *kielbasas*, cottage cheese in cubes, multi-flavoured Jaffa cakes dominating the Eastern European aisles of every corner shop, eyed by faces that felt familiar in their angles, fashion clinging on to *home*.

The commotion of *home* hit me with a strangeness I had trouble dissecting, landing on a moon already known to me, shifting all dimensions backwards, distorting time and, with it, me.

When I ran, when I ran out, I barely knew what it meant to leave your country and your people and here I stood, three years later, thanking and apologising too much, stumbling upon words I had not used for any other purpose than to talk politics and sex with Karol, none of the words helpful trying to make small talk in a taxi.

Poland held no release of being foreign, reminding me that I had never left. I was all in, and everything that had happened up to this moment was a dream, a blur of memories I'd tried to preserve, retelling into fantasy, the only thing that lasts.

My face pressed to the window, lips prised open at the space around me, so unlike London or my southern town, roads and pavements stretched in full breaths, buildings shooting up, one next to the other, and among them The Palace. I was so mesmerised seeing it live in front of me for the first time, as if previously doubting its existence in the modern world. The taxi driver let out a low grunt and said it was a godawful thing and he, for one, hoped to see the day when someone finally turned this communist atrocity into rubble.

The Palace was unlike any other, erect against its definition, defying words and creating new meanings, defying systems and governments who alternatively despised and glorified it. It was the most beautiful building I had ever seen, alien, owning itself against its glossy neighbours, all indistinguishable from one another in their attempt to make more money.

I stole one last glance at it before we got back to John Paul II's alleyway north.

'Nowolipki 12?' The driver turned his heavy moustached face towards me, his wild bushy eyebrows falling freely on small, bright eyes.

I nodded, glimpsing the kebab shops concealed by one straight line of a block and a long stretch of tall glass panes, multicoloured fonts advertising seamstresses, restaurants, bars, and children's toy shops.

I looked up at the block as we took the final corner, different from the grey cubes that surrounded me as a child, majestic, I thought, modernist, they taught us later at school. One of these microscopic balconies was Karol's. I breathed in the air, crisp and fragrant, filling my nostrils with memories of school and the coming autumn. I breathed out, letting them all go.

I walked around the block cautiously, as if I were Alice and this was an unknown Wonderland and here he was, so close. I found the entrance in the courtyard behind, shied away from John Paul and Nowolipki. I pressed the buzzer for 28. The metal door jolted open and I pushed it, quickly tired and gasping for breath. I eyed the lift and pressed the button for the fourth floor.

The door to the flat was ajar.

I hadn't seen him in five months, not since the photographed communist buildings and us not fully knowing how to hold each other. I pushed the door inside, ready for a full rescue mission. I'd rehearsed what I wanted to say to sound reassuring, that whatever was happening, I had this, I was finally *here*, here for him and whatever he was going through, he wasn't going to be going through it alone. I caught myself sounding like Catherine – a mother with solutions, a discipline to getting better.

Karol was leaning on the doorframe before me, smiling faintly, a plain white T-shirt concealing a body that had lost weight and definition, that seemed weaker somehow, thin, skin looser on muscles that had once stretched into healthy weaves and knots, turning men's heads in thirst and hunger.

He had never looked worse, his face sunk even deeper than the last time I saw him, his dark eyes bigger in his face now, cheeks arching underneath them, lips pale and cracked, the edges of his eyes crinkled.

My body wanted to jolt forward towards him and hang myself on him, embrace him completely in the way bodies press themselves to each other, transmitting warmth and safety. My eyes pricked, but as I stood there in the doorway no tears fell.

'I can't believe you're here.' His lips stretched in a smile, cracking his face into an unfamiliar expression.

I sighed in relief. I didn't understand. Did he not call me only nine hours ago and ask me to come urgently?

And urgently I came.

Here we both were.

'I am,' I said. 'Of course I am. What happened?'

'I'm sorry.' He straightened up and retreated into the kitchen, asking me to come in and make myself at home. I closed the door behind me, hearing him thanking me. He was feeling a little better after he'd finally slept. He couldn't sleep for forty-eight hours before that and it had taken him a year to wean off sleeping meds so he wanted to get through it cold turkey.

I walked into a small kitchen with long pine cabinets to my left. There was a small table right in front of me by the door, with four retro school chairs tucked underneath. I pulled one out and sat down.

Karol placed two white ceramic cups filled with coffee on the table and sat down.

'I don't understand,' I said. 'Get through what?'

'I'm sorry, I must've frightened you, I was… well, frightened. I was really scared last night.' His smile sad and punctured, he took a loud sip of coffee, his sooty eyes darting all over me, stopping at fragments of my face and body, as if to ascertain all of me was sitting in front of him in this new world.

I didn't say anything, reciprocating his gaze with the same intent, inspecting his face for signs of illness.

'They switched my meds a few days ago. They said this could happen.' He paused. 'I'm sorry about Apollo.'

Apollo's name felt so out of time here that for a second I wasn't sure who Karol was talking about.

'Oh, yes, well, it's alright, it doesn't matter,' I said with an indifference only granted by time or a sudden shift in perspective. I was curious whether I had gained it by travelling east, if motion stretched those twenty-four hours into a safe distance.

'Can you stay? Are you able to stay?' He took another loud sip of his coffee, his eyes still on my face now, a rare vulnerability between us. How long could we have this time?

'If you want me to stay, of course, of course I'll stay,' I said.

He nodded and said:

'I do.'

33

We spent the following week mostly sleeping, days languid and unreal, our bodies heavy and relaxed as if they could finally stop running for a while and be at rest. I relished the creak of post-war parquet floors and time punctured by the war, a war that split all time, the entire country, into *before* and *after*, Karol's studio apartment falling shortly after, watching The Palace rise in the distance.

A large living room glanced upon its fragments distant in the skyscraper sky, piling upwards to the neoliberal dream of possibility. We slept in its opposite corners, safe within the four white walls, learning a world in which there were only the two of us, and no one else. The balcony door opened up to a foot of concrete, walled up with metal bars. We sat out on its edge, our bums warm on the parquet, our feet stretched onto the balcony, smoke curling up under our noses in silence, dispersed in seconds by the September breeze, crisp and still warm.

'They gave me a month off,' Karol said, and it was the first time I learnt he was teaching at an art college. He said it filled him with dread, even stepping into that building, but he needed a stable income, the work was easy and the boys, those young boys, were so beautiful, with such keen eyes, their faces so young and strong, arrogant and innocent. 'Before you ask,' he turned to exhale, cigarette smoke dissipating into the night, 'I haven't slept with any of them. I don't sleep with my students.'

I smiled and asked him why he hated it, it seemed like a good job.

'I can't really teach them anything,' he said after a while. 'I had you. The most beautiful thing that ever happened to me.'

He said it with long pauses, tired, cigarette burning at the tips of his fingers, eyes vacantly lingering on the Warsaw skyline.

'You've done a lot since,' I said, not knowing what to say, uncomfortable with my title. The most beautiful thing that ever happened to him wedged into my throat, knotting it shut and tensing my muscles, my skin brushing his.

'It's all commissioned rubbish,' he replied. 'I'm working on something new now but I'm afraid it's completely pretentious and not at all good. I'd love to show it to you. Maybe next week?'

I loved our infinity, week following week, peace I had never felt.

I said that sounded good.

Muranów, a socio-realist, working-class resurrection project on the ghetto's ruins, except none if it was resurrecting anyone anymore.

'My grandparents died here, underneath our feet,' he said one evening, the starless night ominous against the spangled lights of the sprawling city ahead. 'My parents were born underneath us too, on the same day, the tenth of June.' I loved our evenings, feet resting against the metal bars, cold in the fast-falling September light, faces warmed by cigarette smoke. He reluctantly agreed to wine tonight, a half-drunk bottle of red he had been squirming his way through stood between us. 'That's all my dad had on him, a piece of paper with the date on it. No name. He was smuggled out and passed from hand to hand , eventually ending up with my nan. She called him Jan.' I listened, the story like so many we had grown up with, buried in textbooks and erased from the streets. 'He was lucky, in a way. I don't think he could've ended up with a more loving woman.' Karol took another swig of wine, his sips thirsty and nervous.

'What about your mum?' I asked, tapping on the cigarette, ash falling flat in the ceramic bowl between us.

'My mum's sister managed to escape before the uprising. She had enormous blue eyes and blonde hair. It helped. She took my mother with her, headed straight west. Settled in Paris.' Karol gave a low grunt and downed his glass. I had barely touched mine. 'She came back thirty years later. She trained as a therapist but was doing a lot of research into trauma and identity. She met my dad. They married, they moved to Żyrardów, they had me.'

'So, is Rosenmann…' I paused, looking up at him. 'Is that your mother's name?'

'No, her name was Zaltman,' he said. 'My father took my nan's name, Różewicz.'

'Like the poet?' I asked, thinking about Karol Różewicz, this whole new person in this whole new world.

'Like the poet,' he confirmed, smiling. 'I made Rosenmann up. I couldn't bring myself to return.' Smoke escaped his mouth in a steady stream, familiar punctures tearing his sentences apart like bullets. 'I wouldn't know where to return to. It was all rubble here, a complete planned annihilation.'

The word drummed in my head for a little while, the buildings all around us falling, everything mowed to the ground as far as we could see, erased by this new housing utopia, a showcase of the strength and grandeur of the Communist Party.

'What happened with your parents?' I asked, weaving my fingers between his, his hand cold and soft, frail somehow.

'My dad never talked about the ghetto uprising. He never knew who his parents were. He didn't know anything about them. I have never seen him try and find out.' Karol took a long drag and exhaled slowly. 'Maybe he was too afraid of falling nowhere.'

'What about your mum?'

Karol stayed quiet for a moment, his voice thinner when it returned.

'They were happy for a while, but he couldn't live in the past and she couldn't live in the present. She bought this flat, not an easy feat for a Jewish woman after 1968 in Poland, at a time when everyone was dreading living here, too, on foundations laid on the graves.' His voice was so quiet I could barely hear him, sat right next to him, words slipping into one another. 'They divorced and I stayed with Dad in Żyrardów. My mother lived here. She became a doctor and then a professor at the University of Warsaw. She found out what happened to her parents, too. They were sent to Majdanek.' Karol stubbed out his cigarette and refilled his glass. I sipped on mine with unfamiliar caution. 'She didn't live long after that. She died of a brain tumour shortly after. I left for Cardiff the same year.' He took another full gulp before continuing. 'I will never forget seeing her body. I couldn't feel mine for a week afterwards. It became lifeless, like hers. Everything went numb from the neck down.' He looked at me, his voice slumping into a whisper, unpleasant and hoarse as if he was being choked by the effort of each word. 'I couldn't see him like this, I couldn't see his body, Toni.' I couldn't look away from his face, fallen, sinking somewhere away from me. 'I couldn't tell you this then and I couldn't see you after we came back to Cardiff, everything about you reminding me of him.' He squeezed the ridge of his nose and closed his eyes, his breaths heavy. I stretched my hand to touch him but he moved away and stood up, uneven on his feet. He swayed backwards, raising me to my feet with a shriek when he caught the balcony rail and pulled himself forward into the room.

'I'm alright,' he said and took a sharp breath before adding: 'I should go to bed.'

I watched him stumble to the bathroom, my heart running with a familiar fear. I lay awake that night, attentive to every ebb of his breath, making sure it was still there.

34

By the third week, we had fallen into a pleasant routine, sheltered from the world. Karol got up early and made breakfast and coffee. It took him an hour to measure the slices of bread (he didn't trust the already sliced loaf) and make sure the water temperature was exactly right. In that time, I walked downstairs and turned the corner for the local grocer to get everything for dinner, usually a variation on pasta, the simplicity and mundanity of which never seemed to bother him, surprising for someone who wouldn't have coffee that was too burnt or a slice of bread that was either too thin or too thick.

After dinner we usually went to Kino Muranów, the entrance to the cinema buried under the triumphal arch of the new social order. We went through their entire catalogue in those weeks, sometimes going back and seeing a film twice or three times, Karol always recognised and greeted enthusiastically by all staff. He nodded and squeezed my hand, at which signal I pulled him closer to me and started talking to him about something urgent, deterring any opportunities for casual conversation from anyone else.

In that time, we had not ventured beyond the old ghetto lines, and we had seen no one else. I started to believe there was really no one in his life but fuck boys and art people he had to network with.

When Karol went back to work, I walked the square lines of the neighbourhood, majestic blocks resting on green sheets of grass, so different from England's lawns, so much wilder and patchy.

It was the beginning of October when I asked him about his project again. If he was still working on it and whether I could see it.

Karol looked at me as if I'd reminded him of something that had happened years ago, something that bore no relevance now.

'Oh yeah, I am, I mean, it's terrible, but yeah, what day is it?' he asked.

I told him it was Wednesday.

'We've got an exhibition on Friday – the opening, I mean.' My lips prised open.

'You're really good at pasta.' He said it like he wasn't enjoying it, eyes glinting in the deep yellows of the kitchen side lights.

I told him it was all I could cook and asked him to stop being a dick.

'I mean it, I haven't eaten this well in years. Since—'

Our eyes met and he picked up again.

'I could show you around tomorrow if you like?' he asked.

'What do you mean that we have an opening on Friday?' I asked back.

Karol looked at me, surprised.

'Well, you're going to be there with me, aren't you?'

Our first venture into town together through a tram system I couldn't begin to grasp, I clung on to Karol tight, watched and copied his every move like a child, Warsaw so different from the place I'd left.

ABOVE US THE SEA

Wisła on our left, mythical and volatile, so much wider than the Thames, its current cutting through recent histories of creation and ruin, the national stadium bubbling with reds and whites proudly above it, signalling the new threshold accomplished, another point proved, one step closer to the West.

The tram crossed over to the waking streets of the eastern quarter, Praga, holding on to a moment of new Soviet nostalgia, welcoming our post-communist generation into its fantasy, bars and cafes popping up in between pre-war blocks with statues of saints in their yards.

I asked Karol about Praga but he couldn't tell me much beyond what everyone knew. The Praga of his childhood was a risky place to venture into, the Praga of today a creature on the threshold of finding out what it could be. We got off outside a set of blocks leaning heavily on the chipped pavement, the grandeur and elegance of the recreated west bank replaced by rows and rows of pre-war townhouses.

I followed Karol around the corner, his gait springy and agitated today, unlike his usual murmuring amble. He was wearing all black, and hooded up, he looked like a splodge of stain on the empty horizon of naked bricked buildings. When I finally caught up with him, I found myself in an empty yard, square in shape, at the back of one of the blocks, lined by large black garage doors. Karol was already wrestling with a heavy industrial padlock. I stayed behind by the tiny statue of St Mary right in the centre of the square, her hands in prayer, her gown blue, she was rested on a cracked brick column. I noticed her chin was chipped and she was missing two fingers on her right hand, her palms turned upwards.

Karol called my name and disappeared inside.

+

The room stretched out to the size of an ex-factory hangar, white lights lining the ceiling like something extraterrestrial, blinding in their cold brightness. The three walls climbed three metres tall at least, showcasing greying granules of no discerning substance or shape across their enormous plains. Nothing but dozens and dozens of square metres of grey particles. It could've been a monumental three-fold painting.

I came closer.

Karol stood still by the door, his thumb in his mouth.

The unison of the image was the illusion, the photographs were positioned neatly by one another, differentiating substantially in their arrangement and shapes at closer inspection. Cautious of my face touching the photographs, I scanned them as close as I could get to them, moving slowly towards the end of the room and looping back, examining small greying grains in meaningless chaos, sometimes taking on larger, more rectangular shapes, other times reduced to a few dots brushing off each other against the white sheet.

I walked back to him.

'It's very abstract, like nothing you've done before,' I cautioned.

Karol stopped biting on his thumb, smiled and grabbed my hand. Holding it lightly, his skin soft and warm touching mine, he walked me to the end of the room, this time stopping a metre away from the photographs.

'Oh.' I squeezed his hand tighter.

It was all rubble.

Fragments of rubble, some blown up, others parts of something bigger, something glimpsed in the time before, ashes sparkled through; some were cut in half by the edges, others were transformed and morphed into abstract remnants from a different place and different time, separated by hours, months, maybe years, perhaps seconds of personal histories, coexisting cultures, erased.

Karol stood still next to me, his face lifted up.

'They're blow-ups of the photographs I've found in various state archives of the immediate post-war period. Some feature the ghetto.' He cleared his throat, a fist pressed to his lips, his voice the usual monotone, a looping lifeless melody. 'Mostly, they're random buildings, significant in the context of the city's history and those quite ordinary. They have all been previously showcased in their entirety and captioned, given the narrative of their history. They're not my photographs per se, I guess I'm retelling the story.'

'Is that your speech for tomorrow?' I said, breaking into a slight smile. It broke the succinct focus on his face, crumbling now into a crooked smile.

'There'll be no fucking speech,' he muttered through his teeth, which made me laugh in turn.

'Stripped of the narrative,' I carried on, choking my laughter and regaining the poise I thought was required in the gallery space. 'Of meaning?'

'Oh, fuck off,' he said, lips stretched. 'It'll fill some conversations tomorrow.'

We took a step forward, still holding hands, the rubble dispersing into patches and dots squeezed into the neat squares of the photographs.

We started to saunter back slowly towards the door, leaving behind mammoth swathes of grainy ruin encircling the room.

'What did you say this was before?' I asked.

Karol paused, looking up at the lights, arms folded on a slouched chest.

'Car mechanic, I think. Then it was nothing for a long, long time,' he said. 'I bought it when I came back from Wales and laid down the concrete, replacing the old brick.'

'On your own?' My mouth flung open.

Karol nodded.

'It kept me busy,' he said.

I noticed a small marble table in the corner of the room, shying away from the lights. I let go of Karol's hand and walked over to it, eyeing up a stash of neatly layered leaflets, thick and matte, their front coarse to touch.

'*Fragments Two: Warszawa*,' I read out loud. White letters in bold were scattered in between the dots and patches presumably taken out of one of the photographs. 'What were Fragments One?' I glanced over to him, the leaflet in my hand.

'They were you.' Karol looked straight at me, my mind spiralling to my body in parts on the walls in Cardiff, Gav, his face burnt in the sun, Apollo with his promise of the young Pierce Brosnan, the two of us, such kids playing a relationship in Jean Genevieve's fake palace, to the time before the ocean and the rest of London and Frank and the Ultimate Picture Palace. Before.

Now.

35

I put on Catherine's black playsuit, contrasting wildly with my pale skin and platinum blonde hair that I'd redyed for the occasion, my scalp still prickling. The playsuit had puffy shoulders and angular, sharp edges. She told me she had been gifted it in the eighties but never wore it beyond the decade.

I drew two thick black lines above my eyes and splodged my lips red.

Karol stood behind me in the bathroom, padding down his black hair, mirroring mine, his white shirt hanging over the black jeans underneath.

'You should put some lipstick on,' I said.

He glanced at mine and shook his head.

'I have other shades.' I opened the cosmetic bag of everything else I inherited from my London mother. 'For example.' I took out a deep shade of plum.

Karol looked at it intently and shrugged eventually with a faint 'Okay.'

'Do you want me to do it?' I turned towards him with lipstick directed at his face. He took it out of my hand carefully and said:

'Oh god no, look at those uneven edges.' He inched his finger to the bottom right corner of my lip. 'And here.' He moved it across to the middle.

I edged myself closer to the mirror but couldn't see it.

'Suit yourself,' I said, leaving him to it, and walked out of the tiny bathroom.

'We look like two emo twins,' he said in a taxi shooting across the Świętokrzyski Bridge and past the lit-up National Stadium.

'I like that,' I said, smiling.

'Me too,' he said, meeting my smile.

I asked him who would be there tonight. He shrugged and said that he wasn't sure. A manager he'd been working with organised the whole thing. It probably wouldn't be many. Maybe some of his students, some magazine people, it was hard to say.

When we got there the hangar was packed, people spilling out of the gallery space and smoking outside, clamouring around St Mary with the chipped chin and only eight fingers.

Karol gasped at the sight and grabbed my hand, clambering out of the taxi. It was bizarre to see and engage with so many people at once, having only seen Karol for over a month with no contact with anyone else. We got separated as soon as we stepped out of the car, Karol circled like prey by fashionable looking men and women, enthusiastically congratulating him on the work.

Tearing through conversations about stripped meaning and recreation, I reached the marble table, now in a more central position and, as I hoped, stacked with plastic cups and bottles of white wine.

I filled one to the brim when I heard someone call my name.

My assumed anonymity shattered, I glanced around and met the eyes of a tall sandy-haired boy, around my age at first glance, with round amber-framed glasses concealing wide hazel eyes. He smiled at me and stretched out his hand.

'Igor, nice to finally meet you,' he said, his voice firm and confident.

Something sparked up in the memories of conversations with Karol from earlier this year, which now felt like a different decade entirely. The last lover, I almost called him, but caught myself just in time, realising how inappropriate that would be.

I shook his hand and smiled.

I told him I was surprised he knew who I was.

'Everyone here knows who you are, Toni,' he said.

I could feel myself making a face at him.

'You're the muse,' he said.

I snorted at that and took a sip of wine that was surprisingly good and still cool.

I didn't know what to say. I hated the word and the idea, and I knew too many very intimate details about Igor to look him in the eye without mentioning that even though I never even knew what he looked like, I knew him well, too.

'Thanks for taking care of him,' said Igor, an amiable smile pushing through his lips, hesitant. 'He's been looking so much better since you came,' he said. We both glanced around the room in search of Karol but he was nowhere to be seen, dispersing within all black-wearing attendees like a grain of rubble in the blow-ups stretched above.

I wanted to tell him that Karol was all I had, but I shrugged instead and said it was alright.

'I was really worried about him. For weeks he refused to tell me what hospital he was in,' he said. A sharp pang shot through my chest. I smiled and echoed the concerned sentiment, adding in reassurance that he was much better. Igor nodded his head with a smile.

'Well, thank you,' he said and brushed past me. My mind, unscathed by any rational trail of cause and effect, wandered to the statistical inevitability of terminal illness and I tried to remember all our moments together for signs of it, inspecting his skin and the blood cells in his cracked lips, the brittle nails he kept biting. What could have been that I knew nothing about and what was going on that he didn't want me to know.

I spotted Karol in a small group. He glanced at me without expression and angled his head to the side to call me over. I took another sip of wine, sour and warm now, and turned my back to him, walking away in the opposite direction.

Recognised, it was easier to momentarily distract myself from Karol dying and talk about rubble and the abstract within the real, everyone retelling the story already retold. I even managed to enjoy myself despite the quickly disappearing wine and the acute soberness I wasn't used to when around people. They were nice, albeit quickly faceless, anxiously beating hearts concealing one from another as we talked Cardiff and the exhibition and the abstract within the real again until it became a coined term thrown around casually and without curiosity.

The crowd was gradually fizzling out to just us and a few others, one introduced to me as the manager, two other people who had been friends with Karol since high school. I started a conversation with Paweł, one of the old friends, a tall broad man with the widest smile I had seen on anyone, persistently avoiding Karol's eyes on me, darting more and more anxiously.

When we got into a taxi back home, Karol turned in his seat and asked what was wrong.

I couldn't bear to look at him in case I managed to detect it, in case I could see him dying, slipping away from me, too. I was angry, so angry at him for not so much as mentioning any of it at any point in the last month, for being so ill with something he needed to be hospitalised for, and for keeping it a secret, from *me*.

Eyes on the dimmed streetlamps, I told him I was fine, I was tired and didn't want to talk.

'Fine,' he said, and I could hear him shifting away in his seat.

36

the sea

I insisted on taking the small blow-up mattress Karol had bought for himself on the day I arrived, but he was having none of it, instead giving me his double mattress that lay on a high stash of pallets, the exchange cold and matter-of-fact, a collection of short requests and stark refusals.

'Fine,' I said, climbing into bed and facing the wall.

'Fine,' he said quietly, disappearing into the kitchen.

I pressed the snooze button on my phone the following morning and stayed in bed with my eyes shut. When I heard him leave for work, I got up. I noticed he hadn't eaten anything. I walked over to the window and looked out at John Paul II's avenue, busy with cars filing towards the Palace. My timeline still in its lack of decision and ending, Warsaw spilled at my feet in endless possibility, no punctures of places to be and people to see and careers to chase and smiles to force and words to remember and pronounce and accents to imitate. There she was, sprawling before me, reimagining and reinventing and retelling, everything she ever was and everything she will be, standing upright on the bones of the dead with dreams in her heart, *Warszawa*.

I wanted to walk Warsaw's every corner, walk, walk, walk and breathe her in, this strange, beautiful concrete city, new to me like I was to her.

I sauntered out of the flat and started walking onwards, towards Kino Muranów, and beyond into the unfamiliar stretches of the Krasińskich Garden and into the fast-beating heart of the reconstructed Old Town, busier than the long leafy stretches of Muranów's pavements, abounding with people taking photographs and sellers trying to grab my attention. I marched on, my stride purposeful despite my lack of destination. I remembered it was Karol's birthday soon, November the 8th, and thought about how he fit every description of a Scorpio that Catherine had ever read out to me. I didn't have a gift and wasn't sure what to get him. We had never bought each other presents before, but it was the first time in over two years that we were actually together, and since I convinced myself we didn't have much longer, this one warranted a gift, the gift of all gifts. A white T-shirt was probably as good as it could get; however, the likely myriad criteria it would need to meet induced so much anxiety I dropped the idea. I still had three weeks. I got a sandwich in Subway, not knowing where else to go, and walked on, eventually finding myself on the river, lined by a long grassy bank with concrete steps and scattered bars. I had my last wage come through at the end of September, for what I assumed could only be the remaining holiday hours I had never used, but that was it, and even though I didn't want to think about it, I needed to make a decision about whether to go back or to stay and find work.

I watched a dog shake and whirr off the cold, polluted waters of the capital's river, and I shook my body too, trying to shake off the future, nagging and heavy. It didn't work.

I started making my way back, which wasn't easy in the maze of roads and with no phone. I had found myself lost at least ten times after asking at least twenty people how to get back to Muranów, and by the time I got back to our block, the sky was dark.

When I got in, Karol was still out. Maybe he knew that I knew. I itched for my phone, wishing suddenly that I hadn't deleted Frank's number, an urge that surprised me; I hadn't really thought about him for a month and a half.

Maybe I shouldn't have been this cold and maybe I should've looked Karol in the eye, even if I could see it in his face. Could I – could anyone see it? Could I see it in Gav's face before he went to the sea and drowned? It was only a few hours between the melody of his voice tearing through the pub to Cher and his white, cold body dragged out of the sea, his lungs full of water, leaving no space to breathe anymore.

My teeth jittery from the chill of the eastern October night, I turned on the tap and waited for the water to run cold. When it did, I blocked the drain and sauntered over to the kitchen, remembering the freezer had nothing in it but a few plastic squares of ice. It needed defrosting. I wrestled with the three containers and shoved them out on the floor, gasping with satisfaction. I panicked, suddenly worried that Karol would come back any second, but I calmed myself and hoped it was one of the days he held an extracurricular evening class. It must've been, and anyway, if it wasn't, I was just about done.

I carried each container one by one to the bathroom and locked the door behind me, a bread knife gripped in my hand. I turned off the tap and pronged the ice cubes into small pieces. I scraped the frost from the containers' walls and poured everything into the bath. I dropped the knife by the bath and, gasping in pain, I put my feet in, lowering myself into the water, feeling my skin break and burst, my body initially jolting and shaking but eventually stilling in peace, numbness calming my mind, fighting to survive, my ears ringing pleasantly.

Each time I submerged, I tried to make the moment last just a little longer, stretch it beyond the *before* and the *after*, before the time when fear kicked in when *he* drowned, violently, in a scream, and expelled me into the moment when I felt everything all at once, and the moment after, when all was gone and I couldn't feel anything at all apart from when I opened my mouth in icy water and it all came bursting in.

This time, after the calm and before the fear, the feeling, the burning and the anger, I saw a hand reaching down, fuzzy and restless. It wove itself around the back of my neck, but I couldn't feel it, not like a hand, it felt rubbery and thorny to touch. The hand clasped my head firmly and pulled me out into the prickling warmth of the bathroom, a bathroom that didn't exist just two seconds ago.

Nothing did.

It felt like being woken up in the middle of sleepwalking, caught floating in the unfamiliar space between a dream and reality, the slowed heart remembering how to beat again, and once it did, it ran forward in horror as the lungs shrunk and expanded violently.

My arms were now wrought around the bath edges, white and blue in colour. It took me a while to recognise the body lowering down in front of me, another hand coming out of the haze, the grains of abstract coming together to form Karol's body, a body I only knew as calm and controlled until that moment. It was shaking now too, his eyes locked onto me in a terror I had never seen in his face, like he would never be able to move on from this moment, like time had just ended and we had ended with it.

I couldn't speak. The shock of the awakening delayed all physical sensations from kicking in. We remained motionless with no time governing us, the moment had forgotten its beginning and seemed to have no end, time and space crouched and scared like our bodies, shivering louder and louder, disfigured into their own shapes of defence and collapse.

Karol was gasping, fighting for each breath in a panic attack. I sobered up enough to reach my hand towards him. He clutched it greedily, causing me pain, his breathing steadying. He let go of my hand, leaving it red against the veiny blue of my forearm, and lifted himself up abruptly, still trembling as he lowered himself towards me. He wrapped his right hand around my waist, his left hand sliding underneath both my knees, and he lifted me out of the water.

It was only when he held me closer that I felt myself shake, teeth clashing.

I asked him if he could wrap me up in something and told him I would be okay as softly and calmly as I could. I always was. Nobody had ever seen me do this, and he wasn't meant to either.

Karol's neck vibrated on my cheek as he let out a quiet 'Aha' and I felt a warm tear on my cheek, then another one.

His. Not mine.

'I'm sorry,' I whispered in his ear. 'I'm so, so sorry.'

I pulled my face closer to his, our cheeks touching, my arms wrapped around his neck, strained and tense, his cheek wet from tears, salty in taste as they forced their way into my mouth, half open in continuous apology. His arms clutched my body as if I could fall and break into a million fragments he would never be able to put together again.

Karol walked me out of the bathroom and across into the bedroom, laying me down on the bed gently.

His face had changed in that short walk from the bathroom. It was somehow smaller and glistening in sweat, the face of someone lacking Karol's calculation and control, his caution, his quality of being vacant despite his physical presence. This face was fully present and intent. I felt vulnerable and overwhelmed under his scrutiny, scanning my naked body in terrified search of death.

Karol's eyes had turned red around the edges. His veins pulsed fast; he bent forward as if punched in the stomach and curled up on the floor. Then he took one more look at me, stood up abruptly, and sprinted to the wardrobe across the room. He came right back bearing a nightgown and a bunch of blankets I had never seen before. He was so delicate wrapping them around my body, cautiously placing each hand in a cotton sleeve. It smelled of his body wash.

I thanked him, feeling the pleasant warmth that always made room for a few hours of peace, my mind free of thoughts and memories. Karol didn't respond, his face drawn in focus, making it familiar again, as if he remembered who he was and what we were, despite what had happened. Two more blankets followed. He tucked my feet underneath them and patted them down so they were wrapped tight.

Karol disappeared into the kitchen and put the kettle on with the same attention. I was dozing off when he reappeared with a black water bottle tucked into a furry black coat and a cup of tea. He placed the water bottle in between two blankets on my stomach. He handed me the cup, but my hands were still too shaky to take it. He offered to hold it for me and exhorted quietly that I should try and take small sips. Those were the only words between us.

I felt embarrassed and didn't want him to do this, but my body obliged. His arms stopped trembling as he moved the cup slowly towards and away from my face in a calm rhythm, observing me with uninterrupted attention.

I couldn't tell between which sips my eyes closed and body surrendered to ubiquitous warmth, but I fell asleep, my head on his shoulder.

37

I slept a dreamless sleep, a rare restful event. When I woke up, the sun pierced through the sheer curtains in a full beam of midday, flooding the scene with a shimmery pool. Karol's made-up bed at the end of the room was empty, his ankles woven around my calves, his back pressed against mine. I pushed myself up on my elbows, glancing around the bed at the astonishing layers of white blankets I must've freed myself from while asleep.

I looked at the rumple of black hair and Karol's long neck jutting into a braid of muscles on his strong shoulders, both hands curled under his cheek with a childlike quality that I wanted to protect. I pulled the duvet off me and covered his exposed body, rising and falling restfully. I pulled it up to his neckline and tucked his feet in as gently as I could, at which point he flinched and turned around slowly, his eyes still glued together, squinting at my face.

He purred a quiet good morning, looking at me with these big eyes of his, amber brown in the cascading quiet light.

'Thanks for letting me sleep with you,' I whispered back, looking down at his chest, broad and freckled, soft and calm this morning.

'Thanks for letting me sleep with you,' he said quietly, smiling. It was a cautious smile, conscious of everything shifting underneath us. The sheets felt delicate and fragile, woven out of strings that had no physicality, drawing thin lines in an otherwise shapeless snow cloud.

Then it dawned on me, the urgency of the information I couldn't let myself get close to yesterday or the night before. I was tired, so tired I remembered it again and said it out loud to myself, and to him.

'Are you dying?' I asked.

Karol pressed both fists to his eyes and rubbed against them for a few seconds.

'What?' He blinked twice, now brushing his hands through messy spikes of hair.

'Are you dying?' I asked with urgency. 'You would tell me if you were, wouldn't you?'

'What are you talking about?' He opened his eyes at me with a grimace.

'I spoke to Igor,' I said. 'He told me that you were in the hospital for a few weeks.'

'Oh, that.' Karol shook his head now, sounding impatient. 'A couple of weeks. Is that what you were angry about?'

'So you're not dying,' I ascertained cautiously, as he got himself from under the blanket and sat next to me, our feet in a receding pool of light.

'No more than anyone else is,' he said. 'No.'

I looked up at him, eyes crinkled from the night, his right cheek contrasting his left, hot and red from the pillow, thick tufts of hair springing wildly, his lips pale and soft, his strong jawline softened with a smile that took my breath away, and in that moment two tears pushed their way down across my eyelids, making the way for others, making it possible for others to keep falling irrespective of the rest of my body, still and turned towards him and his beautiful, beautiful face. I had missed his face like only one other face in this world.

'Oh, Tosia,' he whispered and his face crumbled, his body shuffling towards mine. He wrapped his legs around my waist and pulled me into his chest.

I squeezed him tight, my fingers digging into his back, strong and tender.

'Can you call me that?' I asked.

Karol blinked at me, surprised.

'Tosia?'

I nodded.

He smiled and said softly:

'Sure. Do you want some coffee?'

I nodded, aware of his wandering eyes on me, something in his face broken. Karol stood up and trudged with difficulty towards the kitchen.

I got up and wrapped the nightgown tight around my waist. I glimpsed the black cabinet shaped like a deer, my favourite piece in this room, which other than a bed on pallets and a single mattress had only a simple pine desk in the corner with an old vinyl swivel chair shoved under it. The cabinet was oddly out of place with its glossy look, two deer heads springing away from each other at the neck, cabinet legs shaped into animals' legs galloping, Siamese twins joined at the core.

Karol never worked at home and there was never anything left around on any surface, but this morning there was a photograph, resting against the deer's rising neck. It was a rough A4 size, black and white. He must've placed it there last night.

I gasped when I realised who the people in the photo were, disguised in youth, innocence and a joy I barely recognised, a fleeting blissful moment between strangers. Their faces stretched in hysterical laughter, their heads dipped in the waves of the sea coming in behind them. The boy, strands wet against a pale face, his body lean and long, his skin dissolving in the captured whiteness of the sand, freckles on his arms sparkling like tiny holes in the paper. The girl lay next to him, their faces inches away from each other. Her hair, wet too, fell across her face, parting in the middle. She was looking at the camera, his face fixed on hers, their moving limbs blurring their bodies, washed out by the grains of sand, reminding me briefly of grains of rubble. If you looked long and hard enough, you could disappear into them completely.

Karol stood beside me, handing me a cup filled with hot black liquid in silence.

I stared at the memory I didn't know I had. It had locked itself away from me, the clarity of that day now wiring itself back, the sunny day in Penarth a month before Gav's death. But there was no death in that photo yet, the laughter too strong, too infectious and genuine to let it in.

I let out a quiet giggle, remembering Gav springing out of the incoming sea seconds after Karol had taken that photo, dramatically shouting that *It* had touched him, leaving me and Karol in stitches. There were not many moments like this, but when they happened, they burnt bright and warm, invincible against time.

Penarth felt close for a brief moment, a distant country I fell in love with and left so quickly, what a fleeting love affair, as if it had never happened, not to me anyway. The wet sand grew coarse under my feet now, washed up by the warm water, cradled by a long streak of hot days.

'I miss him,' I said, and couldn't believe how light it felt when it was supposed to weigh so much. All the years gone by, carrying the weight of all our moments, and it was out now, spoken.

'I miss him too,' said Karol, his shoulder brushing mine. He was looking at the photograph as well, observing a moment between two strangers no longer belonging to us. I squeezed his hand.

We sipped on our coffees in silence for a while.

'I was so happy then,' I said, not sure what it even meant while knowing that happiness was held in the lightness of our manic laughter.

I wondered if that feeling could have only existed entangled in Gav, so intricately I could never come across it again. Maybe it had never belonged to me in the first place. Maybe happiness exists in certain places and people, irrespective of our actions, thoughts and decisions, and we find ourselves in its shadow and bathe in it for a little while, and then, creatures of motion, we move on.

Karol didn't say anything, staring at the photograph. I asked him why he kept it. I thought he hadn't left himself anything.

'I found it in a book after I came back,' he said quietly. 'He was shaking like a dog moments after, wasn't he? Do you remember? I swear he barked at one point.' Karol's eyes flickered and he looked at me, chuckling to himself. I snorted in stifled laughter.

He was alive. We both were.

Peace. I could point at it right there and hold it for a second before it was gone again.

'Should we go grab breakfast somewhere?' he asked, lifting himself up.

'I'm starving,' I said, stealing one more moment in Penarth, mirrored in the warm October day in Warsaw.

38

We walked over to Państwomiasto, a spacious mid-century bistro bar a thirty-minute walk away. Somewhere along the lines it had become our place of return. We sauntered over to its modest wooden tables and long stretches of splotched marble floors for long breakfasts and even longer coffees, and we popped in on weekday evenings after cinema dates, hiding under its white glowing neon, a dimmed lighthouse in the growing October nights.

Today was no different, persistent in our ritual of pancakes and three black filters ordered to be delivered separately every forty-five minutes.

I loved that walk, gliding underneath tall oak trees in the yellowing orange stream of their enormous leaves, covering the wide pavements like snow, the last splashes of paint before the greys of November. We walked in silence, entertained by the rustling at our feet, the wind chiming above.

We grabbed a table by the window, captivated by nature's performance, its permanent motion, the whirrs and tiny whirlwinds, the leaves curling up and falling, always so lightly.

'So.' Karol cleared his throat, but I couldn't peel my face away from the window. 'Oh, thank you.'

I looked up at the waiter and smiled.

'So,' he picked up again, looking straight at me, 'you said last night, you said that no one has ever seen you do it.' Karol was looking down at his plate now, his eyes shifting from his hands to mine. 'So you've done it before?'

He bit his lower lip and looked at me, his eyes bigger somehow, his head craning towards me, investigating my reaction.

I took a deep inhale and breathed out, dabbing a strawberry with a fork, avoiding his scrutinising, worried eyes.

'I haven't done it in weeks – months, maybe – not since...' I thought about Apollo's birthday, the disappointment on Catherine's face, the indifference in Frank's eyes. 'I used to, his face would just appear in random moments, his dead face, on the beach.' I bit my lip, slicing the strawberry in half, and once more. I stopped when it lay there quartered in tiny square cubes and then continued, spurred on by his silence. 'I don't know how it started, but I guess, I wanted to understand, I wanted to know what happened and,' my face flushed hot, ashamed, 'I guess I hoped, against all odds, that if I knew how, I would know why, and—' I noticed that my hands started to tremble, but I couldn't move them, I couldn't even curl them into fists, both of them, like juddering fish out of the water. '—the colder I made the water, the more painful it was, the quicker the stillness came and his face was gone and when I opened my mouth and the water burst in, it was so brief, but I felt so close to him, like he was right next to me and I understood, in that split second, but I would always thrust myself upwards, and everything came back.' I didn't dare look at Karol, my face pinned at the strawberry in a mumbling prayer. 'But he was always gone for a while, at peace, and I was at peace for a while after too, and maybe that is why I haven't stopped, when I'm afraid, when I'm really scared, this is the only thing that calms me.'

I stopped and waited for him to say something, but Karol remained silent across the table, our bodies still, our breath shallow. When I finally looked up at him, he rose abruptly and said he needed a cigarette alone, wiping his face, wet and sunken like the night before.

I nodded, looking away from him and back through the window, to Warsaw whirring its old beautiful trees in a chaotic dance.

He was gone for a while. I finished my pancakes and stared at his untouched plate. We got our first round of coffee and I sipped on mine slowly, my mind pleasantly blank, taking in the tall white pillars that jutted across the space between tables, white walls rising so tall they made me feel calm, Warsaw's lungs expanded and spacious, unlike the constricted interiors of London, always running low, out of breath.

When Karol came back he was whiter, his eyes redder around the edges, and he stank of cigarette smoke. He sat down and, without one look at me, started cutting his pancakes in half with the edge of his fork, shoving them into his mouth, one piece after another, his throat contracting with every bite.

I watched him polish off the whole plate in a matter of five minutes and then down his coffee in one gulp.

'Shit, that's still hot,' he winced, his eyes bulging slightly as he coughed and swore again.

I caught a nervous glance from a waiter who had just come to collect our plates.

'Do you want to know what I was in the hospital for?' Karol turned to me, still coughing, his voice louder than it had ever been, focused and angry, attracting annoyed looks from nearby tables.

I said that I wanted to ask him about it.

'Pleurisy.'

I shook my head, having never heard of it, and asked him what it was.

'I'd had pretty bad pneumonia for about two weeks before that,' he said. 'Then my lungs got inflamed and filled with liquid.'

Karol paused here and our glances parted again.

I wanted to ask him why he never called, but then I remembered that he had, many times, I just never picked up, switched off completely. My fingers started picking the skin of my right arm.

'The pain I felt every time I took a breath,' he said after a while, his face drawn and pale, 'it was unbearable, the worst pain I've felt in my life.' He paused again and our eyes met. 'At my worst moment, I just wanted it to stop, I wanted to stop breathing to stop that pain from rising in my lungs.' He took a beat. 'Then I thought about Gav.' Karol was staring right past me, his eyes stilled and voice fainter by the second. 'I thought about his lungs filling up with water and fighting to breathe. In those moments the pain he must have experienced felt understandable, fear spilled into my body with every breath, each one too weak, too short and painful. It was all I thought about, in that hospital, all I thought about was Gav drowning, time and time again, gasping for breath along with me.' Karol fell silent and pushed his fists in his eyes, rubbing at them with slow determined motions.

We allowed the silence to simmer in the melody of conversations around us. When Karol spoke again, his voice was quiet and soft, his head down, eyes fixed on his cup that now had a muddy coffee puddle at the bottom.

'When I left the hospital, I just lay in bed for days. Igor brought me food and cooked occasionally. He told me it was hot outside, breezy and dry, but I never left the flat and I drew all the blinds down to keep the light just right as I worked.

All I saw was rubble, I spread it all around the flat, it was everywhere, but he was everywhere too, no matter how much I worked. My lungs were not quite right for ages, it was the pain, it just wouldn't let up.' Karol padded at his chest and coughed, glancing around, missing my face. 'It sounds silly, but it was like he returned, lodged in my breath. Then I just cried, for days, with all that fucking rubble around me.' He squinted at the window and started tapping his fingers on the table. 'Igor convinced me to get back in touch with my psychiatrist. Our daily phone calls, those brief conversations in those weeks, Tosia, they were absolutely everything, all I clung on to. The night I called you to come and see me, I could hear the waves lapping all around me and him, gasping for breath. It's a terrifying sound. I had never been so scared in my life.'

I gasped and said nothing, clutching both his hands in mine.

'You should see someone about this,' he said, eyes shifting back to my face with precision, his voice quiet now as if it was running out of steam.

'Okay,' I said, my voice ringing low in sync with his. Together we fell silent.

When the second round of coffee came, we still hadn't said a word, finding an escape in a sudden drizzle that stopped the leaves whirring and dancing, a killer of the colourful crunching autumn, mashing the leaves into pulp, turning their edges into ugly splodges of grey.

'Did I even tell you that Igor and I split up in the summer before I got ill?' he said after a while, sipping on his coffee extremely slowly.

'I gathered,' I said. But no, Karol never told me, and I never asked.

Karol's eyes narrowed.

'I forget that you met him. He insists on being around.'

'Would you rather he didn't?' I asked him.

He shrugged in return.

I suddenly wished that Frank insisted on being around despite everything, that I could bump into him in places, keep him within my periphery of vision until the narrative had run for so long it could be reshaped into a new, impossible outcome, us brushing against one another and watching each other lose all those complicated layers that remained between us. Then my mind wandered to Jo's lips and her beautiful, bony cheeks and her eyes, playful and gleaming with a new promise entirely, already a lifetime ago.

I asked Karol to remind me how long they'd been together.

'Seven months,' he said. He must've told me that before.

I apologised for gaps in my memory. Nothing was a full picture for a long time, memories, scenes of fiction, dramatically enlarged or completely gone. Those gaps used to terrify me, but with time they became part of me and how I thought of anything in the world. I learnt to leap between them and make sense of them, of blown-up photographs and unfinished sentences, words I had studied and no longer remembered, others that had grown with my skin and were now wearing off.

'It's crazy what depression does to your brain,' he said vacantly and looked at me, his eyes inspecting my face again. 'Gav never wanted you to know, but I need you to understand.' Karol took a beat before the words poured out between us, heavy and loud. 'He was depressed. He had been clinically depressed the entire time I'd known him.'

My mind buzzed with his Welsh voice, the talk of antibiotics and time off, the migraines and the colds, the times he would lock himself in his bedroom, too contagious to see me.

'I never knew,' I said, my throat tightening. 'I never put it together.'

'No one did,' said Karol. 'No one knew. He had been on medication for years, but it hadn't always worked well.'

I could barely breathe, a lump expanding in my throat, pushing at the northern vertebrae, cutting the blood flow from my head which was now pounding in pain. The beach was different now, and Gav Evans too, the way he walked towards the sea, sober and determined. Karol looked at me, a flash of recognition in his face.

'We'll never know the truth,' he said, his voice thin and small.

For a second I thought I was going to be sick, but the bile in my throat could have been a scream, or tears, congealed into a ball and stuck now, like a herring in my grandfather's throat, the bone leaving a permanent mark.

'Did he ever try to kill himself?'

Karol's face crumpled under the directness of my question. He looked away and patted the back of his jeans.

'Can we have a cigarette?' he asked, his voice breaking, the release urgent. I nodded, my hands still restless, my muscles twitching under this ruptured narrative, the story retold, my own fantasy. We took our cigarettes and walked out, our bodies tugged into full breaths of fresh air. Karol pulled out a lighter, his eyes fixed on the task at hand, but it was too late, tears had already found their way out and were running down his cheeks. He stood there, sobbing, and with his tears mine came too, now they had learnt how to gather and fall. We stood there, cigarettes limp between our fingers.

We had both run out of tears by the time he spoke, softly, his words weaving themselves around the smoke, calming our exhausted lungs.

'I found him in the room, the room that became yours, three months before we met you. He tried to hang himself.' Karol rubbed his eyes with his knuckles and blinked. 'It was the only time. I called the hospital, and they took him in for three months.' He forced a smile, but it only released more tears. 'The night we found you, it was Gav's first night out after the hospital. I was so scared, I didn't want to let him out of my sight, I always knew where he was, I always knew that he was okay apart from the night…' He took a slow drag, fingers jittered before reaching his face. 'He was scared too, terrified, but then,' he looked at me, 'he found you, with your big eyes and your marvel at everything in our lives, your dancing and loud texting and messiness.' He exhaled, looking back at Warsaw with its wet fallen leaves, blurred in the traffic humming in the distance. 'Gav, he—' Karol's voice rose stronger. 'Hey, look at me.'

I turned back to him, hair glued to my face.

'He really loved you,' he said with conviction that rang unfamiliar in his voice. 'The year we met you was the happiest I had ever seen him.'

'Did you love him?' I asked, my head resting against the wall, too heavy to keep it upwards any longer.

'More than anything in this world,' he said, a smile curving between his tears, his head inching towards mine.

39

Above Us the Sea

For Karol's birthday we went to the seaside. We didn't intend to, and we weren't looking forward to it, but when an offer came for Karol to introduce a showcase of the rising stars of national photography at Gdańsk University, it presented itself as a unique opportunity to avoid seeing anyone or hosting anything, which Karol welcomed with such relief and delight it outweighed any aversion to public speaking or small talk.

The event itself was on the seventh, but the organisers very kindly invited us to a series of talks peppered through the preceding week and paid for our stay in Gdynia. They even extended it to the ninth as a birthday gift to Karol. He looked very embarrassed and completely lost any ability to speak until I remarked that it would be a bit grim to spend his birthday riding a very delayed Polish train with a permanently broken toilet. That made him promptly accept the offer.

Seaside November surprised us with open skies and relative warmth, a pleasant breeze coating our bodies as we walked between galleries and cafes, the cackling of seagulls echoing above our heads.

On the day of his birthday we booked lunch at a restaurant recommended by the photography people, only interested in food, having decided to eat and drink our way through the weekend. In our very committed string of eating and drinking and popping up at various tiny exhibitions where all Karol needed to do was to shake hands and smile, we ignored the sea completely, until the moment they sat us down by a wall-long window overlooking the lapping waves and a short strand of sand, climbing down beyond the restaurant's terrace.

We were silent for a while, looking out at it, the Baltic, with its own smell and childhood memories, dunes and pine forests.

'It's amazing,' he said softly, but I knew he meant scary.

I agreed.

A waitress asked if we wanted anything to drink and I interrupted Karol's attempt at two glasses of wine with a bottle of prosecco. He laughed at that and nodded with a smile as she took our order and walked away.

'You're done shaking people's hands and it's your birthday. Aren't you almost forty anyway?' I teased.

Karol pressed his tongue with his teeth in a grimace.

'I'm thirty-four.'

'You look a solid thirty-three,' I said. 'Let's celebrate that.'

A different waiter returned with our bottle of prosecco and two flutes and took our food order, the biggest plate of curly chips they could give us, the world's finest pairing.

'It's Julia Holter, isn't it?' Karol narrowed his eyes, as if needing to obscure his vision to give way to sound.

I nodded. They were playing the entirety of 'Have You in My Wilderness'. Frank played it sometimes in his Soho apartment, the sounds simmering on a loop, first in the background, then bulging bravely forth, loud and clear until I really heard it and it was all I could listen to for weeks.

'How funny,' I said without context and asked if he knew her. He was familiar with a few songs but not many.

'*Sea Calls Me Home*, obviously,' he said, 'and the upbeat one, I can't remember the title.'

'*Everytime Boots*,' I volunteered. Karol had tickets to see her in December.

'If you're still here then, maybe we could go together?' his eyes sparked up for a second. 'What are you smiling about?' he asked, but he was smiling now too.

'We haven't talked about music in such a long time,' I said. 'It was all we ever talked about when we met.'

He smiled.

I told him I hadn't really listened to anything since Gav's death, until I met Frank and he asked me out to a gig. He'd turned the music back on. Whether I wanted to hear it or not, it was on. That album was the first one I'd heard in a long, long time.

Karol said he couldn't listen to anything either. He no longer kept his notebooks, mind turning blank at every attempt to write anything down. Then he started therapy, and then Igor went home for Christmas, and while he was gone Karol got an album from a British friend who was staying in Warsaw for a few weeks. The band was called Flowers.

I shook my head in ignorance.

'Do what you want to, that's what you should do,' he said in English.

I looked at him.

'That was the title,' he said.

'Did you sleep with him?' I asked. 'The British friend.'

Karol looked away with a reluctant yes.

'Well, you took it to heart,' I said, and his face broke into a sly smile, his tongue grazing the right corner of his lips.

'It was before he got me the record,' he said. 'Well, and then after, I guess.'

'How lovely.' I started laughing.

'It was.' He gave a lopsided smile and asked me if I recognised the album playing now. It was in Polish.

I shook my head.

'Ralph Kaminski,' he said. The album was called *Morze* and it had just come out.

'He's got a beautiful voice,' I said.

Karol thought he was going to be quite a hit. If I stayed, should we get tickets to see him too?

'That would be great,' I said, my heart bounding forth towards our future, excited at its sounds.

We walked out on the terrace with our second bottle of prosecco, lighter in our heads and on our feet, Karol's hair rumpled, our bodies warmed by alcohol and stripped down to T-shirts. We must've been the palest people in sight, two ghosts dressed in black.

A woman who had just walked out with her partner glanced at us in horror, her bronze tan glowing against her short white dress. The man on her side of the table was more orange than bronze, a golden chain around the fat neck glistening in the evening sun.

We stretched out on the reclining chairs and clinked glasses to our first holiday together. We sipped on prosecco, staring out in silence into the waning autumnal sunset, a different kind of celestial performance, modest in its clouded palette, peace palpable. I was scared to move or say anything in case I dropped that feeling and it shattered into a million chaotic thoughts again.

Karol broke the silence after a while. 'You haven't said much about that girl you slept with.'

I had always been drawn to Karol's voice, low and soft; it always seemed to come from deep within, grounded and calming, light and ethereal. It never seemed his, outgrowing his wiry, pale body and sunken eyes, belonging to the better part of history, where men with that voice sang long songs filled with sentiment and melancholy.

I instantly forgot what he asked me. Karol waited patiently.

'What did you say?' I asked.

'You haven't really told me much about that girl,' he said.

'I don't know,' I said, my mind swirling between the moments of that night, seen so clearly, burning my stomach with every return. 'I still think about her and still think about that night. It was probably the most free I had ever felt, without anyone knowing, without any weight.'

'You sounded different when I called you the day after you met her,' he said and topped up our glasses. 'There was something different in your voice. It had a new ring to it.'

I looked at him, surprised to hear it.

'What was it that it had?' I wanted him to put me into words, however likely they were to fall between our two worlds and their languages.

'Future,' he said.

I smiled, struck by the possibility of that alternative universe again, free of death and the sea, the one where you could ease into a tomorrow.

I asked about Igor. He was the only one Karol ever mentioned. There must've been many.

'Not that many,' he winced. 'Well, maybe.' He squinted at the glass, filling it and taking a sip from the bottle. 'But yeah, I guess Igor was the only one I stayed with, the only one I cared about.'

'You never told me what actually happened,' I said.

'Oh, I slept with someone else.' He shrugged and looked away at the sea.

'The British guy?'

'No, someone else someone else.' He cleared his throat. 'What happened to that famous man of yours?'

I told him about Frank, the birthday party, and how we got together that one last time, the spilled wine and the betraying sheets, how it went too far, and how it had always felt impossible to lose Apollo and Notting Hill until that very final moment when all I could do was leave.

'I understand,' he said, his voice quiet.

'Maybe Frank kept me afloat until I was able to fall. I don't know if I would've survived if I'd fallen any earlier. When I broke up with Apollo, I knew I would be okay on my own. I had never felt that, not even the moment I arrived in the UK.'

I turned to him again, raking a few black strands away from his eyes, his cheeks tinged with the warmth of alcohol.

'I couldn't remember months after Gav's death,' I said and drained my glass, alcohol fizzing against my throat. 'I could barely remember my first dates with Apollo, and day by day I remembered less and less until Frank came along and shapes gathered contours again, objects started to contain detail. I started to notice things and I was able to observe them, I was able to enjoy them.' I paused and asked him for a top-up. 'I guess he was my first heartbreak, in a way, in a romantic way,' I said.

'Perhaps he was,' Karol said, lips touching the rim of the flute. He took a swig and swirled prosecco in his mouth for a while before he said: 'Perhaps your heart was broken long before him, Tosia.'

Our eyes met, the newly familiar prickling pronging mine at the corners. I followed his gaze, wondering what we expected from the sea in our silent longing, if it ever knew what we wanted, if it could ever look back at us.

Maybe when we looked away from it, it could only be for a fragmented moment, ruptured by our time, the greying edges of his hair and light wrinkles on his tall forehead, above his dark eyes. Maybe our gaze always returned, our eyes were always finding the sea.

Karol asked if I wanted to stroll down the beach and I nodded, taking his hand in mine, weaving my fingers through his. I took my shoes off and left them on the terrace and he kept his on.

Prosecco buzzed in my head in a pleasant murmur. The sun had set, casting red haze across the sky, the breeze picking up slightly, brushing our faces. We wandered out into a secluded bay, sheltered underneath a crown of cliffs, the black outline of a pine forest looking forbidding on the horizon behind us. We ventured deep into the sandy wilderness, our feet drowning in the grains under the weight of our bodies. Karol stopped and looked up away from the sand with a loud sigh.

I asked him if he was okay, and he nodded with a smile.

'Are you ever surprised at feeling okay?' he asked, picking up the pace again.

'Not yet,' I said, 'but that sounds nice.'

Karol squeezed my hand tighter.

'Let's go in,' he said.

I looked down at his feet, which were tucked inside thick white trainers and secured with white socks that reached his ankles, protecting him from what he currently feared the most: granules. I could just about detect his eyes in the falling dusk, sparking up with a sudden injection of aliveness, so rare in his face. We stared out at the gentle waves that had marginally picked up in their stretch and sound, purring louder now.

'I have already felt the worst I could feel. It can't be worse than that,' he said, new wildness glinting in the side of his eyes. 'I never went into the sea in Wales. I have never gone into the Baltic. I never went to see his body. If I don't go in now, drunk and with you by my side, I'll never do it again. I'll never know.'

I felt tears pressing into my eyes and I looked away from him and towards the sea, foreboding ahead of us, a black moving mass linking places of belonging in the lucid vastness of nowhere.

Karol started to undress slowly, shivering in the November night, taking deep breaths. He started with his T-shirt and finished with his socks. His entire body flinched each time his feet touched the sand as we walked down the sandhill towards It.

I walked close behind him, afraid, so scared now, my breath barely detectable in my chest suspended with his body. Karol turned towards me, and there it was too, fear, shooting across his slender naked shadow lapped by the sea's treacherous tongue.

I came a bit closer, standing on the shoreline. My toes gripped coarse grains of sand, naively holding on to them as they shifted underneath my feet.

I slipped out of my clothes and left them where I stood. I took a step forward and waited for the sea to come to me. Sharp pain jolted through my feet when It touched them. I took a deep breath and started walking towards Karol, desperate not to lose sight of him, my heart racing in my chest, dictating its usual terms of fear, its conditions of complete surrender. I stopped when the water came halfway up my ankles. I bent down, clutching my knees, my nails piercing skin. My chest hurt and my head was pounding. Why did he go in that night? Why did he go in? Did every escape carry that risk? If I was there, with my hands stretched out to him, would he swim towards me?

'Tosia, give me your hand.' Karol's voice boomed close, his hand stretched out to me, the pull of this hand stronger than the push of the sea. I smiled at him and took a breath, ready to let go of his hand. I closed my eyes and went down, salt stinging my eyes. The surrounding darkness wasn't complete, it was eerie and warm and had shades and was painful and cold, dangles of weeds floating all around us. How brilliantly alive, pushed in and out by the sea, calm underneath its surface. I felt a hand on my arm, but the sudden touch didn't spook me. It pulled me out gently. We gasped for breath, holding on to each other.

'Okay?' He grimaced, his face right before mine. I could feel his breath warm on my face, still smelling of coffee and prosecco, his teeth jittering like mine, fear somewhere between us but pulling us together, fearing for each other without a route to run away on our own.

I smiled and said I was. We shuddered under the waves as our legs found the ground, weeds lapping at our feet, the sea's woolly limbs.

'When I said that I couldn't see you,' Karol turned to me, words rising and falling, broken by the rhythm of chattering teeth, 'it was because everything about you reminds me of him,' he said, pushing himself slowly back to the shore. I followed close behind with gentle strokes through the stilling pool of water. 'I'm so lucky it does. I hope that everything about you will always remind me of him.' Our feet touched the sandy bottom and our bodies straightened up, now wading through the receding water, our hands intertwined. 'In a way, I'll always have both of you.' He smiled at me and let go of my hand, diving into his pants and jeans quickly.

I smiled back in understanding. My T-shirt sent soothing warm pangs all over my body as I put it on. I glanced at the sea and then at him.

'You're the only person who knows everything about me and still loves me,' I said.

'Well…' He paused for a long time with his head dropped down, before he lifted it and quietly said, his voice breaking in places:

'You know I sucked someone else's dick on the night Gav died and you're still here,' he took a beat, 'and I don't even know why I did it.' Karol's voice dried up, he was looking straight at me, his chest rising and falling in exhaustion, now everything had been said. I smiled and took his hand in mine, grazing his cold skin with my thumb. Karol pulled me close to him like he had never done, his lips against my ear, arms locking me in a tight embrace.

'It's still your birthday. Let's head to town,' I whispered, stroking his hair gently as he pressed his forehead into my shoulder.

When we reached Sopot, everything was still open. I spotted a big second-hand shop on one of Sopot's corners. I had been wearing nothing but Karol's white T-shirts and Catherine's subdued elegance and I felt a pull to strip down again and walk in naked, flustered by the patterns and colours, all promising *me* as a possibility.

'Let's go in,' I said, looking at the threadbare aluminium sign with a bleached-out cartoon face of a woman with a purple wig.

Karol didn't move, muttering under his breath that he would rather not, it was too full of clothes people had worn before.

I told him not to worry and plunged in, leaving him outside. I flicked through the garments, ignorant of their origin, the process of their creation, fabrics and patterns, overwhelmed by the abundance, contrasting wildly with Karol's black-and-white order.

I wanted to ask Karol what he thought of the jumpsuit I'd just picked out, but he looked engrossed in whatever was happening in the world on his phone, ignorant of my waves. The jumpsuit had a shimmering golden fabric, synthetic to touch, blending golds, bronzes and beiges, bold in its eighties angles with puffy shoulders and a wide belt of a folded fabric.

I spotted it as soon as I came through the door and knew this was it. It was going to be the first.

I tried the jumpsuit on. It was a bit too short, stretching just halfway up my calves and forearms, but fit perfectly otherwise. I stared at myself in the mirror and thought I could wear this every day and night, and then I decided that I would.

I pulled the curtain and stepped back into the shop. I spotted Karol looking up from his phone. He stared at me for a while through the window, looking surprised for a second, but soon shot me a wide smile and returned to his phone.

I asked the shop assistant if I could wear it out and she couldn't see why not. I paid, put Karol's T-shirt and Apollo's jeans in the rucksack borrowed from Karol, and met him outside.

He was relieved to notice we'd stopped looking like a pair of killer twins. Now I could be my own floating cosmic child.

I smiled. 'A very tall cosmic child,' I said, turning a few heads as they passed us.

We sauntered to the pier, surprisingly youthful and noisy on a Tuesday night, still pulling in the last swathes of holiday makers, drifting towards the sea in the last breaths of autumn.

We got waffles. My cheeks were sticky with the whipped cream I dipped my whole face in, even managing to get some on my eyelashes, while Karol wrestled with a whole packet of tissues, craning his neck to nibble at his waffle with caution, chocolate sauce dripping ostentatiously onto the pier's floorboards between us.

We tried to remember the last time we had *gofry* at the seaside, and concluded that it might have been as long ago as the nineties. Our taste in waffles had changed very little since then. We both remained faithful to the Polish classic, covered in whipped cream and chocolate sauce.

Karol had finished his now and was looking around for a toilet to wash his hands.

'Just lick them,' I said, putting all five fingers in my mouth. I worked my way around them with my tongue and proceeded to wipe my face with the back of my hand.

Karol's eyes diluted in disbelief and he followed with a firm shake of head.

'Jesus Christ, hold on. I'll find you some wet tissues,' he said and got up, walking off towards the shops facing the pier.

The crowd grew denser around me. I got up and walked, invisible in my golden cloak, invincible under the foreign glances I met with smiles. The bright lights jittered at the end of the pier in a disco rhythm.

Karol texted to say he was waiting by the entrance to the open-air disco, punters clutching on to the dead remnants of the season. He was staring sceptically at this scene of dead summer dancing when I reached him. He handed me a packet of wet wipes. Our eyes followed a topless man body rolling to Erasure's 'A Little Respect' so successfully that a scarce group of heel-mounted girls gathered around him and started clapping.

'Let's,' I said, 'let's go in.'

'You have to be kidding me,' Karol winced, squinting at the man as if the sight of him was hurting his eyes.

'Let's.' I grabbed his hand and pulled him towards the edge of the dance floor. The DJ was having his own nostalgia trip and Erasure was followed by a Polish disco number we vaguely remembered from school discos but couldn't recall the title or the band.

I hadn't danced in such a long time I wasn't sure if my neurons could fire to any beat. We had never danced together, not since Pride, not since Gav danced between us, and I wasn't sure if we could dance without him. We found the music interesting, disputed its originality, drew elaborate comparisons, had carefully formulated opinions and mercilessly measured judgements, but we never moved along to it. Not truly. Not like Gav, whose whole body seemed to be possessed by Cher every time he heard her flying pitch, his voice loud and clear.

Karol looked paler than usual and most definitely mortified, seeing more balding men with oversized suits joining a fragile conga to the apparent hit we were both too young to remember. He gestured towards a bar and disappeared into the crowd. When he came back with two shots of vodka, the group of girls had encircled me, squealing and pointing at my cosmic playsuit. I swiftly avoided the moustached conga men who swept past us, taking the group of girls with them, by locking arms with Karol and downing the shot. The body-rolling man was closing the snaking parade and had, in between songs, lost his trousers. He danced on wearing only his boxer shorts.

I decided that November seaside holidaymakers, the last of the last, ignorant of the seasons, unaware of fashion or comfort, were my favourite kind.

Karol got a couple more shots each, easing us into the strangeness of this extraordinary ballroom, a defiant party.

'My turn,' I said as soon as we downed the shots. I walked away towards the bar, leaving him standing there under a massive canopy that hung over the dance floor, shaking his head at various women approaching him with an invitation to dance.

The night had set in, all limbs warmed by an evening of drinking, a crowd growing denser and louder. I started weaving my way back to Karol when a young boy wearing a sailor costume crossed my path, almost knocking the shot glasses out of my hands. He turned towards me with a wide smile, baring a perfect set of teeth, his short curly hair climbing into a ruffled quiff, its splayed tips falling to the side of his face. The boy threw a quick apology in English, the tone of his voice playful in the exact same way it had been when we met in Swansea. Unaware of the cosmic crossing, and before I could wrestle my senses alive enough to say anything, he disappeared into the crowd.

Where would I get to if I followed him? I tried to locate him, my eyes darting around the room, but he was nowhere to be seen.

I glanced back at Karol. He gave an awkward wave. I started to make my way towards this body I loved so much, now starting to move side to side, his legs giving into involuntary jerks, his knees bending with the music.

'What happened?' he asked when I reached him. 'You look spooked.' I tried to catch sight of the Sailor Boy again, but he was lost between the swirling waves of people, now gliding their hands up in the air to the slowing beat of a song.

I shook my head and smiled.

'Let's dance,' I said. 'Cheers.' We raised our glasses and downed our shots, vodka burning our throats.

I drew close to Karol in a dance. He smiled at me and it no longer felt like a grimace, it *belonged*, and I belonged with it, safe in his arms. He placed his right hand on my lower back and raised my hand with his, hips drawing closer to mine and pushing away with a confident step that I followed with surprising ease, clutching my hand around his warm neck.

I pulled my head out of the sea and took a breath, our bodies alive in motion, and when the music stopped we didn't, making up serpentine moves that no longer bobbed or jerked but flowed, rose and fell, and when the next song came on Karol let out an audible gasp, his eyes dilating with surprised joy as the lapping sea waves fell all around us, rising from the speakers introducing the beats to the only disco song that was ours, pushing us west into each other's arms. Pet Shop Boys roared and feet thumped, the crowd stretching out in a distorted sea of hands, filling the dance floor with joyful thuds, among them the beloved Welsh voice, the melody carrying the sounds of the promised land from far away crevices of the valleys and lost corners of Eastern Europe, his body young and strong, jumping in the air and singing along, Gav's laughter booming between us. Karol weaved his fingers in with mine and for the final notes of the song we danced to our beat, holding on to each other.

Here he was.

Here I was.

Here we all were, always dancing.

Urgent.

ACKNOWLEDGEMENTS

My biggest thanks to my Mum, I owe you everything.

To my brilliant agent Clare Coombes, thank you for believing in me and my story and being such a fearless champion for underrepresented writers. Thank you to Harriet Hirshman and the entire team at Dead Ink Books for all your work on the book. I love what you do and I have loved being part of it. My thanks to my editor Jack Thompson for challenging me to make this story the best it could be, your astute eye and support. My thanks to my mentor Donna Freitas. I have become a better writer because of you. This story is indebted to your expert eye, enthusiasm and unwavering belief in my ability. I owe a great deal to an early reader Christina Petrie; you made me see value in my own voice as an immigrant writer. Your early feedback was invaluable.

To my husband, no thanks feels enough for the love, happiness and support you have given me over the years and your unshakable faith in everything I do. Jimmy, this story owes so much to your love of storytelling, your sensitivity and skill.

At the beginning, I had no structure or plot, only a few disjointed chapters and love for these two: Ralph Kaminski, you have stuck with me through everything and believed in me long before I believed in myself. Thank you for being my biggest cheerleader. Tomasz Zawistowski. There would be no Karol without you. This is to our Caerdydd and our Warszawa, to all the good times.

To Kasia Tumidajewicz, thank you for twenty years of friendship and twenty years of support, enthusiasm and time for my stories. My thanks to Lucy Spence for your insight and support.

To Jill Goode, for everything.

To the teachers in my life: my thanks to Marta Baran for telling me I would be a writer long before I believed it could be possible; to Dr Barbara Sokołowska, thank you for the love of the literary and the beautiful and showing me what lies beyond; and to Zbigniew Waszkiel, for the shared love of the English language.

My thanks to Karol Romanowski for keeping my head up in the trenches of first edits, your friendship and fearless cheerleading on this book.

Thanks to dear friends who have supported me in the last few years and beyond through various creative endeavours. I am lucky to say that there are many to name, but in particular I would like to thank: Mathew Parangot, Katie Vicary, Gati Varillas, Gizmo Varillas, Aga Szara, Meg Parrott, Victoria McGinness, Steve Hay, Anna Gallon, Louise Griffiths and Paul Morrison.

This book is a love letter to Wales, Cardiff and my south Welsh valleys, to everyone in my life at the time, thank you for making me feel at home. Wales will always be one. Diolch yn fawr iawn. To everyone at the LGBTQ+ community in Cardiff. To outsiders everywhere.

My thanks to my dad and my brother and to Kay, John, Ali and Jon.

To my late Gran, Paulina Makówka, the biggest character of them all, thank you for the cosmic amounts of love.

About Dead Ink

Dead Ink is a publisher of bold new fiction based in Liverpool. We're an Arts Council England National Portfolio Organisation.

If you would like to keep up to date with what we're up to, check out our website and join our mailing list.

www.deadinkbooks.com | @deadinkbooks